MW01106659

Nobody's Children

Joyce Henricks

Copyright © 2016 Joyce Henricks
All rights reserved.

ISBN-13: 9781532956911
ISBN-10: 1532956916
Library of Congress Control Number: 2016908147
CreateSpace Independent Publishing Platform
North Charleston, South Carolina

PROLOGUE

HE SHIVERED, SHRUGGED off the snow accumulating on his well-worn parka, pulled the hood up over his head, and settled down into his cardboard box piled with blankets and other pieces of cloth on top of twigs and old newspapers.

"Shit, it's cold," he said out loud, just to hear his own voice. "I've got to find a warm place, or I'm going to freeze to death." He laughed at the thought of people finding his frozen body all bundled up in rags in his cardboard home. *Too bad I wouldn't see their expressions*, he thought.

He rubbed his hands over the small fire he had produced using the pile of twigs gathered before dark, pulled a sandwich wrapped in plastic out of the pocket of his parka, and settled down for the night. Tomorrow he would make new arrangements. Tonight he would try to forget the cold and sleep.

NOBODY'S CHILDREN

CHAPTER 1

"**S**O WHEN IS she coming home? For the whole summer she'll be here?" Hannah Lowenstein was trying not to show her excitement at the news that Madison, her granddaughter, was coming home from a year away at college. Hannah and her daughter, Janice, were finishing their coffee at the kitchen table, each preparing for the day ahead.

"She'll be here next Saturday, after she finishes her exams," Janice answered. "And she's going to stay for the summer. She's already contacted Dr. Jennings for a job. You remember him. She worked for him last year. She actually enjoyed the job."

"What's not to enjoy? She gets to play with puppies and kittens all day."

"Well, she does more than play with them. She helps with giving shots, answers the phone, things like that. And she learned a lot. If she wants to be a vet, this is good experience for her—although I don't know why she's interested in that. It's not easy to be a vet these days. I hear it's harder to get into veterinary school than medical school."

"Well, she's got time to decide what she wants to do with her life. I remember you wanted to be an artist when you started college—and look where you ended up: a principal of a high school."

Janice laughed. "Well, it didn't take me long to discover that I didn't have any talent."

"Well, maybe Maddie will change her interest, too…So what do you want I should make for dinner tonight? Will Paul be home for dinner?"

"Yes, but don't fuss. Let's just have some of that leftover stew from last night."

"David's not going to be happy about that. You know how he is about leftovers."

"He's fourteen years old! I'm not going to let a fourteen-year-old dictate what we have for dinner. Besides, what's he going to do? Go hungry?"

Hannah smiled. No way would David go hungry. That boy had an appetite.

Janice got up from the table and carried the coffee cups to the sink. "Well, I'm off. I'll be home by six—it should be an easy day." She grabbed her purse and briefcase, tossed a jacket over her arm, gave a wave to her mother, and took off.

Hannah remained at the table, enjoying the comfortable silence, the newly sprouted daffodils in the yard, and the little chickadees at the feeders. *Life is good*, she thought.

She liked the early morning hours when the only sounds were the songs of the various birds in the backyard and an occasional car driving by. Since moving to Brewster, she had found birds. No, they hadn't been lost, and yes, there were birds in New York City. But she had never paid any attention to them—except for the ubiquitous pigeons that pooped on the buildings and streets.

Here she could look out the kitchen window and see birds of all colors—green, blue, yellow, brown, and even red. She didn't know their names and wouldn't be able to tell which bird was a cardinal and which a finch—although she assumed the blue one was a bluebird. But she could pick out some that seemed to be regulars. A pair of red birds—well, one was red and the other more greenish brown—seemed to return every year and were always together; and then there was the big blue one that seemed to chase the others away—he was naughty but pretty. One year she had seen an orange-and-black bird, but he—or she—had never returned. She enjoyed the return of the regulars and the appearance of new ones, and she made sure that the bird feeders were always filled.

It had taken her a while to adjust to life in Brewster, a small Michigan town, after a lifetime in New York City, but she found that small towns had some charming features, although nothing to rival the treasures of a large cosmopolitan city like New York. She had to admit, though, that growing up in Brooklyn had many of the aspects of growing up in a small town, a rather provincial town at that. Neighborhoods became the center of one's life, providing all the everyday necessities: shops, schools, restaurants, churches—in her case, a synagogue—and even a movie theater. For things not provided locally, one went into Manhattan, the "City," which required an hour of travel on buses and the subway. Her mother took her along on these trips, shopping the stores on Thirty-Fourth Street for the latest fashions, eating at interesting restaurants, and occasionally visiting a museum. But they were rare occasions, and Hannah's early life took place within a two-block area in Brooklyn.

But this neighborhood wasn't a real neighborhood, in Hannah's opinion. You never saw people outdoors except when they were mowing their lawns, and children never played in the street; when they weren't at their after-school practices, they were driven by stay-at-home mothers to their appointed activities or were in their houses, immersed in their video games.

It was all so different from what Hannah remembered of her childhood. Home from school at three, grabbing a glass of milk and a homemade cookie, dashing downstairs to team up for a game of tag or stickball in the streets, or jump rope with neighbor kids—boys and girls. Finally, being called in to dinner by your mother yelling your name from the apartment window.

But she had come to like living in Brewster, or, more honestly, living with her family. Her husband, Leo, had been dead for almost ten years when she moved to Brewster. Most of her friends in New York had either died or were in nursing homes. At least here she could make herself useful. Janice had a stressful, almost all-consuming job, and the children were at ages where they needed someone at home—or at least that was what Hannah thought.

"Well, enough woolgathering," she mumbled to herself. She sighed as she got up from the table. There was nothing on her schedule for the day, and she felt at loose ends. The house was clean and tidied except for the newspapers strewn on the living room table, the cupboards and refrigerator were filled with the groceries bought the other day, and the material for the evening's school board meeting had been prepared. She could start the preparations for the evening dinner, but there was nothing to prepare: leftovers. Well, she could make that dessert her friend Ruby had told her about. Now where had she put the recipe?

She spent the next hour sorting through her collection. She found the dessert recipe right away, but she got sidetracked by the jumble of papers stuck into the folder and decided to organize the collection. When she finished organizing and ensuring that she had all the ingredients at hand for the dessert, she looked up at the clock. Only nine thirty. She had the whole day ahead of her. It was too beautiful a day to stay home. Maybe Ruby would be up for a trip to the mall. Hannah was not one for shopping, but she was becoming desperate and knew that Ruby wouldn't pass up a trip to the mall unless she was dying.

She had met Ruby on her first trip to Marty's, the local grocery store. Hannah had been trying to figure out the various cuts of beef—they used different names back in New York—and Ruby had helped her. When Ruby heard the New York accent and learned that Hannah was Jewish, well, that did it. Two old Jewish ladies reminiscing about the old days in New York—it was a friendship made to order, but a most unusual one. All they had in common was coming from New York and being Jewish. Ruby was from a wealthy family and had attended college before getting married; Hannah was from a working-class family and had gone to work right after high school. But the friendship was solid, each one overlooking the other's differences and focusing on what she had now: a friend!

• • •

Hannah arrived at Ruby's condo, parked the car in the visitor's area, and took the elevator up to Ruby's apartment.

"Come in. I'll only be a minute." Ruby was adjusting the angle of her hat, which matched the mauve and yellow scarf she was wearing. She rarely emerged in daylight without a hat, which may be why she still had a lovely peach complexion at the age of eighty-one.

"It looks fine," advised Hannah, who saw no reason to dress up to go to the mall. "Let's go."

"Okay, I'm ready…Oh, where did I put my purse?"

"It's over there on the table." Hannah's impatience was beginning to show. She took a deep breath, a technique she used to settle herself down, and went over to the table to fetch the purse.

"Oh, thank you, dear. I don't know why I keep forgetting things. Maybe I'm getting that dementia problem."

"Don't be silly," scolded Hannah. "So you forget. Everyone forgets. Even kids forget. Come. Let's go." She handed the purse to Ruby, who smiled at her, and after one last look around the apartment, to make sure everything was turned off, they left for the mall.

Ruby had moved in the previous year and was still adjusting to living in an apartment after years in her own house. Apprehensive at first, she quickly found it more than adequate for her needs: two average-sized bedrooms, one and a half bathrooms, a galley kitchen, and a living area that opened onto a balcony overlooking the garden.

The walls were white with a tint of peach, and there was track lighting in all the rooms. There were windows on only one side of the apartment, but they faced southwest, providing sufficient light for the living area even on sunless days. Surrounded by the beloved possessions from her previous house, she had settled in to a comfortable life, made even better by the occasional overnights by Charlie Bernardi, a friend who had become a beau—she couldn't bring herself to call a seventy-seven-year-old man a "boyfriend."

• • •

Hannah arrived home exhausted. How could Ruby, such a frail woman, shop so much? She lacked the energy to do the chores of everyday life— leaving it up to Charlie to retrieve the mail from the lobby mailboxes or fetch her something to drink while she watched TV from the couch. But she was inexhaustible at a mall. It had taken all of Hannah's powers of persuasion to get Ruby to agree to sit down for a light lunch at the food court. Over a shared turkey sandwich, Ruby tried, unsuccessfully, to convince Hannah that Louis Vuitton purses were worth the money. Hannah just shrugged.

"Whatever," she replied—her recently acquired word, compliments of her grandson—but privately thinking, a fool and her money...

Hannah sat down in the burgundy recliner with a cup of tea and turned on the TV to her favorite program: *Walker, Texas Ranger*. Fortunately, Janice had TiVo, and Hannah could watch the reruns at her convenience.

She rarely saw a whole episode, falling asleep midway through the program. She woke up when David tapped her shoulder when he got home from school.

Dinner that evening was uneventful: David had little to report about school, Paul was in a hurry to get back to his law office, and Janice was preoccupied with plans for Madison's arrival.

Hannah cleared the table, put the dishes in the dishwasher, and tidied the kitchen. She sat down in the recliner, planning to watch TV, but was interrupted by Janice.

"What's the matter?" she asked as she looked up at Janice. "Something wrong?"

"No, I'm just puzzled. Maddie was telling me about the apartment she and Tiffany rented for next year—they can live off campus after the first year, you know. There's going to be a third girl living with them, but I can't remember meeting her. I don't think I've heard Maddie mention her name before. It's probably nothing. I thought I met all her friends when I was down in Ann Arbor though."

"You don't think she could have made a new friend?"

Janice caught the sarcasm in her mother's voice and responded, "Okay, you're right. I'm being overprotective. Of course, she could have a new friend. She could even have an old friend I don't know about." She sighed. "Letting kids grow up and become independent is harder than I realized."

Hannah smiled, remembering thinking the same thing when Janice went away to college.

CHAPTER 2

MADISON ARRIVED WITH a bang—literally. Her boyfriend, Jaime, had picked her up in Ann Arbor in his old Chevy, which was clearly in need of a new muffler as well as many other parts, and, in the midst of clouds of fumes, cut the corner into the driveway too sharp, smashing into the garbage cans set out on the curb for pickup.

Hannah stood in the doorway, watching and listening to their conversation as they climbed out of the car.

"Well, I guess we won't be able to surprise them." Maddie laughed.

"I'm sorry—I sure didn't expect them to be so close to the driveway." Jaime was a tall, good-looking, well-built young man, with dark hair that extended down to his shoulders. Hannah knew that he was what young girls would call a "hunk"—especially with his dark, expressive eyes. He wore the uniform of young people: tattered jeans, black T-shirt, and sneakers. She appreciated that he kept his given Mexican name but answered to "Jamie" without comment.

Jaime got out of the car and went around to the trunk to get the luggage. Madison didn't travel light: there were two large suitcases, two cardboard boxes with shoes, and one large box of books. Fortunately, she and two friends had leased an apartment off campus for the next year, and she had been able to leave most of her possessions with the roommate who was staying in Ann Arbor for the summer.

By the time the luggage was removed from the trunk, the family had descended upon Madison as if they hadn't seen her for years, even though she had been home two months earlier for spring break. Paul helped

Jaime with the luggage while Janice hugged Madison, and Hannah stood by beaming. Even David had come down to greet his sister, which he did by nodding at her and walking over to talk to Jaime, who had coached his soccer team last year.

The first thing Hannah said when they had all assembled in the living room was, "How about a little snack. You must be hungry after that long ride."

Madison laughed. "Grandma, it's only three hours, and we had lunch before we left."

"So three hours ago you ate something. You could still be hungry now. I'll bring something out. Maybe you'll eat when you see it." Hannah was not easy to discourage when it came to food. In her opinion, the world's political situation would be solved if everyone had enough—and better—food.

She returned with a platter of rugalach, which she strategically placed in front of Madison and away from David, who was always hungry. The talk revolved around Madison's year at the University of Michigan, especially about how she did on her final exams. Hannah barely listened, just looking at her family sitting there.

What she saw when she looked at Madison was a young woman with long dark brown hair pulled back into a ponytail, tendrils falling softly over her cheeks, slightly on the short side—a family characteristic—but quite slender, with ample curves. Madison wore no makeup, but her full lips and large dark eyes, with lashes so long and full it was hard to believe they were real, made enhancement unnecessary.

Hannah knew Madison had done well; she always did well. She knew pride was, if not a sin—which she didn't believe in—at least inappropriate. After all, what had Madison's accomplishments to do with her? But her heart was filled with admiration for her granddaughter. Was that pride? Or just love?

● ● ●

It was midafternoon when Madison returned from her interview at Dr. Jennings's clinic with the news that she was now a "veterinarian assistant" and would be working full time for the summer. And she would be paid.

To which Hannah responded, "Well, of course you'll be paid—a person should work and not be paid? How much are you getting? You should be paid a good wage for a good day's work, you know."

Madison rolled her eyes. "I know, Grandma. I know. I'm getting ten dollars an hour—and that's above minimum wage. It's not just the money I'm doing it for. It's a great experience for me, and it'll look good on my résumé. I'll be assisting in all the treatments—the checkups, the shots, the surgeries. Just imagine. I'll be assisting Dr. J when he operates on the animals. This is an opportunity that most of the other kids won't have."

"I know, darling, and I'm happy for you. I just want you should not be taken advantage of—but enough talk about that. Tell me more about school. You made friends there?"

"Well, sure. Shelley, a girl we met at a party, and my roommate, Tiffany—she's the one who's staying in Ann Arbor this summer, where all my stuff is—we have this cute little apartment for next year. Anyway, we all get along. Tiffany is an English major, and Shelley doesn't know what she wants to major in yet, but she's an artist. She doesn't go to Michigan. She goes to Eastern, which is in Ypsilanti, but we kind of have the same interests and do a lot of things together. And the apartment has three bedrooms, so we'll all have our own room. It's going to be great."

Hannah listed to Madison as she described her friends and her life at college. Never having been on a college campus, it was like listening to one of the radio programs she was enamored with when she was a little girl, or a fairy tale, only this time about *real* young people: no princesses, no monsters, no life-threatening adventures—at least she hoped not—just real people living real lives. Madison talked about life in the residence halls, about the funny things that happened, about the people she met, and about the parties.

"It sounds like a wonderful place. Aren't you glad you went there rather than to the community college so you could be with Jaime?"

Madison had not wanted to be away from Jaime, who would attend the local community college until he could qualify to transfer to the University of Michigan. She had been afraid they would drift apart. Hannah had reminded her of all the ways they could be in touch: cell phone, e-mail, texting, Skyping, and occasional visits. After all, being on the same campus did not preclude meeting new people. If she and Jaime both wanted to be faithful to each other, that could be accomplished long distance as well as on the same campus.

Of course, this was easier for Hannah to believe. She had loved one man in her life, married him, and stayed in love with him until he died. Never having to question his love and fidelity, it was hard for her to understand Madison's fear that Jaime would find someone else.

Madison smiled. "Yeah, we're fine. He called every day—and texted even more. I had to tell him that he needed to stop spending so much time talking to me and spend more time on his studies. You know, he did real well in his classes—a 2.8-point average. He's going to apply to transfer to Michigan, but even if that doesn't happen for next year, it's okay. He's getting really interested in some of his classes, which will help raise his GPA—he never really was interested in school before. So maybe the year after he could transfer."

"Speaking of classes, what about yours? Did you like them? Did you like your teachers? Did you learn anything?"

After an hour of listening to Madison describe her favorite classes—English, sociology, and biology—and her least favorite—math and philosophy—Hannah was sorry she had asked. So much of what Madison said went over her head

All she could say was, "You didn't like philosophy? That sounds interesting. Why didn't you like it?"

"The readings were interesting, but the teacher was real boring. Just read from his notes. Didn't answer our questions, so we stopped asking them. I ended up with an A because his exams were from the readings, but going to class was a waste of time."

Hannah tsked. "Well, it's a shame they have such teachers at a place like that. A university should have good teachers, for all the money it costs to go there." Hannah was of the opinion that you get what you paid for, and this seemed to contradict that.

"Anyway," responded Maddie, without commenting on Hannah's opinion, "what I need to talk to you about is that I've asked Shelley to come visit next week. I haven't asked Mom yet, but I'm sure she'll say okay if you agree, right? You'll like Shelley. She's like you—tells it like she sees it."

Hannah looked at her, eyebrows raised. "Is that good?"

Maddie laughed. "Yes, Grandma, it's good."

"Well, then she can come," Hannah replied with a smile.

CHAPTER 3

T HE NEXT FEW days went by so quickly that before Hannah realized it, plans were finalized for Shelley's stay. As Maddie had predicted, Janice had no problem with Shelley visiting—in fact, she was anxious to meet one of the girls Maddie would be living with. Her visits when Maddie had been living in the residence hall had limited her interaction with Maddie's friends. A typical visit involved dinner with Maddie and some of her friends, who were quick to accept an invitation to a non-cafeteria dinner. Conversation at the table was always lively, with anecdotes from the week revisited with laughter, but there was no opportunity for Janice to get to know any of the girls, beyond her judgment of their table manners. With Shelley here for a few days, Janice would have a better chance to see what kind of person Maddie would be living with.

Hannah, too, was anxious—but for different reasons. What did Shelley like to eat? Did she have any food restrictions? Allergies? Did she get up early? Go to bed late? When Hannah mentioned these issues to Janice, she was told to stop worrying. Just treat Shelley like a member of the family, she was told. From what Maddie had reported, Shelley would have no trouble expressing her needs.

And so Hannah had returned to the kitchen, baking and stocking up on ingredients for a variety of dishes she would prepare for the next few days.

• • •

Shelley arrived at the downtown bus station on Friday, met by Maddie, Jaime, and Hannah. She had a small suitcase, which Jaime stowed in the trunk, and a humungous brown and yellow flowered tote bag, which Hannah noticed she carried with her into the backseat of the car, cradling it to her chest as if it contained her most precious possessions.

It was midafternoon when they arrived at the house. Janice was at the door, with a warm hug of welcome for Shelley and an invitation for the three of them to sit down and have some snickerdoodle cookies and lemonade. David was already at the cookies—his favorites, though whether that was because he liked the taste or the name wasn't clear—and nodded to Jaime, ignoring his sister and her friend. Maddie didn't seem to notice, but Hannah did.

"David, come say hello to Shelley. She's staying with us for a while." This was said in a quiet, calm voice, but her eyes said more—and David knew what they were saying.

He got up off the chair and walked over to them. "Sorry. Hi, I'm David, her brother." He pointed to Maddie, who rolled her eyes at him.

"Duh," she said, "as if she wouldn't know you're my brother."

"Whatever," he replied as he went back to the tray of cookies.

Hannah chose that moment to ask Jaime to take Shelley's luggage upstairs to the bedroom she'd be sharing with Maddie, and gestured for the girls to sit down and eat a "little something."

Shelley smiled at Maddie. "I see what you mean. It's a good thing I didn't have lunch."

Maddie turned to Hannah and explained that she had told Shelley to expect something to eat as soon as she entered the house.

"Well, of course there'll be something to eat. In fact, if I had known she wasn't going to have lunch, I'd have served something more than cookies. Are you hungry, Shelley? Would you like a sandwich or something?"

"No, no thanks, Mrs. Lowenstein. I'm fine—and these cookies are really good. Did you make them?"

"Of course. For a guest, you don't serve store bought."

David looked up, his mouth full of cookies, and mumbled, "Aren't Oreos store bought?"

Shelley laughed, Maddie just looked at him, and Hannah replied, "Yes, but they're not for company."

• • •

After a dinner of grilled salmon and asparagus, Maddie, Shelley, and Jaime left to visit friends, and Hannah, Janice, and Paul went into the living room to relax and catch up on the week's activities.

Janice and Paul had been married almost a year and had not yet taken time to have a real honeymoon. They had talked about spending two weeks in Fiji, or Hawaii, or even a tour of Europe, but because of the pressure of their jobs, nothing materialized. Paul was a lawyer, and Janice was a high school principal—neither job allowing much free time to newlyweds. They took advantage of whatever time they could to spend together, even if it meant sitting in the living room, talking—with Hannah present.

Hannah, though, knew the importance of time alone for newlyweds and so tonight, after a half-hour, pleaded fatigue and went to her suite, a bedroom / sitting room and bath on the ground floor, where she promptly turned on the TV to watch the latest episode of *Blue Bloods*. She was quite smitten by Tom Selleck, who, although older and heavier, still reminded her of the Tom Selleck of *Magnum, PI*, a favorite show of hers many years ago.

• • •

In the living room, Janice and Paul continued sharing their weekly events. Snuggling a little closer on the couch, Paul turned to Janice, with a smile. "Your mother is a delight. She seems to sense when we want to be alone. Fatigue, my eye. You can hear her TV blaring from here." He laughed.

Janice smiled. "You know, when she first came to live here, I worried that we would get in each other's way—or, more to the point, that she would get in my way. But when she planned to move out last year and move in with Ruby, I realized how much I'd miss her. She's been a lifesaver—not only helping out with the chores, but the kids adore her. I was afraid that I was losing them—they went to her with their problems, not me. But she makes it seem so natural—'that's what grandmas are supposed to do,' she says—that it's not a problem. Speaking of the kids, what do you hear about Sandy? Is she going to camp this summer?"

Sandy was Paul's daughter from his previous marriage. She lived with her mother but spent alternate weekends with Paul and Janice. The arrangement worked out fine, both parents living in the same small town, each parent happily remarried and willing to overlook past mistakes for the sake of their daughter, who was a happy eleven-year-old apparently unaffected by her parents' divorce.

Janice had made Sandy feel a part of her new family, and even though David tended to ignore her, Hannah more than made up for that. She spent time with Sandy, baking, biking (yes, Hannah biked!), and coloring inside the lines of the abstract coloring books she found for her, where any color went anywhere. During these activities, they talked about Sandy's teachers, friends, and her consuming interest in animals, preferably small rodents like squirrels and chipmunks. Sandy idolized Maddie—her older sister, now—and was delighted when Maddie took her to the vet's office to help with the animals boarded there.

"Well, that's still up in the air," Paul replied. "Sandy doesn't want to go, especially now that Maddie is home and can take her to work occasionally. But Deb is determined to send her. I think she wants some time to herself."

Paul stretched out his arm and pulled Janice closer. "Fortunately, it's not up to me. That's in Deb's ballpark."

Janice snuggled closer. "So what do you think of Shelley?" she asked.

Paul shrugged. "Seems like a nice-enough girl. Why do you ask?"

"I don't know. She seems nice and all that, but there's something about her that puzzles me. For example, why does she carry that bag around with her all the time? Did you notice that she brought it down to dinner—put it in the corner—and took it with her when they left? It's a big bag and it seems quite heavy. What's in it that's so important she has to tote it around with her?"

"I don't know. I guess I wasn't paying attention. Is the bag any bigger than the one you carry?" he asked with a grin.

"Yes, it is. And I'm not glued to it, as she seems to be. I don't know. It's probably nothing. But I've seen kids who carry things that have special significance for them and I wonder what it is that Shelley has to have with her. I'm probably overanalyzing again."

Paul smiled. "Let's go to bed," he suggested. "You can do your detective work tomorrow. There are more important things to do tonight."

CHAPTER 4

"**G**RANDMA, I HAVE a problem." Maddie had joined Hannah at the kitchen table, after Janice and Paul had left for work. David and Shelley were still asleep.

Hannah stopped washing dishes, wiped her hands on the towel hanging from the refrigerator door, and, with her second cup of coffee in hand, sat down at the table next to Maddie.

"So, darling, tell me. I knew there was something important going on—you being up so early. What's the problem?"

"Well, it's about Shelley. You know she's living with us next year—and I really like her. But she's had a hard life—she's an orphan, you know—and I'd like it if she could stay here longer than planned. You know, like maybe the whole summer. She could look for a job in town so she could pay…"

"Nobody pays to stay with us," Hannah interrupted. "If she stays, she stays as one of the family. So what's the problem? She seems like a nice girl."

"She is. She's really nice. But I don't know how Mom will see it. She's fussier about these things than you are, and the house is already crowded, especially when Sandy returns from camp. Maybe Mom won't want another person around all the time."

"You want to know what your mother would say? Ask her. She may surprise you. But tell me more about Shelley. You said she was an orphan. Who raised her? A relative, maybe?"

"No, she grew up in foster homes. The last one was real good to her. They're the ones who sent her to college, or at least encouraged her to go—they didn't pay. She has an art scholarship—she's real talented—and she gets financial aid because of her situation. But she was in a lot of foster homes before, and some weren't very good at all. She would have liked to stay with this last family, but they moved to Florida, and at eighteen you're no longer in the foster care system—you're on your own."

Hannah shook her head with disapproval. "In my day, being on your own at eighteen was normal; but today—today everything's so different. Eighteen is too young today."

Hannah's youth had been so different from that of Maddie's that she often had trouble understanding what life was like for young people today. She had gone from living at home with her parents to living with her husband until his death ten years ago. And now she was living with her daughter. She realized she had never really been on her own, not like Maddie, who at least was on her own at college, or Shelley, who, it seemed, had been on her own most of her life.

"Well, you're just going to have to talk with your mother. In the meantime, aren't you going to work today?"

"Yeah, but later. I don't have to be there until this afternoon. I thought Shelley and I would check out the mall, see if any of the stores are hiring—just in case she stays, you know."

"Well, I hope it all works out for her. It sounds as if she hasn't had an easy life so far. But it's up to your mother, so I'd suggest you take it up with her this evening. Speaking of evening, what about dinner? Will you be home for dinner?"

"It depends on what we're having," she replied with a grin.

"Miss fancy pants. Now that you've seen the big city, you're fussy about what you eat, huh? Well, we're having spaghetti—or pasta, as they call it now. Any objections?" Hannah said with raised eyebrows and a smile.

Maddie got up from the table, put her coffee cup in the sink, and gave her grandmother a hug. "Your spaghetti is yummy, to die for. Of course I'll be home for dinner." She blew a kiss as she left the room.

● ● ●

Janice entered the living room, wineglass in hand. "Well, I'm glad that's over. These schedules are a bother—not difficult, but time consuming.

And if you assign teachers a class at a new time, they complain. Our math teacher claims you can't teach math in the afternoon—the 'numbers brain' only works before noon."

Hannah smiled and patted the couch, indicating where Janice should sit. She ignored Janice's complaining and asked, "So, how did your talk with Maddie go?"

Janice sat where indicated, took a sip of her wine, and sighed. "I don't know. We left it open. I don't think Maddie was happy, but I just don't know. Am I being overprotective? Paul thinks so. He thinks my suspicions of Shelley are unreasonable. I just have a feeling that something isn't right...and I don't think Maddie knows very much about Shelley either. The idea of their living together next year makes me uncomfortable."

"Well, one way of getting to know more about her would be to let her spend the summer here—at least you'd know more before they go back to school," Hannah suggested. "What are you afraid of? Why are you— what did you call it—suspicious?"

Janice didn't respond immediately, and Hannah waited patiently. Janice was one of those rare people who considered what they said before they said it. Hannah envied that. She, however, often just blurted out whatever came into her mind. In her defense, she claimed that at least she was honest, but she had to admit, if only to herself, that she often caused hurt feelings, albeit unintentionally. Her husband, Leo, whom Janice resembled in looks as well as temperament, had cautioned her many times about her "honesty," but she remembered his advice only after the damage had been done.

Finally Janice looked up and moved closer to Hannah. She whispered so softly that Hannah had to strain to hear what she said. Janice took a deep breath and listed her concerns: Was Shelley really enrolled at Eastern? How did she get an art scholarship, given her situation? If she had such good foster parents that they encouraged her to go to college, why did she seem not to have any contact with them? If Maddie knew her mostly from parties, was that all she did? Did she use drugs? Where did she get her money? Scholarships didn't pay for everything. And perhaps most intriguing—what was in that damn tote bag that she carried around with her all the time?

"She has some of the characteristics I've seen in kids who have had trouble at home—abuse, neglect, things like that. They usually drop out of school, but there have been a few who stayed in school but crashed on friends' couches, or worse, lived on the streets. I'm not judging Shelley, although I think Maddie thinks I am. If she needs help, I'll help. I'm just not comfortable with Maddie's friendship until I have answers. Am I being unreasonable, Mom?"

"Darling, of course not. You know these young people today better than I do. If you have a funny feeling, then there's something funny. Your concern about Maddie comes first. Then you can help Shelley if she needs it."

"You know, Mom, you're right. Having Shelley here for a few weeks— or more—is a good way to get to know her better. It'll be crowded, but if Maddie doesn't mind sharing her room, it'll work."

Problem solved, at least temporarily, the conversation turned to their mutual concern over David's love of video games. He was on the school soccer team and had a circle of friends, but his real passion was video games. And the more violent—at least in their eyes—the more obsessed he was. Hannah agreed with Janice that this was not unusual for boys of his age, but she still worried. She was concerned about the violence, believing that watching violence caused violent behavior. She had also seen the lack of social development in some of these boys and attributed it to an unhealthy addiction to these games. She didn't want this to happen to David.

She didn't have the evidence to support her assumptions, but that didn't shake her confidence in believing them.

They ended their discussion when Paul entered the room, returning from a late night at the office. He greeted both women and went into the kitchen in search of something to eat. "There's leftover spaghetti," Hannah called out. "Just heat it up in the microwave."

Janice kissed her mother good night and got up to join Paul. "Thanks, Mom. I know how to get some of the information, and now I'm going to tell Shelley she's welcome to stay."

CHAPTER 5

THE NEWS THAT Shelley could stay was received by Maddie and Shelley as a reason to celebrate, which they did on Maddie's next day off from work. A visit to the mall was always one of their preferred ways to while away time, if not to purchase new must-have items, then at least to see what were the new trends. Today, however, their mission was different: Shelley was looking for a job.

Hannah tagged along, not sticking too closely to the girls. After putting applications in to as many stores as possible, Hannah and the girls celebrated with a lunch of pizza and coke and a visit to a Bath & Body Works store, where the girls each bought fruity-smelling body lotions.

Within a week, Shelley had received a call for an interview with a women's apparel store. Interview successful. Job attained.

"It's only a part-time, minimum-wage job, but it's more than adequate for me," she explained to Hannah and Maddie, "especially since your family is letting me stay with them. The only problem is what to do with my bag…I won't take the job if I can't keep it with me."

Not that Hannah cared, but she didn't understand Shelley's obsession with that tote bag. Not only was its omnipresence awkward, it was ugly.

Fortunately, Shelley later explained, she was assigned a locker at the store, where she could stow the bag, and even though it wasn't secure, she managed to protect its contents by inserting a small lock through the bag handles and keeping the key on a chain around her neck, a chain she found at Claire's at the mall.

Now that both girls had jobs, the mornings became more hectic. Neither one was inclined to eat much breakfast, but Hannah made sure that they had "a little something" before they left for the day: a bagel or toast, a glass of juice, some yogurt with fruit. She wasn't always successful; most mornings they left with just a cup of coffee downed quickly as they raced out the door.

Maddie's job required her to be at work at nine, whereas Shelley didn't have to report until eleven—and only three days a week. But they left together; Maddie dropped Shelley off at the mall and picked her up after work at five. As far as Hannah knew, Maddie never asked Shelley what she did on the days she didn't work at the store, and apparently Shelley never raised the issue.

But Janice did at dinner one night. "So, Shelley," she started, "how do you like your job?"

"It's great," Shelley responded between mouthfuls of mashed potatoes. "I'm getting better at sales, and they're going to give me more hours. And I get discounts on whatever I buy at the store. You know, at first I wasn't aggressive enough, but now that I know they want you to push people to buy, I've been doing that. And it works."

Hannah raised her eyebrows. "How do you push people to buy? If they don't want to buy, they shouldn't buy."

Shelley looked uncomfortable and glanced around the table to see if others agreed with Hannah. Seeing nothing but neutral expressions on faces, she took a deep breath. "Well, sometimes a woman comes in and looks like she can't decide if she should try something on. We're supposed to encourage her to try it on. And then we're supposed to help her make the decision, you know, tell her it looks good, or get another size, or another thing like it. And if she decides to buy the thing, try to get her to buy an accessory for it—you know, a blouse or belt, or scarf. Yesterday, I sold a woman a blouse and a scarf to go with the skirt she was buying. My supervisor liked that and told me she would recommend me for more hours."

Hannah wasn't satisfied, but she said nothing, turning her attention to passing the platter of green beans around the table.

Janice, however, used the opportunity to pry a bit.

"Will you be working every day, then?"

"Well, no. Probably just a few more hours a week."

"What do you do on the days you aren't working? It must be boring waiting for Maddie to pick you up after she's finished working."

"Oh no," replied Shelley, "it's the best part of the week. I can sketch all day. You can't imagine the people you see at the mall—fat people, skinny people, young, old, all sorts of people. I finish about five sketches each day that I'm not working."

The expression on her face transformed her from an awkward young girl to a confident, mature young woman. She got up from the table and reached for her tote bag, which was in its usual position in the corner of the dining room. She pulled out three pictures, saying these were the most complete. She spent the next twenty minutes telling about some of the sketches.

"There was this old man at a table in the food court. He was reading a newspaper and sipping coffee. I don't know what it was about him, but he looked so happy and contended, I had to capture that. This next one," she said, holding up a sketch of two children, a boy and girl, playing by the fountain, "just made me smile, watching them. And this last one is simply a woman looking at shoes in a store window. Nothing special, but there was something about her look that intrigued me."

All were in charcoal, complete with details down to the wrinkles on the face of the man, the dimples on the knees of the little boy, and the expression of desire on the face of the woman. They were good!

She passed the pictures around the table, clearly proud of her work.

After comments of "This is very good," "Beautiful," and "Nice work," Maddie, with a twinkle in her eye, declared, "I told you she was an artist."

Janice looked across the table at Shelley. "Shelley, these are very good, better than good. You have a real talent. We need to talk about showing some of these. There are people who can help you sell these, if that's what you want."

After a pause, Shelley responded. "I have done a little selling—at street fairs, things like that in Ann Arbor and Ypsilanti. I sometimes do caricatures for people—five dollars a picture."

Janice smiled. "I think you can get more than five dollars for these sketches."

• • •

"Well, what do you think of Shelley now? Are you still concerned?" Hannah and Janice had just finished the dinner dishes, Hannah washing, Janice wiping and putting away.

Janice stopped what she was doing and leaned against the counter. "I don't know. She's a nice young woman—that seems clear. But there are still big blanks in her background. I haven't heard back from my contacts at Eastern, but so far I haven't found any record of a Shelley Kingsley taking courses there. It may just be a glitch in the records, and they're short of staff in the registrar's office in summer, so maybe they haven't looked very hard. I have a call into a friend there who could be of help when she returns from vacation."

"Well, I like her," announced Hannah.

"Mom, you like everyone." Janice laughed.

On that note, both women left the kitchen, Hannah to watch a rerun of *Walker, Texas Ranger*, Janice to her office to prepare for the next day's meetings

CHAPTER 6

"MADDIE, I CAN'T find it. It's not in my locker."

Maddie listed to a hysterical Shelley on the phone. "Hold on. Let me go outside." She looked apologetically at Dr. Jennings, who was trying to hold down a very frightened cat so that he could give it its yearly shots. "I'm sorry. It's my friend—she's really upset," she explained.

"Go. I can handle this monster," he replied, as he pinned the animal down with one hand, syringe at the ready in the other.

Once outside, Maddie listened to Shelley's recounting of events: she had placed the tote bag in her locker as usual when she reported for work, but when she clocked out at four after her shift, the bag was gone.

Maddie tried to calm her and reminded her of other times she had "lost" the bag only to find that she had forgotten where she had put it: leaving it on the floor in a bar after imbibing too many beers was probably her most foolish "loss."

Since it was almost time for Maddie to pick up Shelley, Maddie promised she would help look through the locker room for the bag. That seemed to at least reduce Shelley's level of hysteria.

• • •

That evening at dinner—Shelley's tote bag in its customary place in the corner—Maddie regaled the family with the day's main adventure, told with exaggeration and humor. Even Shelley was laughing.

"Well, I'm glad you found it. I know how important that bag is to you—I've never seen you without it," said Janice. "What's in it, though, that's so important you have to have it with you all the time?"

Shelley glanced around the table, everyone waiting for her response. Hannah wondered if she'd answer.

"Well, all my art supplies, for one thing. I never know when I'll want to sketch something, so I want to have things with me," she answered.

"But it must be quite heavy. Surely you don't need such a large bag for your sketch supplies," persisted Janice.

Hannah thought that Janice's pursuing the point now was awkward, but she sensed that her temptation to sneak a peek at it was quickly growing into an obsession.

Hannah, noticing Shelley's growing discomfort, tried to change the topic, but she was interrupted by David, who jumped up from the table, grabbed the bag, and emptied the contents on the floor.

Hannah shouted at him. "David. Stop that. That's Shelley's bag."

Janice followed suit, jumping up from the table to restrain David, who seemed surprised that his action had met with such a reaction. "Okay, I'll put things back. Jeez, I don't know what's you're so angry about. I've seen lady things before," he said, referring to the panties and tampons that had spilled out of the bag.

"That's not the point," said Janice as she knelt down to put everything back into the bag. "You don't touch other people's things—you know better than that."

David, clearly embarrassed at this point, tried to defend his action by claiming he was tired of people wondering what was in the bag; he just wanted to show people so they'd stop talking about the stupid old bag.

Only Hannah was watching Shelley; everyone else was focused on the scene David had created. Seeing Shelley's reaction—the sharp intake of breath as David grabbed the bag from the corner of the room, her eyes staring in horror as the bag's contents spread out on the floor, her face the color of bleached linen—Hannah reached over and put her hand on Shelley's arm. "It's all right, dear. It doesn't matter," she murmured.

"Okay, that's enough," Hannah announced. "Put the bag back in the corner where it belongs, David, and apologize to Shelley for *invading her privacy*—I think that's what it's called—right, Paul?"

Paul, not wanting to get any more involved than was necessary, simply nodded, and David, looking down at the floor, said, "Sorry, Shelley."

"Well then, let's have dessert. Come, Shelley. Help me get the ice cream." Hannah rose from the table and headed for the kitchen, followed by a very shaky Shelley.

• • •

Later that evening, Janice knocked on Hannah's bedroom door. "Am I interrupting your program?"

"Yes, but I've seen it before. I just can't get over how much the Texas man looks like your father."

"Yeah, Dad was a real cowboy." Janice smiled, seeing absolutely no resemblance between Chuck Norris and her father, a gentle, medium-sized, bookish man. But if Chuck Norris brought pleasant memories of her father to her mother, who was she to disagree?

"I wanted to talk to you about this evening. Forget David—I don't know what got into him. He's usually oblivious to what goes on around him. I don't know what precipitated his concern with the bag."

"You know, ever since the girls came home, dinner conversations have focused on them—Maddie's job, now Shelley's job, school stories. No one's asked David what he's into."

"Well, you know what his answer would be: *nothing.*"

"Yes, I know. But sometimes he might want the opportunity to say *nothing.*"

Janice looked at her mother and nodded. "Yeah, you're right. But right now I'm concerned about the contents of the bag. Did you see what was in there?"

"Not too much. I was worried about Shelley."

"Well, I think you're right to worry about her. I don't know why, but she carries around in that bag a little household: food, clothing, personal items, and a wad of bills—more than spending money—in addition to her art supplies. I don't know. There's something going on with that girl that's not right."

"Well, what have you found out?"

"That's just it. There's no record of her attending Eastern or any college in the area. There's no phone listing, although that's not unusual with all the cell phones today. I've even checked with the Ypsilanti and Ann Arbor police departments: nothing..."

"Well, that's good, isn't it?"

"Well yes, but it doesn't tell us anything about her—except that she hasn't been in trouble. Where does she live? How does she support herself? What does she do? And is it okay for her to live with Maddie?"

At this last question, Hannah nodded. "Yes, that's our main concern... You said she had food in her bag. What kind of food? Candy? Snacks?"

Janice sighed. "Yes, but more. I didn't want to say anything—you get so concerned about the kids getting enough to eat. But she's been taking food from the house. We've been going through a lot of fruit and cheese lately, and I assumed David was the culprit. That's not a problem, but I worried that maybe he was hungrier than usual and wasn't eating enough at mealtimes. I didn't want to tell you. You'd worry and make sure he was getting what he likes to eat. And I don't want you catering to him. He can eat what we eat. But when I asked him about it, he was genuinely surprised. He admitted he raided the cookie jar frequently—but we knew that—but he denied taking any of the other items. And when I saw the little baggies of cheese in Shelley's bag, and the packets of sugar and ketchup, and the cookies, I was surprised. Especially since she and Maddie are always so careful about not gaining weight."

"Well, you know a lot of young girls have that eating problem—what's it called? You know, where they eat and then throw up so they don't get fat."

"Bulimia. But I don't think that's what's happening. She doesn't rush from the table to the bathroom after dinner, and she's not skinny as so many of them are. I think it's some sort of psychological thing, like insecurity or fear—oh, I don't know. This is outside my area."

"So talk to someone in the area. You've got a doctor at the school, don't you? Ask him."

"Don't assume every doctor is a man. But no, we don't have a doctor. We have a nurse—and don't assume that's a woman, although it is. But that's a good idea. I'll check with her and with the counselor tomorrow."

"And how should I refer to your counselor—her or him?" Hannah asked with barely disguised humor. "It's so hard these days to know what to call anyone. Mr. Kempler at the Senior Center was complaining about people calling him 'visually challenged.' He said—and I quote—'Visually challenged? Hell, I'm blind.'"

Janice smiled. "Well, we do carry it too far at times. But I'm trying to get the next generation to avoid gender stereotypes…Look at Maddie. In your generation, and even in mine, you wouldn't usually think of a doctor being a woman, no less a veterinarian. And today, young women think nothing strange about being doctors, engineers, scientists—well, that one still needs work."

"Point taken," Hannah replied. "But getting back to Shelley. Do you think she's in trouble? On the lam? Maybe she's a runaway. How do we help her?"

"On the lam? You've got to stop watching those cop shows, Mom. But no, there's no indication that she's in trouble with the police, and she's over eighteen, so technically she's an adult and can't be a runaway. I'm going to have to talk with Maddie, get some more information about what she knows about Shelley."

After she left, Hannah remained in her recliner, lost in her thoughts. She was concerned about Shelley. There was something familiar about her—not her looks, her behavior—but she couldn't think what it was. After a short while, she got up and prepared for bed, still trying to retrieve that buried memory.

As she brushed her teeth, it came to her: Helen. She was a few years younger than Hannah and lived in one of the houses across the street. Hannah's family lived in an apartment building on a busy street in Brooklyn. The houses that faced the side street were considered luxurious, although they would be considered merely modest in today's market. But to Hannah's family, having your own detached home on a street with little traffic was truly luxurious.

Hannah babysat Helen when she, Hannah, was fifteen years old. Helen was a shy little girl. Small, skinny, with uncombed stringy hair and bitten nails, she was often seen wearing tattered clothes a size too large. She idolized Hannah, called her "my big sister," and looked forward to the treats that Hannah would bring when she babysat.

One day Helen saw Hannah jumping rope with friends. Hannah had waved to her, and Helen took that as an invitation to cross the street to watch the game. She sat on the curb and watched the girls, laughing along with them when they missed and got tangled up in the ropes. Double Dutch was the latest fad, and the girls were just getting the hang of it.

When the game was over, Hannah sat down on the curb next to Helen. She liked the little girl but found her shyness difficult to break through. However, that day she saw a different Helen—a happy one. They chatted awhile, Hannah explaining the rules of the game, Helen listening. As Hannah was getting up to go home, Helen started talking: how she wished she lived with Hannah's family and how she wished she had nice hair and clothes like Hannah.

Hannah hadn't known what to say. She smiled, said something vague, and waved good-bye.

She reported the conversation to her parents that evening over dinner. Her mother looked at her father and then back at Hannah. It seems that they and some of the neighbors had been concerned about Helen for a while. The little girl had been suspected of stealing from the local candy store—things such as chewing gum, candy, and once a small package of barrettes for her hair. The owner was reluctant to tell Helen's parents, as he, along with the neighbors, felt sorry for the child. It was clear to them that she was neglected. Her hair was never combed, her clothes, even when clean, were in need of mending, and her timidity bordered on pathological. Her parents kept to themselves, not interacting with the other families in the neighborhood. Not sure of their reaction to the news that their daughter was stealing, everyone just kept quiet.

All of this came back to Hannah as she stood at the sink, toothbrush in hand, looking into the mirror. It was years later that she understood that Helen had indeed been neglected, that she was starved for love, and that the stealing and the big-sister friendship of Hannah were the only bright spots in an appallingly bleak life.

She wondered what had happened to Helen. Helen's family had left the neighborhood by the time Hannah was a senior in high school, and with all the excitement of senioritis and preparation for graduation, she had forgotten about Helen.

Now she wondered if Shelley was another Helen—frightened and starved for love.

CHAPTER 7

SHELLEY HAD LEFT the house after the scene at the dinner table and taken refuge in the school playground a few blocks away. The playground was empty except for a young boy who seemed equally despondent. Perhaps he, too, had a secret he couldn't share with anyone.

She sat on the swing, feet touching the ground, rocking back and forth, clutching her tote bag. Humiliation and fear rivaled each other for dominance in her mind. (How embarrassing to be found with packages of cookies in one's bag. Would Hannah think she wasn't feeding her enough? What would happen now? Would Janice ask her to leave? Where would she go? Would Madison still want to live with her in Ann Arbor?)

Rocking back and forth always calmed her. As a child she had found solace in sitting on the bed in the orphanage, rocking herself to sleep, pretending she was in the arms of a mother who loved her, a mother who would not give her away because the new man in her life didn't want her around anymore—now that she had told her mother what he did at night. They called her a liar, that she made up terrible stories, that there was something wrong with a four-year old who made up stories about sex—wasn't that an indication of something terribly wrong with her?

She, however, was one of the "lucky" ones. At four it was difficult to be adopted: people wanted newborns, not children with problems. But she was pretty, blond, and petite. Adoption wasn't in her future, but foster care was—many times. It was never clear to her why the foster parents rejected her: she was obedient and didn't get into trouble, didn't ask for much, and didn't get in the way.

At first, the couple who took her in was prepared to file for adoption, but when the woman got pregnant with her first child, Shelley was sent back to the orphanage. The message: our own child is better than someone else's. Subsequent placements failed for various reasons: she was too moody; kept to herself too much; didn't fit in with the other children in the family; the couple decided they didn't really want any children; and the money provided for the care wasn't worth the amount of work involved.

Over a period of fourteen years, Shelley had been in seven foster care homes. Her last placement, from the time she was sixteen, had been in the home of the Colliers where there were three other foster children, all younger than she. She liked the idea of being the big sister to the two girls and one boy and didn't mind that she was made the primary caretaker for them. This cut into her schoolwork though, as she was forced to miss many days when one of the other children was sick or had a doctor's appointment during school hours. She had mentioned this, hoping that Mrs. Collier would take over during school hours, but the request was ignored: Mrs. C had "things to do."

Shelley enjoyed school, which made her an oddity among her fellow students, and managed to pass her courses with above-average grades. She listened to the other students planning college and envied their assurances that they would be admitted somewhere. She knew the only way she could go to college was on a fully paid scholarship—and her grades were not high enough for that.

At that time, she was living in Ypsilanti the home of Eastern Michigan University, only a short distance from the University of Michigan–Ann Arbor. She would observe the college students as they sat in coffeehouses, laughing, engaged in exciting discussions, having the life she wanted for herself. In the summer, when there was no school, she would take the younger children to the campus area and treat them to ice cream—with the money Mrs. C had had given her to "do something with them." This was where she belonged, and without even realizing it, a plan was forming in her mind.

In her spare time, Shelley had taken to sketching the things she saw around her. With the meager allowance given to her she had bought pencils, papers, and, finally, real sketchbooks. After a few years she had three books filled with her sketches of people. She showed these to no one, keeping the sketchbook as her version of a private diary. Her depiction of people captured the emotions of the moment—the sadness of the children when punished for taking cookies without permission; the anger of Mrs. C. when interrupted while talking on the phone; and the gluttony of Mr. C as he sat in his recliner, watching TV and eating a huge plate of nachos, sauce dripping down his chin. There were happy images too: the smiles of the children when she took them to the park, and their looks of delight when they tried to lick the melting ice cream before it dripped on their shirts.

She dreamed of the end of her senior year, when she would have more free time. She could still take care of the children, and if she got a part-time job, maybe she could afford a class at the local community college. She would take an art class.

Unfortunately, the week before her graduation, Shelley was presented with the news, by Mrs. C, that now that she was eighteen and finished with high school, she was on her own. They were bringing in a new girl to take care of the children. Shelley would have to leave by the end of the week. Shelley knew that the state no longer provided funding for foster care after eighteen, but she thought the Colliers would want her to stay on to take care of the children. She could get a job and contribute toward her keep.

She was shattered, her plans in complete disarray, her future in jeopardy. What would she do? Where would she live? *How* would she live? She would have to get a job, but one that would pay enough for her to live on, not the part-time one she had planned on.

Graduation was on a Saturday; she left the Colliers on the following Monday. It was June, and the weather was unusually warm. She slept on a bench in Peninsular Park, across the Huron River from the EMU campus, and used the restroom in the shelter to freshen up in the morning before going on her job search.

All she owned was stuffed in a yellow-and-brown tote bag she had received as a Christmas gift from one of her foster parents years ago. The bag went with her wherever she went.

Not having access to laundry facilities, she didn't impress employers of the clothes stores she applied to. But she did manage to get a part-time job as a waitress in a coffeehouse on the campus. She was paid less than minimum wage but was allowed to have a sandwich or bowl of soup when she finished work at two. It wasn't enough money for a roof over her head, but she found that if she ate a big sandwich for lunch—and filled her tote bag with crackers, jelly packages, and the salvageable leftovers on the plates—she could manage until the end of the summer.

On her afternoons she would head over to the other parks in the area and quietly sketch. One day a woman approached her and asked to see what she was doing. Shelley panicked, as she had sketched the woman and was afraid the woman would complain and report her to the police. She had no idea if what she was doing was illegal. To her surprise, the woman was delighted with the sketch and offered to buy it. After that experience, Shelley made her presence more noticeable and became comfortable approaching people with the sketches she had made of them. And many were willing to pay the $5 Shelley charged for a very good likeness of themselves.

At first she used the money to buy more paper, but after a few weeks she had enough money to treat herself to a proper dinner at one of the restaurants on campus. She still didn't have sufficient funds for housing, but that didn't bother her. The weather was warm, and she had established a routine that worked: sleeping in the park, eating at—and taking food from—the coffeehouse, and showering at the EMU gym, where for two dollars a day she could buy a pass to use the pool and showers. She had her afternoons free to sketch. Even on the days it rained, the pavilion at the park provided enough protection, and she could always remain at the coffeehouse, sipping a cup of coffee for hours.

It was there on one of those rainy days that she met April. She had seen April and her group of friends before, but they had never talked. On this day, Shelley sat at a table in the corner, sketching. When April walked by her table, she stopped to look at what Shelley was doing—it was a picture of her. Impressed and flattered, she called her friends to come over and look at the sketch. Within a few minutes of admiring the sketch, they all requested sketches of themselves and invited Shelley to join them at their table.

They were students at EMU and lived together in a big house on Sherman Street, a short distance from campus. The women were in social work, the men in law enforcement, with one lone English major with no idea what she was going to do with her degree when she graduated.

Shelley never said she was a student but, with vague answers to their questions, gave the impression that she was an art major and that she lived close to campus.

She looked forward to seeing them and went out of her way to be at the coffeehouse on the afternoons she knew they would be there. She had checked on the classes that were being taught in the art department and had picked up information on both the classes and the professors by listening to the students at the coffeehouse. She could easily pass as someone taking classes in the art department.

As September approached, nights became uncomfortably cool. The park shelter bench was no longer adequate. She had to find somewhere to sleep.

The problem was solved when April mentioned that Steve, one of the men in the group, was dropping out of school and would be leaving the house. Would Shelley be interested in moving in with them?

Shelley fought the impulse to say "Yes, yes, yes" and replied that she would think about it. However, she did let April know that she paid very little rent where she was living and wouldn't be able to pay much more.

Within the week, Shelley moved into the house with the understanding that she would contribute to the cost of food but could pay her rent portion by being the official "housekeeper." Shelley was ecstatic; she had plenty of practice taking care of a house, as Mrs. Collier had required her to do the cleaning as well as take care of the children.

Now Shelley's life was perfect. She had food and a home. She worked at the coffeehouse in the mornings, and her afternoons were spent sketching in the parks or in her room. No one asked when she had classes, assuming that as an art major she had a flexible schedule. She met April and the others at the coffeehouse on the afternoons when it wasn't her turn to prepare dinner, and was invited to the parties held on the weekends.

And her tote bag was always with her.

It was at one of those parties that she met Maddie. By that time she had established a significant clientele for her sketches. When she reached fifty dollars a week by doing family sketches, as well as individual ones, she worried about carrying all that money, in addition to the money she earned at the coffeehouse, in her bag, but the thought of putting it in a bank or under her mattress worried her even more. And so she clutched the tote bag even closer to her heart as she went through the day.

The meeting with Maddie was memorable. April had invited Shelley to drive over with her to a party in Ann Arbor. At first, Shelley was hesitant, not sure that her clothes were appropriate for what she assumed would be a fancier party. April, however, just laughed and said, "Wait until you see what they wear over there." And she was right. Shelley's jeans and T-shirt, old but clean, blended right in.

April introduced Shelley to Maddie, who took an immediate liking to Shelley, saying she was impressed by the fact that Shelley was a *real* artist and that she was supporting herself through college. And Shelley was impressed by the fact that Maddie was preparing to be a veterinarian. Never having had a pet, Shelley was fascinated by the stories that Maddie told about her experience at the Dr. Jennings's clinic. They talked well into the night, comparing stories of their families: Maddie's real, Shelley's imaginary. It was past 2:00 a.m. when April interrupted them to say she was leaving.

Maddie and Shelley looked at each other in surprise. They had so much more to talk about they hadn't realized how late it was. It was decided that Shelley would stay over and Maddie would somehow get her back to Ypsilanti the next day.

The next day turned out to be two days later, when Maddie corralled one of her friends with a car to drive Shelley back for her pretend classes. The budding friendship blossomed throughout the next few months, with Shelley spending her free time in Ann Arbor with Maddie and her roommate, Tiffany, and sketching in the Arboretum and other parks in the area.

The invitation to join them in a house in Ann Arbor, with the assumption that Shelley would be transferring to the U of M, was easy for Shelley to accept. She could pretend to go to classes in Ann Arbor as easily as she had in Ypsilanti.

But now, would all that change? Would they know she had lied about being a student? That she was homeless? Would Maddie still want her to live with her? Would she still want to be friends?

It had grown dark while she sat on the swing, and the early summer evening was cool. She pulled a sweatshirt out of her tote bag and put it on over her T-shirt. She knew she had to return to the house, but wanted to wait until she could avoid everyone. She didn't want to answer any questions or offer any explanations.

CHAPTER 8

THE HOUSE WAS quiet, everyone asleep or in their own bedrooms. Only Hannah, whose bedroom was on the first floor, was stirring. Ready for bed, she had tried to sleep, but her worry about Shelley kept her awake. It was almost eleven when she heard the front door open. She had decided that the best course of action was to let Shelley go upstairs and speak to her in the morning. However, before she knew it, she was out in the hallway.

"Shelley, come here, darling."

Shelley had clearly hoped to slink away without notice. She stopped and waited.

"Darling, I just wanted to make sure you were okay. We can talk later, but I just wanted you to know that everything's going to be okay. Okay?'

Shelley smiled weakly, nodded, and went upstairs to her room. Hannah went to bed, finally able to sleep.

• • •

The next evening, everyone in his or her preferred place—David playing his latest video game in his room, Paul watching *Rachel Maddow* in the living room, Maddie and Shelley doing whatever in Maddie's room—Hannah and Janice settled in Hannah's room and talked.

The day had gone by without mention of the tote bag incident of the previous evening, Shelley apparently too embarrassed, everyone else too uncomfortable to mention it.

Hannah was in her recliner, feet up, leaning comfortably into the pillow behind her back. Barely five feet tall, most seats were not made for her. As she claimed, "They make me feel like that Lily Tomlin character where the little girl's feet don't reach the floor."

Janice was stretched out on the bed, shoes flung off, head cradled on her arms folded behind her head.

"So you want to say something?" asked Hannah.

"Well, we haven't talked about it since last night. What time did she get back?"

"Ah, language. 'It,' 'she'—but I know what you mean. Shelley got home around eleven. I was up—I couldn't sleep—and heard her come in. I said good night to her, and she went upstairs. And that was that."

Janice stared up at the ceiling, jiggling her legs on the bed, saying nothing.

The room was silent but for the jiggling of the bed and the whirling of the ceiling fan. Finally Hannah leaned forward and sighed.

"I was thinking of Helen the other night after you left. You remember I told you about Helen?"

Janice shrugged. "Yeah?"

"Well, Shelley made me think about Helen. I think there's something like that in Shelley's background.

"What? Parents who ignored her?"

"Well, I don't know about that, but something made her insecure, made her afraid."

"But what's she afraid of? She's bright, attractive, clearly talented, and even if she's not in college—I'm still checking on that—she has friends and enough money to live on."

"Darling, think about it. What's in that ugly bag that's attached to her like Velcro? You like detective stories—think."

Janice sat up. "Okay. Let's see: food, clothing, her art supplies…what else?'

"Soap, money—it was sticking out of the pocket inside the bag—tampons, a blanket…Why would a young girl need all those things with her every day?" asked Hannah as she looked at Janice.

Without waiting for an answer, she continued. "I think she doesn't trust people, or she doesn't really have a home."

Janice sat up even straighter, legs now hanging over the edge of the bed. "You think she might be homeless?"

"I don't know, but one could live out of that bag for quite a while: food, clothing, personal items, money, and a blanket—that's what people take when they go camping, isn't it? All she's missing is a tent and a bed."

'My God, I never even considered that…I should have though. We've had kids at school whose parents threw them out of the house. They basically survived on junk food and showering after gym class. And crashing on couches with friends' families. They could get away with that for months before we'd find out."

Hannah leaned back in her recliner. "So what do we do?"

"I don't know. But we have to do something. First thing, though, is to try to talk to Shelley…Do you think she'd talk to you? I think I intimidate her."

Hannah sighed. "You can be intimidating, darling. You're so smart and organized and you look like a movie star…"

"For heaven's sake, Mom, only you see me that way."

"Whatever," replied Hannah with a shrug. "But I'll try to talk to her. Who knows—maybe she wants to talk about it," declared Hannah.

● ● ●

The next morning Hannah took the opportunity to talk to Shelley. Well, she didn't *take* it, she *created* it. Feigning a bad back, and knowing that Shelley didn't have to report to work until noon, she asked Shelley to stay behind and help her with some chores, promising that she would drive Shelley to work in plenty of time.

What could Shelley say? Assured that Maddie would pick her up after work, she stayed behind to help Hannah.

"Darling, get that look off your face. This isn't the inquisition. You're not in any trouble. I'm just a nosy old woman who has questions, and you have the answers. Now, do you want more coffee? Maybe a danish—there's cherry and prune, which is better than the cherry…Come and sit down. Everybody's gone. It's just you and me, kid—I heard that in a movie somewhere—so let's talk."

Shelley helped herself to coffee and sat down at the table, across from Hannah. Taking a deep breath, she said, "Okay, I guess you don't need help with chores—although I can help if you want, but," she started.

Hannah interrupted her, waving her hand. "See, I knew you were smart. You pick up on things. You watch people. You know what's going on. No, I don't need help. But I think you do, so here goes." Hannah leaned forward and looked Shelley in the eyes. "I may be wrong—and I know you'll tell me if I am—but I think you've been living a lie...no, don't interrupt. Let me finish. Then you can interrupt. I think you've been on your own, maybe not even going to school, living on the street, somehow. I don't know. But you're good at surviving. That bag you carry around all the time—it's got everything you need to survive: food, clothing, money—even your art things. You're intelligent, pretty, and smart—that's different from being intelligent, you know—and I think you've been living by your smarts. I think you're what they call 'homeless'...So how did I do? Am I way wrong? Before you answer, there's nothing wrong with being homeless, if that's what you are. But if that's true, you need help—and that's what we do in this family: we help each other."

With that, Hannah sat back and waited for Shelley's response.

Shelley sat in silence for what seemed like an hour to Hannah, but was actually less than a minute. To Hannah's credit, she restrained her impatience, quietly sitting and waiting for Shelley to respond. At least Shelley didn't get up and bolt—that was promising.

When Shelley did respond, it was with an apology. "I thought you'd be mad at me for stealing food. I thought you'd want me to leave."

"Nonsense," cried Hannah. "Why would I be mad at you? Although at first I worried that maybe you weren't getting enough to eat here. But when I saw what else you had in the bag, I thought...well, I don't know what I thought. So do you want to talk? Can we have a conversation?"

Shelley smiled and told her story. Hannah listened. After an hour, Shelley sat back, took a deep breath, and wiped her tears. Hannah, too, sat back, took a deep breath, and wiped her tears.

"Look at us, two weeping women," said Hannah as she reached for the box of tissues, extending it to Shelley after taking a few for herself. "Enough tears, darling. I'll drive you to work, and then tonight we'll make a plan."

She walked over to Shelley, put her arms around her shoulders, and said, "Don't worry. I make good plans."

CHAPTER 9

HANNAH HAD JOINED Ruby and Charlie for lunch at the Senior Center. After lunch, Ruby would stay for her bridge game and Charlie for an afternoon of poker. Hannah, not interested in card games, would leave. But she looked forward to these lunches.

Charlie was still attractive, kept trim by daily visits to the gym. Today Ruby's influence on his wardrobe was noticeable. Instead of his usual outfit of brown slacks, brightly colored Henley shirt, green plaid sports jacket, and white tasseled loafers, he sported a light-green shirt with a chocolate cardigan over tan slacks, and brown loafers. No longer looking like the used-car salesman he had been, he appeared to be a retired success-ful businessman—until he opened his mouth. But Ruby loved him, and Hannah liked him, so the threesome continued.

"Charlie," scolded Hannah, "if you eat all that, you'll make yourself sick." She pointed to his plate, piled with lasagna, a thick slice of ham, a pile of mashed potatoes, and a spoonful of green beans.

Charlie grinned. "But look. I'm eating my veggies."

"And a plateful of desserts. Why do you need a brownie, cookies, and bread pudding?" she persisted.

"Oh, Hannah, it's okay." Ruby interrupted. "He had a checkup last week and he's fine. The doctor said he had the body of a man ten years younger." Ruby smiled at Charlie as she said this and was rewarded by a smile in return as he shoveled food into his mouth.

Hannah resorted to her now favorite word, "Whatever," and changed the topic. "Did you know that foster care only lasts until the child is eighteen years old?"

"That's not true," responded Ruby. "My friend in New York had a foster care boy who lived with them until he finished college. They had wanted to adopt him, but there was some legal problem. Anyway, they had him from when he was six or so until he graduated. I think they continued to see him even after that."

"Well, they were obviously good people; but the law doesn't require—or I should say, they don't pay for kids after eighteen. So people who do it for the money just kick the kids out at eighteen. And what's an eighteen-year-old to do? How are they going to live?"

"Well, they can go to college—there's financial aid for that—or they can get a job like everyone else does."

Hannah was about to respond, when Charlie interrupted. He lifted his head from his plate. "That may have been true in our day, Ruby, but not today. Financial aid doesn't cover everything, and the kids have to take out student loans, which can add up, and then they're stuck with them for years. And you know how the job market has been lately. No, it's not easy for young people today—especially if they don't have a family to help them. Remember I was telling you about that article I read last week about the number of college graduates returning to live at home with their parents? Well, these kids—the foster kids—don't have a family to return to."

Hannah was nodding her agreement throughout Charlie's comments. She loved Ruby but had no patience with her naïve—in Hannah's eyes, ignorant—views on social issues. It was another example of how strange friendships could be: What *did* they have in common except the fact that they were both New York Jews living in a small WASP midwestern town? But Hannah found that if they avoided social and political issues, they enjoyed each other's company.

When Charlie finished his comments, Ruby nodded. "Well, maybe you're right," she conceded.

"Maybe? You're darn tootin' he's right. You ought to listen to him—you got a real *mensch* here," Hannah replied, patting Charlie on the shoulder.

Charlie went back to the rest of his lunch. Hannah knew that to continue the discussion would be difficult for him. Pursuing his point would seem to be correcting Ruby, and he would want to avoid that. He and Ruby had a good relationship, and he wouldn't want to jeopardize it by pointing out how far apart they were on certain issues, issues that didn't really make a difference in their lives. He knew, however, that Hannah saw that as a weakness in him, but, as he had told her, he was the one who had to deal with Ruby afterward, not Hannah.

Lunch finished, Ruby settled at the bridge table, and Charlie returned to the dessert table, filling a plate with cookies to take to the poker table. Hannah said her good-byes and left.

It was one thirty, and she wasn't sure what she would do with the rest of the afternoon. Her talk with Shelley that morning had left her restless. She couldn't get Shelley's face out of her mind: the tears, the shame, the guilt. As if being homeless had been her fault, something to hide. Surely there was something to be done—not only for Shelley—that would be easy—but also for others in similar situations.

Hannah sat in her car, thinking. She was anxious to talk to Janice about Shelley, having a plan of action in mind, but Janice had a meeting after work and wouldn't be home until late. She needed to do something *now*. But what? Well, it was always good to get the facts. After all, she was on the school board. Why not start at the high school? There must be a counselor or teacher who could tell her if there were any students in the position Shelley had been in. In fact, didn't Janice say that she knew of some kids who had been kicked out of their homes? Yes, that was the place to start.

She drove to the high school, adrenaline working its way through her system. She almost missed a stop sign. *Calm down*, she told herself. *You don't want to show up all flushed and excited. They'll think you're a dotty old lady—and not only won't you be taken seriously, but you'll reinforce the stereotype of old women.*

She slowed down, driving more cautiously than necessary, to the frustration of the driver behind her, whose attempts at passing were doomed to failure in the heavy traffic. She figured she would be mortified to hear what he was probably saying about her driving: *Get the hell off the road, you crazy old biddy. You shouldn't be driving at your age.* But she didn't hear him and continued at her own slow pace, ignoring his many attempts to pass.

Brewster High was located on the edge of town, a large brick building in the shape of an *H*, surrounded by farmland. The city had bought up some of the farmland years ago to allow increasing the size of the school's football field, without which—in the eyes of most people in the city—there couldn't possibly be a high school. The reduction and elimination of such programs as art, music, and foreign languages didn't anger people, but any decrease in funding the sports program brought out irate parents and concerned citizens.

Hannah entered the building in the middle of the *H*, the reception area. Fortunately, Brewster hadn't experienced the violence in schools that other cities had, and there was no metal detector or armed guard at the door. Instead, she entered a quiet hallway. Classes were in session, and few students were walking around. Having been to events at the school before, she was familiar with the layout and walked to the main office.

"Well, hello, Hannah," the receptionist said with a warm smile. Hannah was known to the teachers and staff, as the mother of the principal and an outspoken member of the school board. She was the one who always asked for the input of the people who actually knew what was going on in the schools, which frustrated those who thought of schools as simply another business, preferably one that made a profit.

"Heather, how nice to see you. I see you've got another grandbaby," she said, looking at the picture of a fat, cross-eyed, bald baby so ugly it was cute.

"Yes, that's Alfred—Freddy for short." Heather beamed. "He's such a wonderful little guy: sleeps through the night, already eats solid foods—and he's only three months old. And he has such a pleasant temperament. We're so lucky with this one. His sister was a pistol: a fussy eater and a fussy sleeper until she was almost two."

"Well, each child is different, but we love them all, right? By the way, maybe you can help me. I need to talk to someone—counselor, teacher—anyone who can give me some information about students who don't live at home. You know, kids who might have been kicked out by parents."

"We do have some of them. Usually they've been in trouble—drugs, shoplifting, fights—and their parents just can't handle them. Is the board going to do something about those kids? They're really a problem."

Hannah quickly realized that she didn't have an ally in Heather, so she let the assumption that she officially represented the school board remain uncorrected.

"Well, we're looking into it," she replied—honest but misleading. "But I need some information. Who would be good to talk to about that?"

"Probably Diane Cassidy, our counselor. She sees most of the problem kids. Let me check her schedule…You're in luck, she has a free hour now. You can probably find her in the faculty lounge."

Hannah thanked her and went in search of the counselor, hoping to find a more sympathetic attitude than she had seen in Heather.

• • •

Diane Cassidy, in her forties, was dressed in a flowing yellow tunic over jeans, had short, spikey gray hair, and wore an infectious smile that gave her plain face a patina of beauty. She greeted Hannah as she entered the lounge.

"Mrs. Lowenstein," she said as she rose from the table to welcome her. "How nice to see you. Are you looking for the boss?"

"Oh, so my daughter's the boss here. No wonder she thinks she's the boss at home too," Hannah joked. "No, I'm here to see you. Heather thought you might be able to help me."

"Come. Sit down. I don't have an appointment until two thirty, and this place is usually quiet, so we can talk here. What's the problem?"

Hannah took a seat at the table and explained what she was looking for: How many students were considered homeless? Where were they living? Why were they homeless? What other information could Diane share about them?

She made it clear this time that she didn't represent the board, only herself, but that she would raise the issue with the board after she had sufficient information.

"I don't have numbers at hand, but I could certainly get them for you," Diane said. "I'm surprised—but glad—that you're looking into the issue. Most people don't realize that we have a problem with homelessness here, especially that it affects young people. I've talked it over with Janice, and we agree that in addition to the usual problems connected with not having a home, it has an especially cruel effect on our students. It's hard to keep up with schoolwork when you're worried where you're going to spend the night, no less how you're going to eat. Many of these students drop out of school, and those that don't drop out usually don't do well, which affects their opportunities when they do graduate." She leaned back in her chair and sighed.

Hannah could see that Diane was going to be an ally: no blaming of the students, sympathy for their situation, and maybe willing to do something. Yes, she had found the right person.

"Well, if you could get me some numbers that I could present to the board, perhaps we could do something. I don't know what, but it's shameful in a town like this—"

Diane interrupted her. "Mrs. Lowenstein, believe me. I'm with you. If we can do anything to help these kids, I'm with you. But you have to realize that there's not much support for homeless people in general. People don't want to know about them. It's easy to blame them for their problems: they're lazy, use drugs, drink too much, et cetera. People don't want them in their neighborhood. They don't want to spend money on them. They don't want to think about them. So it's not easy to fix it."

"I know, I know. I get too excited about things—that's what Janice always says—and I want quickie fixes. But what else do I have to do these days? I can certainly spend some time *trying* to do something. At least I'll be able to sleep at night."

Hannah got up from the table, leaned over, and hugged Diane. "When you have the information, please call me. And thanks for caring," she said as she left the room.

CHAPTER 10

IT WAS ALMOST five when Hannah arrived home. She had stopped at Marty's to buy groceries for dinner and had got stuck in traffic. The shift at Delfield's, a factory that produced widgets of some sort, had just changed, and traffic was backed up as cars streamed out of the parking lot.

She was exhausted and not up to preparing a feast for the family. Fortunately, she had part of a roasted chicken in the refrigerator, which, combined with the veggies she had just bought, would make an easy casserole. The family would just have to do with store-bought cookies she kept hidden in the pantry for emergencies.

She quickly threw the casserole together and into the oven, and she retreated to the living room to relax with another repeat of *Walker*, which was where David found her when he returned from soccer practice: TV blaring, Hannah sound asleep. Hannah stirred when she heard David go into the kitchen. "I wasn't sleeping, darling. Just resting my eyes. Come, tell me how your practice went."

"I'll be right there, Grandma. I'm just getting a snack," he replied. A few seconds later, he emerged with a plate of last night's lasagna in hand.

"Darling, what are you eating? You'll spoil your appetite. I made chicken tonight—and a special dessert," she added.

"I'm starving," he said, diving into the lasagna. "The coach really made us run a lot. He thinks we're getting lazy, but he's wrong. We've been winning games, more than last season, so I don't know why he's being so hard on us."

Hannah resisted the temptation to engage in a discussion of hard work, instead turning the conversation to school. "So, how's summer school? What are you learning?"

"Nothing, the usual."

"So the usual is nothing? For that you're going to school? Better you should go out and get a job."

"Grandma," pleaded David. "I don't mean *nothing*, just nothing that I'm interested in."

"Ah, that's different. So what aren't you interested in?"

David took another large bite of the lasagna, wiped his mouth with his hand, and sighed, settling in for a long talk. There was no putting Hannah off when she was asking questions.

"Well, I don't see the reason for taking algebra, I'm never going to use it. And poetry. All those strange people writing in ways like nobody talks—who needs that?"

"Well, I don't know much about poetry, but algebra—I use it when I do grocery shopping: If one can of tuna fish costs a dollar and ten cents, how much should four cans cost? And when the special says four cans for five dollars, I know it's a scam."

"Yeah, but I can do that without algebra."

"Okay, good. You can do my shopping for me." She laughed. "But what *does* interest you, besides soccer?"

David paused for a second. "Science. I've decided I want to be an engineer, and you need science for that."

"You also need math for that, if you want your bridges shouldn't fall down," Hannah reminded him. "But good, an engineer is good. We need engineers, especially ones who know enough math so their bridges don't fall down."

Just then, Maddie and Shelley came in. David quickly took the opportunity to grab his lasagna and dash upstairs, where his latest video game was waiting. He'd said he was anxious to get to level six—which would put him a level ahead of his best friend, Billy.

"Don't eat any more. Dinner will be ready soon," Hannah shouted as he raced up the stairs.

Maddie plopped down on the couch, kicked off her shoes, and sighed. "You can't imagine what a day I've had. The meanest cat I've ever seen.

We had to put a muzzle on her just to take her temperature. I'm not in favor of declawing kittens, but that one…all her claws should have been removed—and her teeth."

"I assume you don't take temperatures in the mouth, right? Well, the poor thing doesn't know why you're poking around back there. No wonder it's scared," Hannah said with a smile.

"Well, anyway, it wasn't fun."

Shelley had been quiet since entering the room, still standing in the doorway.

Hannah motioned to her to sit down next to Maddie. "And how was your day? Better than Maddie's, I hope."

Shelley walked over to the couch and sat down. Head bent down, she responded with a nod, followed by a quick glance at Hannah. Hannah smiled gently, not intending a follow-up conversation. She was pleased to see Shelley relax.

Hannah looked at the two girls. They were pictures in contrast: one blond, one brunette; one tall, one short; one short hair, one long—but both young and beautiful. But there was a contrast that made all the difference in the world: Maddie had a loving family; Shelley had no one.

• • •

The casserole was a success. Even David asked for seconds.

But when the cookies were brought out, David frowned. "You said there was a special dessert—these aren't special."

"David, stop complaining," Paul scolded. "Your grandmother can't bake something special for you every day. If you don't like the cookies, don't eat them."

"No, I like them. But she lied…"

"That's enough…" Paul said, his voice rising.

Hannah interrupted Paul. "No, Paul, he's right. I did say we had a special dessert. I was trying to get him to stop eating the lasagna, but he's right: I lied. So I apologize, David. I shouldn't have said that."

David, not sure what was happening, only that he was no longer on the hot seat, looked uncomfortable. "Ah, that's okay, Grandma. These cookies are okay."

Hannah saw the change in David. Last year he would have worn his disappointment for the rest of the meal. Now, he was starting to realize that there were other people in the world beside him. And, she realized that one of those people who really mattered to him was his grandma. When she had decided to move out of the house and live with Ruby last year, David had been devastated. He had confessed that he looked forward to the strange conversations they had. She was like a friend, only old and funny.

The conversation reverted back to a discussion of the latest movies in town and whether *X-Men VII* would be as good as its predecessors, David the only one optimistic—in fact, the only one who cared.

By the time the table was cleared and the dishes were taken care of by Maddie and Shelley, Janice returned home.

"Are you hungry?" was the first thing Hannah said. "We can heat up some of the casserole."

"No, I had dinner at the meeting," Janice replied as she hugged her mother. "I see you got the girls to do the dishes. You'll have to share your secret." She laughed.

"I heard that," Maddie shouted. "We always do the dishes...when we're not going out."

"And why aren't you going out tonight? It's Friday. Speaking of going out, I haven't seen Jaime lately? Everything okay?"

Maddie and Jaime had been seeing each other for over a year. Maddie's worry that going to different schools would change their relationship had faded. She'd confided to Hannah that texting, skyping, and visiting when possible had strengthened the relationship until now she couldn't remember that she ever doubted the strength of their commitment.

"He's fine. He works nights at the store and doesn't get out until after nine. He's hoping to change his hours, but so far..." Maddie shrugged.

"Well, he's a nice young man," interjected Hannah. "You should invite him to have dinner with us when he's not working. One more mouth to feed, no problem."

Janice smiled. "Maybe Mom should open up a soup kitchen. That way she could feed more people."

"That's not a bad idea—I don't mean I should do it—but I bet there are a lot of people who could use a good hot meal…*Is* there a soup kitchen in town?"

Shelley, who up until this point had not engaged in the discussion, looked up at Hannah. Her unspoken question was clear to Hannah: *Where was Hannah going with this?*

Paul answered Hannah's question. "Yes, there is. It's over on Willow Street, next to the water department office. I've had some clients who volunteer there—you know, help prepare the food, serve it, clean up. They're always looking for people to help out."

Dishes put away, Maddie turned to Shelley. "Come upstairs. I want to show you something before we leave. Tiffany sent pictures of some furniture she got for the apartment at a garage sale. They're kind of neat."

• • •

Hannah sat at the kitchen table, preparing a shopping list for the next day. "Orange juice, toilet paper, maybe some fish, berries—I could make a pie," she muttered to herself as she added to the list. Her mind wasn't on the task; she kept coming back to the discussion she'd had with Shelley. It was only her awareness that Janice and Paul needed some time alone that kept her from interrupting their conversation in the living room.

She liked Paul; he was good for Janice, as well as a fine man. And the kids had accepted him as a stepfather. Their own father made such infrequent attempts to see them that they appreciated Paul's caring, constant presence in their lives. And he was always willing to help Hannah in her various "investigations." It paid to have a lawyer in the family!

The list finally finished, she went into the living room to say good night. Janice was cuddled up on the couch next to Paul, empty wineglasses on the coffee table, TV turned to a black-and-white movie that no one was watching. They looked up when Hannah entered.

"Night, Mom. Sleep in tomorrow. I don't think anyone will be getting up early," Janice predicted.

CHAPTER 11

HANNAH WAS UP at six—her usual time—everyone else still asleep. She put the coffee on, whipped up a batch of cinnamon rolls for the traditional Saturday breakfast the family liked, and sat down at the kitchen table.

The early morning hours were the time for planning her day, and today was going to be busy: grocery shopping, baking a pie with the raspberries she had bought at the local farmers' market, calling Diane Cassidy for the information on homeless students—yes, she had asked Diane to call when she had the information, but it couldn't hurt to remind her, could it?—and finding time to talk to Janice about Shelley.

Shelley had seemed fine at dinner, although uncharacteristically quiet. But Hannah sensed a tension in her that had not been there before. Perhaps, she wondered, Shelley was unsure what Hannah would do with the information she had shared. If that was true, Hannah had to do something. She had promised to make a plan and now had to do that.

By the time she had finished her second cup of coffee and removed the batch of cinnamon rolls from the oven, she could hear movement from upstairs. Janice and Paul, she guessed. The girls had come in late the night before and would probably sleep in, and David never appeared before nine on the weekend, unless there was a soccer practice or game.

A few minutes later Janice and Paul appeared: he in jeans and a black T-shirt, she in a light-green robe over her blue-striped pajamas, long hair tangled, giving her the appearance of the teenager Hannah remembered.

Paul greeted Hannah with a kiss on the cheek as he filled two cups with coffee. "Cinnamon rolls!" he cried. "You sure know how to please a man."

"And a woman," added Janice as she reached up to take her coffee from him.

"So easy to please? You come cheap," quipped Hannah, joining them at the table. "So what are you two up to today?"

Janice looked at Paul. "Well," she said, pausing for effect, "I think Paul is going to fix the garage door. Right, honey?"

Paul responded with a nod, his mouth filled with cinnamon roll.

"You can do that?" asked Hannah. "I didn't know you were handy. And what's wrong with the garage door? It works okay."

"It works now, but if the hardware isn't tightened, it's going to come crashing down one of these days. Haven't you noticed the noise when it's opening and the shudder when it's closing?"

Janice rolled her eyes at her mother. It was a source of family fun to remind Hannah that she was unobservant of her surroundings.

"I don't have time to notice such things," Hannah responded defensively. "I leave that up to you."

Janice exchanged smiles with Paul and changed the subject.

Didn't they know it was useless to try to get her to be more observant of things? She knew she lived in her head, making plans, conducting internal dialogues with herself, oblivious to what was going on around her. She liked it that way.

But she also knew that she was observant about people. She could always tell if someone was in a good or bad mood, happy or unhappy, comfortable or not, truthful or hiding something. Janice used to complain how, as a child, she had never been able to hide anything from her. She claimed that her reputation for honesty was due to the fact that growing up she realized it didn't pay to lie, because Hannah would always know.

"So, what are you doing today," she asked.

"Nothing special. Groceries—you need to tell me what to add to my list—and I'll make a pie for dessert and maybe try that recipe Ruby gave me for a shrimp dish—it's got shrimp, peppers, tomatoes, and it all goes on rice. It sounded good, so I thought I'd try it. Not too spicy though. I know the kids don't like spicy."

"You mean David doesn't like spicy. You know, Mom, you spoil him. He has to learn to eat what the rest of us are eating."

"I know. I know. But he's still young. He'll learn...and I'm going to check up on the homeless kids in town." Hannah waited for a response. She hadn't yet told Janice about her talk with Diane Cassidy and didn't know how she would respond.

"What do you mean 'check up'? Check up on what?"

"Well, this isn't the time to talk about it—we *do* need to talk—but I spoke to your Diane Cassidy yesterday about the kids who don't have homes. She's going to give me the facts, but I thought I'd start with some of the people at Listening Ear...you know, the place people call when they're in trouble. She told me about that place. Maybe they know something about these kids. But that's for a longer discussion, when we have more time. The kids will be coming down soon, and I don't want they should hear this."

With that announcement, Hannah got up from the table, put her cup in the dishwasher, and proceeded to bustle unnecessarily around the kitchen.

Janice took the hint: discussion ended. She went upstairs to get dressed, while Paul went to the garage to check on what was needed for the repairs.

Hannah could tell that Paul wasn't excited about fixing the garage door. But any opportunity for a trip to Home Depot, where he could roam among all the power tools he didn't need but coveted was okay to him. He may be a lawyer, she smiled, but he was also a man.

● ● ●

After everyone had finished breakfast and gone off to whatever they were doing that day, Hannah put in the call to Diane Cassidy, who was surprised to hear from her. Diane explained that she would get to it on Monday and would call then. Hannah, realizing that she had been unreasonable to expect any results yet, apologized for bothering Diane and promised that she would wait for her call.

She sat by the phone, waiting for an inspiration. What to do? Whom to call? When it hit her: Listening Ear. Why not talk to people there today?

After checking that she had her grocery list with her, Hannah took off to visit Listening Ear. Hannah had discovered it had been founded in the seventies to handle crisis calls that were not handled by the 911 number for the police department: calls from people who were depressed or suicidal, from rape victims who were reluctant to go to the police, from anyone who needed help or someone to talk to. It also provided limited temporary housing for those who needed it, when funds were available.

When Hannah walked into the office on Birch Street, on the edge of the downtown area, she was surprised to find it empty except for a large young woman at the desk, talking on the phone. She had expected to find a row of people answering crisis calls.

The young woman finished her call and turned to Hannah. "Hi, can I help you?" she asked, clearly surprised to find someone like Hannah, who didn't look like she was in crisis.

"I hope so. I want to know about homeless students—you know, kids who are in school but don't live at home, or anyplace." Hannah could tell from the young woman's expression that she didn't know what Hannah was talking about and may have even thought that Hannah was eccentric. So she took a deep breath and started over.

"Dear, I'm on the school board, and we're concerned about the students who are technically homeless. We believe that some of them contact your agency for help. Would you have any information on that? Not their names, of course, but perhaps how many have called for help, say in the last year or even the last few months."

Hannah knew she was on questionable grounds, as the school board knew nothing about this, but she planned to raise it at the next meeting and could justify, at least to herself, that she was simply gathering information.

The young woman nodded, but replied, "I don't have that information, but if you come in on Monday when the director is here, I'm sure he'll be able to help you. Perhaps you should make an appointment though, to be sure that he has time to see you."

"Good idea. Put me down for whatever time he has available on Monday—I'm flexible. And where are all the phones that you take the calls on? I don't see any here."

"Oh, this is the office. The actual calls are picked up in another room where there's a whole bank of phones. Would you like to see it?"

"That would be lovely," Hannah replied, smiling warmly.

They entered a room with five cubicles. Only one was presently being used, by a young blond man reading a magazine.

"Saturday morning is usually a quiet time," the young woman explained. "By tonight all five phones will be in use. On the slow times, we just need one person to handle emergencies, but we always have another person on call."

It pleased Hannah that the young woman was proud of the work Listening Ear did, and it also pleased her that young people worked there. Not that older people wouldn't do a good job, she reminded herself, but it helped to maintain her faith in young people: not all of them were self-involved, narcissistic, irresponsible hedonists.

• • •

Serving leftovers had a strange effect on Hannah. On the one hand, remembering her mother's tales of life in the depression years, she refused to waste food, leading her to develop unusual but tasty meals of remnants from previous dinners. On the other hand, because the wanted to serve only the best to the family, she felt guilty serving leftovers, thinking she should have put time into preparing something from scratch.

So today she would cook and bake. After she left Listening Ear, she stopped at Marty's for groceries. Once home she set about baking two blueberry pies, to be served with ice cream, and a pan of enchiladas, David's favorite. She knew that she spoiled him, but…well, no excuse. She just spoiled him.

She had never made Mexican food before coming to Brewster, but she had enjoyed eating it in restaurants. So how hard could it be to make enchiladas when there were recipes in all of the magazines? By her third attempt, she had mastered the process, and now it was on her list of go-to recipes. With a green salad to accompany the enchiladas, and pie and ice cream for dessert, she felt better about the leftovers of the previous night.

David was the first one home. Between soccer practice three times a week, summer school, and video games every day, Hannah worried that he barely had time for things like movies, swimming, and the other summer activities he had looked forward to.

Hannah woke when she heard him approach. "I wasn't sleeping. I was just resting my eyes." He smiled and turned off the TV.

"So, how was your practice? Did you make a home run?"

David rolled his eyes. "Grandma, home runs are for baseball. We make goals in soccer."

"So, did you make any goals?"

"It wasn't a game, only a practice. But yeah, I did get one into the net—that's where the ball goes to make a goal, you know."

"Of course I know…So you had a good practice, good. You have homework to do?"

"I have to read this stupid poem about fences. I have to write a paragraph about what I think it's about. That's going to be easy. It's about fences."

Hannah peered at him over her glasses. "Fences? That's all you got out of it? You can write a whole paragraph about fences? Maybe you should talk to your mother about it. I don't know much about poetry, but the writer must have meant something more. Maybe 'fences' means something else?"

"I don't know. Anyway, it doesn't matter what I write. I just have to write something." With that announcement, he waved at Hannah and went upstairs to either write his paragraph or return to his video game.

• • •

Hannah managed to get Janice alone after dinner, before she got immersed in something else. It was a challenge for Janice to spend enough time with the children—especially David. Maddie seemed to thrive on her independence and didn't need "quality time" with Janice, whose resolution not to bring work home with her had been broken the week after it was made. The choice was to either stay at the office late or bring work home. At least at home, she rationalized out loud to Hannah, she was available to others.

The discussion was brief: Hannah apprised Janice of her talk with Shelley, her meeting with Diane Cassidy, and her visit to Listening Ear;

Janice reported on what she had found about Shelley's college record—there was no record.

Janice looked at her mother. "So what do we do? What can we do? It's clear she's been technically homeless since she graduated high school. It's also clear that she's been resourceful in hiding that and has found a way of surviving. But what do you think of her—is she a person Maddie should be living with? In fact, how will she even pay her part of the rent?"

Hannah listened to Janice's concerns, but didn't respond. This was her daughter, a woman she knew was concerned about Shelley, but who had a fierce determination to protect her children. Janice's divorce had been precipitated by Jim's neglect of the children more than his flirtations and affairs. Hannah would tread lightly when she made her suggestions regarding Shelley, and tonight was not the time for that.

She nodded agreement with Janice's concerns and ended the conversation by saying she didn't know what they could do, but she would think about it. Janice rose from her chair, kissed her mother on the cheek, and went to join Paul in the living room.

CHAPTER 12

WHEN HANNAH ENTERED the front door of Listening Ear, it was quickly apparent that this was a different place than she had seen on Saturday. It was bustling with activity: the same young woman was at the desk, but this time she was busy attending to a long line of people, some requesting help, others seeking applications to work at the agency. She was pleasant, efficient, and compassionate when appropriate. She looked up and nodded at Hannah, indicating she should go down the hall to the director's office.

Hannah knocked on the door with the sign *Director, Mr. Abramson*, and entered when she heard a voice. She didn't know what the voice said—her hearing wasn't what it used to be, even though she wouldn't admit it—but she assumed it was an invitation to enter.

Mr. Abramson, seated at a desk behind a pile of papers and books, got up to shake Hannah's hand and offer her a seat, from which he had to first remove a pile of papers. He appeared to be in his late fifties or so, with a mop of salt-and-pepper hair, a large belly, and a warm smile. He wore a white shirt, with sleeves rolled up, and brown trousers that appeared to be well worn but of good quality. Hannah smiled back at him as she sat down.

"Angela tells me that you were in on Saturday and had some questions for me. Are you thinking of volunteering? We could use someone of your experience here, you know. Some of our clients would respond better to a mature woman than to our youngsters."

"Ah, a flatterer. Mature, not old, nice. But no, I'm not here to volunteer. I'm here for information." She decided to continue the image of being there on official business for the school board and presented her request for information on the homeless student population in the area.

"Well yes, we do have quite a few young people seeking assistance with housing, but adults form the larger percentage of the homeless in town," Mr. Abramson informed her. "You know, with the economy the way it is, we're seeing a different sort of person here. It used to be largely men who sought us out for shelter—you know, those who had been released from our mental institutions and were left to fend for themselves, or those who had alcohol or drug-related problems. Now we see women, and women with children, coming in for help. Why just the other day, a young woman with a toddler—couldn't have been more than two years old—came in. She had lost her job—obviously lost her husband earlier—and couldn't pay the rent. She and the baby had been sleeping in her car and getting food at the soup kitchen in town for two weeks. We were able to provide a few nights at one of the local motels that works with us—they give us a discount rate. But that's not a real solution, only a Band-Aid for a wound that's hemorrhaging."

It was clear to Hannah that he cared about the people who came in for help, and also clear that he was frustrated at how little he could do for them. Her first impression of him as a typical slick administrator concerned with the bottom line was being replaced by that of a committed, caring individual.

"I know you do other things here than deal with homeless people, like help people with problems like suicide and depression, things like that. And from what I hear, you do a lot of good for those people," Hannah said, smiling at Mr. Abramson. "What I'm trying to do is small, dealing with students, primarily because I'm on the school board. I wish I was on the City Commission—then maybe we could get the city involved in the bigger picture. But for now, I have to focus on the young people, and I need numbers to present to the school board: How many students…in fact, how many young people have dropped out of school and are homeless. What happens to them? What can you do for them? And do you know of any other places where they might go for shelter? Any information you can give me will help when I talk to the school board next week."

She sighed, sat back in the chair, and looked at him with expectation on her face. He looked at his watch, looked up at her, and looked away, as if considering whether to spend any more time on the issue. He seemed tempted to just send her away with a promise that he would get back to her when he had more time—a promise he would conveniently forget. But the look on her face and the concern she had expressed must have impressed him. While she might be naïve in her assessment of what the school board could or would do, what harm would it do to give her the information she requested? Stranger things had been accomplished by naïve people.

He got up from his chair, indicated to her that he would be right back, and left the room. Hannah fought the impulse to get up and follow him. But she could not sit in the chair any longer. She paced the room, looking at the photos on the wall, mostly of staff and volunteers, and was ready to leave, when Abramson returned. She smiled when she saw that he held a folder in his hand, which he handed to her.

"This is the data we have available for the last three years. I don't know if it will help you, but you're welcome to use it however you think best. I hope it helps."

She took the folder in her hands and smiled at him "You're a *mensch*, Mr. Abramson. Thank you."

• • •

It was still too early to meet Ruby for lunch, and it was also too early to bother Diane Cassidy again for information. Hannah sat in her car, pondering her choices: stop for a cup of coffee and a danish at the new bakery on Mission Street or browse some of the shops at the mall. The mall. She could drop in on Shelley at work. But would Shelley think she was checking up on her? *Oh, for heaven's sake*, she scolded herself, *if I considered every possibility of my actions, I'd never do anything.*

She arrived at the mall and wandered around trying to find Shelley. It would have helped if she had remembered the name of the store, but without that information, she had to enter every store that sold women's clothing until she found Shelley in one of them, helping a customer pick out a sweater. The woman was looking at a green sweater, and Shelley was holding up a variety of alternatives, trying to convince the woman that the blue was more flattering for her complexion. The sale finally concluded, and Hannah walked over to the counter and, with innocence exuding from her face, expressed surprise at seeing Shelley.

"I didn't know you worked here," she declared. "I have a few minutes before meeting a friend for lunch, and I thought I'd see what people are wearing today. I'm afraid Maddie is right: I'm stuck in the eighties with my style."

Shelley smiled. "Yes," she replied. "But it looks good on you. Those brown slacks, with the pale blue shirt—and that lovely beige scarf—work beautifully together... Now if you just got more fashionable shoes, you could be a model."

Hannah ignored the suggestion and asked, "So, how's business?" Hannah asked as she looked over the sweaters on the counter. Picking up a yellow cardigan and holding it up to her face, she asked, "Is this color good for me?"

Shelley frowned. "No, look in the mirror. See how it drains the color from your face and makes you look sallow."

Hannah looked, and nodded agreement. "I see what you mean. Who knew different colors changed how you looked. I just never wore yellow because I didn't like the color. Though come to think of it, maybe I didn't like the color because my mother always told me *she* didn't like the color. Maybe she was telling me it didn't look good on me. She was always very tactful."

Shelley laughed. Before she could say anything, a customer approached the counter. Hannah took that as her cue to leave, mentioning her lunch appointment as she waved to Shelley.

Once back in her car, Hannah let out a sigh of contentment. Shelley was fine. All she had to do was find a way to get her into college or at least an art program somewhere. How hard could that be?

• • •

Hannah arrived at the Senior Center late. Ruby was already seated at the table with two other women, eating her chicken-salad sandwich and a cup of tomato-basil soup. She waved at Hannah and pointed to an empty seat at the table. Hannah deposited her purse on the empty chair and proceeded to the food line, where she filled her plate with chicken salad, potato salad, and a large scoop of peach cobbler—which she justified by not taking any bread.

The two other women at the table were regaling Ruby with the latest gossip. This time it was about Phyllis Parkins, who was on a mission to charm or, in their eyes, trap the new man in town. Phyllis was the subject of much of their gossip. In her seventies, she dressed like a teenager: short skirts, bare midriff in summer, tight sweaters in winter, always high heels, lots of makeup, and poufy blond hair—not a pretty sight, but somehow attractive to men. The women at the table couldn't understand what it was that men found attractive, and they were offended by Hannah's suggestion that it was sex.

"Men aren't interested in sex at that age," Mrs. Ladimer declared, "that age" being the age of most of the men at the Senior Center. "Besides," she continued, "it's unfair to suggest that men are so shallow that they'd be attracted to a woman like Phyllis."

Hannah restrained herself from reminding Mrs. Ladimer that her husband was of that age and seemed to enjoy looking at Phyllis. She simply replied, "Well, I'm not saying that all men are interested in someone like Phyllis, but some obviously are. You have to admit it's not her intelligence or stimulating conversation that's seducing them. The poor woman can't string three words together to form a sentence. Which leads me to think that it's something else that the men are interested in. Is she a good cook? No—you've tasted the chicken casserole she brings to every potluck. Is she nurturing, making them feel important? No—she talks only about herself and the gifts that she receives from them. So I'm left with the only attribute she has: sex.

"But you know, I feel sorry for her, for anyone who can't accept growing old. I'm sure she's lonely after losing her husband, and if this flirting makes her feel better, what harm does it do? Me, no one could compare to my Leo, so I don't even think about other men."

With that, Hannah returned to her chicken salad. Mrs. Ladimer, still not convinced that men in their seventies were interested in sex, just shrugged. Hannah caught Ruby's eye and smiled. She knew that men in their seventies were still interested in sex. Ruby and Charlie had taught her that.

• • •

That afternoon Hannah received a call from Diane Cassidy, with the information she had requested. There had been five students in the last two years who had been considered homeless by the school: three had dropped out, and two had successfully completed high school. Diane had checked with the school's attorney and been told it was okay to release the names of the students, although she didn't have any information on their present addresses. Hannah thanked her and, armed with the information, proceeded to form a plan to track down the students.

With nothing to do until David returned from soccer practice, she turned her attention to Shelley. Surely there were scholarships or financial aid for people like Shelley. She was talented, had graduated high school, and with sufficient resources she could have gone to college. So what if she incurred student loan debts? At least she would have had an opportunity to get some credentials and, perhaps even more important, some training that would help her support herself in the future.

Hannah didn't underestimate the importance of a college education. She had insisted that Janice go to college when all Janice had wanted to do after high school was get a job and move out west. Fortunately, Leo had sided with Hannah, and off Janice went to NYU on an academic scholarship and student loans. She did well and went on to get a graduate degree at Columbia, partially covered by a fellowship. But even if it had cost them more money, it would have been money well spent. Janice had been introduced to a world she would not have known, a world that awakened her to books and music, experiences that Hannah and Leo could never have provided.

• • •

Hannah was watching a rerun of *Walker*, when she heard the door slam and David toss his backpack on the floor in the hallway. She had been anxiously awaiting his arrival and quickly got up from the recliner to greet him in the hallway.

"David, are you hungry? I have some cookies for you. Come into the kitchen. We have to talk—after you pick up your stuff."

David retrieved his backpack from the floor, put it on the shelf, and followed her into the kitchen, where he sat down to a glass of milk and a plate of homemade chocolate chip cookies.

"Wha's up?" he mumbled.

"Don't speak with your mouth full," Hannah scolded. "I need your help...in an investigation."

That was a magic word to David. Last year, he had helped Hannah in finding out information about Ruby's son, and it had been exciting, he'd said. Some of the information was easily found on the Internet, but some required what he'd called "creative hacking."

"I need to find out how I should get in touch with these five people," she said, showing him the list of the names Diane Cassidy had given her. "They may be living in town, but I don't think you'll find them in the telephone book. You have ways of finding this out?" she asked.

"Sure, but why do you want to find out?"

How much to tell him, Hannah wondered. He was a young fourteen, but you've got to give children responsibilities if you want them to learn to be responsible. So she explained that these five people had been kicked out of their homes when they were still in school, and she wanted to know how they were doing.

"What kind of parent does that to a child? Terrible," she said.

"Yeah, I knew a guy in my class who was kicked out by his dad for something—I don't know what—and he couch surfed. Everyone knew this. He came in early and used the shower in the gym. I haven't seen him recently though, so I don't know if he's coming back to school in the fall."

"Couch serve? What's that?"

"No, couch *surf*—you know, like surfing the net. You find friends who let you spend a few nights on their couch, then a few nights on someone else's couch. This guy I was talking about did it for almost a year. He was lucky. One of his friend's parents didn't care who he brought home."

"Ah, another wonderful parent. Anyway, here are the names. Find out what you can. But remember, homework first—and maybe we shouldn't tell your mother just yet?"

David gulped the last of the milk, took another cookie from the plate, and rose from the table.

Hannah looked at him. "Remember, homework first."

"Aye, aye, Captain," David replied as he saluted Hannah and walked out of the kitchen.

• • •

That evening, the talk at the dinner table focused on David's achievement at reaching level six.

"No one's interested in hearing about your silly game," Maddie exclaimed.

To Hannah's surprise, Shelley came to his defense.

"Oh, it's okay, Maddie. It's hard to get to that level." She turned to David. "Not many people get there, right?" She smiled at David, who looked at her as if he had never seen her before.

"Uh, yeah, right," he replied, now somewhat self-conscious about the attention he was getting. He was used to being ignored, or at least humored. To be taken seriously was clearly a new experience for him.

Janice used the break in the conversation to announce that she had something to discuss with Shelley after dinner. Shelley, ever wary, looked across the table and seemed somewhat relieved to see a smile on Janice's face.

After dinner, Janice, Hannah, and Shelley—and Maddie, at Shelley's request—moved to the living room. Janice started the conversation.

"Shelley, I have a confession to make. I've been doing some digging into your background…"

Shelley turned pale and looked as if she wanted to flee.

Hannah, who had intentionally seated herself next to Shelley, put her hand on Shelley's arm and whispered, "It's all right…You'll see."

Shelley sat back in the chair and waited to hear what Janice was going to say. Maddie was obviously clueless and just sat quietly, looking mystified.

Janice started again. "Honey, I had to check. You told us so little about yourself, and you're going to be living with Maddie. I had to know more about you. And what I found out is okay. I know you aren't enrolled at Eastern or any other college. I know you were in the foster care system. And I know you don't have enough money for college—or for much else, I would guess. I also know that you are a very talented artist."

Janice stopped here and leaned forward. "I don't know how you've been able to make a life for yourself since you left the foster care system, but obviously you have other talents than your art. Anyway, I have a proposal. Nothing is settled. It's up to you to decide if you want me to go ahead—"

Shelley interrupted her. "You don't mind that I lied? That I don't go to college? That I've basically been living a lie for the last year?"

Turning to Maddie, she asked, her eyes filling with tears, "And you?"

Maddie looked at her, puzzlement on her face. "So you don't go to college. Why does that matter?"

"I lied to you. Can you forgive that?"

"Well, you had your reasons. There's nothing to forgive."

Janice took back control of the situation and repeated, "I have a proposal. Do you want to hear it?"

Hannah nudged Shelley, who replied, "I guess so."

"Okay, here it is. I've spoken to people at Michigan...no, wait," she said as Shelley started to object. "Nothing is done. All I did was find out what the options are. It's up to you to decide which, if any, you want to accept. Okay?"

When Shelley nodded, Janice continued. "There are always scholarships at universities that go unused, usually because no one knows about them. My contacts at Michigan tell me that there are a few art scholarships that haven't been used. The one I think is a possibility for you requires there be financial need—which applies to you—and that the person show an aptitude in art, which I also think applies to you. All you would have to do is submit some of your sketches for their approval, and if they like them, you might qualify for the scholarship. If you're interested, let me know, and I'll set up an appointment for you."

Janice sat back and waited for Shelley's response.

Shelley turned to Maddie and asked, "Would you still want me to live with you and Tiffany?"

Hannah looked at Janice and shook her head. Such insecurity. She couldn't imagine what Shelley had gone through to be so fearful of acceptance. But she could imagine what Maddie's response would be and was rewarded by Maddie's reply: "Don't be silly. Of course I want you to live with us. This'll be even better. You'll be at the same school as us, and you won't have to travel back and forth to Ypsilanti. It'll be great."

Shelley wiped the tears rolling down her cheeks, gratefully using the tissues that Hannah had pressed into her hand. She had trouble controlling her voice and simply nodded her acceptance, at which point Janice rose, walked over to her, and hugged her.

"Okay, tomorrow I'll contact them and set up an appointment. What you have to do is select which of your sketches you want to show them—pick the best ones—and we'll get the ball rolling. We need to do this quickly. It's late for typical fall semester admissions, and even though yours is a special case, let's not waste any time. We don't want someone else to realize there are unused scholarships available."

CHAPTER 13

TRUE TO HIS word, David came up with information on three of the students who were still living in town. Two—those who had graduated high school—had jobs: a young woman worked as a cashier at the local Walmart, and a young man had a job as a mechanic's assistant at the local Ford dealership. The other person was still homeless. David had tracked him down at the local encampment in the park, a place where people set up makeshift tents which, in Hannah's opinion, worked in warm weather but which did nothing to protect them from rain or cold nights. David said he found out the encampment was in violation of city regulations, but the police turned a blind eye toward its enforcement until some indignant citizen filed a protest. The tents were then taken down, only to be resurrected once the police left.

He was still trying to find the other two students, who had fallen off the grid. With no address or landline phone, he had resorted to searching e-mail addresses and Facebook and Twitter accounts, but had not yet had any success.

Hannah reluctantly concluded that they were not going to be found, at least not in time for her to interview them before the school board meeting.

She showed her gratitude to David by baking some of his favorite snickerdoodle cookies, and she proceeded to make arrangements to interview the three available students.

The first thing she did was enlist the aid of Shelley, who, having been homeless, might be able to establish a rapport with the students, which would help the interviews go more smoothly.

• • •

The interviews did go smoothly; all three of the students were comfortable talking about how they dealt with being kicked out of their homes while still in school. In fact, they were almost too willing to describe how they felt about their parents: none of the students had any contact with their parents, even though they all lived in Brewster. Their anger and hurt were apparent throughout the interviews, and it took some finesse on the part of Hannah to get them to focus on how they managed to live while homeless and still in high school.

What she found was that being homeless required creativity in order to survive. Derek, the young man who had dropped out of school, had the easiest time during that period, as he just floated from couch to couch, getting some income from mowing lawns in the summer and shoveling snow in the winter. He also resorted to petty theft when possible, leading to a few stays in the county jail.

The two students who had finished high school now had jobs that paid enough to provide housing, but they had had a hard time in school. They had needed time to do homework and to keep up a presentable appearance—more important for the young woman than the young man, who, like many of his age, seemed to thrive on looking like he slept in his clothes and who thought that washing his hair was, at most, a monthly affair.

Friends, and families of friends, had been their main support, as were people like Diane Cassidy at school.

She had admitted to Hannah that she knew about their situations and that she should have reported them to the local Children's Protective Services. She knew not doing so could get her into trouble, even fired. But she had seen too many children lost in the system. So long as she kept her eye on them—made sure they weren't in any danger and that they had managed to find shelter—she kept quiet. She had, however, reported students when it became clear that they weren't able to make it without official help. For some, foster care was the solution; but there were others who just remained wards of the state. So long as there was an option, she kept quiet.

• • •

The girls returned home from work. Hannah was again asleep in front of the TV. Fortunately, Hannah was a light sleeper and woke easily. "I wasn't sleeping, just resting my eyes," she said as she leaned forward in the recliner. The girls smiled.

Hannah looked at Shelley with interest. "So, what's the news?" she asked, as she turned off the TV.

"You know that student that I told you about the other day, the one who just graduated, who was the nanny?"

Hannah nodded, trying to remember what Shelley had told her.

"Well, I ran into her at the mall. I was on a break and saw her with two little kids. They were playing in that area for kids, you know, and she was just sitting watching them. Anyway, I went over and said hello and sat down next to her. We talked—nothing special, just talk—and I told her that I had been a nanny too. Well, to make a long story short—"

"Yes, please," interrupted Hannah.

Shelley made a face and continued. "Well, she really opened up. Told me about her situation, why she's in Brewster, and all that. It's terrible, the situation she's in. Something should be done…"

"Shelley, darling, I don't know what you're talking about. Slow down. Start from the beginning, go to the middle, and then end it."

Shelley took a deep breath. "Okay, what I found out is that Sage— that's her name, Sage Barker—is the oldest of eight kids. Her mother is part Ojibwa—that's Native American, you know—and her father is a white man, but he deserted the family, and she doesn't know where he is now. She left home—up in Gladwin—at fifteen to take the job as nanny. That way she could go to high school in Brewster. I got the impression her family was pretty poor and having one less to feed made it easier for her mom. She says she has no contact with her family in Gladwin. She's angry and ashamed, I think."

"Why is she ashamed? I can see angry—but ashamed?"

"Because of the sex," replied Shelley with indignation.

"What sex? What are you talking about?" Hannah was fighting to hide her frustration with Shelley. She took a deep breath and started over. "Okay, let's start over. This girl, Sage—strange name, but nice—she comes from a place called Gladwin, right? And she left home at fifteen to be a nanny here in Brewster, right? Then what happened?"

Shelley sighed. "Okay, she took this job as nanny—for a rich family here—and they were nice to her. Gave her a nice room of her own and some spending money. The kids were in school, so she could go to high school and take care of them after school and on weekends. The only problem was that the man started hitting on her after a few months, and it's been going on ever since."

"'Hitting on her' means sex?"

"Yeah, it means he's forcing her to have sex with him in order to keep her job."

"And the mother knows this? Has she told anyone?"

"She thinks the mother doesn't know—"

"Or maybe doesn't want to know."

"And she hasn't told anyone else," continued Shelley. "I think that's why she's ashamed. She doesn't want to have sex with him, but she doesn't want to lose her job. She's enrolled in the community college for the fall and won't be able to go if she loses her job."

Hannah was quiet, her feelings ranging from compassion to anger to helplessness. What could she do? Something had to be done, but what? Hannah came from a different time, a time when women were not expected to be sexually active—even though many of them were—but a time when sexual relations were not so casual. She felt out of touch with the sexual mores of young people today and was reluctant to voice her views. But this wasn't right!

"I think there's a name for this—I heard it on NPR—something about traffic?"

Shelley laughed. "Yeah, it's called sex trafficking—that's when you bring in a girl from another country to be a nanny or work someplace and end up making her a prostitute."

"Well, she's not from another country, but it's the same thing. We have to help her, but I don't know how. We need to think…Who is this *schmuck* she works for? Do you know?"

"She told me his name, but it didn't mean anything to me. I could find out though," Shelley responded.

"Do you think she'll talk to me? I hear that Indians—excuse me, Native Americans—respect their old people. Or would it be better if you were to talk to her again?"

Shelley hesitated before answering. "I could ask her if she'd be willing to talk to you." Shelley smiled as she added, "I could let her know that you're okay. That you're not a typical old lady."

"Oy, what a compliment! But go ahead and ask her. In the meantime, I've got some other places to check with."

CHAPTER 14

HOW COULD ANYBODY keep track, Hannah asked herself. She had visited three agencies in search of data on homeless people, and each agency seemed to know only about itself. The agencies apparently failed to coordinate with each other.

While her initial interest had been with young people, she realized—thanks to her interview with Derek, who was still homeless—that there were many reasons for homelessness. More importantly, she learned that, contrary to public opinion—and her opinion before she started this project—most homeless people were not drunks or drug addicts. Especially in bad economic times, the ranks of the homeless were filled with people who had lost their jobs, their homes, and, for some, their families. Veterans were another major category of the homeless, as were GLBT young people. Women with small children were a new addition to these numbers.

What was becoming clear after her meeting with the other agencies was that nobody really knew how many people were homeless in the area: the homeless were truly invisible.

• • •

Before the meeting that Shelley had arranged with Sage Barker, Hannah spent some time Googling information about Gladwin, Sage's hometown. What she found was that it is about a hundred miles north of Brewster, with a population of less than three thousand people. It was established in the nineteenth century during the lumber boom and had declined in population and fortune since then. Sixty percent of the households had incomes of less than $35,000, 26 percent of the people were on food stamps, and a high percentage of people and families were living under the poverty level.

Hannah understood why Sage had left home and moved to Brewster to be a nanny and attend high school. The opportunities at home seemed quite limited for her, especially as the oldest of eight children in a family living in poverty.

But that wasn't what she was going to ask her. Hannah wanted to know about the family Sage was working for here in Brewster.

Hannah knew she had to keep her anger under control. If Sage didn't want to upset her situation—as wicked as it was—Hannah could do nothing. She hoped, however, that she could persuade the girl that she didn't have to put up with sexual abuse, that there were options for her. But what were the options? Hannah had to have something specific to suggest. Otherwise, this meeting would be pointless.

She came up with only two options: find another job for Sage or report the man to the police. The first one was difficult, as it would have to be a job that paid enough for rent and food and enough to allow her to attend college, and the second one was dependent on the girl's willingness to go public. Hannah struggled to come up with other options that would be more appealing, but came up empty.

Beneath the surface, but uncomfortably rising to her consciousness occasionally, Hannah realized that her prime motivation seemed to be to *get* the bastard. Sure, she was concerned about Sage and wanted to help her, but she had to admit, if only to herself, that if she could do so without disgracing the man, she would not be satisfied. What that said about her she didn't want to consider.

• • •

The meeting with Sage took place at the mall in order for Shelley to join them on her break. It was two, and the food court was relatively empty. They found a table that allowed them privacy and sat down, each with a drink: coffee for Hannah, Diet Coke for Shelley, and Mountain Dew for Sage.

Sage was an attractive young woman with long black hair framing a round face. She had a light-copper complexion, which was highlighted by the pale-yellow T-shirt she wore. Jeans and flip-flops completed the outfit.

They sat in awkward silence for a few moments until Hannah started the conversation by asking Sage about the children.

"I hear you take care of some children. Are they in school?"

"Yes, they both go to the Montessori school in town," Sage answered.

"I hear that's a very good school. So you can go to school, too, while they're in school. That's good. Getting your education is important. Are the children easy to take care of?"

Questions about the children had the effect Hannah was aiming for: to relax Sage. It was clear after a few minutes that Sage was fond of the children. In fact, fond was perhaps too mild a term: she loved them. When she talked about them, it was as a loving parent would. They were beautiful. They were talented. They were bright. They were above average in every category she could think of. Even when they were naughty, they were adorable.

Hannah realized that this was going to be more difficult than she had first thought. Sage was not likely to want to leave this family, the only family she now had.

Shelley, barely hiding her impatience while Sage extolled the virtues of the children, chose the first opportunity to announce that she had to get back to work.

"That's all the time they give you? Not even enough to finish your drink?" Hannah tsked. "Bosses—they're all the same."

She just smiled, shrugged, waved, and left to go back to work.

Shelley's leaving had broken the mood. Hannah looked at Sage, not sure how to broach the topic she had come to talk about. Never one to be deterred by possible embarrassment, she plunged right in.

"So," she started, eyes focused on Sage, "I can tell you like the children. But what about the parents? Do you like them?"

Sage fidgeted in her chair, grabbed a lock of her long black hair, and wound it between her fingers. "Yeah, they're nice people," she replied as she looked down and continued to twirl her hair.

Hannah continued to look at Sage until she looked up. Eyes locked in silence, Hannah patiently waited for Sage to take the next step. She knew the information would have to be volunteered by her.

After what seemed like hours, Hannah decided to risk losing the rapport already established and got up from the table. "Are you hungry? How about a snack? Nachos? Pizza? Ice Cream?" she asked.

Sage looked at Hannah as if she were a crazy old lady, but then laughed. "Ice cream sounds good," she said. "Chocolate, please."

Hannah smiled. *Ah yes, food always does it.* She returned with two Styrofoam cups of chocolate ice cream and proceeded to dig in. Sage seemed lost in thought.

They sat there in awkward silence, each seemingly engrossed in eating ice cream. Finally Hannah, realizing that Sage wasn't likely to confide in her, started to talk about herself—about why she came to Brewster, about her family, and about how she had trouble staying on the sidelines when she saw someone in trouble. This segued into a brief description of the homeless situation in town and how terrible it was for young people who tried to finish school when every day they worried about where they going to sleep that night.

Sage nodded and seemed about to say something, but remained silent.

"Shelley tells me you come from Gladwin?"

"Yes."

"Where is that? I don't know much about Michigan—just Brewster and this area. I did get down to Ann Arbor once to help Maddie, my granddaughter, move in, but we didn't see much of the city."

Sage described Gladwin in very general terms, so general that Hannah couldn't tell what feelings she had about the town.

"Do you have family there?" Hannah persisted. "And if I'm asking too many questions, just don't answer. I wouldn't want I should be too nosy."

Sage smiled at Hannah. "I don't mind. I don't get a chance to talk about my family very often. Kids at school know I'm Native American, but they think we all live in tepees on reservations, so they don't want to hear about what we're really like—it's not so 'romantic.'"

"What about the family you live with here? Do they ask about your family?"

"No. Obviously they know all about my background. They had to investigate before they hired me. But no, they never discuss it."

Here was at least a partial opening for Hannah to continue the discussion. "How did you come to be a nanny here? Did you know them—what's their name?"

"Campbell. No, I didn't know them. There was a website advertising jobs, and I applied for the nanny position. I had a lot of experience with my seven younger brothers and sisters, and I thought it sounded like a good job."

"Did Mr. and Mrs. Campbell meet with you before they hired you?"

"No, they asked for some references—my pastor and one of my teachers wrote letters—and a recent picture. And then they sent money for a bus ticket and picked me up at the station here."

Hannah kept her dismay in check and simply asked, "Did they explain what your responsibilities were going to be?"

"Mainly take care of the children." Sage sighed. "You see, my mother was having a hard time supporting eight kids on a waitress's salary, and I would have had to drop out of school and get a job to help. This way, she'd have one less kid at home. My brother is almost sixteen, so he's bringing in some money to help now. And the Campbells allowed me to go to school here. The children are in school—preschool and first grade, and there's an after-school program for the preschool boy, so I can pick them up after my last class. It was a great opportunity...I love my mother, but I don't want to end up like her. I want more. And Mr. Campbell said he wanted me to stay on after I graduated and that he would pay for me to attend the local community college in the fall."

Sage fiddled with the melting ice cream and sat back in her chair, her eyes imploring Hannah to understand her decision.

Hannah understood: Sage was not about to jeopardize her situation by biting the hand that was literally feeding her. Well, okay, she thought. No point in pressing the issue. She would just have to work on getting Sage's trust, which she set about doing right now.

"That sounds like a smart move on your part, dear, though I'm sure you miss your family. But college in the fall. That's going to open a whole new world for you. I never had the chance to go to college, and I've always wondered where I would be today if I had. But I've had a wonderful life, with a wonderful daughter and grandchildren, and I'm glad they've had the opportunities I didn't have. And I'm glad you'll have that opportunity too. Who knows—maybe we'll hear great things about you in a few years."

Sage laughed. "I don't know about that, but I am excited."

"Well," said Hannah as she stood and gathered her purse, "I don't want I should keep you any longer. I'm sure you have something more fun to do on your time off than eat melting ice cream and talk to an old lady."

Sage pushed her chair back and smiled shyly. "I enjoyed talking to you. I don't get to talk about myself very much. It's like…well, like talking to my grandma. She knew how to listen, like you do."

Hannah went over to Sage, put her arms on her shoulders, and asked, "Can I get a hug?"

Sage beamed as she hugged Hannah. They started to leave the food court, when Hannah stopped and turned to Sage. "You know, dear, you can always call me if you want to talk again. Here's my phone number," she said as she scribbled the number on a napkin she picked up from the table.

They left the mall together, each going her own way—Sage to pick up the children from school and Hannah to get the groceries she needed for dinner and to assign David another "investigation."

CHAPTER 15

THE DAY HAD been hot and humid. Maddie and Shelley arrived home and headed for the shower as soon as they entered the house, each one racing up the stairs to be first. Hannah looked up from the TV and was about to ask if they were hungry, but before she could get the words out, they had vanished.

Satisfied that food was not the top priority for them, she returned to the program she was watching—*Dr. Phil*, where a woman whose husband was having an affair with her sister was being interviewed, a situation Hannah found fascinating and was curious to see what advice Dr. Phil would offer. She wasn't impressed with his suggestion that the woman give her husband an ultimatum: stop the affair or get out. Hannah thought that the woman might have some reason for not wanting to risk a divorce, financial reasons being uppermost in her mind. While things had changed for women—more independence, for example—there were still some who were financially dependent on their husbands, especially if there were children involved.

She was frustrated that with all the changes that the women's movement had brought, there were still women in these situations. Then she remembered that there were many women, like Janice, who were financially independent and who could support themselves and their children and who, when they married, did so for love or at least companionship, rather than economic necessity. And again she thanked whoever or whatever had favored her by bringing her Leo, the man she married for love against her family's protests that he wasn't "well-established" enough—which translated meant "not rich enough to give their precious daughter the life she deserved."

Well, she thought, they were right in a way: What had she done to *deserve* such a wonderful life with such a wonderful man?

By the time Janice and Paul arrived home, the girls had showered and were helping Hannah set the table for dinner. She had prepared one of David's favorite meals—enchiladas with the usual accompaniments—and was disappointed when Janice reminded her that he had an evening soccer practice and wouldn't be home until later. Hannah was careful to put aside a portion for him, in case he should be hungry, she explained to Janice, who rolled her eyes. She had given up telling Hannah that she was spoiling David.

The conversation at dinner was dominated by Maddie, who described how she had helped Dr. Jennings neuter a cat. "It was awesome," she exclaimed. "It was done so quickly. The cat was unconscious, duh, and he just snips away, and before you know it, it's done."

"You didn't faint or get sick?" Hannah asked, wondering how she would have reacted.

Maddie looked at her with mock scorn. "Of course not. You learn to focus on what's being done. It's really like carving a chicken, only one who's alive."

"Oy, that's not such a reassuring picture. I'll have that in my mind the next time we have chicken for dinner."

Hannah was glad that David was not present, as she knew he would want to know more of the details of the surgery than she was prepared to hear about at the dinner table.

Dinner over, table cleared, dishes in the dishwasher, Maddie announced that she and Shelley were meeting friends at the Wayside, a bar that allowed underage customers but had a strict enforcement for buying and consuming alcohol.

Hannah was concerned about the Wayside. She had heard rumors in the past of young people being served alcohol there. But she said nothing, having been assured by Janice that the monitoring had improved.

Jaime was picking the girls up at 9:30, after his shift at the store. Hannah found this disturbing. "At such a late hour, they go out?" she protested to Janice, who explained that this was the typical pattern of dating for young people today. That explanation didn't convince Hannah, but, as she liked to say, "Well, you know I don't like to interfere," to which Janice just smiled.

• • •

With the girls off to the Wayside, and Janice and Paul watching a rerun of Masterpiece Theater's last season's production of *Downton Abbey*, in preparation for the new season, Hannah sat in her room, waiting for David.

It was almost ten, and David wasn't home yet. She had questions for him, but right now her main concern was that he wasn't home yet. Reluctant to raise the issue with Janice, she tried to busy herself with tidying her room, making a list of what she had to do the next day—all chores that needed attending to but, unfortunately, not ones that diverted her attention from David. However, when she heard the clock chime the hour, her good intentions flew out of her head, and she marched into the living room.

"So where's David? At this hour he's still practicing his soccer? What if he's in trouble?"

"He's with the team. They probably stopped off for pizza—the coach treats them if they had a good practice. I'm sure he's okay."

"And this coach—you trust him?"

Janice looked at her in amazement. "What are you suggesting? That Coach Benson is molesting the boys?"

"I'm not saying he is or he isn't. You know I don't like to interfere. I'm only asking," Hannah replied. "You hear so much about coaches—like that man in Pennsylvania who molested those young boys—I'm just asking."

Fortunately, the conversation was interrupted by David, who announced his arrival by slamming the front door.

"Don't slam the door," Janice yelled.

"Sorry, Mom," he replied as he entered the living room.

His light-brown hair was still wet from the shower he had taken an hour ago, and the curls seemed alive as they bounced around his head. He usually kept his hair short, claiming he wouldn't have to comb it, but this summer he had let it grow long enough to reach his chin. He had inherited his father's blue eyes and, combined with the full eyelashes of his mother, showed signs of becoming a handsome young man. At present, however, all that one could see was a small, thin boy in constant motion, dressed in whatever was at hand when he awoke. No matter how much time Janice spent making sure he left the house with at least clean clothes and matching socks, by the time he arrived at school, he looked as if he had just finished a ten-mile marathon, smudges on his clothes and face. Hannah had seen this transformation with her own eyes.

He smiled at everyone and declared that he was the star of his team today. "Coach allowed me to select the pizza tonight—only the star of the day gets to do that." He was clearly pleased with himself and could hardly stand still, shifting from foot to foot as he stood in the doorway. "I made three goals—three. That's more than anyone has made in a long time."

"Now don't get a big head," Janice warned. "Remember, soccer is a *team* sport."

'Yeah, I know. But you should have seen me. I was hot!"

Janice smiled. "Yes, I wish I could have seen it. I'm sure you were hot."

David then turned to Hannah and asked, "What did you make for dinner? Did I miss something good?"

"No, darling, I made something bad." Hannah laughed. "I made your favorite enchiladas. I forgot you wouldn't be home for dinner, but I can make them again next week."

"Didn't you save any for me?"

"Of course. I always do. But they won't keep for tomorrow. They'll be too soggy."

"I could have some now. They're still okay now, right?"

Hannah looked at Janice. No way was she going to answer him with his mother right there.

Janice shook her head. "You just filled up on pizza. You don't need enchiladas too. You can't be that hungry."

"You don't have to be hungry to eat, you know."

"You'll make yourself sick"

"It'll be like a snack before going to bed. I'll be fine. In fact, it'll help me sleep. I always sleep better on a full stomach."

Janice looked over at Hannah, who had been silent throughout this exchange, and shrugged. "What do you think, Mom?"

Hannah knew what she thought: a growing boy can always eat more. "Well," she said, "maybe just one?"

Janice nodded in exasperation, and David bounded for the kitchen to await his enchilada.

CHAPTER 16

HANNAH WAITED UNTIL the next morning to talk to David, at first patiently, now not so patiently. Everyone had gone off to work. The breakfast dishes were washed and put away. Hannah sat at the kitchen table, trying to read the morning paper but finding it difficult to focus. After her talk with Sage yesterday, she was anxious to find out more about Larry Campbell. It was times like this that she resolved to learn more about computers and how to access all the information that was so deviously hidden in them; but "times like this" passed, and she found herself dependent upon the skills of a fourteen-year-old.

She checked the clock again—only three minutes later than the last time she checked. But it *was* after ten. Surely he had slept enough. She got up from the table, went into the utility room, and came out with the vacuum cleaner. She smiled as she remembered the tricks her mother had used on her and how they had come in handy in raising Janice, and now David. The old vacuum cleaner ploy—how could anyone complain about housework when it was ten in the morning? And, well, it was easier to get the upstairs done before doing the downstairs. Everyone knew that.

She felt guilty though. She had hated it when her mother woke her that way, always suspicious that the primary intent was not to clean but to wake. And now she was doing the same thing, and clear on the intent: to wake David.

It worked. David emerged from his bedroom, curly hair all tousled, rubbing the sleep out of his eyes. "What are you doing, Grandma?" he asked. "You woke me up."

"Oh, darling, I'm sorry. I thought you were already up. It's after ten, you know." Guilt was taking front stage for Hannah. Guilt at using the vacuum cleaner ploy and guilt at lying to him.

"But Mom said you weren't to carry that thing up the stairs—you're too old and might get a heart attack."

Now Hannah really felt guilty. He wasn't angry—he was concerned about her. Oh, she would have to make amends, but not now.

"Too old? I'll have you know that I am perfectly capable of carrying this vacuum cleaner up the stairs, young man. Now why don't you wake up and come downstairs for breakfast?"

"Okay, but remember, Mom said that if you insisted on doing too much work around here, she was going to hire a maid."

"We don't need a maid. I've never had a maid and don't intend to have one in my house, reorganizing everything and doing things the wrong way," Hannah huffed.

"Whatever," mumbled David, apparently happy to leave the argument for his mother to pursue. "I'll be down in a minute."

In an attempt to assuage her guilty feelings, Hannah prepared David's favorite breakfast: buttermilk pancakes with strawberry syrup. She placed them on a plate when she heard him slam the bedroom door and fly down the stairs, obviously drawn by the aroma.

"Pancakes!" he exclaimed. "What's the occasion?"

"Why does there have to be an occasion?" Hannah shrugged. "I can't make pancakes when I'm in the mood? Come. Sit down—eat."

He sat. He ate. Finally, he pushed his plate away, wiped the milk mustache, and sighed. "Boy, I'm full."

Hannah laughed. "You should be. You ate the whole batch—ten pancakes. I don't know where you put it. You're so skinny."

He pulled himself up and leaned across the table. "I'm not skinny, Grandma. I'm wiry. That's what Coach says. I'm wiry and strong." He looked so hurt that she wanted to hold him in her arms, as she did when he was a baby, and comfort him. But that would make matters worse.

"You're right. 'Wiry' is better—wiry and strong."

She started to clear the table, but hesitated and sat down again. "David, are you up for another investigation?"

His eyes opened wide, all indignation gone. "Sure. What is it?"

As Hannah explained what she wanted, his excitement increased. "So is this a bad guy?" he asked. "Is that why you want to know about him? A crook, maybe…or worse?"

"Whoa, boy. I don't know what he is. That's why I want you should find out whatever you can about him. You know, like what kind of a lawyer he is—does he defend bad guys? And who are his friends, his business associates? What about his family, his wife? Has he ever been in trouble with the law? You know, even lawyers can have a record. I know that from TV. Sometime lawyers are corrupt."

David nodded, obviously having seen the same TV programs. "Okay, I'll start looking today after I get back from the quarry."

He and Billy were meeting some friends at the quarry, a favorite place for swimming. Janice had determined that it was safe to swim there, but Hannah, not familiar with quarries, wasn't so sure—swimming was done in a pool, a lake, or the ocean, not a quarry. But all she said was, "Be careful, darling. Don't dive in and hit your head."

David guffawed and said, "Sure, I'll be careful," smiling as he got up from the table.

● ● ●

The data gathered from Listening Ear and other agencies in town had provided sufficient evidence for Hannah to conclude that there was a need not being met. She had started with a focus on the students who were homeless but had expanded her concern and investigation to encompass anyone who was homeless. What she had learned surprised and shocked her. At least three hundred people in Brewster did not have homes. No addresses, except in some cases the license numbers of the cars they lived out of. Most seemed to congregate in the various parks in town, putting up temporary shelters out of cardboard boxes, hanging blankets from trees to create makeshift tents, or using their bundles to provide soft places to sleep on the ground. It was warm now, but come winter these arrangements would not be sufficient. Clearly a better solution was needed.

But the official number accounted for only those who could be identified as homeless. What surprised Hannah was that some of the people who were homeless were also employed, usually at low-paying jobs, but not making enough to afford housing, though often qualifying for government assistance. These were the truly invisible homeless, indistinguishable from one's neighbors, except that the homeless washed up in public restrooms and slept in cars and all-night restaurants and stores (those that didn't turn them away).

Hannah had not interviewed any of the adults, getting her information from Derek. But not having easy access to the adult homeless, she was prepared to go to the school board with the information she had. Surely that would be enough for them to realize that there was a problem in Brewster and that they had the means to remedy it.

• • •

On that optimistic note, she set off to the Senior Center. Ruby was scheduled to give a presentation on how to grow perennial plants indoors. Many of the people at the Center lived in condos or small apartments with no yards in which to grow flowers. Ruby's love of gardening had been the main obstacle to her selling her house and moving into a small condo, where there was not sufficient light or room for plants. She had found a condo where she could work in the garden. What had started out as a volunteer effort to keep the premises looking good had turned into an almost full-time job as the official gardener, which granted her a discount on her maintenance fee—thanks to Hannah's negotiations with the manager.

Even in late fall the garden was alive with color: the rust of sedum, the gold of hardy mums, and the pale pink of autumn crocus, against the bright green of the holly bushes with their red berries and glossy leaves. She had added some viburnum and heather for the winter and spent hours creating a profusion of colorful arrays of flowering bushes and beds of peonies, hostas, and grasses.

Hannah was not interested in getting her hands dirty, indoors or out. She had always lived in urban areas where the only things growing were the weeds between the sidewalk cracks. Hannah knew little about flowers, except what she gleaned from Ruby, and was content to appreciate the beauty that others created with nature's gifts.

So her reason for attending Ruby's presentation was not to gain any tips on growing plants indoors but simply to support her friend. Ruby was a gentle, rather timid person, and even when possessed of knowledge and know-how, she needed encouragement.

CHAPTER 17

WHEN HANNAH ARRIVED at the Senior Center, the parking lot was full, which required her to park across the street. As she hiked across the crowded parking lot, she reminded herself how smart she was to have worn her sensible shoes; they might not be what Maddie would consider fashionable, but they were comfortable.

The lunchroom was filled with people Hannah had not seen in months—snowbirds back from Florida, she thought. Seeing Ruby and Charlie at a table with a chair reserved for her, she made her way through the horde.

"I got food for you already. I figured there might not be any left, with all these people today. Is that all right?" Ruby asked, a worried look on her face.

Hannah looked at the plate and laughed. "Am I that predictable? You got everything I like."

"I tried to convince her that you would like extra dessert, but she didn't listen," piped in Charlie.

'Yeah, extra dessert—for you," Hannah retorted. She was met with a sheepish grin from Charlie, who received from Ruby a smile a mother might bestow on a beloved but naughty child.

"I didn't expect so many people to come. I don't know if I have enough to say to so many people," fretted Ruby.

"What, you decide how much to say depending on how many people you're saying it to?" chided Hannah. "You say what you're prepared to say, and that's it."

"But what if they can't hear me—so far back there?"

"Well, most of them can't hear you, even if you're standing next to them," contributed Charlie, "so don't worry about it."

None of this seemed to lessen Ruby's concerns, but it did dissuade her from continuing to voice them.

When the lunch dishes had been cleared and the projector set up for Ruby's presentation, she and Charlie walked up to the front of the cafeteria. Charlie was in charge of the slides. He'd whispered to Hannah that he'd transferred the slides to a disk once it became clear to him that Ruby was not comfortable with any technology developed after 1950.

Hesitant at first, Ruby mumbled a few words barely audible to Hannah in the front row. She had intentionally sat there in order to provide a friendly face in case Ruby got nervous—flummoxed, as Hannah would say.

"Louder," she shouted. "We can't hear you."

Ruby looked at Charlie, who smiled back and nodded encouragement. Taking a deep breath, she started over. Once she was finished with the introductory remarks about why she was there and what she was going to be doing, and apologizing for not really knowing much about what she was going to say, she transformed into a confident speaker, clearly knowledgeable about the topic she loved: gardening. She spoke for almost thirty minutes—longer than the ten minutes she's planned, thought Hannah—and answered questions from the audience for another half hour.

The possibility of wintering over their favorite plants—and herbs, such as basil—was well received by the thirty or so people who remained behind to ask questions. All in all it was a success, and Ruby left the Senior Center excited about the event, making plans for a repeat performance.

Hannah was pleased for her friend, but she didn't look forward to another horticultural lecture.

• • •

Hannah arrived home to an empty house. The other adults were at work, and David was swimming at the quarry. Only Max, the family golden lab, was home—and he wasn't up for conversation, curled up in a tight ball on the living room couch. He wasn't supposed to be up on the furniture, but he looked so comfortable that she didn't have the heart to disturb him. *Anyway,* she figured, *he's probably on the furniture when no one is home.*

She was all sixes and sevens, wanting to do something but not knowing what. What she wanted was information about Campbell, but she had to wait for David to get that. In the meantime, she had to focus on her talk with the school board the next day. She felt prepared—she had enough evidence and documentation to at least raise the issue of homelessness in town—and if she didn't get too nervous with her presentation, she was confident that she could convince the board to set up a committee to investigate the issue. It would have the authority to get more information.

She settled into the recliner and turned on the TV. Dr. Oz was on with a new cure for insomnia, a problem she fortunately did not have. Bored with the program, she let her mind roam. She had done all she could on the homeless issue; she had to wait for information on Larry Campbell; Shelley had sent in her application to the University of Michigan and was waiting for a reply. She had dinner under control: salmon, asparagus and corn, and strawberries and ice cream for dessert—the veggies and fruit fresh from the local farmers market.

But there was something she should be worrying about.

She closed her eyes—to rest them—and awoke with a start. Jaime. What was happening with Maddie and Jaime? She hadn't seen Jaime in the past few weeks. Usually he was over at the house, picking up Maddie to go out or joining them for dinner at least twice a week. And Maddie hadn't mentioned him recently. Could there be a problem?

Hannah was a romantic underneath her practical exterior. She mourned the news of every divorce or separation as deeply as she did of deaths. Since her marriage had maintained the romance until the death of her husband, she couldn't imagine an ending of a marriage—or a relationship—not resulting in pain. Was Maddie hurting? Was Jaime? While her first concern was Maddie, she was also very fond of Jaime. His mother was Mexican, and he had stood out when the family first moved to Brewster. And being different in high school was clearly not the path to acceptance. The fact that he kept the Spanish spelling of his name— even though it was pronounced by most people as "Jamie," ignoring the fact that the name was pronounced "Hymie"—had impressed Hannah: he wasn't denying his background—or, in her eyes, his mother. She had been pleased when Maddie had first befriended Jaime, welcoming him into her circle of friends. Of course it helped that he was an excellent soccer player and had led the team to the state finals, only to lose to a downstate powerhouse team.

Yes, she had approved of the growing romance between the two teenagers and was pleased that the separation for the past year hadn't affected the relationship. Or had it? Well, she would just have to wait until Maddie decided to talk to her. *Or*, she thought, *I could ask an innocent question. That's not interfering.*

Contented, she closed her eyes again and was awakened when the door slammed, the standard announcement of David's arrival. Before he could tease her about falling asleep while the TV was on, she rose and greeted him.

"So, how was swimming? You didn't hit your head?"

David rolled his eyes. "I'm fine, Grandma. I know how to dive without getting hurt. I've been doing that since I was a kid."

She didn't remind him that he was still a kid, but simply looked at the backpack he had deposited on the floor in the hallway. David, ever alert to her looks, sighed as he picked up the backpack and put it on the shelf.

"Are you hungry? I have some oatmeal and raisin cookies—a few won't spoil your appetite."

"Yeah, sure. Although I like them with chocolate chips better than with raisins," he replied.

Now it was Hannah's turn to roll her eyes and sigh as she followed him into the kitchen.

With David seated at the table, mouth full of cookies, Hannah brought up the topic of Larry Campbell again.

"So do you think you'll have time to look up that man I told you about?"

"Sure, I'm going to get to it as soon as I shower. You know, Grandma, I think I'm going to be a detective. But not one like those guys on TV who talk to people and do stakeouts all night. I want to do cybercrime—well, not the crime, but catching the bad guys. You know, like that guy on NCIS, the one who gets all the info on his computer. That's what I want to do: tracking them on their electronic gadgets, checking their records, piecing together all the clues that are out there in cyberspace. And you know it is all out there. Everything you buy, every time you sign onto a site, every e-mail you open—it's all stored there and can be found if you know how to look for it."

"Well, that's a little scary. I don't know that I should want someone to know everything about me."

"But I wouldn't be looking at your stuff. You're not doing anything illegal."

"But how would you know? I could be a Mata Hari—she was a spy in the Second World War, you know. It's like on the airplanes. Who would be a better person to have a bomb in her underwear than an old grandma? Should that allow them to frisk me? I think that's the word."

The gulp of milk David had just ingested came spewing out of his mouth as he collapsed in giggles.

Hannah went for the towel, and when David regained his control, she suggested he take his shower and get to work. He wiped his mouth, took a cookie from the plate, and bounded up the stairs, still giggling.

CHAPTER 18

HAIR STYLED BY Maddie and Shelley, dressed in her version of a power suit—a navy pantsuit, pale blue shirt, silk scarf with bright slashes of color, small gold earrings, and black pumps—Hannah was prepared for the school board meeting.

She had refused Maddie's suggestion that she buy a pair of navy pumps. "I should buy a pair of shoes I'm going to wear once a year?" she'd asked. "Besides, who's going to be looking at my feet?"

She checked her folder again, making sure that she had all the documentation needed to make her case: statistics about students from Diane Cassidy: statistics from Listening Ear and the other agencies she had contacted, a list of possible places she had thought of for a shelter, and a tentative budget for what it would cost to buy or build a shelter in the area. This last item was to be paid for by the city.

She thought she hid her nervousness from the family, but Janice saw through her cheerful facade. "Now, Mom, you realize that this might not be successful. Don't get your hopes up too high."

Hannah smiled. "Darling, you know me. I don't expect to change the world on the first try—or the second. But eventually anything is possible—even that the school board might do something useful for a change."

Hannah left early for the seven o'clock meeting in hope of finding a parking spot close to the building. She usually parked far from the building in order to get a little exercise, but today she found she was out of breath and wanted to be relaxed and in control when the meeting started.

When the other members of the board started filing in, they found a smiling, relaxed Hannah seated at her place at the table, sipping a cup of decaf coffee. The first ten minutes of the meeting were devoted to greetings, jokes, and chitchat until the chair, George Cotter, called the meeting to order.

"Well, it looks like we have a fairly short agenda this evening. We could be out by eight, in time for the second half of the game."

"Not so fast, George," Hannah interrupted. "We have a lot to discuss. I called in and put the homeless issue on the agenda—official-like—and I'm going to take the time to explain. So maybe you won't be home for your football after all."

George was a heavyset man with sparse gray hair and a pink complexion, which was now turning an unattractive shade of purple. He had never had to deal with someone like Hannah. He was used to his decisions and orders docilely accepted by people, and, as president of the local bank, he expected the proper respect from others. Hannah upset his expectations.

After Hannah's presentation, which took almost thirty minutes, one board member used parliamentary procedure—rarely done—to remind the group that there was no motion on the floor and therefore no business to be conducted. Fortunately, the youngest board member, probably out of sympathy for Hannah, who clearly didn't know anything about Robert's Rules, suggested that perhaps Hannah would like to make a motion.

"Sure, I make a motion," she said.

"You need to be specific as to what you want us to vote on," said George as he shook his head.

"Okay, I make a motion that you agree that we need to get a homeless shelter in town and that we ask the city to pay for it. How's that for a motion?"

Jane Meyers, the board secretary, suggested a restatement of the motion and asked Hannah if that conveyed her intent, and when Hannah agreed, the motion was voted upon and defeated—10–2, with the only board member under thirty voting with Hannah.

George quickly called for a motion to adjourn, and everyone dashed out to catch the last minutes of the football game.

Hannah sat at the table, gathering the papers into her folder. What had she done wrong? What should she have said that would have convinced them—at least more of them? Her young ally came back into the room when he saw that she was still sitting there.

"Don't knock yourself out about this," he said. "This board is full of old fuddy-duddies who are here to put some service on their résumés. I've been on the board for two years now, and nothing has been done. No curriculum decisions, no policy revisions, nothing. It's usually worse. The superintendent usually attends, and then he runs the meeting. Everyone kowtows to the guy. Whatever he says, they take as gospel. No one listens to the teachers—or the students—and they just rubberstamp whatever he wants."

"Such a way to treat education." Hannah tsked. "Well, there are other things I can do. I'm not one to give up so easily, you know."

"I can see that," he said. "Good luck."

• • •

When Hannah arrived home, she found Janice and Paul waiting for her in the living room, watching the football game.

Janice was the first to talk. "Mom, are you okay? How did it go?"

"Darling, I'm fine. It takes more than a bully like George Cotter to stop me—oy, such a *putz* he is. And the other people? Who knew there could be so many *schlemiels* in one group?" Hannah could find no synonyms in English for these Yiddish terms.

She nodded when Janice suggested they have a cup of tea. After two cups of herbal tea and a danish, Hannah had completed her report of the meeting. It was too soon for her to see any humor in the situation, but she no longer found fault with her performance. After all, they hadn't even taken her seriously enough to ask any questions.

She kissed Janice good night, went to her room, and slept well.

CHAPTER 19

I T WAS FRIDAY evening, and the house was silent, except for the music that came from David's room upstairs. Janice and Paul were spending a rare evening out with friends. Maddie and Shelley were at the movies—without Jaime. Hannah and David had the house to themselves. David had done his investigation, and while they sat at the kitchen table munching on trail mix, he explained what he had found out.

Larry Campbell was an influential lawyer in town, considered to be a shoo-in for a judgeship in the next election. Brewster was an example of the new politics: while the population was fairly split down the middle in terms of Republicans and Democrats, the voting districts had been drawn in such a way as to guarantee Republican victory in local and state elections, thanks to a majority Republican legislature. As such, Republican-backed candidates usually won the judgeships. And Larry was well backed.

David had also found out that Campbell was married to the former Suzanne Poynor of Poynor Paper Products, a rival company to Kimberly-Clark. He could finance a campaign with his wife's financial support alone.

He had a son at Brown University and a daughter in her senior year at a local private high school. Campbell didn't appear to be a devoted father—there were no records of his attending his children's activities, and there had been an article in the local newspaper on absentee fathers in which a Campbell-like lawyer had been used as an example. David was thorough in his investigations.

Hannah took notes and nodded, shook her head, and tsked at each new piece of information.

"But," David continued, "there's more. I just haven't been able to get to it yet, but I found out how to get it—you know, follow-the-money stuff."

"Remember, nothing illegal. I don't want I should have to explain to your mother why you've been arrested."

"Don't worry. It's not illegal. My computer guy told me how to do it, and he's a teacher."

That didn't comfort Hannah, as she was well aware that David's "computer guy" was self-employed and gave private lessons. And who believed that even regular teachers were law-abiding these days? However, she let David continue describing what the next steps would be.

"You see, I can find out where he gets his money—probably from his wife—but also where it goes. That could tell us something, right?"

He looked at Hannah with such pleading that she replied, "Yes, darling, it could tell us something. Just make sure that you're not violating his privacy. Even if he's a bad guy, he deserves the same rights as the rest of us, and I wouldn't want someone should pry into my personal business."

"Yeah, but this is public stuff, all available on Google."

"Well, if it's on Google, I guess it's all right," she conceded.

David beamed, clearly delighted that he had the go-ahead for more intensive snooping.

Hannah remembered that David's "computer guy," had helped before when Hannah had asked for information on Ruby's son. David had been able to find out that the son was in financial trouble and was trying to swindle Ruby out of his inheritance—before she died. Like so many elderly widows, she had allowed her son to have complete power of attorney over her affairs. When she had been in a nursing home recuperating from a fall, he had sold her house, intending to keep the money for himself. Not knowing what to do, and not wanting to think ill of her son, Ruby had turned to Hannah for advice.

"Stop the bastard," she'd advised, and she—and Charlie—proceeded to help Ruby act on it. The upshot was that the house was sold, Ruby got back enough money from the sale to buy the condo she was now in, and Charlie became a much-appreciated fixture in her life.

Hannah let David think it was all due to him.

• • •

"Why do you think she likes that program so much?" Paul asked, The TV was turned to a rerun of *Walker, Texas Ranger*, and Hannah appeared to be sound asleep.

"She says it reminds her of my father—good looking, smart, strong. But Dad wasn't at all like that. Oh, he was good looking and smart—and strong, but not in a physical way. He was the gentlest man I've ever known—aside from you, of course. But I think it makes her feel better. I know she misses him, even after all this time. I think that's why she came out here. With nothing to do back in New York, she was bored, and I think the memories were painful. Here, we keep her busy and don't give her much time to reminisce."

Paul laughed. "I can't imagine her being idle wherever she is."

Janice smiled and went over to Hannah. She bent down, put her hand on Hannah's shoulder and whispered, "Mom."

Hannah looked up, pretending to be startled. "Oh, I must have dozed off."

"It's 11:30. Do you want something before you go to bed?"

"Well...I guess I could have a little something to nosh on, since I won't be able to sleep after my little nap. Come. I'll get you something too," she said as she got up from the recliner.

"Thanks, but not for me, Hannah. I'm still full from dinner," Paul said as he patted his stomach. "See you upstairs, honey."

Janice followed her mother into the kitchen, where Hannah removed cookies from the cupboard and milk from the refrigerator. They sat at the table facing each other. As Hannah nibbled on cookies, Janice looked at her.

"So, how was your evening?" asked Hannah.

"Wonderful. That new Thai restaurant in town is really good, and we always enjoy Harriet and Sam. They just got back from a river cruise in Europe. Raved about it. Maybe Paul and I will do that someday."

"You two should take more time for yourselves. Marriages need tending to, you know. They don't stay perfect without attention."

Janice smiled. "I know. We're planning to take a little time off later this summer, when Paul's workload lightens up and before school starts again...So tell me, what did you and David do this evening? Did he come out of his room at all? Once he gets into a video game, nothing pulls him away—except food."

Hannah didn't want to lie, but she was also not willing say what she and David were up to. So she smiled and said, "We talked while he had a little to eat—you know, the usual, like swimming, soccer, that sort of thing. He's really growing up. You can have a real conversation with him, at times."

"Yeah, at times. Well, I'm bushed. Don't stay up too late. See you in the morning."

Hannah watched as Janice left the room. Should she have told Janice what David was doing? Was he doing something illegal? Hannah would be devastated if he was doing something that could get him into trouble, but she had ignored that possibility. *Oh, what kind of a grandmother am I, using my grandson to get information, knowing that he's getting it in a not-so-kosher way?*

Oy, now her head hurt. *Okay, that does it.* When her body reacted, she knew it was telling her something. And now it told her she couldn't let David go ahead with his hacking—yes, she knew it was hacking.

CHAPTER 20

SATURDAY MORNING, ONLY Hannah was up, enjoying the sunrise. What a marvelous idea, she thought, building a house so that the kitchen faced east. Even on days that would later turn gray, the sunrise always put her in a good mood. How could one not marvel at the pinks, mauves, and golds that filled the sky and filtered through the trees, creating a fairyland of the backyard?

She had lived most of her life in apartments where all one could see out the windows were other tall buildings—some apartments, some warehouses, some just tall buildings whose function she didn't know. She found delight each morning in Brewster as she watched the sun rise.

Before making the family's breakfast, she sat at the kitchen table with her coffee, enjoying the sight and planning her day. After her decision to stop David from further investigation into Larry Campbell's finances, she had felt better and slept well. She would find a way to help Sage without involving David.

First she had to deal with the school board and its reluctance to take seriously the concern of homeless people in the community. How could she force the issue?

She heard David coming down the stairs, loud and bouncy.

"It's not even seven," she said in surprise. "Are you all right? Does something hurt?"

"I'm fine, Grandma. I'm just excited. Couldn't sleep anymore. I got the down and dirty on that guy," he said, beaming with satisfaction.

"'Down and dirty'? What kind of expression is that? And what does it mean?"

"It means I found out what he does with his money and where it comes from. He makes a lot of money as a lawyer—about three hundred thousand dollars a year—but his wife is even richer…Yeah, I checked up on her too. She's like a millionaire. They spend a lot of money on their kids' schools—they go to private schools. And they're members of the Brewster Country Club, which costs"—he looked at the papers in his hand—"fifty thousand a year. That's a lot of money for a club, isn't it?"

"A lot of money for us, but maybe not for them."

"Well, anyway, the only other thing I could find was that he gives to a few charities, not a lot of money, except to one that he gives about"—he consulted his papers again—"almost a hundred thousand dollars. It's called People for a Free America. I looked it up, and it's like a political group."

David looked at Hannah and shrugged. "I couldn't find anything bad about him." He looked disappointed.

"Well, not everyone who does bad things leaves a public record. But this was helpful, darling. Now what would you like for breakfast?"

He looked around the kitchen.

Hannah shook her head. She knew what he was thinking: This was Saturday. Where were the cinnamon rolls? She got up from the table with a sigh, went to the oven, and removed the pan of cinnamon rolls she had been keeping warm.

"Here, darling, have one. How about some cereal or scrambled eggs too? You need more than cinnamon rolls for breakfast."

"How about pancakes?" he asked.

Hannah put her hands on her ample hips. "No pancakes today. Cereal, eggs, or french toast—that's it."

"Okay, okay," he replied. "French toast, please—with syrup."

She smiled at him and went to the refrigerator for the eggs. While she whipped the eggs with a fork, she turned to him and asked, "So what are your plans for today?"

"Nothing special," he replied as he reached for a second cinnamon roll.

• • •

She cleared the table after David left, set out the coffee cups and cinnamon rolls, and went to her room. She needed to talk to someone, but whom? Could she burden Janice with her knowledge about Sage? She had already shared her involvement with the homeless issue with Janice; could she add the Larry Campbell issue? Or would Janice advise her to refer Sage's situation to the police? But she couldn't go to the police. She only had Shelley's report—Sage had said nothing about sexual abuse.

Her musings were interrupted when Maddie knocked on her door.

"Are you all right, Grandma?" she asked. "Do you want to join us for breakfast?"

"I'll be right there, darling. I'm just getting organized for the day," Hannah replied. She pulled herself together, put a smile on her face, and joined the family in the kitchen.

Hannah smiled at Janice. "David was down early this morning," she explained. "I had breakfast with him and lost track of the time. But now I'm ready for a second breakfast," she joked as she reached for a cinnamon roll before sitting down.

"So what are the plans for today?" she asked as she looked around the table at the most important people in her life.

Maddie looked at Shelley before responding. "Well, we're going to the lake this afternoon. Shelley has the day off, and I only have to work until noon. So we'll join the other guys at the lake."

Hannah put on her innocent face and asked, "Will Jaime pick you up, or will you meet him there?"

Maddie looked down and mumbled something.

"Darling, my hearing's not so good. What did you say?"

"I'm not seeing Jaime any more, Grandma. I don't know if he'll be there."

"Oh," said Hannah, looking at Janice, resisting the urge to ask more.

"And Paul? What about you? Any plans?"

He smiled and turned to Janice. "Honey, do I have any plans for today?"

"Well, the lawn could stand mowing. If you do that, I'll do the weeding. How's that for a deal?"

"Best deal I've had so far today." Paul laughed.

Hannah's day brightened when she saw how happy Janice was with Paul. So different from her first husband, Jim, a decent man, but not ready for the responsibilities of marriage and parenthood.

"How about you, Mom?" Janice asked. "Any plans?"

"Well, I don't know. I have to speak to some more people about the homeless issue, so maybe I'll get busy on that...Will you be home for dinner?" She looked over at Maddie and Shelley and said, "I'm assuming you two won't be home for dinner. Right?"

"Yeah, we'll probably eat at the lake or grab some pizza later," answered Maddie, Shelley nodding her head.

After ascertaining that Janice and Paul would be home for dinner, Hannah started to list the possibilities for dinner, when Janice interrupted her.

"Mom, anything you make will be fine. Surprise us."

"You want I should surprise you? Okay, kiddo, you got it—a surprise dinner."

Shelley laughed.

Dishes washed and put away, family dispersed to their various activities, Hannah sat down to plan her surprise dinner. She pulled out her recipe collection, perusing all the old favorites. But that wouldn't do—that wouldn't be a surprise. *What wouldn't they expect?* A different ethnic dish? Italian, Chinese, Jewish, even Mexican had become regulars in her itinerary; what would be new? And it should be light—it was going to be a hot day.

She was still sitting at the table when David came down again, on his way out to a soccer practice.

"What are you doing, Grandma?" he asked as he gathered up his equipment.

"I'm looking for something to make for dinner. Your mother wants she should be surprised. Any ideas?"

"Nah, I like all your dinners—well, almost all," he acknowledged. "But why don't you look online?"

"Online? What would I find online?"

"Things to cook. There's lots of sites for recipes and stuff. You might get an idea there, some inspiration."

"That's what I need—inspiration. So how do I find these recipes, darling?"

David put down his equipment, went to the laptop on the little desk in the kitchen, and brought up one of the more popular food sites.

A whole world of new recipes! Surely she could find something here to surprise Janice. She hugged David, who shrugged and waved as he left the kitchen.

Hannah spent the next hour reading recipes, most of which she rejected: too much cream, too much sugar, too much butter. Finally, she found one that seemed a possibility: a chicken salad with curry, chutney, raisins, cashews, and an acceptable amount of mayonnaise. It was different, it was healthy, it was light, and it should taste good. She decided to make it in advance in case it didn't taste as good as it looked in the picture. She could always prepare a nonsurprise dinner in an emergency. And a cherry pie would provide a nice finish to any meal.

She made a list of groceries needed and set out for Marty's. She was trying to avoid thinking about the homeless shelter issue. She didn't know what the next step was—how to get the school board, or even the City Commission, on board. Preparing a surprise dinner seemed a more productive use of her time.

While Paul mowed the lawn and Janice weeded the garden, Hannah prepared the chicken salad. A surprise should be a surprise, she thought, so she hurried in order to hide the dish by the time Paul and Janice finished their chores. She tasted the salad, found it delicious, and placed it in the refrigerator in a covered dish. Now on to the cherry pie.

The aroma of cherry pie baking in the oven filled the room as Janice and Paul entered. Hannah chastised Paul as he went to the oven to peek in. "No, no, no," she cried. "You don't open an oven while baking a pie."

Paul made a sad face. "But it smells so good. And I'm hungry after all that mowing," he whined.

Hannah laughed. "Just like a kid. Okay, what do you want for lunch? We have cold cuts and cheese for sandwiches. Is that okay?"

"Sure," he replied.

"Well, here they are," she said as she removed the ingredients for sandwiches from the refrigerator and put them on the table. "Make your own—after you wash your hands."

Paul laughed and left to wash his hands.

Janice shook her head. "They're really always little boys, aren't they?" she said with a smile as she walked over to the sink to wash her hands.

Hannah joined them for lunch. Paul might know Larry Campbell—after all, they were both lawyers in town. "Do you know a lawyer by the name of Larry Campbell?" she asked. "Ruby said something about using him for some question she had about her condo."

Paul took some time to answer her. She attributed that to the fact that he had a mouthful of sandwich, but revised that when he still hesitated after swallowing. She raised her eyebrows and looked at him in anticipation.

"Well, I might be biased—I don't like the guy—but I think Ruby could do better with almost any other lawyer in town."

"Oh, what's wrong with him?"

"Nothing proven, mind you. But there are rumors about some of his business deals being shady, if not outright illegal. But as I said, I don't like the guy, so I'm inclined to believe the rumors. But there's no proof of anything illegal that I know of. I just don't trust him."

"Okay, I'll tell Ruby to look elsewhere. Do you have any recommendations?" She had to follow up. She didn't want to tip her hand in the investigation yet.

"Well, Kevin Moore is pretty good at contracts. I'm sure he could help her. Tell her to mention my name, and he'll probably give her some free advice if it's not too complicated."

"Thanks. I'll do that."

· · ·

That evening after dinner—which did surprise and delight Janice and Paul, and which earned a "not bad" from David—Hannah sat down with Janice for one of her "conversations."

"What's up, Mom?"

"It's Maddie. What's happened that she's not seeing Jaime anymore? A fight?"

"You know kids of that age. They're in love one minute and out of love the next. She doesn't want to talk about it, but she seems okay with it. "

"What about Jaime? Is he okay with it?"

"I don't know. We haven't seen him in weeks. Why do you ask?"

"You know I don't like to interfere, but he was like a member of the family last year. I like the boy, and I wouldn't want he should think we don't care about him."

"Well, there's not much we can do about that. If Maddie doesn't want to see him, we can't invite him over for dinner," Janice protested.

Hannah sighed. "I hate that people treat friendships like Kleenex—when you're finished, you just throw them away. But, as I said, I don't like to interfere…"

Janice smiled at that.

CHAPTER 21

HANNAH WAS FRUSTRATED. Not only was she getting nowhere with the homeless issue, she wasn't helping Sage either. She felt helpless. She couldn't go to the police. She couldn't confront Campbell. She couldn't do anything.

Well, she could get more information. She marched over to the computer on the desk in the kitchen and accessed People for a Free America. It seemed innocuous—a conservative political site. She didn't agree with its views—against gun-control legislation and advocating more restrictions on immigration—but she couldn't find anything that could be used against Campbell. After all, free speech protected even the ignorant. But something bothered her.

• • •

The day had started out overcast, but by noon the sun had peeked through the clouds and promised a lovely summer afternoon. Hannah had been busy baking, her go-to activity when she was frustrated, angry, or just plain bored. Today she was frustrated and angry. So she baked a strawberry-rhubarb pie (for dinner), snickerdoodle cookies (for David), and rugalach (for general noshing).

By three she had finished, the aromas of the baked goods wafting through the house, creating warm memories of her mother's kitchen. If that didn't lift her spirits, nothing would, she thought.

She sat in the recliner, turned the TV on, and then immediately turned it off. Now was not the time for escape TV; now was the time for thinking. And she sat back in the recliner, put her feet up, and thought—and fell asleep.

She awoke when Maddie returned early from work.

"Darling, you're home early. Everything okay?" Hannah asked as Maddie entered the room.

"Sorry to wake you, Grandma."

"I wasn't sleeping. I was just resting my eyes," Hannah replied, which caused Maddie to smile. "So how come you're home early?"

"It was a slow day, and Dr. J said he would handle things so I could go home…What smells so good?"

"Oh, I've been baking: pie, cookies, rugalach. You know, the usual."

"Uh-oh, that means something's wrong. You do that when you're in a bad mood."

"No, darling, just when I want something to keep my mind occupied. Sometimes one shouldn't think. One should do something. And if I don't know what to do, I bake. And then, like a miracle, a solution comes to me."

"Well, I'm glad that's what you do. So did you come up with a solution to…whatever you're thinking about?"

"Not yet, but it's coming," Hannah said with more confidence than she felt. "So," she continued, "what's with you and Jaime? Come. Sit down. Talk to me."

Maddie shrugged as she sat down on the couch next to the recliner. "I don't know. We're just not getting along any more. He complains that I spend too much time with Shelley, but he's busy all the time working at the store—even doing overtime when he doesn't really have to…I don't know. It's just not the same."

"Do you still like him?"

"Well…I don't know. I like how he was before, when we would spend time together and talk and…you know. But now…"

"So, have you told him this? Have you told him how you feel? Maybe he feels the same way. Maybe he would like things to be like they were before. Maybe you have to find out how to make it better. Or maybe it's over…feelings change. You have to decide what you want. But you should talk to him. Don't just stop talking to each other. You'll have many boys—men—in your life. You're a beautiful girl. Jaime may not be the one for you. But how you treat him will be a lesson for how you'll treat others. But I don't like to interfere…"

Maddie got up from the couch. Hugging Hannah, she whispered, "I love you, Grandma…especially because you never interfere."

"Oy, I think that's sarcasm." Hannah laughed. "Okay, enough talking. I have to get dinner started. Do you want to help?"

"In a minute. I have to make a phone call," she called out as she went upstairs.

Hannah smiled and went into the kitchen to start the preparations for the curry shrimp creole dish she was trying out. She had gotten the recipe from a woman who had served it at a fundraising luncheon. It was good, it was easy, and it was perfect for a change. She was getting tired preparing the usual dinners.

By the time everyone finished dinner—some asking for seconds—and had their fill of strawberry-rhubarb pie with ice cream, Hannah proclaimed the meal a success and added the recipe to her collection. Before leaving the table, Maddie announced that she would be going out for a while.

Shelley frowned. Hannah could see that Shelley was surprised that she wasn't being included. Hannah wished that Maddie had talked to Shelley before announcing it at the dinner table. The girls would have to learn how to *live* together without *being* together all the time. But it was done, and she didn't like to interfere.

After dinner, Hannah approached Paul. "Do you have a few minutes for some legal advice?" she asked.

"For you? Always," he replied as he escorted her out of the kitchen and into the living room, which was presently empty. Hannah headed for the recliner, but reconsidered. This was not a time for relaxing. It was a time for serious discussion.

Perching on the edge of the couch next to Paul, she took a deep breath. "I want you should tell me about an older man forcing himself on a young woman. I mean, what does the law say about that?"

Paul leaned back and looked at Hannah. "You always surprise me, Hannah. That's not a question I would have expected of you."

He paused, then continued. "I don't know if you're asking about rape—independently of the ages involved—or about older men and younger women. If it's consensual, there's no law against it, unless the woman is underage. But you said the man 'forced' himself on her. I assume you mean he forced her to have sex with him. Well, that's rape—or sexual assault, as it's called in Michigan law. But why are you interested? What cause are you involved with now? I thought it was the homeless shelter issue."

"Yes, I'm working on that, but this came up along the way...Imagine, hypothetically, as they say, a young woman who would be homeless—there's the connection, hypothetically—but she has a job in a rich man's house taking care of the children, and he, you know ...takes advantage of her. She's only like eighteen or nineteen and doesn't have family who can take care of her. She was able to finish high school because of living with this man's family, and she could probably go to college if she stayed there. But what he's doing is wrong..."

Paul leaned forward and placed his hand on her arm. "Hannah, this story is sad, but do you have any reason to suspect that there's rape involved? Did this 'hypothetical' young woman tell you that?"

Hannah hemmed and hawed. "Well, yes and no. Not really. But she told someone else who told me. The young woman—hypothetically, remember—doesn't want to lose her job, so she's not likely to report it, official-like. So I want to do something about it." This last statement was asserted with a series of nods.

Paul paused, then explained that if the young woman wasn't willing to file a complaint, there was nothing Hannah could do—unless she had independent proof of the rape. And that was not very likely.

"I don't see what you can do about this," he said. "Perhaps the person who told you can convince the young woman to report it. Otherwise, there's nothing that the law could do. If she won't come forward, and if this has been going on for a while without her reporting it, it's going to be difficult to even prove that it was rape. After all, it could be seen as consensual sex. The fact that he's older—even much older—is irrelevant, especially if she's over eighteen. Under eighteen, a person is considered a minor, unable to give consent, but at eighteen she's no longer a minor.

I wish I could be more helpful, but I don't see anything you can do, given what you've told me."

"What if it started when she was younger, like fifteen? Would that make a difference?"

"Well yes, but you'd still have to have some evidence. Would she be willing to report it?"

Hannah sighed. "Probably not. I think she might be afraid of him. He's rich and well known in town. I think she'd be afraid no one would believe her."

Paul frowned. "Could this hypothetical rapist be Larry Campbell?"

When Hannah didn't respond, Paul continued, "If it is, please don't do anything by yourself. Campbell is a powerful man in the community. He could cause a lot of trouble for you if you go about accusing him of rape without any evidence. If you get confirmation, if the woman is willing to report it, you should go to the police. But remember, it's going to be hard to prove. It'll be a case of 'he said, she said,' and Campbell is well connected with important people in town, including judges."

Hannah nodded, thanked Paul, and started to rise from the couch. When Paul helped her up, she kissed him on the cheek, murmuring, "Janice is lucky she found you—such a *mensch*."

He hugged her. "She didn't find me. I found her, and it wasn't luck. It took great perseverance on my part." He laughed as they left the room.

CHAPTER 22

HANNAH SPENT THE next few days meeting with various agencies she hoped would have some information on the number of homeless people in town.

Armed with this new information, she marched into the office of the editor of the local newspaper, the *Daily Sun*. Her previous experience with newspapers reminded her to have not only the data available but also a carefully written statement that outlined the issue. She knew that small-town newspapers often didn't have sufficient staff to do the research.

Joe Machewski was a large man with a frown etched on his face. He wore a rumpled white shirt, khaki trousers, and a pencil behind his right ear. He looked up as Hannah entered his office. He pushed his glasses to the top of his head and deepened his frown.

"Who are you?" he demanded. "If you've got a complaint, go to the front desk. They'll take care of it." He pushed his glasses down and returned to the papers on his desk.

Not one to be intimidated by size or rudeness, Hannah stood in the doorway, rising to her full five feet one inches, glad that she had dressed in her navy pantsuit, with a pale-yellow blouse instead of the flowered print she had considered.

"Mr. Machewski," she started, pronouncing his name with the proper "v" sound, "I do have a complaint, but it's not with your newspaper, which is very fine for a small town. I'm here to enlist your aid in exposing a terrible shame in this community."

At this, he looked up. Perhaps it was the proper pronunciation of his name or the fact that the woman standing in front of him reminded him of his mother, but he pushed his glasses up again and motioned to a chair in front of his desk.

"Let's start again, okay? Please sit down, Mrs...."

"Lowenstein, Hannah Lowenstein. Thank you. I know I should have made an appointment, but that never works. I don't like to be rude, but sometimes it's necessary."

He shrugged. "Okay, so what's this terrible shame you're so upset about?"

"Did you know that there are over three hundred people in this town who are homeless, *officially* homeless? They have no place to sleep. Now in this weather it's not so bad—they camp out in the parks, places like that—but in the winter, can you imagine what it's like? And many of them are children. Some with their parents, but the older ones are often on their own. Some drop out of school. Others continue school but with a great disadvantage. I want you should print an article on this in the paper... Here, I have a statement you can use if you don't have time to write one yourself. You can change it any way you like, as I'm not a writer like you. And here is the information and the numbers I got from Listening Ear, Eight Cap, and other groups in town to show that I'm not making this up," she declared as she handed the folder to him.

"Mr. Mackewski..."

"'Mac to friends." He grimaced in what was intended as a smile.

"Mac, if you would print an article on the need for a shelter in town, I could go back to the school board—they didn't want to hear about this when I spoke to them before—and maybe embarrass them for not taking the issue seriously before."

"Ah, Lowenstein, I thought I heard the name before. You're on the school board, aren't you?"

"Yes, but don't believe what they say about me. I'm not one of their favorite members."

"So I've gathered. Well, let me look at this information, and I'll get back to you. If we decide to take this on, I'll assign a reporter who would work with you. I'm not promising anything—we're short-staffed—but we'll see."

Hannah knew when not to push an issue. She got up, thanked him, and made sure he had her phone number. "You can call anytime. We have a machine," she announced as she left.

• • •

Well, that went well, she thought as she sat in her car outside the newspaper building. And it was only nine thirty. She had the whole day ahead of her with nothing to do except check on Larry Campbell's connection to the People for a Free America website—but she didn't know how to do that.

Maybe a little something to eat would help. She started the car, intending to drive to her favorite diner, but instead headed towards the Senior Center. It was too early for Ruby to be up and about, but Charlie was an early riser and a poker player. There was always a game going on and therefore a good chance that Charlie was already there.

At this hour, parking close to the building was easily available. Hannah backed into a space, praising herself for her driving ability. Many of her elderly women friends couldn't back up or parallel park. She had been taught to drive by her father, who had mastered the art of driving in a big city, and she had reaped the benefits of his knowledge.

As she scanned the parking lot, she didn't see Charlie's green 2003 Mercury Grand Marquis. Well, there would be others she could join, and they did serve good pastry. She entered the Center, walked up to the buffet table, and helped herself to coffee and a cheese danish. She was startled when someone came up from behind and gave her a hug, almost causing her to drop her danish. She spun around and came face to face with Charlie, a big smile on his face.

"Sorry. I didn't mean to scare you. What are you doing here so early?"

"You didn't scare me. It's just that I don't usually get hugs this early in the morning.

"After lunch is a different story," she joked. "I didn't see your car outside. Did you walk?"

"Nah, the monster's in the shop again. Ted gave me a lift today."

"Are you in the middle of a game? When you're finished, I'd like to talk to you about something."

"Nah, I'm tapped out. My luck isn't with me today. Let's sit down," he said, pointing to a table in the corner. "It'll be quiet there, and we can talk. But let me get some coffee. Do you want something?"

"No, I'm fine. Go get your coffee."

Coffee in one hand, two glazed donuts in the other, Charlie joined Hannah at the table. "So, what's up?" he asked as he finished off one donut in two bites.

Hannah didn't know what she expected Charlie could contribute, but he always surprised her with his resources. He had been a successful used-car salesman at one of the big dealerships in Detroit and kept in contact with his former coworkers. He also kept in touch with friends from his Navy days. So who knew? Perhaps he could help get information on Campbell.

"Okay, now this is confidential. You know what that means, right? Don't tell anybody, not even Ruby. You know she can't keep a secret, even when she tries."

"Yeah, I know what confidential means, Hannah. Get on with it."

"Well, it has to do with finding out about a website."

"Oh, that's real helpful," he said, rolling his eyes."

"Let me finish," she whispered as she leaned forward. "I need to get information about a group called People for a Free America. They have a website, and it looks like a typical conservative group. You know, don't want gun laws or any more immigrants, want to 'take the country back'— whatever that means—things like that. But I have a bad feeling about them. I'd need to find out more, but I don't know how."

Charlie laughed. "How did you find out about this group? Just idle curiosity?"

"No," Hannah replied indignantly. "I was interested in finding out about a particular person and found out that he belonged to this group. Now I need more information about the group."

Charlie smiled. "So David's been hacking again, huh? That kid's gonna go far, if he doesn't get in trouble first."

"I know. I know. I shouldn't have asked him to help, but now I'm stuck. I know this person is rotten, but I don't want David should get any more involved."

Charlie paused for a moment and then said, "Hell, there's got to be a way to get that information. I know some guys who are savvy about getting information like that. I'll check with them and get back to you. Okay?"

"Wonderful. I knew you'd come up with something."

"I can't promise anything. It may be just what it seems: a right-wing group. You may not like it, but there's nothing illegal about being a Tea Party conservative."

"Whatever you can do is more than I can do," she said as she got up to leave. "Do you want this?" she asked, pointing to her plate. "I forgot all about it, and now I'm not hungry."

"Sure," he smiled as he reached over and grabbed the danish. "Maybe it'll change my luck," he laughed, as he headed for another round of poker.

CHAPTER 23

RIVING HOME, SINGING along with Tony Bennett on the one CD she had in the car, Hannah was more cheerful than she had been for days. What if Charlie could find out something about Campbell that would be publically embarrassing? How could she use that information? Should she make it public? Or should she confront him with it? Would that be blackmail? She didn't like the idea of blackmail, but what else could you call it?

She was startled by a horn blaring. She looked in the direction of the blare and saw a blue SUV at her passenger side, the driver shouting something she couldn't hear. She looked around, noticed the stop sign she had just run, and waved her hand in what she hoped the driver would realize was an apology and drove off.

Well, if I don't concentrate on my driving, there may not be an opportunity for me to do anything about anything, she thought. Driving slowly— even slower at intersections—she managed to get home without any further incidents.

She realized how shaken she was when she attempted to get out of the car. She was so unsteady she had to hold on to the car door to prevent falling. She sat down, took a deep breath, and tried again. She walked with mincing steps, successfully navigated the pathway to the front door, opened the door, entered the living room, and plopped down into the recliner, her heart pounding throughout her body. She was frightened; this had never happened before. Her heart was strong—the doctor had told her so—so why was she reacting this way? Was she having a heart attack? Doctors were known to be wrong, she thought.

She sat there for a while, her heart beat slowing, her breathing returning to normal. Okay, she thought, what was that about? *So I nearly had an accident. So? That's happened before.* Not often though, she reminded herself—so why that reaction? Not finding a satisfactory explanation, she decided to simply attribute it to an overreaction on her part and got up to eat a little something.

• • •

By the time the family had returned from work and play, Hannah had completely recovered. She was particularly pleased to see that Jaime would join them for dinner, and was glad that she had decided to prepare quesadillas—one of his favorites.

The conversation at the dinner table focused on Shelley's promotion from clerk behind a counter to salesperson on the floor. Shelley was clearly delighted with the promotion and with the congratulations from everyone at the table. Hannah joined in the festive atmosphere, even though she thought that a promotion without a raise didn't really count. But she was happy for Shelley; clearly, her work was appreciated even if not rewarded.

Jaime sat quietly, occasionally glancing at Maddie, a smile on his face. David tried to engage him in predictions about the success of the soccer team's next game, but Jaime just smiled and said, "Don't know. We'll have to see." After three attempts to generate more of a response from Jaime, David gave up and turned his attention to eyeing the last quesadilla on the platter.

Hannah noticed his interest and asked, "Does anyone want the last one?"

David nodded in gratitude as he reached for it.

• • •

The house was quiet. Maddie and Jaime—with Shelley—drove off to meet friends. Janice and Paul worked in the study they shared. David played video games in his bedroom, aiming for level nine. David said Billy had reached that level last week, and David was determined not only to match his accomplishment but to better it.

So Hannah had the living room to herself. Relaxed in the recliner, feet up, a cup of tea on the table by her side, she took stock of what had to be done. She ticked them off in her mind: check with Charlie, check with Machewski—both of which required patience on her part—and check with Shelley about Sage, though she had no news to share yet. This was frustrating, she thought. Wasn't there *anything* she could do without waiting? Hannah was not one to ignore her faults, and she easily acknowledged her lack of patience as one of them. So what could she do now?

The only answer she came up with was to turn on the TV and watch a rerun of *Walker*.

● ● ●

It was after ten, and the predicted heat wave had arrived. Hannah was restless. The house was almost empty, everyone off to work and David still asleep. The dishes were cleaned and put away. She had even rearranged the cupboards, tossing out anything beyond its expiration date and organizing items according to some plan only she would be able to reconstruct.

But what to do now? It was too soon to contact Mac at the newspaper, and she knew that Charlie would call her as soon as he had any information. She wondered how Sage was doing, but she didn't know how to find out. That frustrated her, and when she was frustrated, she acted. Of course, she thought, she knew how to contact Sage—she was at the Campbell house.

A brief look through the telephone book—she didn't trust online information, preferring to believe that the written word was more likely to be accurate—showed the Campbells lived on Orchard Drive, referred to by the locals as "Pill Hill" because of the number of doctors who lived there. Fortunately, Brewster had not yet developed gated communities—which would have presented a problem for Hannah. There was no way she could visit Sage if she had to be announced.

She changed her housedress for a pair of tan slacks and an emerald-green blouse with a mandarin collar, adorned by a long gold necklace—real gold—that Janice and Paul had given her at Christmas. She would have preferred to wear a loose cotton dress to accommodate the predicted heat, but as she looked in the mirror, she was pleased: she appeared to be a respectable, wealthy elderly woman who would certainly be admitted to the house—by servants, even if Mrs. Campbell was not home. In fact, she hoped that Mrs. Campbell would not be home; she wanted an uninterrupted visit with Sage.

She left a note for David with instructions for his chores for the day, gathered her purse, and left the house. Her car had GPS, which she rarely used, but today she entered the Campbells' address. She didn't want to be seen driving up and down streets, looking for the house.

Orchard Drive was on the outskirts of Brewster, a secluded community all its own. The houses were large and ostentatious, with columns in front and turrets on top and four-car garages at the end of seemingly endless driveways bordered by tall fir trees. If the intent was to impress, it failed on Hannah. As she drove down the driveway, she tsked. Too overdone, she thought; it was like wearing too much jewelry to show that one could afford it. These must be very insecure people—or just people with bad taste—she concluded.

She arrived at the front of the house, parked the car, and rang the doorbell, which was quickly answered by Sage. They looked at each other, each one startled. Hannah was the first to recover. "I was surprised—I didn't expect you to answer the door," she explained with a smile. "I was in the neighborhood, and I thought I'd drop by to see how you were doing."

Sage gathered herself together and smiled at Hannah. "Please come in," she said as she held the door open. "I was just getting the children's lunch ready. Then we're going to the country club—they're taking swimming lessons there."

"I won't take up much of your time," Hannah assured her. "Just a few minutes."

"That's all right. No one else is home, and we can talk while they eat. Come into the kitchen."

After walking what seemed like the length of a football field, they entered the kitchen, where Hannah found two young children seated at the table jointly working on a coloring book. They looked up at her and then at Sage, who assured them that Hannah was a friend. Content with this information, they returned to their coloring.

While Sage prepared the children's lunch, Hannah fussed over their coloring techniques, praising the beautiful colors they used and especially the creativity shown in coloring outside the lines. It must have been the first time they hadn't been criticized for their "sloppiness." They looked at her in puzzlement but then smiled at the praise being bestowed upon them.

Sage smiled at Hannah, obviously pleased that the children liked her. "They don't get to meet many people," she explained, "and are kind of shy with strangers. But they seem to like you."

Sandwiches cut into quarters, sliced banana on the side, and a chocolate chip cookie as dessert, the children turned their attention to lunch, and within ten minutes had devoured everything on their plates.

Sage turned to Hannah and laughed. "They love their lunch. Mrs. Campbell doesn't let them eat between meals, so I try to give them enough so that they're not hungry. They don't have dinner until six—which is a long time between meals for them. Mr. and Mrs. Campbell don't eat until eight, when Mr. Campbell gets home from work."

"When do you have dinner?"

"Oh, I eat with the children."

"Who does the cooking? Does Mrs. Campbell, or is there a cook?"

Sage laughed. "You're looking at her. Mrs. Campbell prepares the menu, and I do the shopping and follow the recipes that she gives me. I don't mind. I like to cook, and I've learned a lot about preparing food that I never knew before. I could probably be a chef someday."

Hannah silently added up the responsibilities that Sage had taken on in addition to being a nanny for the children, namely housekeeper and cook. She wondered what else Sage was expected to do for the family and how much she was being paid—if anything.

Sage sent the children out to play in the enclosed backyard. She grabbed a Diet Coke from the refrigerator and offered it to Hannah, who declined. Sage opened the can and sat down across the table from Hannah. She smiled nervously and fiddled with the can.

Hannah took the opportunity to get to the point. She took a deep breath and asked, "Are you all right, dear? I don't like to pry, you know, but I have a feeling that something's not right. Is there a problem with the children? Or the parents?"

Sage looked down at her hands holding the can of pop and shook her head. "No, everything's fine," she responded. But when she looked up, the tears filling her eyes started to flow down her cheeks.

Hannah reached over and took the hands holding the can into her own hands. "Darling," she started, "I don't know, but I think I know what the problem is. And you need to know that it's all right. You've nothing to be afraid of—certainly nothing to be ashamed of—and if you'll let me, I'd like to help."

Now she felt foolish. What if Shelley had misunderstood what Sage had told her? What if Sage was just embarrassed by Hannah's awkward intrusion? Would Sage think she was an interfering old woman with dirty thoughts on her mind? She waited for Sage to respond.

After a few agonizing seconds—Hannah waiting to be told to leave— Sage lifted her head and looked at Hannah.

"I don't know what to do," she whispered, taking a deep breath. "I have something to tell you, but I don't want you to tell anyone else. I don't want to lose my job…"

"Darling, you have my word. If you don't want it to go any further, it won't—but I may try to convince you otherwise."

Sage started to talk. Once started, she couldn't stop. Hannah listened quietly, not interrupting to ask for clarification for fear of scaring Sage into silence.

The whole story poured out: the initial flirtation turning into unwanted fondling, the uninvited nightly visits to her bed. The man was a prominent lawyer in town. Who would believe her story? Maybe she had led him on? Maybe she had unconsciously wanted it?

When Sage finished, face flushed, eyes shining with tears, Hannah leaned over the table and again put her hands on Sage's.

"Nonsense, darling. It's nothing to be ashamed of. You were—are—a child. He is a grown man. He's your employer. What he did was wrong— and against the law—"

"No, please," Sage interrupted. "I don't want the law to get involved, no police. Please."

"What did I promise? I don't break promises. What you just told me was in confidence, but that doesn't mean I can't make suggestions, give advice—which you can ignore. Okay?"

Sage wiped her eyes and smiled. "Okay."

"Tell me something about this man—and his wife."

"Well, as I said, he's a lawyer in town. He must be pretty good, because they're very rich, and they go to a lot of events where they have to dress up, and they have lots of dinner parties for other rich people in town. I don't know who all those people are, but I see some of their names in the paper—other lawyers, even judges, and important businesspeople, like the guy who owns all the motels in town and the one who has that oil business."

Hannah nodded her understanding. "Yes, I can see why you're concerned. Now I'm just asking. Don't get upset. Would you mind if I did a little checking up on this Mr. Campbell? Nothing public, just checking newspapers—they're public documents—to see what they say about him? I want I should help you, but I don't know how without risking your job, and I know that's important to you, but maybe I'll get an idea if I can look into him a little bit. You never know what a person could find out. But I won't do anything without asking you, okay?"

Sage blew her nose on a table napkin and smiled. "I feel better telling you about it—like I would my grandma. I just don't know what to do."

"Well, we'll figure something out. But let me ask—does Mrs. Campbell know what's going on?"

Sage's eyes grew large with fear. "No," she gasped. "She would fire me if she knew. She's very jealous. They fight a lot when they get home from parties. I can hear them. She's always accusing him of flirting with some woman at the party, and he's always denying it. But I've noticed that after those fights she always receives a gift from him—a bracelet, a purse, something like that."

Hannah shook her head and tsked. Buying silence from a wife, she thought. She wasn't convinced Mrs. Campbell was as unaware as Sage thought. Jealous women had an extrasensitive antenna for a husband's dillydallying.

At that moment, the door opened, and the children rushed in, anxious to be taken to the pool for their swimming lesson. Hannah got up from the table. "Well, I don't want I should take any more of your time. I'm glad we had this talk, and I'll let you know if I think of anything. And remember, I keep my promises."

With that announcement, she hugged Sage and waved at the children. As she left the house, she could hear the children laughing. To all appearances, a happy home.

CHAPTER 24

DINNER WAS ALMOST over when Paul arrived. "Hannah, have you seen today's paper?" he asked as he sat down and filled his plate with salad and rolls.

"No," she answered. "I haven't had time to see the paper. What's in it?"

"Your story. It's got an editorial on the homeless situation in town, and it mentions you and your attempts to get a homeless shelter. It was really a decent editorial, for a change."

Hannah was speechless. She had hoped Mac would pick up the story, but she was unprepared for such a quick and effective response.

Janice leaned over and placed her hand on Hannah's. "You should be proud, Mom. Now they won't be able to dismiss you so easily. Go get 'em." She laughed.

"Well, I didn't expect that so soon. Mac—the editor, you know— seemed interested, but you're never sure if they mean what they say. Although I had a good feeling about him. Gruff, even rude, but he seemed sincere. I'll have to thank him tomorrow. And call in to put the issue back on the agenda for the next board meeting. You're right. This time they won't be able to ignore me."

"By the way," interrupted Paul, "great dinner. I didn't know a salad could taste so good."

Janice laughed. "When I told him we were having salad for dinner, as it was too hot to have the oven on, he panicked. Maybe now," she said as she turned to Paul, "you'll appreciate veggies more. They can be tasty."

Hannah smiled. She knew it was vanity, but she loved being com-plimented on her cooking—although preparing the salad didn't require cooking, just a lot of chopping and using the right ingredients.

• • •

Another hot day, but the oven was on. Hannah, in her cotton caftan, was hot but determined. Preparations had started two hours earlier, and the chocolate babka was now ready to be baked. In another hour she would be able to pay a visit to Machewski, gift in hand.

Paul's news last night had thrown Hannah off schedule. Now was the time for action, and she didn't have a plan. Thanking Mac was first on the list, but that was the easy part—except for baking on a hot day. She knew she would have to raise the issue again at the next school board meeting a week from tomorrow, but she needed more community awareness before that. She knew from experience that yesterday's news was quickly forgot-ten in the public's mind.

Sitting at the kitchen table, third cup of coffee in her hand, she stared out the window at the lush rhododendrons in the backyard. She was amazed that they had survived the year. Neither Janice nor Hannah was a gardener.

When Ruby had moved from the house she'd lived in for many years to an apartment, her main concern had been the gardens. She had cre-ated a wonderland of beauty around her house: front, back, and sides. Not able to take everything with her—Charlie refused to dig up the large flowering shrubs and trees—a compromise was reached, with Hannah's approval: some of her favorites would be transplanted at Janice's house. And so Janice was the recipient of rhododendrons, azaleas, and roses—all of which required considerable care. The only flowers Janice had planted herself were peonies, which were not only beautiful but also loyal: they bloomed every year without much fuss.

Hannah, out of respect for Ruby, had taken on the job of watering the plants throughout the summer. At first an onerous task, she now looked forward to the evening ritual of turning on the hose and walking around the backyard, giving what she hoped was the proper amount of water to each plant. She had lost some of the rhododendrons—the pink ones—but the white and violet ones were thriving. And with the lilacs, azaleas, and red and yellow roses, combined with the white, pink, and red peonies, the backyard was a blaze of color in the spring and early summer. It was now the beginning of July, an unusually hot July, and she was afraid that the blooming season was over. The flowers would fade and die, and the yard would return to a solid green, with no bright colors to break up the monotony.

Hannah was not fond of lawns—she thought them to be an unnecessary use of water—but she wasn't about to suggest planting anything that required maintenance throughout the whole summer.

She did, however, enjoy the many trees that Janice had planted when the house was built. They were all mature now, with roots deep enough that they could survive both a hot summer and a cold winter. And they provided housing for the many birds that returned each year to the feeders scattered around the backyard.

Hannah sat at the table, deep in thought, inspired by the beauty of the flowers and their survival. If these delicate beauties could find a way to contend with the vagaries of weather, surely she could manage the quirks of the school board, she decided, oblivious of the non sequitur involved in that reasoning.

She rose from the table, washed her cup, removed the babka from the oven, and strode to her room to get ready for the day. She now had a plan and hoped the babka would do double service: a thank you and a bribe.

● ● ●

Machewski was barely visible over the piles of papers on his desk. He looked up at Hannah's gentle knock on his open door.

"Am I bothering you?" she asked.

"Bothering, no. Interrupting, yes," he barked. "But since you've already interrupted my train of thought, you might as well come in," he said as he pointed to the chair across from his desk.

"So what can I do for you? And what is that package you're carrying? Not a bomb, I hope."

Hannah smiled. "I wouldn't know how to make a bomb. But a babka I can make. You know babkas?" In answer to his nod, she went on. "Well,

I want to thank you for the article in the paper about the homeless shelter, so I brought you the babka. I don't know if it's the kind you like. It's chocolate…"

"What's not to like? Thank you. It's our anniversary. I'll give it to my wife as a present. She'll love it. Now what can I do for you? I have a feeling there's more coming."

"Well, now that you asked…" Hannah paused, not sure how to proceed.

Mac raised his eyebrows. "Come on now. Where's that moxie that I saw last time—you came barging in, making demands. Come on. What's up?"

Hannah laughed. "Okay. I want you should advertise a public meeting so that I can make people aware of the homeless situation before the school board meets next Tuesday. You could advertise it in the paper, and I could put flyers up around town. Then people might come to the meeting, and they wouldn't be able to dismiss what I have to say. I've seen these things work. In New York, my husband, Leo, was in newspapers. He was a printer and a union rep. We learned how to hold meetings for the public before the city council took a position on something. And I'm proud to say my Leo helped to change the council's mind quite a few times. It's all politics, you know."

Mac smiled, the first real smile Hannah had seen from him. He looked at her and raised a finger, indicating he needed silence to think, and pulled out a sheet of paper from one of the piles on his desk. "Ah, here it is," he muttered. "Okay, if you have a hundred dollars, I can give you a half-page ad on Wednesday. That's a good day for ads."

"What about Wednesday and next Monday, for a reminder. Can I get a deal?"

"You drive a hard bargain, Mrs. Lowenstein. Okay, for a hundred and fifty dollars, I can put the ad in Wednesday and next Monday. Okay?"

"Well, now that we've got the days settled, let me ask. How much would it cost to make the ad a full page?"

"Are you made of money, woman?" he thundered. "Do you have any idea how much that would cost?"

"No, that's why I'm asking," she calmly replied. Blustering men didn't faze her. She just focused on the content, not the form of response.

Mac consulted a chart on the top of his desk. "A full page ad costs two hundred and fifty dollars. We're talking about five hundred dollars for two days. Are you sure you want to spend that much?"

"Mac, don't get so excited—you don't want blood pressure problems. Look, I have my social security and a small pension from my Leo. My daughter—she's the principal of the high school—is wonderful. I couldn't ask for a better daughter. She won't let me pay for anything, so I have no fixed expenses. My money is mine to do what I want with. I'm not rich, but I don't need much. Everything's provided for me: food, a comfortable room, the run of the house. I have a home with my family, who treat me like a queen. All I have to do is cook, which I would do anyway—Janice isn't a very good cook. So if I want to spend five hundred dollars—or maybe three hundred dollars—on what I think is an important cause, what's wrong with that? It's better I should spend it on a fancy new outfit?"

Mac looked shook his head. "You're a pistol, Mrs. Lowenstein. Maybe you should go into politics. You could teach them a few things about negotiating."

"No, I couldn't do politics. They're not my kind of people. So how about it? Three hundred dollars? For two days, full page?" When Mac didn't respond, Hannah added, "I can pay full price if necessary."

Mac sighed, shaking his head. "This coming Monday is a slow day, so why don't we compromise and say…three hundred and fifty dollars?"

"It's a deal." Hannah laughed. "It's been wonderful negotiating with you."

"Okay, but if you want the ad to go in Wednesday, you have to have it in by five today."

"No problem," she replied. She picked up her purse and waved as she left an Mac shaking his head, an uncomfortable smile on his usually frowning face.

• • •

It was almost noon when Hannah left Mac's office. She needed to talk to Ruby, whose writing skills were more sophisticated than hers. After all, Ruby had had two years of college before she married.

Hannah sat in her car and used her cell phone to call Ruby. It was times like this that she realized that modern technology did have some advantages. When there was no answer at Ruby's end, Hannah headed for the Senior Center, remembering that Monday was bridge day, and Ruby never missed bridge day.

Charlie's green Chevy was parked close to the entrance, a good sign that Ruby was with him. She'd had a hip replacement last year and had fully recovered, but she liked the special attention received when she reported that she "was recovering from surgery." Charlie just smiled and accommodated her.

Hannah found Ruby at the bridge table and Charlie at the poker table. She waved to Ruby and pointed to a table, indicating that Ruby should join her when the game was over. Not a bridge player herself, she didn't realize that bridge games could last for hours.

Poker, however, was a different game. Charlie nodded to Hannah when she arrived and soon joined her at the table.

"Is your game over?" asked Hannah.

"It's not over until there's no one left playing. I'm just taking a break—I've lost the last two hands; need a rest to regain my mojo. So what brings you here? Lunch?"

"I'm not hungry. I need to talk to Ruby about getting an ad out about a meeting—she's better at that than I am. And what's with your mojo, whatever that is?"

Charlie chuckled. "Oh, that's what the kids say. I don't really know what it means, only that it sounds cool—which doesn't sound so cool." He laughed. "So what's the ad for—a yard sale?"

Hannah shook her head. "Of course not. I could write that by myself. It's so people will know that at the next school board meeting we're going to be talking about a homeless shelter in town. I need to get the word out so that people will attend the meeting. Otherwise, there won't be any real discussion of it, and they'll dismiss the issue like they did last time. Did you see the editorial the other day? Well, I want to act while that's still in the minds of people."

"Good idea. Say, listen, I talked to my guys downstate. I was going to call you later with the info. That group you mentioned—People for a Free America—it seems it's just a right-wing political group, nothing illegal or, given recent politics, not even unethical. In fact, it's pretty mainstream Tea Party."

Hannah received the information with a frown. "So that's it, huh? Nothing negative?"

"Well, the guys checked Campbell's finances too—don't ask. Good ratings, good income, no debt to speak of. Most of the stuff online is about lawyer stuff." Charlie reached into his shirt pocket and pulled out a crumpled sheet, which he consulted after smoothing it out.

"Let's see," he started. "He belongs to the Rotary, the American Bar Association, attends Sacred Heart, the big Catholic church downtown, not the one on the college campus." He paused, reading his notes. "And that's it. The rest is about dinners and events he and his wife attended and cases he defended. Nothing questionable that I can see," he concluded.

"Well, that's not going to help. Paul doesn't like him, and I trust Paul's opinion. But…thanks anyway. Give me the list though. Maybe it'll give me some ideas."

Charlie shrugged. "Whatever you say, Boss," he replied and handed her the list.

Hannah peered at the list and shook her head. "I can hardly read this. Didn't they teach you how to write in school?"

Charlie laughed. "They tried. But I'm up to date now. Kids don't write. They text, and so do I."

Hannah tsked and put the list in her purse. "I'll figure it out."

Just then Ruby sat down at the table. "You two were so involved you didn't see me waving. I wanted to know if you wanted something for lunch, Hannah. I was going to get it for you."

Ruby was wearing a new outfit, one Hannah hadn't seen before. A pantsuit in a light blue that brought out the blue in her eyes and complemented her fair complexion and white hair. Hannah admired—and envied—how Ruby looked: always dressed to bring out her best features, of which there were many.

"Oh, thank you, dear. No, I'm not hungry. Charlie and I were just catching up, nothing important." She glanced at Charlie, hoping that he got the message, and was relieved when he nodded. "That's a lovely outfit. Is it new?"

"Yes. Do you like it? Charlie bought it for me. Well, naturally I picked it out—he doesn't know much about women's clothes—but he bought it. He's such a dear," she said as she smiled coyly at Charlie.

Enough, thought Hannah. If she didn't change the topic, she'd be hostage to a long recounting of all the wonderful things Charlie did for Ruby, and never get down to business.

"I need your help," Hannah said, trying to get Ruby's attention off of Charlie. "I need to get an ad done for the newspaper, and you're better at that than I am. Here's what I want it should say." She handed a sheet of paper with the essentials of the ad to Ruby and waited while she read it. Ruby was a careful reader, but slow. How long did it take to read a paragraph? She restrained herself with considerable effort; after all, she was asking Ruby for a favor.

Ruby took out a pen from her small purse and made some changes to the wording. "Here, see if this works. I've added some things for clarity and changed some things for emphasis. But I think it works. What do you think?"

Hannah looked it over, nodded, and thanked Ruby. "This is much better. Do you think this would work on a flyer too? I want to put them up around town so even if you don't get the newspaper, you'll hear about the meeting."

"Yes, but be sure to have it printed on colored paper, with large print—here, let me show you." She proceeded to indicate what should be in large print, bold, and italics, even making suggestions about the font and the paper color.

When they had finished, Hannah had an ad and a flyer done. She sat back in her chair, pleased and, all of a sudden, hungry. "After all that work, I need a little something to eat. Anybody else?"

Not one to pass up food, Charlie stood up and, in his best imitation of a waiter, took their order.

Anxious to get the ad to Mac, Hannah downed her cinnamon roll, gulped her coffee, hugged Ruby, waved at Charlie, and left.

She dropped off the copy of the ad at the receptionist's desk. Fortunately, Ruby's handwriting was beautiful—the product of an education at an elite private school in Manhattan—and didn't need deciphering. Hannah did, however, request a copy of the ad in order to prepare the flyers that would be distributed around town. She was sure she could get Shelley's help in designing the flyer; after all, Shelley was an artist. And she thought that David, with his friend Billy, could be persuaded to help distribute the flyers, especially if she paid them. Now she had to be sure to get the homeless issue back on the agenda for next week's meeting.

CHAPTER 25

I T WAS DONE. The agenda was finalized, with the homeless issue at the beginning of the session, thanks to the publicity given by the *Daily Sun* and the massive display of flyers around the town: in stores, churches, schools, hospitals, laundromats, and any place where people would see them. David and Billy had outdone Hannah's expectations, thanks to the twenty dollars she gave each of them, and to the competition between the boys to see who could find more places for the flyers. While Hannah wasn't an advocate for competition—she preferred cooperation—she had to concede that competition had its place.

At first the issue had been relegated to the end of the agenda, the place where old business was discussed, on the grounds that the issue had been brought up before. But with all the publicity and the awareness that there was a possibility there would be a reporter and a full house present, George Cotter, ever aware of how his reputation would be affected, had moved it up on the agenda. No one would be able to say that he stood in the way of open discussions.

Hannah had done more than publicize the event; she had recruited "experts" to testify. Derek had agreed to describe how being a student without a home had affected his performance in school, leading him to drop out. He had convinced some of the older people to describe how they survived living in parks, sleeping in the train station and all-night stores, and migrating from couch to couch until they had used up friends they could depend upon.

She had also sought the help of Mr. Abramson from Listening Ear and Diane Cassidy from the high school, both of whom had agreed to talk at the board meeting. Armed with statistics and narratives, she approached the meeting with more confidence than she had the last time. At least the issue was going public. Unless she was the only one concerned about people not having a home, or at least a place to sleep, there was a good chance that something would come out of the meeting. Surely the stories, if not the statistics, would move people to act.

• • •

Again dressed in her navy pantsuit, this time with a mauve blouse and the gold necklace, Hannah entered the boardroom fifteen minutes before the start of the meeting. Already the room was filling up. It was clear that the word had gotten out and that there would be a full house at the meeting. In fact, it was clear that they were going to need more chairs.

Hannah put down her bag, waved to the people she knew in the audience, and went in search of the janitor.

She found her in the maintenance room down the hall, half-asleep. Hannah apologized for disturbing her and reported on the need for more chairs.

Marcy was a large woman—not fat, just large and strong. She groaned as she got up from the sofa she had been resting on, retrieved the keys to the storage room, and followed Hannah. By the time the official meeting started, twenty more chairs had been delivered, filling the room to capacity.

Hannah thanked Marcy and took her assigned seat at the table. Her young colleague, sitting two seats to her right, leaned forward to get her attention and gave her a smile and a thumbs-up sign.

The meeting started with a welcome to the audience from George, who took the opportunity to give the impression that he was responsible for the evening's agenda.

"Welcome, friends. I can see that I'm not the only one who's concerned about the plight of our fellow community members. That's why we're doing away with protocol this evening and will be getting to the issue of our homeless friends as soon as possible. Bear with us while we do the required approval of minutes and other housekeeping details. As you can see from the agenda displayed on the screen, we'll get to the main issue very quickly."

The official meeting called to order, minutes approved, a brief discussion on a new curriculum change—action on which was postponed by Hannah's young ally—George turned the meeting over to Hannah, who was introduced only as "Mrs. Lowenstein, a member of the board whom we have asked to introduce the issue," making no mention of her involvement in getting the issue on the agenda in the first place.

Hannah proceeded to correct that impression. She took the first two minutes of her talk to explain, in general terms, how she got involved and how she had presented the issue to the board at its last meeting, with no success, but thanks to the response from the community, it was finally getting a hearing.

She could see Janice shaking her head. Hannah knew she was not behaving professionally, not being a team player, but she didn't care. What could they do? She had another two years on the board, and she couldn't be more ignored than she already was. But Janice's warning was enough for her to get to her prepared talk, which was short. She used the time to introduce her experts, who could, as she explained, present the facts better than she could.

She had not indicated that she was going to do this, and George was caught off guard. He rose to object but realized that would look as if he wanted to stifle discussion. So he sat back down, a smile plastered on his face, and welcomed Hannah's team of experts.

Abramson presented the data from Listening Ear, and Cassidy reported the data from the high school, but the high points were the stories told by Derek and his friends.

Derek had at first been reluctant to talk of his own experiences, wanting to concentrate on how he had survived when he dropped out of school, but Hannah had convinced him that the details of how he survived *now* would also have an impact on what the board decided to do.

He stood up, cleared his throat, looked around the audience, and began.

"It was easy when I dropped out of high school. I had lots of friends who let me stay with them, and I earned money by mowing lawns in the summer and shoveling snow in the winter. But now"—he hesitated—"it's harder. Not so many couches to crash on. Summer's not too bad. It's warm, and the police don't bother you if you camp out in Island Park. But winter's different."

He hesitated again and looked at Hannah, who nodded encouragement.

"I live in a cardboard box, with lots of blankets and other rags. I build a fire with old newspapers and twigs so that I can heat up some water for coffee and to clean up a bit. Sometime it's so cold, I can't stay there, so I go to one of the stores that are open all night. I can usually stay there for a few hours before someone asks me to leave. Then I go to another all-night place and do the same thing. I don't get much sleep, but at least I don't freeze to death."

Hannah knew he wouldn't announce that he stole food from super-markets: fruit, granola bars, small packages of anything that would fit in the pockets of his oversized parka. He'd said he had been caught a few times but let go with a warning not to return.

Joey, a fifty-year-old man who had been surviving for over ten years living in the local park, shocked people when he told them he had a job. Unfortunately, it was a low-paying job that didn't allow for housing but did provide him with the means to buy food and, more importantly, a tent and a propane heater that made it possible to survive the winter months "camping out."

As the others talked and shared their stories of how they had become homeless and how they survived, it became clear that there was consider-able resilience—and creativity—involved. All of these people were long-time survivors with strategies developed over the years. But Hannah had wanted to include the stories of the newly homeless, those who had lost their homes because of medical costs or job layoffs or divorce—people who didn't have the survival skills of the speakers. And they needed to talk about a shelter. She needed to get the floor again but didn't know how.

When the speakers had finished, George got up and was about to close the meeting. Hannah saw her chance. "I think we should give a few minutes to the audience, George," she interrupted. "They might have some questions—or even suggestions. They might"—she smiled—"know how to get a homeless shelter started. Wouldn't that be great?"

George had no alternative than to say, "My thoughts, exactly. The floor is now open for comments from the audience." He smiled and sat down.

One of the first to rise was the minister of the Methodist church, Reverend Dwayne.

"Since reading the editorial in the paper last week, the Brewster Interfaith Council has met and discussed the problem. We are interested in forming a group to look into what other communities have done to provide shelter. You don't have to be affiliated with a church. Anyone interested in working with us is welcome. In fact, see me after this meeting is over, and we can start getting names and contact numbers."

Other clergy stood up and echoed Dwayne's invitation. The Catholic priest, the Presbyterian minister, the Jewish rabbi, the Unitarian lay leader, and a few ministers of churches that Hannah had never heard of all joined in. By the end of the meeting, there would be the start of a group to work on getting a shelter in town.

Other members of the audience arose and told of friends who were living with them while they sought assistance. A recently divorced woman with children and no child support told about how she and the children lived out of their car. A family who had lost their home because of unexpected medical expenses shared their story. It seemed as if everyone knew of someone in need of help.

After forty minutes of audience responses, George rose again and, looking at Hannah and receiving a nod of approval, asked for a motion to adjourn, which was quickly made and seconded.

Hannah was about to leave with Janice and Paul, when Reverend Dwayne called to her.

"Mrs. Lowenstein," he shouted. "Do you have a minute?"

Hannah turned to Janice. "This won't take long. I'll meet you outside in a minute."

She walked over to the group surrounding Dwayne, who parted the waves for her—or at least it looked that way to her. People patted her on the back, congratulating her, thanking her.

Dwayne took her aside. "Mrs. Lowenstein, we would love to have you join our group. We feel you have done so much and know so much more than we do that it would not only be an honor to have you but also a necessity. I know you're probably very busy, but do you think you could meet with us in the next week or so to at least get us started?"

"Of course," she replied. "I'm not so busy I can't do something important. Just let me know when you'll be meeting. But now I have to leave. My daughter's waiting."

Janice and Paul were waiting outside, Janice pacing on the sidewalk, Paul sitting in the driver's seat, looking uncomfortable, probably hoping to avoid being asked to be the mediator in what was going to be a confrontation between the two women.

Janice's body language was clear. Hannah took a deep breath, pulled herself up to her full height—glad she was wearing heels—and braced for the inevitable clash of wills and values with her daughter.

Paul jumped out of the car and opened the back door for Hannah, giving Janice an imploring look.

Janice sat down in the front passenger seat and said nothing. The tension in the car was palpable. No one spoke, and while Hannah was anxious to get the argument over—or even started—she kept silent. Better to wait until they were home. Fighting in a car could cause an accident.

Once inside the house, Janice let loose. "You can't be a team player, can you? You embarrassed George tonight. You're going to have to pay for that, you know."

"Darling, calm down. It's not so serious. So George was a little put out. He covered well, didn't he? In fact, he came out looking like the meeting was all his idea."

"Yes, he covered well. But he was seething. You could see he didn't like being upstaged by you, and he certainly didn't like the way the meeting went—because of you."

At this point, Hannah's level of tolerance for frustration was reached. "When did you ever know me to kowtow to an arrogant blowhard like George Cotter? What, I should worry about how he feels and ignore the fact that he doesn't give a tinker's damn—I think that's an expression— about homeless people or about the education the young people are getting? That all he cares about is his public image? If I hadn't stopped him from closing the meeting, there wouldn't have been any follow-up. People would have just gone away, and that would have been the end of it. They would have tsked, tsked—isn't it terrible about the homeless—and then forgotten about it. This way, there's action. Something can get done."

"Yes, but did you have to point out that the board had refused to discuss the issue and it was only because of the publicity you created that they put it on the agenda for the public meeting? You could have graciously thanked the board for holding the meeting."

Hannah shrugged. "Well, yes, I did get carried away. I could have been more gracious. Maybe my vanity got the best of me. But you know what? It felt good. I've been ignored, even dismissed, for over a year now. None of the questions I've asked about the high school curriculum has ever made it to an agenda. It's as if I'm not there, as if no sound comes out of my mouth when I raise an objection or even a question. Yes, it felt good to deflate that big bloated ego of his, if only for a while. He'll fume for a bit, but he'll be back to his old self by the morning. And I'll pay for it? What can happen? They'll ignore me? We won't be friends? So what else is new?"

Hannah sat down, out of breath. She looked up at her daughter and smiled gently. "I know you're worried about me, that I'll get into trouble, that maybe that I'm not aware of what I'm doing. But, darling, have you ever known me to avoid a fight when I think something is important?"

When Janice didn't respond, Paul, who had been standing in the doorway, entered the room and put his arm around Janice. "I think you've both said what you needed to say. It's late. Let's go to bed. See how you feel in the morning."

Janice looked at him, nodded, said good night to Hannah, and went upstairs.

Paul went over to Hannah and helped her up from the chair. "Are you all right?" he asked. She nodded, patting his arm. "I'm fine, and Janice will be fine too. We've always disagreed about these things. Neither one of us is wrong. We just handle these things differently. She's more diplomatic—if she did what I do, she'd lose her job. I have the luxury of not worrying about that. It's like in the civil rights movement. The adults couldn't risk losing their jobs if they demonstrated, but the kids had nothing to lose, especially when the teachers were behind them. So I'm like a kid with nothing to lose."

Paul grinned. "Good night, Hannah. See you in the morning."

• • •

She couldn't sleep. She had followed her usual nighttime routine: wash, brush teeth, brush hair, place a glass of water on the night table, and make a to-do list for the next day. But her mind was rehearsing all the things she would say at the first meeting that Reverend Dwayne would call, and imagining all the things she had to find out about shelters before that meeting. She got up, put on the light, and added something to her list: get help on getting information on other shelter programs. She wasn't the lone ranger—or, if she was, she needed her Tonto. It was time to enlist the help of others. She made a list of the people she knew who were more computer savvy than she. It was a short list, but she wasn't doing a research paper; she was just looking for ideas.

CHAPTER 26

"ARE YOU SURE you want to go? It's going to be a lot of boring talks, and the food won't be as good as yours." Paul had just invited Hannah to attend the Brewster Lawyers Association Banquet, an annual event used by local lawyers to network and congratulate themselves on what a good job they were doing. He had to attend, and Janice's presence, as principal of the local high school, was also expected. But Hannah? She knew he had invited her out of politeness, not expecting her to want to spend time with lawyers.

"Sure, though I might not eat much."

"You don't have to go…and," he added with a mischievous grin, "you won't have a chance to talk to anyone. It's a large group, and they're all seated at reserved tables…"

Janice looked at him. "What's the problem? If she wants to go, of course she'll go. I've already reserved a ticket for her."

Hannah smiled. Obviously Paul hadn't shared their previous conversation with Janice.

"It's okay, Paul. I understand the situation. But I think it would be nice to go out to a fancy event for a change. I might even get a new outfit."

"Okay, then it's settled. A week from tomorrow, I'm escorting the two loveliest ladies in town to a boring lawyers' dinner."

Janice looked at her mother. "You haven't bought anything new since Maddie's graduation party last year. I think it's time to go shopping. How about Friday after I get home? I'd suggest Saturday, but with summer school in full swing, there's always so much to do to make sure classes are set for the second session that I need the weekends for that."

"Friday's fine. It shouldn't take long. I just need maybe a new blouse or scarf—something to dress up my navy outfit."

"Oh no, you don't. You're not wearing that navy pantsuit to this event. You're going to get a new outfit, a new dress even. Some women will be wearing long gowns—and plenty of diamonds. This is where the men show how successful they are by what their wives are wearing."

"So, what are you wearing? Something fancy?"

"I don't do fancy. I have some dresses that this group hasn't seen. One of them will do just fine. This shopping trip is for you."

Hannah sighed. Shopping was not on her list of fun things to do. These days there was not much need for new clothes: she had enough slacks and tops for all seasons, with a few things for special times like birthdays, funerals, and the occasional fundraising dinners she was invited to.

Even when she was younger, clothes were not a major concern for her. Her husband encouraged her to go shopping more often, claiming that he liked to show her off to his coworkers at the newspaper, but she always found an excuse to wear something she already had. Part of her reaction was her reluctance to spend money on something that wasn't essential—she preferred to use the money to support her political candidates and causes. And part was due to the fact that she didn't think there were any clothes that would make her short, stocky body look any better. Leo thought she looked fine in anything but liked to occasionally surprise her by buying something special, like a new scarf in the bright colors she liked. She pretended that he shouldn't have wasted his money, that she didn't need any more scarves—but, to his delight, wore them frequently.

• • •

The shopping trip was successful. After two hours at the mall, Janice and a salesperson finally convinced Hannah to buy a long A-line dress in a violet, which brought a soft glow to her cheeks and highlighted the salt in her salt-and-pepper hair. Janice had trouble convincing her that black pumps did not go with the dress, but finally had success when Hannah found a pair of silver sandals at Payless that she agreed looked better with the dress, and which was cheap enough that she wouldn't mind if she never wore them again.

Purchases stowed in the back of the car, the two women left the mall, stopped at the Bistro for drinks, and arrived home tired and happy.

"Good night, Mom," said Janice as she hugged Hannah. "We should do that more often."

"Yes, darling, that was fun," Hannah replied, returning the hug. "But let's leave out the shopping next time."

● ● ●

The night of the banquet arrived. Hannah and Shelley helped Hannah get dressed, making sure that the silver combs Shelley had bought for Hannah's hair were placed correctly so that they were noticeable, and applying rouge to her cheeks—not too much, insisted Hannah. The girls acted as excited as if they were attending the Banquet.

Hannah enjoyed their excitement and accommodated them by spinning around so they could see her from all angles, and even posed long enough for Maddie to take a few pictures. Laughing, Hannah said, "You'd better take them now. I'm not likely to be dressed like this again."

By the time they arrived at the banquet, Hannah was having second thoughts about her decision to attend. Already her feet were hurting, and she was so worried about not tripping on the long dress that she walked with hesitation. Brief introductions were made as they entered the room, after which they took their seats at their assigned table. She relaxed once she was seated, and looked around the room. She didn't expect to know anyone and was surprised to see George Cotter, the school board chair, and his wife, as well as some members of the City Commission. And Mac was there—with a pretty redheaded woman, quite a bit younger than he. Clearly a trophy wife, thought Hannah, who was disappointed. She had thought he was above that nonsense.

People were milling around, men shaking hands and patting backs, women air-kissing. Paul and Janice brought friends over to meet Hannah, who decided that she could stay seated and still shake their hands.

Drinks were served, and after thirty minutes of informal networking, people were asked to take their seats—the food was about to be served. Hannah took the opportunity to ask Paul to point out Larry Campbell. He pointed to a silver-haired, tall, well-built man in his midfifties, who was holding a drink in one hand and patting the back of the man he was talking to with the other. He exuded confidence; Hannah instantly disliked him.

"I would have disliked him even if I didn't know anything about him," she said to Paul, who smiled and quietly cautioned her to behave herself.

Hannah had to admit the food was wonderful—though not as good as hers, of course. The Brewster Lawyers Association had gone all out: a delicious seafood bisque, large portions of prime rib and lobster, perfectly prepared potatoes and vegetables, and a variety of desserts. The wine was also wonderful. Hannah had never liked wine, having been raised on Mogen David, until Janice introduced her to Pinot Noir and Cabernet Sauvignon. But this was something else. Maybe there was something to higher-priced wines after all.

Plates cleared away, after-dinner drinks were served as people settled down for the obligatory speeches.

Paul was right: there were a lot of self-congratulations and inside jokes, which Paul tried to explain to her until she relieved him of the responsibility by patting his hand and saying, "Doesn't matter, dear. I'm not really listening."

As they got up from the table to leave, Mac and his redhead came over to talk to Hannah.

"Honey, this is the woman I was telling you about. Mrs. L, I'd like you to meet my daughter, Andrea. She was asking about the woman who started the homeless project."

"How nice to meet you," Hannah smiled as she extended her hand to Andrea. "But your father deserves most of the credit. If he hadn't published that editorial, I would have been dead in the water—I think that's the expression. Anyway, no one would have listened to me. He's a wonderful man, your father."

Mac started to say something but was cut off by his daughter. "I know. He's an old grouch, but a good one."

"Enough bullshit. We've had our share of it this evening. Can you believe these guys? But we've got to get going. Andrea lives in Cleveland and has an early start in the morning. Good to see you, Mrs. L."

So a daughter, not a trophy wife. Good, thought Hannah, pleased that her positive impression of Mac could remain unchanged. She got up to use the restroom, which required her to walk past the Campbells' table. Reminding herself of Paul's admonition, she started to walk past the table. But, she couldn't resist.

"Good evening, Mr. Campbell, Mrs. Campbell. I'm Hannah Lowenstein, a friend of your nanny, Sage. I just wanted to tell you what a treasure you have in her. You're so lucky to have someone you can trust with your little ones."

"How do you know Sage?" asked Larry, clearly disturbed by her comments.

"Oh, I met her in the park, when she was there with the children. I was so impressed with how she got along with them—you know sometimes the nanny doesn't do anything with the children, just sits there and talks to the other nannies. But I could see that Sage was different. And so we got to talk and...well, you know. After a while I looked forward to our little talks...such an interesting life she'd had, don't you think? And such a strong girl to put up with...so much."

Hannah was looking at Mr. Campbell, who stared at her. Mrs. Campbell interrupted. "Yes, she is a remarkable young woman. And with all that she does for us, she's excelling in school—going to college in the fall. We're so proud of her."

Campbell frowned at his wife and started to lead her away, but Hannah continued the conversation. "Will she continue to take care of the children next year?"

"Oh yes. She's like a daughter to us. She'll live with us and help with the children. They'll both be in school, so that won't demand as much of her time."

"Suz," Campbell interrupted. "We've got to get going. Nice to meet you, Mrs...."

"Lowenstein, Hannah Lowenstein. And nice to meet you—both of you."

As she walked away, she could feel Campbell staring at her. She felt a chill, which if she had been superstitious would have worried her. But she just pulled her shawl around her shoulders and continued to the restroom.

That went well. Nothing was done that Paul could criticize, she concluded.

CHAPTER 27

REVEREND DWAYNE, TRUE to his promise, had called together a group to follow up on a homeless shelter in town. The group, composed of clergy, representatives of various agencies in town, and interested citizens, spent the first two hours of the meeting selecting a name for itself. By an almost unanimous decision—Hannah was the only dissenter—they came up with the Committee for Providing Shelter for the Homeless— which Hannah pointed out was not even a pronounceable acronym. The next hour was spent fumbling around the issue of what to do next.

The Listening Ear representative pointed out that if they wanted to receive public and private grants, they had to register as a nonprofit group, requiring the filing of a 501(c3) form. In true bureaucratic form, a subcommittee of one was designated to look into that issue. The next item on the to-do list was to look at other communities to see what they were doing. Again, a subcommittee of one was assigned that task. And the last thing was to establish a meeting schedule for the future. That took another hour, until it was finally decided that since so many people were able to attend this meeting, perhaps this time each week should be set as the official meeting time.

Hannah left the meeting with mixed feelings: pleased that something was finally being done and yet concerned that winter would be here before anything really got underway. But, as she told herself driving home, slow progress was better than no progress.

• • •

The shelter committee finally settling down to business, Hannah turned her attention to family matters. While she hadn't neglected the family—there was always dinner waiting for them when they returned, and she was always available for advice when asked—she hadn't initiated any discussions.

Well, that would change, she decided. That evening at dinner, she made a point of asking everyone: "So, how did your day go?"

David replied, "Okay."

Maddie replied, "Fine."

Shelley replied, "Fine."

Janice looked across the table at Hannah. "What's up, Mom? Why the interrogation?"

"What interrogation? I can't show interest in what my family's doing?" she huffed.

"Sorry. It wasn't a criticism. It's just that you seemed on a mission, that's all."

"No mission, just interest. Normal family interest—there should be discussion at dinner, sharing things. How am I to know what's going on if I don't ask questions? No one tells me anything unless I ask."

Hannah knew that she was overreacting. Clearly her perceived neglect of the family had brought guilty feelings to the forefront. She had read enough pop psychology to have a name for her reaction: a defense mechanism. There was probably a more precise name, but that one was sufficient to calm her down. She took a deep breath and looked at Janice.

"Okay. Sorry. I've just been so busy with the shelter stuff these past few weeks that I haven't kept up with what's been going on here." She looked at the kids. "Didn't mean to put you on the spot. You have something to tell me, you'll tell me," she said. "If I have something to ask, I'll ask. Okay?"

Maddie laughed. "You can ask anything you want, Grandma. And if I don't want to answer, I won't. Right?"

"Right. So now we understand each other," she replied as she bobbed her head up and down a few times for emphasis.

All through this interchange, Shelley had been silent, looking from Janice to Hannah to Maddie and back to Hannah, glancing for comfort at her tote bag, still sitting on the table in the hallway.

Hannah noticed Shelley's discomfort, turned to her, and changed the topic. "So, Shelley, have you seen Sage lately?"

Shelley looked up and shook her head. "No, she hasn't been to the mall with the kids for a few weeks, I think."

"Hmm, I hope everything's okay." She frowned.

"Mom, there are a lot of reasons why she hasn't been to the mall, so don't go investigating, okay? Maybe the kids are sick. Maybe the family's on vacation. Maybe she takes them other places instead of the mall."

"Maybe." Hannah shrugged and helped herself to another slice of raspberry pie. But she wasn't convinced. Something told her—maybe her gut, maybe her subconscious—that something wasn't right. She would talk more to Shelley, but not now, not here.

CHAPTER 28

THE COMMITTEE FOR Providing Shelter for the Homeless had proved to be more productive than Hannah had expected. The papers for the incorporation of the group as a nonprofit had been submitted, and information about shelter programs in other communities had been gathered.

The most promising information they had received was that many communities had success with rotating shelters, utilizing churches as host sites to provide food and shelter for a week at a time.

Hannah had balked at this last bit of news. "We don't want people should be made to be lectured to about religion, you know, try to get them to believe things or…"

Reverend Dwayne interrupted her. "No, the churches would be told up front that there is to be no proselytizing. We visited the Traverse City shelters. Their rules and regulations seem acceptable, and they explicitly forbid proselytizing."

"Okay then." She nodded.

Now the focus of the Committee for Providing Shelter for the Homeless was to find host sites in town.

After only a few weeks, with members of the committee meeting with their own churches, four churches had indicated interest in being hosts. There was still much to do in order to implement the program before the cold weather set in, but the committee was fortunate that it had members who were willing to work as well as talk.

One member, however, drove Hannah to distraction. Eddie—who in other situations would have been a delight—couldn't focus on the fact the committee did not have, and would not have, enough money to buy a building that could be used for a shelter right away. He came to every meeting with another house he had found that would be perfect. When pushed for details, he would admit either that the house wasn't up for sale or, if it was for sale, was priced at $500,000. Somehow he thought they could raise enough money for a down payment on a mortgage—forgetting that they would also need money to operate the shelter and to pay staff.

This discussion usually took at least twenty minutes, during which time Hannah would fidget, searching through her purse for something or getting up to refill her coffee. But eventually she would shout, "Point of order, Mr. Chair"—she had heard this on a TV program—and get the meeting back on track. She knew she was not the only one who was frustrated with Eddie, but realized she was the only one willing to stop him. Midwesterners were so polite, she thought, shaking her head.

• • •

Now that people were assigned their respective tasks, she was free to focus on Sage. No way was she content to assume that all was well in the Campbell household.

Again, when struggling with a problem that resisted solution, she turned to food—preparing it, not eating it. After three hours she had a kitchen filled with the aromas of a pesto sauce for the evening's pasta dinner, snickerdoodle cookies (for David), a peach pie made with peaches from the neighbor's fruit trees, and two loaves of bread.

Exhausted, she sat down in the recliner and, without even turning on the TV, fell asleep, awakened only when David announced his arrival by slamming the front door.

"Snickerdoodles," he shouted. "You made snickerdoodles," he repeated, as he made a dash for the kitchen.

"Hang your things up," Hannah called after him. "And wash your hands." She was amazed that he could smell the cookies from the mélange of aromas drifting through the house.

"So tell me about your day," she said as she followed David into the kitchen. He had already attacked the cookies and was filling a glass with lemonade. He looked at her and shrugged.

"I don't know. There's nothing to tell. It was just a day."

"Just a day? A day without anything in it?" Hannah wouldn't let it go. It was about time he learned to engage in a little conversation. She sat down at the table across from him, leaned forward, and, with a serious look on her face and a bubbling laugh in her heart, continued to press him for details.

"So how's soccer? How's your video game? Is Billy still ahead of you?" She knew that would get a response.

"He's not ahead of me. I'm on level ten now. He's still stuck on nine," he replied as he put down the cookie to face Hannah and set her straight.

"That's good, right?" Hannah asked. "Level ten is pretty high?"

"Yeah, no one in the group has gotten higher than that. And I think I can make eleven soon. I just have to watch out for traps. That's the hard part."

David proceeded to describe the pitfalls he had to escape and the strategy he had developed to accomplish that. Hannah listened but was more interested in the passion he showed than in the explanation he offered. *See you can have a conversation with him. You just have to choose the right topic. But isn't that true of most people? The key to conversations is to find a topic that both you and the other person are interested in.*

Explanation finished, cookies consumed, David got up from the table, put his glass in the sink, and looked at Hannah. "If you're interested, I could show you how to play," he offered tentatively.

"That would be nice." Hannah smiled. "I need to learn new things. It keeps a person young."

• • •

David ran off to his room to reach level eleven before leaving for soccer practice, and Hannah returned to thinking of Sage. Well, it was still early. Perhaps Sage would be alone in the house again. It was worth a trip out there to see how she was doing. She changed into slacks and her green mandarin-collared blouse—in case she ran into Mrs. Campbell, she wanted to look good—and headed for Orchard Drive.

Sage was not there. But as Hannah turned the car around to return home, she noticed a park at the end of the cul-de-sac. She remembered Sage talking about taking the children to the park in the afternoons, and she slowed down, carefully perusing the area. There she was. The children on the monkey bars, Sage sitting on the bench, watching them.

Hannah parked the car, walked over to Sage, and sat down next to her.

"So how are you doing? I thought I'd drop in and see you at the house, but here you are. Lucky for me I don't drive too fast, or I would have missed you."

Sage smiled politely. Hannah realized immediately that Sage wasn't in a mood to talk about her situation again, perhaps regretting that she had told Hannah anything. But here she was. She might as well get on with it.

She glanced at the children, made sure that they were not able to hear her, and asked, "So how are you doing?"

Sage looked at her and shook her head. "I don't know. I'm sorry I ever said anything. It's really not so bad—it's only once in a while now—and I really like it here. Most of the time he treats me good—and he's going to pay for my going to the community college in the fall. And Mrs. Campbell is quite nice, lets me have time off, doesn't demand too much…I don't know. Maybe we should just let it go."

Hannah listened as Sage talked, barely keeping her frustration in check. She knew this was not the time to push Sage, to remind her that what Campbell was doing was not only illegal but wrong, deeply wrong; that she had the right to dignity and to decide when and with whom she would have sexual relations; that there were other ways to get a college education. But she kept silent. She would do this on her own but without compromising Sage's position.

"Well, dear, I can see you have two children who want your attention. I'll let you go. Just let me know if anything changes or if you need anything." Hannah hugged Sage, smiled at the children, and walked away

CHAPTER 29

"**W**HY DO I get involved in these things?" Hannah muttered to herself as she drove through the streets, underground sprinklers doing their job at keeping the manicured lawns green. "So much for a water ban. I guess such things don't apply here," she complained. All of her frustration at Sage was being redirected at the neighborhood she was driving through. "Look at that one," she continued, focusing on a building with turrets and what looked like a moat, only composed of hedges, not water. "They must think they need a fortress to protect them from…" She couldn't think of the appropriate danger, so she just shook her head.

She arrived home in a foul mood, partly caused by the houses in Pill Hill and partly by Sage's reaction. She was greeted by a blast of ninety-two-degree heat when she got out of the car, which added to her already foul mood. She quickly removed the mandarin-collared blouse as soon as she reached her room. "So much for fashion," she grumbled as she tossed the blouse and slacks on the floor and reached for a cotton caftan. She fanned herself with a magazine and sat down on the bed. "Well, that was a waste. It would have been better not to talk to Sage at all," she concluded. "Now what do I do?"

She got up from the bed and stepped on the green blouse. Hannah was a neat person, and the sight of clothes on the floor jarred her into the present. She bent down to retrieve the discarded clothes and placed them in the laundry bin in her bathroom. It was now almost four, and she had the rest of the afternoon to herself. Or so she thought, until she heard David slam the front door.

"David?" she called out. "Is that you?"

"Yeah," he responded, out of breath.

"Where were you? And why are you breathing so hard?" she asked as she came out of her bedroom.

"Practice was called off—Coach decided it's too hot."

Hannah's second question was answered by Max, the family's golden retriever, who had plopped down, panting, tongue hanging out. Clearly, David and Max had been running.

"In this heat, you're running? And making Max run? You could give him a heart attack. He's no spring chicken, you know."

"Aw, he's okay. It's good for him. We only ran for a few blocks. We stopped for an ice cream on the way back. That made him feel better," David said as he leaned down to pat Max on the head.

"Well, okay, but give him some water. Ice cream is fine, but water is better."

David shrugged, signaled for Max to follow, and went to the kitchen, where Max ran to his water bowl, slopping most of it on the floor in his excitement.

Well, there goes my quiet afternoon, thought Hannah. *I may as well get started on dinner.*

Max had retired to his blanket, placed strategically near an air vent—warm in the winter, cool in the summer. David could be heard upstairs, music blaring, most likely engrossed in his game. The house was no longer quiet, but Hannah found comfort in the sounds floating down from upstairs.

CHAPTER 30

I T WAS UNUSUALLY hot for July. Usually a comfortable seventy-five degrees, temperatures had remained in the low nineties for the last three weeks, bringing threats of water rationing as well as rising tempers. Conversations started with "Hot enough for you?" and ended with "Keep cool."

Hannah had arrived at the farmers' market minutes after it opened at eight. She went early before the produce was picked over, and today she wanted to be home before the temperature rose.

She was engrossed in picking out the perfect melon, shaking and smelling it to guarantee ripeness, when a woman jostled her, reaching over her head to get the attention of the farmer. Hannah turned to admonish her but stopped when she recognized Suzanne Campbell. Although annoyed, she was more curious.

"Why, Mrs. Campbell. Nice to see you," she cooed.

Suzanne looked at her, trying to remember who Hannah was and where she had met her. Hannah toyed with the idea of leaving Suzanne in confusion, but thought better of it—she wanted information about Sage, and here was her opportunity.

"I'm Hannah Lowenstein. We met at the lawyers' banquet."

"Oh, of course. Nice to see you."

"We talked about Sage and…"

"Don't talk to me about that girl," she cried. Suzanne's reaction surprised Hannah.

"Why, what's happened?"

"Well, I can't go into details. But she was not the person I thought she was. I loved her like a daughter, and she…" Suzanne stopped.

"Oh, my dear—come. Let's go into the shade. We need to talk. You know I, too, was very fond of her. Please tell me what happened." Hannah gently led Suzanne to a bench under a maple tree, which provided temporary shade.

Suzanne dabbed at her eyes with a handkerchief—no tissues for her—and took a deep breath. "Everything was fine, but then I couldn't find the diamond necklace I had worn to the banquet. I'm sure I had put it away, but it was so late when we got home, and Larry was in such a foul mood, that maybe I just left it on the dresser. But either way, when I went to wear it to the annual Founders' dinner at the country club, I couldn't find it. I looked all over: jewelry box, behind the dresser, even under the bed. Larry was furious. He always wanted to put it in the vault—it was worth a lot, you know—but I kept saying what's the use of having a beautiful necklace if I have to go to the bank every time I want to wear it."

"Of course you'd want it handy. But what does this have to do with Sage?"

"Everything. Angie, who does our cleaning, found it under the mattress in Sage's room! It was a fluke. Usually she just makes the beds, but this was the time to turn the mattresses. Otherwise, we'd never have found it."

Hannah couldn't hide her disbelief. "What did Sage have to say? Surely she had an explanation."

"What could she say? Of course she denied everything, said she had no idea how it got under her mattress. Well, we had no recourse but to let her go. We couldn't have someone in the house whom we couldn't trust. Now I have to start over and find another nanny for the children."

Hannah was stunned—and suspicious. She fought the impulse to defend Sage, to argue that it was a setup—probably by Larry—but kept quiet. She needed to know where Sage was, if she was safe; she needed information from Suzanne.

"How terrible," she managed to say. "It's hard to believe. She seemed like such a responsible young woman. I can't imagine why she would do such a thing. And the children seemed to really love her. It must be hard for them. What did you tell them?"

"What could I say? I just said she had to leave and we would get another nanny for them. Of course they were upset, but they'll adjust."

She turned to leave, but Hannah reached out to detain her. "What's happening to Sage? Are you pressing charges? Do you know where she is?" Hannah couldn't hide her concern. She had to know how to find Sage.

"Well, we're not pressing charges—we did find the necklace, and Larry doesn't want the publicity that would result—and I have no idea what's she doing. Maybe going back home. You know she's an Indian, don't you? I should have never hired her—those people are known to be thieves. I had thought she was different...well, I won't make that mistake again."

Hannah stood there, mouth open, looking at Suzanne as she walked away. Did she hear right? *The woman trusts Sage with her children and yet harbors such prejudice?* Did she ever really like Sage? Trust her? Hannah would never understand such people. Better she not spend time with them, she thought. She wasn't good at hiding her contempt.

But the important issue was finding Sage. She wandered through the market in a daze, picking up tomatoes, corn, spinach—without squeezing, smelling, or looking for defects. She wanted to get home. She needed to find Sage.

● ● ●

Hannah sped home, dropped the produce on the kitchen table, and took off for the mall. After circling the parking lot for ten minutes, she saw a spot just being vacated near the entrance. She nosed into it just before the car with the turn signal could move, and gestured apologetically— ignoring the raised middle finger of the driver—and dashed off for the entrance.

She was out of breath, perspiration staining her cotton top, and looked frazzled. When she entered the store, Shelley ran over to her, frightened at her appearance.

"What's the matter? Are you all right? You don't look good. Let me get you some water."

"No, I'm okay. Let me sit for a minute, though, catch my breath. Oy, I'm not so young anymore I can run like that."

"Let me check with my supervisor. I'll take my break now, and we can go to the food court and talk."

Hannah smiled. "Thank you, darling. I'll just sit here and wait for you."

Shelley returned in a few minutes, and they set off for the food court. Hannah handed Shelley a ten-dollar bill and insisted that Shelley get something to eat and bring her back a black coffee and a donut, preferably a glazed one—after all, one had to keep up one's energy when one was upset.

Coke for Shelley, coffee and donut for Hannah, the two sat down in the corner, away from the other customers. Hannah was still having trouble catching her breath, and her eyes were filling up.

"What's wrong?" Shelley asked. "You're scaring me. Are you okay? Should I call 911?"

Hannah reached over and put her hand on Shelley's "No, darling, I'm okay. Just need to catch my breath." Within a few minutes, Hannah's breathing returned to normal. She took a bite of her donut, followed by a sip of coffee, and turned to Shelley.

"I must look a wreck." She smiled. "Sorry if I scared you, darling. I'm fine now. I just had a shock and needed to talk to you." She took another bite of the donut and continued. "I just found out that Sage was fired. They accused her of stealing a diamond necklace—I think it's a put-up job, but that's not the point for now. For now, I'm worried where she is. She has no money that I know of—they just kicked her out—so where is she staying? Do you know if she has any friends, anyone she might stay with? Did you ever see her with anyone when she was here with the children?"

Shelley leaned forward, staring at Hannah, mouth open. "Oh my God," she whispered. "How terrible. Are they going to go to the police?"

"No, they don't want the publicity, and they found the necklace—under her mattress, they claim," she replied with disdain. "Those people are not nice. I think they framed her. Why I don't know...But you see, I might be responsible." Here Hannah's eyes filled again, and she stopped to sip her coffee.

Shelley frowned.

Hannah regained her composure. "Forget that for now. The main thing is to find her. Do you have any idea where she could be or who she could be with?"

Shelley sat back, eyes moving back and forth, thumb finding its way to her mouth, deep in thought. Finally she looked up at Hannah.

"Well," she said, "there was this guy that would sit with her when she let the kids play in that area in front—you know, where they have the slides and balls for kids to play with. I don't know his name though."

"Does he come here often?"

"I've seen him a few times. I think he works here—but I don't know which store."

Hannah considered her options: ask Shelley to walk with her into every store in the mall, get a description of him from Shelley and walk into every store herself, or be patient and wait until Shelley called her when she saw him again. None of these options satisfied her. But at least she could get a description of him.

"So, what does this man look like?"

"Just an average guy. Medium height, kind of scrawny, longish hair—kind of brown, I think. The usual clothes: jeans, T-shirt, sneakers. Nothing that would stand out."

"Oy, this is going to be difficult. I'll have to think some more…But you'd better get back to work. I wouldn't want you should get fired because of talking to me so long."

Shelley nodded, got up, and hugged Hannah. "Are you all right now? You scared me, you know."

Hannah laughed. "Yes, I'm fine now. Back to normal. Go. You don't want you should be late. I'll see you tonight."

Hannah remained at the table, sipping her coffee. How could she find this man? If he looked as scruffy as described, he wouldn't be working in any of the finer stores, at least not dealing with the customers. But he could be working in the stockroom—or he could be working in one of the technical stores: they didn't care what you looked like so long as you knew what you were doing. So she needed a list of all the stores at the mall.

Hannah spent the rest of the afternoon, map of the mall in her hand, walking in and out of the likely stores. It was after four. Her feet hurt. She was tired. She was frustrated. She sat down on a bench and tried to think. "There must be a better way to do this," she mumbled. If Mr. Scruffy was working at the mall, she couldn't find him.

With a loud sigh, she lifted herself from the bench and walked toward the exit. It was time to head home. With all the activity of the day, she hadn't paid any attention to dinner. Her original plan of a rice pilaf with all the produce she had bought at the farmers' market was no longer possible. It would have to be something simple—pizza? Why not? Everyone loved pizza.

Remembering the lesson learned from her last driving-while-frustrated experience, she drove slowly and carefully—probably too slowly for the other drivers anxious to get home after work.

David was already home, in his room, most likely attempting to reach level eleven and stay ahead of Billy. Maddie and Shelley were just driving into the driveway.

They entered the house laughing.

"What's so funny?" asked Hannah as she washed her hands at the kitchen sink, preparing to start on a salad to accompany the pizza.

"Didn't you see us? We were right behind you almost all the way from the mall. You were going so slow, we thought we'd never get home," Maddie said.

"I look in front of me, not in back. And I drive carefully. What's the hurry, anyway? An extra few minutes won't make a difference in the long run." Hannah knew she was being peevish, but she couldn't tell them about her real reasons. Trying to change the topic, she turned to the refrigerator and pulled out the ingredients for a caesar salad. "Here, make yourselves useful. We're having pizza tonight, and we need a big salad. I'll leave the salad to you two—so have at it," she announced as she left the room.

But she could still hear the girls.

"Did we do something wrong?" Shelley asked.

"Not really. Sometimes she doesn't like to be teased—especially about her driving. Mom says that she's afraid we'll think she shouldn't be driving if we tease her. Anyway, she'll get over her snit in a few minutes. She never stays mad long…"

"I can hear you," yelled Hannah as she closed the door to her room. *This is ridiculous*, she thought. *Yelling at the girls for something so silly. Of course I was driving too slowly…Well, I'll apologize later—maybe defrost some of those cookies Maddie likes. I just have to calm down, focus on first things first: dinner, then finding Sage.*

• • •

Hannah slept fitfully. Thoughts of Sage sleeping in the park, wandering through dark streets, alone, frightened—and the thought that she was somehow responsible for Sage's situation—kept her tossing and turning throughout the night.

She was on her second cup of coffee when the sky started to lighten. It was going to be another hot day. The family wouldn't be up for another hour, so Hannah just sat there drinking and thinking. How could she find Sage? She realized that returning to the mall was a waste of time. Who else might Sage have turned to? She had to admit she was hurt Sage hadn't sought her out. Surely she knew that Hannah would have helped. But she also had to admit she had poked her nose in where it wasn't wanted. Perhaps Sage resented her interference. But surely Sage had some friends, or at least some classmates she might turn to. And it finally hit her: Diane Cassidy might know who they were.

All of a sudden the sky seemed to cast a soft pink haze over everything, and Hannah could see that it was going to be a beautiful day. She quickly showered and dressed, prepared the batter for buttermilk pancakes—usually reserved for weekend breakfasts—and waited until she could call Diane.

CHAPTER 31

SAGE CAREFULLY FOLDED the bedding, made up the couch, show-ered, and dressed. She made sure that everything was in order and quietly left the apartment. She appreciated Diane's generous offer but couldn't stay there much longer. She had to find a job, one that would pay enough for her to afford her own place, even if it were only a room somewhere.

She was still reeling from the shock of being accused of stealing. She had not put that necklace under the mattress—she knew that. But who would have done that? Mrs. Campbell always said how glad she was that Sage was there to take care of the children. And Mr. Campbell…well, that was more complicated. It's true she didn't like having sex with him, but he did treat her well—little presents, her favorite chocolates—and he was gentle with her. He said that he had a special love for her, that he wanted to see her happy, and would do what he could to help her with college expenses. She thought the Campbells loved her; they had said as much. But now? Mrs. Campbell had called her a "dirty Indian," and Mr. Campbell had just stood there, not saying a word.

So who could have put the necklace there? The children? They wouldn't do something like that, and besides, they couldn't have lifted the mattress high enough to hide the necklace. Angie? Why would she do such a thing? No, it didn't make sense. It was just so unfair. Just when she thought her life would get better—college, living at the Campbells, taking care of the children—it would have been perfect.

Questions filled her mind: What do I do now? *I can't stay at Diane's forever—I need to find a place to live, I need a job. I miss the kids. I wonder if they miss me. Oh, how could this have happened?*

Tears filled her eyes. *Stop it*, she told herself. *What's done is done.* "It's time to find a job," she muttered as she locked the door behind her.

She didn't realize that she was crying until she was approached by a woman pushing a toddler in a stroller.

"Are you all right? Do you need help?"

Sage wiped her tears and smiled. "No, I'm fine. I'm okay."

The woman looked skeptical but walked away, frequently glancing back to reassure herself that Sage was okay until she was no longer in sight.

Sage was embarrassed. She didn't like calling attention to herself, especially in public.

She quickly glanced at the other people on the street. Was anyone else looking at her? Were they creating stories about a crying girl—an Indian girl? She missed her family. All the time at the Campbells' house, she'd felt at home, almost forgetting that people saw her as an Indian. But when Mrs. Campbell accused her of stealing, she had called her a "dirty, sneaky Indian." That shook her. How could she say that? Had she thought that all along?

She sat down on a bench by a bus stop and tried to clear her head. *Okay*, she thought, *I've got to get control of myself. There's no point in trying to figure out what happened—it happened.* She concentrated on thinking of options, but each time she came up with one she found a reason why it wouldn't work. She could move back home, but without any money to get there, and without any job, she would just be adding to the burdens her family already struggled with. She could stay with Diane for a while longer, but that was only a temporary solution. Even though Diane had not specified a time limit, she couldn't impose on her much longer. She hadn't made many friends in Brewster, since most of her free time had been taking care of the children, and the friends she made at school didn't know of her situation. They thought she was somehow related to the Campbells and took care of the children as an older sister would. No, she couldn't ask them for help.

She couldn't think of any other options—except getting a job. Fortunately, the Campbells had allowed her to pack up her clothes and personal belongings. She at least had decent clothes to wear to interviews.

She got up from the bench, continued walking, and entered the McDonald's on the next block. She didn't have money for food, but she knew they had clean restrooms. She washed her face, combed her hair, and refreshed her makeup. She straightened her shoulders, looked in the mirror, and, satisfied with what she saw, left MacDonald's to find a job.

● ● ●

Hannah received the answering machine when she called Diane Cassidy. She hung up without leaving a message, but then thought again and redialed.

"Hello, this is Hannah Lowenstein. Would you have some time to meet with me? I don't want to go into detail on the phone—it's rather complicated—but it is important. Thank you."

She hung up the phone and then realized she hadn't left her phone number. Did Diane know that she lived with Janice? She picked up the phone again and said, "I forgot to give you the number. You should call me at Janice's home—763-4892. Thank you."

Now she had to wait. But what if Diane was out of town? What if the message didn't go through—Hannah didn't trust machines. She faced a day of waiting with extreme frustration.

She busied herself with cleaning and cooking. She dusted and rearranged cupboards in the kitchen, cleaned out the refrigerator, and defrosted the freezer. She was starting on the pile of magazines lying around the living room...Janice! Why didn't she think of that? Surely Janice would know where Diane Cassidy was.

She ran to the phone and dialed the number of the school. The receptionist answered.

"Hello, Heather," Hannah said, trying to catch her breath, "is Janice available? I need to speak to her. It's important."

"Sure, Mrs. Lowenstein, I'll transfer you right now. I hope it's not an emergency."

Hannah knew that Heather lived for gossip, and calmly said, "No, nothing like that...I need to know what she wants for dinner."

Now why did she say that? *I didn't have to give her any reason to want to talk to my daughter. Oy, I'm not thinking clearly.*

Janice came on the line, worried about Hannah. "Mom, are you okay? Heather said there was an emergency? Are the kids okay?"

"Darling, calm down. There's no emergency. It's just Heather's need for drama in her life. No, all I need is information. Do you know where Diane Cassidy is? I need to get in touch with her. She doesn't answer her phone at home…"

"Well, that's because she isn't at home. She's here at work. Kids need counseling during the summer too. Do you want me to transfer you to her office? She may be with someone, but you can leave a message, and I'm sure she'll get back to you as soon as she can."

"Oh, that would be wonderful. Yes, transfer me…But while we're talking, what would you like I should make for dinner?"

Janice laughed. "Anything you want. I'll see you this evening, Mom. Got to run. Bye."

Hannah was immediately transferred to Diane, who answered the phone on the first ring. "Hello, Diane Cassidy. How may I help you?"

"Oh, it's you. I'm so glad. I hate to talk on those machines." Hannah took a deep breath, realizing that she hadn't even introduced herself. "I'm sorry. How rude of me. This is Hannah Lowenstein. I don't know if you remember…"

"Mrs. Lowenstein, of course I remember you. What can I do for you?"

"Well, it would be better to talk in person, but I'm so worried. I'll tell you over the phone. It's about a young lady who needs help. She was unfairly kicked out of the place she was living and I don't know where she is or what she's doing…She's a student—although I think she just graduated and was planning on going to college, but that's not going to happen now—"

"Are you talking about Sage Barker?" Diane interrupted.

"Yes, Sage, that's her. Do you know anything about her situation? I'm really worried about her."

"She's fine, Mrs. Lowenstein. She's staying at my place for a while until she can find a job. She doesn't know many people outside of her classmates and the family she lived with."

"It's a long story—and not a nice one. But I've talked with her and was trying to help her, and then this happened. You know why she's not working with that family anymore?"

"Well, yes I do."

"Then you know it's a trumped-up charge. That girl didn't steal anything. She was framed, and I think I know who it was."

"Can you come down here, or could I meet you somewhere?"

"It has to be a quiet place, somewhere we can be confidential."

"Why don't you come to the school? We can use my counseling room—confidential and soundproof. What time works for you? I'm free after two this afternoon."

"Then two it is. I'll be there. Thank you, Diane. I'm glad Sage has you for a friend."

"Good-bye, Mrs. Lowenstein. See you at two."

• • •

Hannah had two hours to kill before her appointment with Diane. Well, it was time for lunch. She would see if Ruby was at the Senior Center. She hadn't caught up with the local gossip for a while, and what better place to hear it, and what better person to hear it from than Ruby?

But Ruby wasn't at the Center, nor was Charlie. She scrutinized the place and found no one who would provide a pleasant hour of discussion—she didn't want to listen to the latest tales of ailments and doctors. She caught a glimpse of Phyllis Parkins, who was at least interesting, and walked over to sit with her. Hannah could use an amusing update on Phyllis's latest adventures in man trapping.

And she wasn't disappointed. She could concentrate on what she was eating, listen with half an ear, and still enjoy the latest tale of Phyllis's attempt to convince the new man—what was his name?—that he really would enjoy being married to her.

After forty minutes, Hannah excused herself, citing a previous appointment, and wished Phyllis luck.

She sat in her car a few minutes, realized she still had an hour before meeting Diane, and drove to Marty's. There was always something she could get for dinner.

Armed with two bags filled with what she would call "junk food," she drove to the school for her appointment. She arrived a few minutes early and strolled around the building, observing for the first time the shrubbery and flowers, the murals painted on the side of the building with sidewalk chalk, and the students on the field. She wondered if David was out there with the soccer team. She thought of going over there to find out, but she didn't have the time and was concerned that David wouldn't appreciate his grandma watching him at practice.

Following the path, she came upon an area filled with rows of vegetables: corn, peppers, beans on stalks, cabbages, carrots, and more. Each row was clearly labeled with a name, a date, and a number, which she assumed catalogued information regarding the growing conditions. She was impressed, even though she didn't know whether it was the work of students or staff. Either way, she thought, the students at the school were made aware that one could grow one's food—something she hadn't realized until she was almost an adult!

It was time to see Diane. She hurried back to the front of the building and reached Diane's office on the stroke of two, slightly out of breath. Diane was just finishing up with a young man who seemed to have received good news, grinning as he left the office.

"Come in, Mrs. Lowenstein. I'll be just a minute. I have to get these notes in the right folder while I remember. I can never find anything if I don't do it immediately."

"Don't rush, dear. I have plenty of time." She sat down in the chair next to the desk, using the time to catch her breath. *Oy, that was more exercise than I get in a year.*

"Okay, that's done," Diane said as she leaned back in her chair and looked across at Hannah. "What is it you wanted to talk about? As I told you, Sage is okay. She's staying at my place until she can get settled on her own. As I understand it, she's enrolled in the local community college for the fall, and then she can live in college housing."

"I think it's wonderful that you should let her stay with you. And it's also good that she'll be going to college in the fall. But…how should I say this? Do you really think that she'll be able to earn enough money to pay for tuition, a room, and extra money for…whatever?"

"Well, I'm helping her with applying for financial aid and student loans. And there are scholarships for Native American kids. I'm hoping that with piecing things together, she can afford college."

Hannah wasn't convinced. She had ideas of her own as to how Sage could afford college, but said nothing. No sense saying anything until it was done. She wanted to raise the issue of the Campbells but didn't know how much Sage had confided to Diane. So instead she said, "Do you think I could talk to Sage? I don't want I should upset her, so if she doesn't want to talk to me, that's okay. But could you ask her? Maybe she could call me, and we could meet someplace? There are some things I need to tell her." Her voice trailed off, and she sat, expectation on her face, waiting for Diane's answer.

"Of course I'll ask her. I'm sure she'd like to talk to you. She mentioned that she knew you and that you were, in her words, 'a cool lady.'

"Well, that's a new one. I guess that's better than a 'nice old lady.' Hannah laughed as she rose to leave. "Thank you, dear. It relieves my worries now that I know there's someone looking after her."

Hannah walked to her car. She hadn't raised the issue she was really concerned about, but somehow she hadn't felt that Diane would understand. Oh, Diane would probably agree that Sage hadn't stolen the necklace, but would she understand Hannah's suspicions about the Campbells? Better not to show one's hand yet. And Sage was safe, so that was good. No, she would have to do the rest on her own—at least until she had some real evidence, not just suspicions.

CHAPTER 32

ANNAH WAITED TO hear from Sage. She left the house only when necessary, hovering by the phone like a teenage girl waiting for her boyfriend to call. After two days, her patience gave out. If Sage didn't contact her, she would contact Sage. But how? Where? She knew Sage was still at Diane's apartment, but Hannah couldn't bring herself to barge in there uninvited. A person's home should be a sanctuary—unless you brought a gift.

What could she bring? Nothing personal—that would be inappropriate. Something for the house? No, too formal. Food? Of course! Food was always an appropriate gift. Having settled that, she rummaged through her recipes. Cinnamon rolls and cookies were always appreciated, but pies made with fruit just harvested at a local farm—perfect.

She grabbed her purse, dashed for the car, and headed to her favorite local farmer. The farmers' market wasn't until tomorrow, but she couldn't wait that long. She was sure there would be fresh berries of some sort available.

Armed with a basket of rhubarb and strawberries—and green beans, onions, and broccoli—she arrived home and set to baking two pies: one for Sage and one for the family.

While the pies were baking, she treated herself to a glass of iced tea and a cookie and tried to think of how to approach Sage. What she wanted was for Sage to agree that Larry Campbell had raped her and that he should be reported to the police; what she wanted was for Larry Campbell to be revealed as a rapist; what she wanted was to feel that justice had been served and that the balance of good over evil in the universe had been at least temporarily restored. But forced to return to reality, she realized she would have to settle for something less. She just hoped it wasn't for nothing.

● ● ●

It was now four thirty. Dinner wasn't until six thirty, which left Hannah enough time to deliver her pie and talk to Sage. She didn't know if Sage would be home, but it was worth the attempt even if it was just to calm herself down. She had to *do* something.

She arrived at Diane's, pie in hand, and was confronted with a building that allowed access only if a resident buzzed you in. Would Sage let her in? What a silly question, Hannah thought. Why wouldn't she? *It's only natural that I'd be concerned about her—and she did tell Diane that I was "cool."*

Hannah rang the bell and announced herself, and Sage buzzed her in.

"How are you, dear? I heard about what happened, and I was worried...Oh, here's a pie I made for you and Diane," she said as she handed the pie to Sage.

"Oh, thank you. It looks delicious. Diane's not back from work yet, but she'll be delighted. I'm doing the cooking, and we haven't had dessert for over a week," she replied as she placed the pie on the counter.

"So how are you?"

Sage shrugged. "I'm fine. I just can't understand what happened. I didn't steal that necklace..."

"Of course you didn't—anyone who knows you would know that. Do you have any idea how it got under your mattress?"

When Sage looked at her in confusion, Hannah realized that an explanation was needed. "I ran into Mrs. Campbell at the farmers' market last week, and she told me the whole story—her version of the whole story. It didn't make sense to me, and when she told me that they had fired you, I was concerned. And then Diane told me that you were staying here, and so here I am."

"What did she say—Mrs. Campbell?"

"Well, she told me that she couldn't find her necklace and that the maid found it under your mattress. And that she fired you."

"Did she say anything about the children?"

"She said they missed you."

Hannah didn't want to say anything about Mrs. Campbell's comment about Indians or about getting a new nanny. No sense in upsetting Sage any more than she already was.

Hannah looked around the small apartment kitchen, glad for the large one at Janice's.

"Forgive my lack of manners. Please, come sit down," Sage said as she led Hannah into the living room.

"Sage, dear, I need to speak to you. I think you have some important decisions to make. I think you were set up. I don't know why, but it seems that, for whatever reason, they wanted you gone. Whether that was Mrs. Campbell's decision or her husband's, I don't know, but it's all too suspicious. What would you do with a diamond necklace? Hock it at a pawnshop? Wear it? And why would you hide it there? You've been with them long enough to know the routine—when the mattress gets turned, for example. How convenient that it's found so quickly after she noticed it was missing. No, something's not right."

"But why would anyone want to do that? I thought they liked me. They treated me as if I was part of the family."

"Yes, darling, but you aren't. And that leads me to the next question: Are you sure Mrs. Campbell didn't know what her husband was up to? I mean, you told me how jealous she was. Could she have found out what he was doing and decided to get rid of the 'competition'—after all, you are an attractive young woman, and she's no spring chicken."

Sage was silent, chewing her lip, and looked down at the floor. When she raised her head, tears flowed down her cheeks.

Hannah was startled. "What's the matter?" she asked. "Did I say something?"

Sage shook her head, unable to say anything. Hannah waited, her own tears starting to form. What could she have said to precipitate such a reaction?

Sage gained her composure after a few minutes and apologized. "I'm sorry. I feel so stupid," she said as she reached for a tissue to wipe her tears.

"Why stupid?" Hannah protested. "It's stupid to show a genuine feeling? No. What's stupid is to deny one's feelings…What can I do to help?"

Sage took a deep breath. "You don't understand. It's all my fault."

Hannah was puzzled. "What's your fault?"

"You're right. Mrs. Campbell might have found out about Mr. Campbell and me. The last few days before she fired me, she changed. She was cold, not friendly like before. I told Mr. Campbell about it, but he said not to worry—he'd handle it. And then that last day she called me a dirty, sneaky Indian."

"So how's that your fault?"

"Because I liked Mr. Campbell. Because he liked me. When I told you what he did, that was only in the beginning. It changed recently. We came to like—maybe even love—each other. He's been kind to me. He brings me presents. He said that he didn't love Mrs. Campbell anymore but that he couldn't leave her because of the children and his job—it would ruin his chances for being a judge."

Hannah was stunned. She hadn't expected this. Perhaps, though, she should have. She had heard of the Stockholm syndrome. While Sage hadn't been a prisoner of Campbell, he had obviously used the same techniques that emotionally bound prisoners to their captors. But how to explain that to Sage. No, Hannah realized, this was the job for someone more experienced.

Oh, what a mess, she thought as she watched Sage go through a box of tissues. What a bastard Campbell was—to manipulate a vulnerable young woman to think he was acting out of love and not self-gratification. And how did he respond to firing Sage? Obviously he hadn't done anything to protect her.

Hannah felt helpless, conflicted: anger, sympathy, frustration. Say something? Do nothing? Stay? Leave? She sat there as if paralyzed until she realized Sage was looking at her, expecting a response. But she had no response. Fortunately, she was saved from further awkwardness by the arrival of Diane.

"What's this lovely pie doing here? Did you bake today?" she called out.

Hannah looked up at Diane as she rubbed Sage's back.

"What's happened? What's wrong?"

Sage blew her nose again and tried to smile. "I'm okay. Just having a pity party. Hannah brought the pie over for us. Wasn't that nice. It looks delicious."

"Yes, thank you, Hannah," Diane said, keeping her eyes on Sage. "But forget the pie, Sage. Why were you crying?"

Sage looked at Hannah, imploring her not to say anything. *Aha—she hasn't told Diane about Campbell.* Well, Hannah wasn't going to raise the issue; that was up to Sage.

Hannah rose from the chair, picked up her purse, and headed for the door. "I'd better be getting home. They'll be wondering where I am. I just dropped by to see how Sage was doing and to deliver the pie. You know when you're baking a pie for dinner, it's always easy to make two, and then you have too many." Feeling that she was engaged in the same prattling as Sage, she finished by saying, "I'll let myself out. Keep in touch, darling," she murmured as she hugged Sage and waved to Diane.

• • •

Hannah arrived home minutes before Janice and Paul. Still shaken by Sage's reaction, she hurried into the kitchen to get dinner on the table.

Janice took one look at her and asked, "Mom, what's the matter? Are you all right?"

"I'm fine, darling. Just a bit tired. The heat really gets to me."

"Sit down. Let me get the dinner," Janice said as she guided Hannah over to a chair. "Sometimes you forget that you're almost eighty years old," she scolded. "You can't go running around in this heat—and you can't solve all the world's problems by yourself."

"Thank you for reminding me I'm old—not eighty though. And you're right. I can't solve all the world's problems. I can't seem to solve any problems," she grumbled, which caused Janice to peer at her more closely.

Janice started to press Hannah for details but was interrupted when Maddie and Shelley entered the kitchen, each laden down with an armful of packages. Their laughter was cut short when they noticed the serious atmosphere.

"What's wrong, Mom? Is Grandma okay?"

Hannah rose from the table and smiled at her granddaughter. "Nothing's wrong, darling. Your mother was just yelling at me to remember I'm no spring chicken and that I shouldn't go out in this weather. Come. Let me see what you girls have got in those bags."

Janice proceeded to set the table and put out the food that was already prepared, while the girls displayed the "bargains" they had found.

"It was such a good deal, we couldn't resist" was the report they gave as they held up each item.

Hannah gave the appropriate approval each time, and by the time everyone was assembled for dinner, the atmosphere had been restored to normal: laughing and sharing of the day's events.

• • •

"Well, whose turn is it to do dishes tonight? David? Paul? Girls?"

Hannah started to volunteer, but Janice put up her hand. "No, not you, Mom. You and I have some business to discuss."

Paul looked at Janice and then said to David, "Well, big guy, how about you and I doing dishes tonight? Let's show them that we men can do it faster than the women."

"But then they'll want us to do it all the time," complained David, who reluctantly got up and started to clear the table.

Paul nodded to Janice. "We've got it covered, honey. Go have your talk."

• • •

"Stockholm syndrome? Yeah, I'm familiar with that. Why are you asking?"

Janice and Hannah were in Hannah's sitting room, the door closed for privacy. Hannah had raised the question without any prelude.

Hannah sighed. "Well," she started, "someone told me about a young woman who's in a bad relationship, and they mentioned Stockholm. I'm just curious about what it is. I think it has something to do with liking the bad guys, but I'd like to understand more about it."

Hannah kept her face composed as Janice glared at her suspiciously.

"Okay. What I know is that it's named for a situation in Stockholm where the hostages—I think it was in a bank, but I'm not sure—sort of emotionally bonded with their captors. It's now used to explain why people in abusive relationships remain in those relationships. They begin to agree with the abuser's perspective, even develop sympathy for the abuser. They often interpret the abuser's behavior as an expression of love. That's why victims of domestic violence, even after they've sought protection in a shelter, return home. It's not uncommon for a woman to enter a shelter three times before she finally leaves her husband or boyfriend."

Hannah frowned. "Why do they do that?"

Janice shrugged. "I know it's hard for us to understand, Mom. But a lot of women—men, too—are vulnerable. Whether it's low self-esteem, or insecurity, or an actual or perceived threat to their safety, I don't know. Sometimes people just don't see a way out of a bad situation, and if the abuser shows kindness to them at times, it's easier to "adjust" to the situation and perhaps persuade oneself to see it as something other than abuse.

"I think the data show that it's more likely to occur when an individual is isolated from others, when the relationship with the abuser is the main relationship. I know from my contacts at the domestic violence shelter in town that the women who come into the shelter are usually alienated from their families and have few friends whom they can confide in. After all, if you have a supportive family or independent means of survival, you don't need to go into a shelter. But domestic violence occurs among the affluent as well as the poor. It's just that it can be hidden better if you have money. It's sad to think that we believe this happens only among poor, uneducated people. I personally know of instances among professors, doctors, you name it. Often the victim is embarrassed to report the abuse, or they believe no one will believe their story. It's gotten better than it was, but still, unless you can show physical damage, it's hard to convince someone you've been raped or emotionally hurt."

Janice stopped talking and looked straight at Hannah. "So why are you really interested in this? Who do you know who's being hurt?"

Hannah hesitated, then sat up in her chair and leaned forward. "This has to be confidential. It would cause a lot of trouble for someone if it should became public too soon. Okay?"

"Okay."

Hannah then proceeded to relate all she knew of Sage's situation, from how she came to be in town, to the conditions of her employment with the Campbells, to the sexual abuse, to the charge of Sage stealing the necklace, to her living with Diane Cassidy, to her reluctance to report Campbell, and finally to her feelings of guilt and her confession of love for Campbell.

"And she's a student here?"

"She was. She graduated this year and is scheduled to go to college—the community college, I think—but that's not clear now because she doesn't know how she's going to afford it if Campbell doesn't pay for it. Of course, she thinks he loves her and will pay anyway, although his wife may have other plans. I don't know what to think or do. But I have to do something, no?"

When Janice spoke, she leaned forward, put her hands on Hannah's, and said, "Mom, I know you want to help this young woman—Sage? But you have to be realistic. What can you do? You know, I'm concerned that a student in my school had to go through this and I didn't know. And Diane didn't know either, or she would certainly have told me. To think that this had been going on while she was a student and no one knew, no one could help her, really concerns me. How many other young people have troubles that they don't share with anyone?"

"Darling, you can't blame yourself. You can't know everything that goes on at the school."

"No, I should know everything that goes on. Maybe not directly, but certainly indirectly. We have staff meetings every week. I meet with teachers whenever they have concerns. We have to do better in training the staff to spot kids who are troubled—including those who are homeless—and then report it to me so we can figure out a way to help. If nothing else results from Sage's terrible situation, you've made me aware that the school has to do something."

"That would be wonderful," Hannah agreed. "But what should I do about Sage?"

Janice sighed. "I don't know. Let me think about it. Would you mind if I talked to Paul about it? See if there is a legal angle we could use?"

Hannah smiled. "I like the "we" part. And yes, you can tell Paul, but remember the police can't be involved. I promised Sage that. In fact, I think she'd deny the whole thing if it became public."

"Okay, I understand. Now how about joining Paul and watching TV? I think we recorded that movie you wanted to see—*Harold and Maude*."

Janice was pleased when Hannah nodded agreement. She knew that her mother would pursue her search for something to do to help Sage, but she hoped that, at least for this evening, she could relax and put Sage and her situation on a back burner where it could simmer instead of reach a full boil.

CHAPTER 33

SIMMER WAS PERHAPS not the best way to describe Hannah's worries about Sage; a slow boil might be more appropriate. But at least it wasn't taking all of her attention, which left some time to focus on the latest developments for the Committee for Providing Shelter for the Homeless.

At the last meeting, the subcommittee for the rotating shelter program reported that twelve churches had signed up, each to host a week, in some cases, two weeks, of shelter for up to thirty people. Now the emphasis was on how to provide the supplies and volunteers to aid the host sites. Sufficient donations had been received after the newspaper had announced the latest developments—Mac was still a great supporter— and the necessary supplies had been purchased. Now the task was to find volunteers for overnight supervision, on-site registration, laundry, transportation, and food.

Much of the meeting was spent on suggestions for attracting volunteers. Hannah had checked the local telephone book and found that there were at least forty churches, one synagogue, and one mosque listed. Since twelve churches had agreed to host sites, that left, in her view, almost thirty possibilities that could be tapped for volunteers.

A subcommittee was formed to follow up recruitment from these sources. Hannah had been prepared for the adjournment of the meeting, when Eddie raised the issue of a permanent shelter again. He had again found a house, which, he assured everyone, would make a great shelter.

Everyone listened politely. Reverend Dwayne thanked him for his efforts and suggested that he pursue the issue. Hannah didn't expect Eddie to have success, but she agreed it was important to keep Eddie's energy invested in the work of the committee. And if Eddie succeeded in finding an appropriate building, and funding for it, that would be wonderful. Hannah resisted the temptation to ask Eddie what it would cost. It was late, and she wanted to get home.

• • •

The next few days went by without incident. It was still unseasonably hot, which meant less baking and cooking for Hannah. Salads had become a standard for dinner, although she did find recipes online for interesting variations that transformed a plain old salad into a tantalizing main dish. And following that with cookies—store bought—and ice cream warded off any complaints.

She had not heard anything from Sage, nor from Diane. The shelter program was taking shape and, with the promise of enough volunteers signing up, was set to open as soon as the cold weather arrived. There was nothing for Hannah to do, which frustrated her.

She sat at the kitchen table with her third cup of coffee and looked out the window at the remains of the early summer flowers. The yard was now largely green, with occasional patches of brown. There had been no rain for over three weeks, and the lawn was slowly becoming parched. Hannah didn't believe in watering lawns, claiming that it was a waste of precious water, but Janice liked a green lawn. But since neither Janice nor Paul took the time to do the maintenance, Hannah just sat back, listening to their complaints about the appearance of the yard but not volunteering to do anything about it.

But the yard was still visited by the birds. Hannah meant to keep a list of all the birds that gathered at the feeders, intending to look them up in a book Janice had, but she never got around to doing it. She just watched and enjoyed them as they ate and splashed in the birdbath she filled with water every day.

Eventually she roused herself to action. She could at least make a list of groceries needed. And maybe she could find a new treatment of a salad online.

She sat at the computer, looking for recipes. She finally found one that looked promising, although she planned to make changes. She knew that tuna fish would be preferable to sardines for her family.

She looked at the clock, surprised to see that it was almost noon. Although not particularly hungry, she felt the need for company, which she could find at the Senior Center. It took her less than ten minutes to comb her hair, put on some lipstick, gather her purse, and get out the door.

• • •

As she had hoped, Charlie's car was parked in the handicapped area, which meant that Ruby was with him. She had been so busy with the shelter and Sage that she had neglected to return Ruby's call. That wouldn't do, she chastised herself. Friendships needed nourishing as well as flowers did, and Ruby's friendship was important to her.

Her recriminations disappeared as Ruby smiled and waved at her, pointing to an empty seat at the table.

"I was worried about you," Ruby said as Hannah sat down. "Is everything all right?"

Ruby made no reference to the unreturned phone call, probably out of politeness, as her memory was still sharp.

Hannah shook her head. "No, no, I'm fine. Just so busy I can't keep things straight. Sorry I didn't get back to you the other day…"

Ruby interrupted her. "So if it had been so important, I would have called back. As long as you're okay. So what are you so busy with, if I may ask?"

Hannah hesitated. Ruby was so good hearted that she answered any question asked of her, which meant that she didn't keep secrets.

"Let me get some lunch first," she replied, using the time to consider her response. "Can I get you something?"

"No, Charlie is getting me a salad. He's up there at the counter."

Hannah got up and walked over to the counter and said hello to Charlie, who was filling his tray with a salad for Ruby and a burger and two brownies for himself. Hannah ordered an egg salad sandwich.

Once they were all seated at the table, Charlie dominated the conversation with tales of his luck at the poker table. Hannah knew Ruby worried about his gambling, but she couldn't bring herself to actually admonish him. At most, she would remind him of the losses that balanced out his winnings. Hannah usually interrupted Charlie when he monopolized the conversation, but today she was grateful for the diversion he provided.

It was almost two when they all got up from the table and headed for the door. Hannah hugged Ruby and promised to go shopping with her on Saturday. She wasn't a shopper, but she did look forward to spending the time with Ruby, and to the lunch that would follow the shopping. And who knew? Maybe she would find something to buy for someone. There was always a birthday coming up.

CHAPTER 34

"SO HOW IS Jaime?" Maddie had come into the kitchen while Hannah was preparing dinner. Shelley had gone upstairs to shower, and Hannah grabbed the opportunity to pump Maddie for information. It was a rare occurrence to catch Maddie alone since Shelley had come to live with them. Not that Shelley's presence would have prevented her from prying, but it was better this way. While Hannah didn't think prying was interfering—she was just asking a question.

Maddie rolled her eyes. "He's fine, Grandma."

"Well, that's good to know. So how are the two of you? Still like each other?"

"You're impossible, you know," Maddie replied. "You're so nosy."

"Nosy? Nosy is if I ask you what you and Jaime do. I don't ask that, just if you and he are getting along. A normal question, no?"

Maddie shrugged. "Okay, a normal question. I'll give you a normal answer. We're doing fine. In fact, I took your advice and talked to him. We came to an understanding." Here she hesitated, looking at Hannah. "It seems his nose was out of joint because I was always with Shelley. He thought that my going to the U of M had caused a sort of wall between us, with him being at a community college and not being in Ann Arbor. He thought that I had 'grown beyond him,' as he put it."

"And you set him straight?"

"Of course. You know I met lots of guys at school, went out with a few of them. None of them compare to Jaime. He's smart, kind, and gentle— good looking, obviously—and fun, when he's not moping about losing me. I guess I thought he was losing interest in me when he was always so busy to join us—Shelley and me. Now that he realizes how I feel about him, he doesn't mind Shelley."

"Good. But the two of you need to have some time together without Shelley. She's a smart girl. She'll understand if you explain it to her. Now go, let me finish getting dinner ready. I don't want I should make a mistake with the seasoning...And you could invite Jaime for dinner more often," she added. "I like the boy, and he seems to need a good meal every so often—he could use a few more pounds on him," she pronounced.

Maddie looked at her grandmother, as if prepared to defend Jaime's physique, but shook her head and instead said "Whatever" as she left the room.

Hannah smiled, pleased that Maddie and Jaime had worked out their problems. Young people today, she thought, had a harder time with relationships than in her day. Why, she didn't know. Perhaps they had too many options.

She switched her thinking from Maddie to Shelley. She hoped that she was right in assuming that Shelley would understand Maddie's relationship with Jaime. But at least Shelley was establishing some security in her life: she seemed to feel comfortable in the family, she had made friends at her job, and she had received a full scholarship—for tuition—at the University of Michigan to pursue her degree in art. Her other expenses would be provided by getting a part-time job, selling her caricatures, and applying for student loans. Hannah wasn't happy about the student loans, having read that they charge interest, but Janice had convinced her that it was necessary. Otherwise, Shelley would have to work too many hours, which would affect her academic performance.

Hannah marveled at how Shelley had changed since first coming to live with them. No longer working so hard to hide the fact that was homeless, she had relaxed when she realized that the family did not hold that against her. And while the yellow tote bag was still packed with provisions, she no longer carried it with her wherever she went.

Yes, Hannah thought. Shelley was going to be okay. If only she could say that about all the other homeless children.

• • •

Paul was late getting home. He arrived while Janice and Hannah were watching the *Rachel Maddow Show*. Hannah could see he looked worried about something, though he was obviously trying to hide the fact.

"Come on in," Janice said. "She's interviewing the guy who wrote that book on climate change being a hoax. She's politely tearing him to shreds, and the guy isn't even aware of it." Janice laughed.

Paul smiled at her. "I'm going to get something to drink. Any orders?"

"Well, if you're going to get a *drink*, I'll have one too. Mom? How about you? Some wine? Scotch?"

"So it's party time? Sure, I don't have to get up early tomorrow. I'll have a scotch on the rocks—one rock, please. And if you're hungry, there's some stroganoff left over in the fridge. Just heat it up."

"Thanks, but I had dinner earlier," Paul replied and went to get the drinks.

Janice turned off the TV when Paul returned with the drinks. The three of them sat and chatted, Paul and Janice on the couch and Hannah in the recliner. After extracting the last drop of scotch from her glass, Hannah got up.

"Well, I certainly can't drink like I used to. I'm going to bed."

Janice laughed. "Dad would be ashamed of you, Mom." Turning to Paul, she continued, "My Dad was so proud of how Mom could have two scotches and still be able to hold her own in an argument with his friends. She was the only woman in the crowd who drank—Jewish women, at least at that time, didn't drink much, except Mogen David wine."

Hannah smiled at the memory. "I'll have to get back into shape—two drinks a night for the next month should do it," she joked as she headed for her bedroom.

• • •

Janice and Paul went upstairs where their bedroom was far enough away from the other rooms that they could have a conversation without fear of being overheard. Paul lost no time in explaining his behavior.

"I didn't want Hannah to hear this, not yet. I don't know the best way to tell her."

Janice was now worried. "Tell her what? Paul, what's going on? What's happened?"

Paul realized he was frightening Janice. He took a deep breath and said, "Sage Barker was the victim of a hit-and-run this evening and is in the hospital. I know Hannah is fond of her, concerned about her. I know she has to be told, but I didn't want to just dump it on her. You'll know better how to break the news."

"How is she?"

"She's in serious condition. Some broken bones, maybe internal injuries. We heard about it at the office because one of our associates was at the station, and he thought she might need a lawyer—he's a high-class ambulance chaser. Anyway, I recognized the name and thought of Hannah."

"Mom will be devastated...I'll have to tell her before she reads it in the paper tomorrow. Oh, that poor girl. She's been through so much, and now this. Were there any witnesses? Did anyone see the accident?"

"All I know is that someone called 911 and reported it. I think they described the car as a 'big black sedan.' I'll get more details tomorrow. There's nothing we can do now. Let's get to bed. You'll have to get up early tomorrow if you want to talk to her before she reads the paper."

"Yeah, I'd better set the alarm for six. She'll get up early—even after a scotch."

CHAPTER 35

JANICE DIDN'T NEED the alarm to awake before Hannah. She hadn't slept more than an hour at a time, tossing and turning throughout the night. By five she gave up and went downstairs to prepare the coffee.

She sat at the kitchen table and rehearsed how she would break the news to Hannah. She was concerned about Sage, but there was nothing she could do about that. However, her main concern this morning was Hannah. She knew her mother would not rest easy once she heard about Sage. She wasn't worried that she would spend too much time at the hospital monitoring Sage's recovery—that was a given. She worried what she would do about the hit-and-run. Given the information Hannah had shared with her, Janice knew that Hannah would leap to the conclusion that Larry Campbell was somehow involved in the accident. And even without any evidence, Hannah was likely to make her suspicions public and cause serious problems for herself.

Her mother made friends easily but alienated people with her tell-it-like-it-is talk. Living in Brewster for only three years, it seemed to Janice that the only true friends she had were Ruby and Charlie. Oh, Hannah was respected by many people in town, but not necessarily liked. Janice remembered the school board meeting where Hannah had ruffled George Cotter's plumage. He was obviously upset, but who knew how many other people were annoyed by Hannah's behavior at the meeting.

And Larry Campbell would not just be upset—he would use his arsenal of resources to save his reputation. Janice didn't know him personally, but she knew of him. And what she knew was enough to know that he had the money and connections to make life difficult for Hannah.

"Darling, what's wrong? Why are you up so early?" Hannah appeared in the doorway, hair disheveled, concern showing on her face as she wrapped her robe around her.

"I'm fine, Mom. I just couldn't sleep and came down for some coffee...I made a pot. Would you like some?" she asked as she started to get up from the table, heading for the coffeepot.

"Sit. Sit. I'll get it." Hannah helped herself and sat down at the table facing Janice. "So tell me what's bothering you so much you can't sleep."

Janice took a deep breath and told Hannah about Sage's accident. Concerned with Hannah's reaction—a gasp and a hand going to her heart—she hastened to add that Sage would be fine, without mentioning that she had no grounds on which to base that opinion. She put her hand on Hannah's free hand and tried to reassure her.

"Sage is young and healthy. She'll get excellent care at the hospital. She'll most likely have a full recovery."

Hannah nodded, smiling feebly. "I'd better get dressed. She should have someone with her—to make sure there are no mistakes. You know they're always cutting the nursing staff, and then there are mistakes."

Janice smiled. "Okay, you go ahead. I'll get breakfast for the others when they come down."

By seven Hannah was showered, dressed, and ready to head to the hospital. Reminded by Janice that she would probably not be allowed to visit Sage so early, she just nodded. "So. I'll wait. They have magazines I can read. I should be there when she's ready for visitors. After all, she thinks of me as a substitute grandma."

Janice let that comment go and asked Hannah to call her when she had any news—and not to do anything more—which elicited a frown from Hannah as she left the house.

• • •

It was after nine when Hannah was finally allowed to visit Sage. She had represented herself as a relative—not as a grandmother, even for her that was going too far, but as an aunt. Her obvious concern for Sage, manifested by asking about her condition every ten minutes, must have convinced the staff that she really was related to Sage and therefore qualified to visit her in the ICU.

Sage was lying in bed, casts on her right leg and right arm, tubes running in and out, head bandaged, with scrapes and bruises on her face. She appeared to be asleep. Hannah hesitated in the doorway, reluctant to wake her. Instead, she returned to the desk to inquire about her condition.

Assured that Sage was out of danger, but still in a serious condition, she returned to the room and sat quietly in the chair by the window. She didn't care how long it took; she would stay there until Sage awoke. That she sat there for over an hour without making a sound testified to her commitment; she was not one to sit quietly for any length of time, at least not without falling asleep. She occupied herself by observing Sage's breathing and her vital signs on the monitor. At one point she worried when she saw a change in the oxygen rate, but relaxed when it shortly returned to normal.

At about ten thirty, a nurse appeared to change the intravenous solution, waking Sage as she did so. Hannah tsked, believing that sleep was the panacea for everything, but didn't say anything when the nurse turned to her, obviously interpreting her sound as one of concern.

"She's doing fine," she assured Hannah. "You can talk to her now that she's awake. Just don't let her get too excited. She's still in a serious condition."

Sage looked up at Hannah and started to cry. Hannah was devastated. "Do you want I should leave? I don't want I should upset you."

"No, no, I'm just so glad to see you.

"You—and Diane—are the only people who care about me," she said between sobs.

Hannah brought the chair over to the bed, sat down, and patted Sage's left hand. "Two people who love you is better than fifty Facebook 'best friends,'" she replied. "So, tell me, what did the doctor say? How much damage is there?"

Sage removed her hand from Hannah's grip and wiped her tears. "I don't really know. I haven't seen a doctor—at least I don't remember seeing one. It's all a blur. All I remember is hearing a car behind me. Then nothing."

Hannah suppressed the impulse to push for more information. Instead she asked, "Has Diane been to see you?"

"No, I don't think so. You're the first person I've seen."

"Well, she might not even know about the accident. I'll call her when I leave."

Seeing Sage begin to nod off, Hannah bent down to kiss her on the cheek and said, "Get some rest, darling. I'll come back later." As an afterthought, she asked, "Do you want I should bring anything?"

Sage shook her head. Hannah nodded. Enough time for those things later. She had some thinking to do, and that was always more productive with a little something to eat.

• • •

She arrived at the Senior Center just as Charlie's long legs were emerging from his car. He waited for her to catch up, and together they walked into the building.

"What brings you here?" he asked as they sat down at a table, donuts and coffee in hand.

"I need some information—about police procedure."

"And you're asking me?" Charlie replied in surprise.

"Well, I don't have anyone else. So here's my question: When there's a hit-and-run accident, is that public information?"

"The fact that there was an accident is usually in the paper—the local paper, anyway. But I don't know what you're asking."

"I want to know how I can get the information the police have. What kind of car...did they try to stop...were there any witnesses...what are they doing to find the driver..."

Charlie scratched his head and frowned. "I don't know if all that's public information. I'd guess it's not, at least not until the police decide it is. After all, they might not want the driver to know what they know—if they know anything."

He leaned forward, narrowing his eyes as he looked across the table at her. "Why do you want to know this?"

She brought him up to speed on what she knew about the accident and shared her suspicions about Larry Campbell's involvement, to which Charlie asked: "Why would he want to hurt the girl?"

She scowled at him. "There are a lot of reasons," she sputtered, trying to think of some that would make sense to him. "Like," she continued, "he doesn't want his wife to know what he was doing with the girl, or maybe she knew something illegal he was doing, and he didn't want her telling anyone, or maybe..." She spread out her hands in frustration. "I don't know. I just don't trust the man."

Charlie hesitated. "Be careful, Hannah. I don't think you know what you're getting into. Suspicions aren't evidence, you know."

Hanna sighed. "I know. I know. But I have to do something...Thanks for listening—though don't tell Ruby about this. She'll only worry."

Charlie smiled and nodded as Hannah got up and left the Center.

She sat in her car, air conditioning going full blast. Where to now? She reluctantly started to head toward home but then remembered something Charlie had said: accidents were reported in the newspaper. Mac, she thought. *Maybe he knows something that hasn't been in the paper yet.* It was a long shot, she knew, but worth it. Besides, whom else could she ask? Even if she went to the police, whom should she talk to? Would they take her seriously—an old lady with no real connection to the victim? Maybe Mac would have some advice, even if he had no information.

She marched past the receptionist, straight into Mac's office. He was seated at his desk, barely visible above the clutter of papers. He looked up in annoyance when he heard the door open, shaking his head when he found Hannah standing in the doorway.

"I should have known. No one ever dares enter my office without knocking—except you, Mrs. Lowenstein."

"Sorry, but this is important."

"Of course, what else could it be? So what is it this time? More shelter publicity?"

"No, not yet. This is about police protocol. I need to know if you have any information about yesterday's hit-and run-accident—you know, the young girl who was run down?"

"All I know is what we put in today's paper—did you see it?"

"I didn't have time. I was in a hurry to visit the girl—I know her, you see. I don't think it was an accident. I think it was intentional. But I don't know how to prove that without the evidence the police may have. And they might not make the necessary connections…"

Mac leaned back, pushed his glasses to the top of his head, and looked at Hannah. He didn't say anything for what seemed like an hour to her, finally got up, closed the door, and sighed. "Okay, tell me your story," he said as he settled back in his chair.

CHAPTER 36

HANNAH LEFT MAC'S office with a new bounce in her step. He hadn't promised anything, but he had listened. And, she thought, at times he had almost nodded. Maybe she had found an ally, not simply someone who agreed with her, but someone who would do something to help.

With that thought in mind, she drove to the high school in search of Diane Cassidy. At least she could tell her about Sage's condition and perhaps get access to the apartment so she could take some of Sage's personal items to her.

She was once again impressed by the landscaping at the school and made a mental note to mention this to Janice. A pang of guilt accompanied this thought: with all of her concerns about Sage and the homeless shelter, was she neglecting her family? When had she recently sat down and had a good conversation with Janice, one that didn't revolve around her own concerns? Had she even asked Janice how her life was going—what was she dealing with at school? Was everything okay with her and Paul? And what about Maddie and Shelley? She hadn't talked much with them recently, except to ask what they wanted to eat. Well, she resolved, that was going to change. Family came first—although followed very closely by others.

She found Heather at the reception desk and, without stopping, waved as she walked through to Diane's office. She knew Heather would have her nose out of joint. The rules required everyone to sign in when entering the building, but today Hannah had no time to make idle chitchat or to follow rules.

Diane was in her office. She looked up from the computer screen when Hannah appeared in the doorway. "Mrs. Lowenstein. I'm so glad to see you. Do you have any news of Sage? Janice told me you went to see her this morning. Is she all right?"

"Well, she's pretty messed up—broken bones, and maybe something more. But they say she's going to recover, although it'll take time. I'm going to go back this afternoon. That's why I'm here. I was wondering if there was some way I could get into your apartment so I could take her some things—you know, hair brush, personal things."

"Oh, of course. I'll call the manager to let him know you'll be coming by. He'll let you in."

"Wonderful." Hannah started to leave, but turned back. "Has Sage told you anything about the family she lived with?"

Diane looked surprised. "Only that they treated her very well, and that she loved the children. I know she was devastated when they accused her of stealing that necklace, but I think she accepts their firing her as reasonable, given the facts."

Hannah nodded, thanked her, and left. She was so preoccupied with thinking about Diane's response that she just walked out of the building, oblivious of Heather's attempt to get her attention.

A counselor so unaware of what was going on in a young girl's life that she just accepted the surface explanation given? Diane had just gone down considerably in Hannah's estimation. Well, there would be no help there.

• • •

It was late afternoon by the time Hannah found the personal items to take to Sage, who was sleeping so soundly she didn't respond when Hannah tried to wake her. Concerned, she tracked down a nurse in the hallway and inquired about Sage's condition.

"Is it okay that she's sleeping so soundly? Is she maybe getting too much pain medication?"

Fortunately, the nurse she had approached was familiar with meddling families. She smiled, somewhat condescendingly, and assured Hannah that Sage was being watched very carefully, the pain medication allowed her to sleep, and that sleep was the best medicine in the first few days of such an injury.

"Why don't you leave that stuff here, and I'll see that she gets them when she wakes," she suggested. Hannah thanked her and reluctantly left, after taking one last look at Sage.

• • •

What are you doing, Grandma?" David was clearly surprised to see Hannah at the computer, busily writing notes on a pad.

"Oh, just checking something." She looked up at him. He had grown in the last few months, she realized. "Are you hungry? There's fresh fruit in the fridge."

"Nah, I just had a coney dog with Billy. So what are you checking? Is it that guy again?"

Hannah sighed. Should she tell him? But all she was doing was getting the names of the people Campbell defended—that wouldn't be a problem, she decided.

David's response to the information was a bored "Oh," which Hannah took as a challenge. "It's important information. I want to see if there's any canoodling going on—you know, if he's involved with gangsters or…"

That grabbed his attention. He ignored the comment about *canoodling* and said "Oh, that's different" as he pulled a chair over and sat down beside her. "What did you find out?"

"Nothing of use. He defends all sorts of people, but it's mostly small-time things like divorces, drunken drivers, a few robberies. I don't see how he gets much money from these cases."

"Yeah, but remember his wife has the money."

"But even so, why would he be such a big shot in town if he's just a run-of-the-mill lawyer?"

"Maybe he has the right connections," David suggested, raising his eyebrows up and down in a Groucho Marx imitation.

Hannah sat up in her chair. "Of course! It's the connections, not the cases. You're brilliant, darling," she said as she reached over and hugged David. "But how do I find out about his connections?" she wondered aloud as she chewed on her pencil. "Oh, this is too much for me right now. I need a little something to eat while I think. Join me?"

"Yeah, I am getting a little hungry," David acknowledged as he followed her into the kitchen. "That coney dog wasn't really big."

CHAPTER 37

*C*ONNECTIONS. HOW DO *you find out a person's connections?* Hannah sat at the kitchen table, oblivious to the dishes piled up on the counter, of the coffee cooling in her cup, of Max's repeated efforts of begging for some of the uneaten bacon. All she could think was *connections.*

Finally she noticed Max and declared, "Enough of this woolgathering, Max," and she got up to retrieve two strips of bacon from the dishes on the counter. "It's a good thing we have you," she said as she patted his head and let him take the bacon from her hand. "Otherwise I'd have to throw this away, and that's a waste." She laughed as she said this. She remembered her mother always reminding her of the "starving children in the world"—different parts of the world, depending on the year. Well, her mother was right—one shouldn't waste food.

Once up from the table, she was energized. Dishes done, Max put out in the shaded part of the yard with a bowl of water, she showered and dressed. Her head was clear. Of course there were ways to find out about a person's connections. Family, friends, business associates, and clubs and organizations one belonged to. The question was how to access this information. Well, that was what a library was for, right?

Armed with determination and a notepad, she drove to the public library. It was smaller than the college library, but she always felt uncomfortable among the students and faculty there—an outsider, or worse, an imposter. So, at least for a start, the public library would do.

Parking was a problem near the library—too few spaces and too many people who didn't know how to park, straddling two spots, making it impossible to fit a car into the remaining space. She drove around the block hoping someone would move, but after two times around gave up and parked three blocks away. She calmed down when she persuaded herself that the walk was good exercise for her.

She arrived at the information desk, slightly out of breath, wiped perspiration from her forehead, and presented herself to the young librarian.

"Good morning, dear," she started and then stopped. She hadn't thought what to ask for. She threw herself on the mercy of the young woman and asked, "How can I see old newspapers?"

The young woman frowned. "Which newspapers?" Her frown jiggled the dangling silver chain hanging from her left eyebrow, which matched a small chain implanted in her right earlobe.

Hannah quickly realized that the young woman wasn't a "real" librarian and, more importantly, that she needed to start with the local papers first. Once that was clear, the young woman pointed to the back of the room where current newspapers and magazines were displayed.

"And what about old ones?" Hannah persisted.

"Oh, they're probably on microfiche."

"And what's that?"

After a frustrating exchange of questions and answers, Hannah had honed her questions to greater specificity, and the young woman, with a sigh, had agreed to show her where the microfiche machine was, how to find the files she wanted, and how to use the machine.

Seated at the machine, pen and notebook at her right side, Hannah started to scan for any mention of Larry Campbell. Thirty minutes of searching produced three mentions of Campbell in connection with clients he represented and the beginning of a headache for Hannah.

There had to be another way, she thought as she sat back, took off her glasses, and rubbed her eyes. She lasted another twenty minutes, sighed, packed up, and left. She felt slightly nauseous from the microfiche experience and decided she could use something to settle her stomach—and it was almost noon anyway. Perhaps she could catch Charlie at the Senior Center.

• • •

Charlie was sitting at a table with Ruby, his plate overflowing with goulash and french fries. Ruby looked up from her salad when Hannah entered the room; Charlie didn't lift his eyes from his food.

"Here, over here, Hannah," Ruby called out, half rising from her chair.

Hannah, seeing Ruby's smile and excitement at seeing her, was overcome by such a feeling of love that it brought tears to her eyes. Not one for emotional responses, she took control of herself and walked over to the table, resolved, however, to show her appreciation for Ruby's friendship more frequently. Good friends were not to be taken for granted, and appreciation had to be shown, not just felt.

When she returned from the buffet table with her lunch of a tuna salad sandwich and a cookie, Charlie finally looked up from his plate, which was now empty. "That's what I need," he said as he eyed the cookie on Hannah's plate. He asked Ruby if she wanted one and, receiving a shake of her head, went to fetch a few for himself.

Hannah involved Ruby in a discussion of the new nutrition guidelines on the importance of fats in one's diet. Charlie returned and announced, "Never having doubted the importance of fats"—he grinned at them—"I knew that."

They ignored him.

The conversation moved from nutrition to sales at the local shoe store to reports of Ruby's son's family. Ruby had two grandsons, whom she saw very rarely. Her explanation was that they were in college and were too busy to visit. Hannah had a different explanation: Ruby's son was a nogoodnik who didn't go out of his way for his mother ever since he was thwarted in his attempt to get his inheritance before she died. And he made sure that his sons saw their grandmother with the same jaundiced eye as he did. But she said nothing. Ruby didn't need to be reminded that her son was a selfish, greedy man.

Ruby was in such a good mood that Hannah didn't have the heart to change the topic in order to pump Charlie for advice on finding connections, especially as it wasn't a topic she wanted to discuss with Ruby present. She convinced herself that there probably wasn't much that Charlie could have contributed anyway and just went with the flow of conversation until she could find a polite way to leave.

"Look at the time," she announced. "It's one thirty already. I'd better get going—and leave you two to your games." Hugs all around, she left them, Ruby to bridge and Charlie to poker

• • •

By the time Hannah arrived at the hospital, it was after two. She smiled at the nurses as she strode down the hallway to Sage's room. She stood in the doorway and watched Sage struggle with the food on the tray. With only one good arm—the left one—she was having trouble getting the soup spoon to her mouth.

Hannah marched into the room, pulled the chair away from the window to the bed, and sat down. "Here, darling, let me help you," she said as she took the spoon from Sage and proceeded to feed her. "Soup isn't easy to eat when you can't use your right arm," she declared, indignant that the nursing staff would have ignored that fact.

Hannah was rewarded with a smile and was pleased that Sage was alert enough to respond and that she had an appetite. Soup finished, Hannah turned to the red Jell-O injected with pieces of yellow something—possibly pineapple? She didn't express her disapproval of the food served; she was just satisfied that Sage ate any of it.

"So how are you feeling?"

"I'm okay," Sage responded. "They give me stuff for the pain, so it's not so bad. My arm and leg don't really hurt. It's my stomach that hurts when I try to move."

Hannah nodded, making a mental note to ask the nurse about internal injuries and how serious they might be.

"I dropped off your hair brush and some of your things when you were sleeping yesterday. Did you get them?" Receiving a nod from Sage, she continued. "Diane called the manager so he would let me into the apartment. Have you seen her?"

"No, but maybe I was sleeping when she came. And she's probably busy," Sage said, anxious to defend Diane.

"Yes, that's true. Any other visitors?"

Sage hesitated, looked down, and mumbled, "Mr. Campbell came by."

What? Did she hear that right? "I'm sorry, dear. I didn't hear you—I don't hear so well, you know."

Sage looked up, took a deep breath, and said—loud and clear: "Mr. Campbell came by."

"How nice. That was very thoughtful of him."

Sage smiled, obviously pleased that Hannah didn't say anything negative about him. She continued, "Yes, he's been very nice to me. In fact"—she beckoned Hannah to come closer—"he wants to pay for my hospital bills, and he still wants to pay my tuition for the fall, and…" She paused. "He has a friend who has an apartment I can use when I get out of the hospital."

Hannah expressed her surprise by raising her eyebrows and whispering, "Wow." She wanted to say more but didn't. No sense in warning her of Campbell's likely agenda. How convenient to find an apartment for Sage, where he could "visit" her away from the jealous eyes of his wife. She casually changed the topic from Campbell's questionable philanthropic behavior to the day of the accident.

"Do you remember any more about the accident—the color of the car, whether it was a man or woman driving, anything?"

Sage leaned back into the pillow. "No, all I remember is hearing it behind me. I didn't turn to look. I just kept walking. I was real close to the edge of the road. I thought the car would just go around me. I don't remember anything after that, until I woke up here. Have you heard anything?"

"No, it's just a hit-and-run—no more information. But don't worry. I'm sure the police will follow up. Besides, you shouldn't be worrying about that. You just get your strength back. Which reminds me that I should be going so you can rest. I'll see you tomorrow."

Hannah kissed Sage on the forehead and headed for the nurses' station, where she proceeded to lecture the woman behind the desk about the importance of giving Sage food she could handle without her good arm. Satisfied that she had made her point, she left.

CHAPTER 38

F RUSTRATED WITH HER failed attempts to get information about the accident or about Larry Campbell's connections, she slowly drove home. Frustration combined with anger at the news that the man she thought responsible for Sage's accident was now playing the kindhearted philanthropist: paying the hospital bill and tuition was all well and good—although most likely a bribe, she thought—but conveniently finding an apartment? That was too much.

But what could she do? Sage was clearly besotted by him—probably because of the absence of a father in her life. Hannah had not taken any psychology courses but had known enough women who looked to older men to provide what was missing in their childhood. She had to admit that sometimes it worked out fine—her friend Selma had married a man twenty years older than she and, except for the fact that he died almost twenty years before her, had had a wonderful marriage. But this was different. Sage wasn't making a rational decision, as Selma had. Sage was vulnerable and Campbell was taking advantage of that.

The more she thought about it, the more questions arose. Why would a wealthy couple seek out a nanny on the Internet? And what kind of an "investigation" could they have conducted? It was hard to believe that a couple like the Campbells would entrust their children to a poor, uneducated, Native American young girl from Gladwin. Didn't people like the Campbells opt for au pairs from Europe who could teach their children a foreign language, or at least a college girl looking for a job and a place to live while attending the local college? No, it didn't make sense. Unless they were looking for something else. She knew the something else that Campbell was looking for, but what about Mrs. Campbell? She couldn't have had the same reason for hiring Sage. Was she that insecure in her marriage that she would give in to her husband on a matter as important as the welfare of her children? Oh, this was giving her a headache.

She pulled into the driveway, behind a strange car. Realizing that she would have to come out and move her car when whoever belonged to the strange car wanted to leave, she backed up her car and parked in the street.

When she entered the house, she was surprised to hear a familiar man's voice in the kitchen. Mac was sitting with David, enjoying one of Hannah's prune danishes.

"Mac. What are you doing here?"

"That's the greeting I get? No, hello, how are you. Nice to see you?"

"Hello. How are you? Nice to see you. What are you doing here?" she responded with a smile.

Mac smiled back. "This young man came to my office with a story that I thought needed more detail—he's going to be a great investigative reporter when he grows up—and so I came here to talk to you," he said while reaching for another danish.

David flashed a wide grin at Hannah, who frowned and asked, "What story?"

Mac turned to David. "You tell her, son."

David stuffed the last bit of the danish into his mouth and said, "You remember Derek, the guy who was living in the park? Well, I saw him today—"

"Where did you see him?" interrupted Hannah.

"That's not the point, Grandma. The point is he saw something, and nobody's paying any attention to him. I thought it should be reported to the police, but Derek didn't want to get involved. He said he told the police, and they ignored him. So I thought of the paper—you said good things about Mr. Mac—so I went there, and he wanted to talk to you. I told him you're usually home by four and invited him here. That's okay, isn't it?"

"Of course it's okay, darling," she replied, going to the refrigerator to bring out the carton of milk. "Here, have some milk with the danish."

"So what's the story?" she said, pouring him a glass.

"Well, Derek says he saw an accident—a hit-and-run. He's the one who called 911. He said he told this to the police, but they didn't seem interested—maybe because he looks like a bum, you know, and maybe he was a little stoned. Anyway…" David faded off at this point and looked at Mac.

Mac picked up the conversation. "I think this might be related to what we were talking about the other day. David says that you've talked to this Derek kid, so I thought he might be more willing to talk to you than to me or a reporter."

"Of course I'll talk to him. Oh, Mac, this might be the break I'm—we're—looking for."

Hannah was having trouble hiding her excitement from David. She didn't want him to be any more involved with her suspicions about Larry Campbell than he already was. It was one thing to investigate someone's financial affairs, another to investigate an attempted murder. In a clumsy attempt to divert David's further curiosity, she turned the conversation to talk about the weather, which only raised the level of David's curiosity.

After a third danish, Mac got up, shook hands with David, and smiled at Hannah. "I expect I'll be hearing from you soon, Mrs. L."

"As soon as I find Derek."

• • •

David looked up at Hannah as she bustled around the kitchen, preparing for dinner. She avoided his eyes, not wanting to continue the conversation, but he managed to get her attention by asking, "What's going on? Is Derek in some kind of trouble? I know he uses drugs and has a record—but only for small things. I don't think it's fair that people pick on him and think he's lazy and dumb. He just looks bad because he doesn't have clean clothes and a place to wash up. He's really smart. I've learned a lot about things from him. Did you know that he spends a lot of time at the library reading and going on the Internet? He knows more about animals than anyone I know and…"

Hannah stopped bustling about and sat down at the table opposite David. "You're right about Derek, darling. It's not fair, and I wish I knew how to help him and all the other Dereks out there. But he's not in trouble. No, that wasn't what Mac and I were referring to."

Here, she paused, not sure how to assuage David's concerns about Derek without saying too much about the accident. "It's just that we're interested in an accident that happened to someone we know, and it looks as if Derek has some information on that. That's all—no trouble for Derek. And so, since you know him so well, perhaps you could ask him if he would talk to me about what he saw. Okay?"

"Well, sure. I'll ask him tomorrow."

"So where do you meet Derek? At the library?" she asked with raised eyebrows.

David lowered his eyes and mumbled, "Well, not there—other places."

"Other places? Like the park? Do you arrange to meet at a certain time or just happen to run into each other? You know I like Derek. I think he's had a hard life, and I admire how he manages to survive. But how did the two of you get so—what's the word I want—close?"

David looked up, leaned forward, and hesitated. Hannah could see that he wasn't sure how much to tell her. As difficult as it was for her, she resisted the temptation to encourage him to talk. She had to depend on the strong connection they had and the trust that had developed between them. He would answer her when he was comfortable doing so. And so she waited.

Finally, David sighed and said, "I ran into him a few weeks ago when I was walking Max. It was that really hot day, and Max was panting a lot. I had stopped to get ice cream for him—and me—and Derek saw us and came over to pet Max. We started talking about how a lot of people don't know how to take care of their pets—you know, don't provide water for them, keep them cooped up so they can't get any exercise—and he told me that he wanted to be a vet, but couldn't afford it, but that he took care of a lot of the animals in the park. That was awesome—taking care of squirrels and birds. He said he'd show me the place where he was taking care of a bird that had a broken wing."

David's eyes grew larger as he described the protected area Derek had made for the recovering bird and how Derek provided the food—worms—for the bird. "And then, well," David continued, "every once in a while I would go to the park and check out the bird. That one was gone—Derek said it had recovered—but there was a baby squirrel he was taking care of. He's really good with animals. He reads about them at the library. You know you don't need to buy food for animals, at least the animals in the park. You just need to find out what they eat—you know, like nuts or leaves or worms—and get it. Anyway, we talk a lot about animals, and he likes dogs a lot, so I take Max to the park when I know Derek's going to be there."

David paused, waiting for Hannah's response. When he saw her smile at him, he relaxed and sat back.

"I'm glad you got to know Derek, and I wish there were some way to help him be a veterinarian. But my first concern is to know that you're safe, that you're not going to the park when it's dark, that you're not doing something foolish and putting yourself in danger. Okay?"

He smiled back at her. "Okay," he said. They both got up from the table, and as he headed up the stairs to his room and video game, he called out, "Did you find the connections you were looking for with that guy?"

"No," she answered as she returned to the preparations for dinner. "I'm still looking."

● ● ●

And she was still looking. Microfiches had triggered headaches and frustration, but a little bit of Internet snooping had produced better results. She had been able to find the ad for nannies that had brought Sage to the attention of the Campbells. Surprised that it was still running, she attempted to trace the source for the ad, but found only that it was an agency, the Good Nanny, with a PO box in Brewster. So it was local, she thought. Strange. How many people were there in a small town who would need the Internet to find a nanny? Didn't people know other people—neighbors, friends, family—who could give them contacts? And how could she find out a name connected with the agency and a PO box? Surely there had to be a person signing for the PO box. Well, that was something she could check with the post office.

Armed with the PO box number and fortified with two cups of strong coffee, Hannah took off for the post office. Compared to New York, the

Brewster post office was small, which presented a dilemma. In New York, if one wanted to browse around the PO boxes, one could be invisible among the hundreds of people lined up for service. Here, however, an elderly woman standing by the PO boxes would be hard to ignore. Most likely someone would come over to see if she needed help. Hannah wasn't averse to asking for help, but she thought it unlikely that asking for the name of the person connected to a particular PO box would get her very far. After all, wasn't privacy one of the reasons people used PO boxes?

So she sat in her car outside the post office, strategically positioned to observe who entered and where they went. After two hours of watching people go in and out without any success, she decided this would not work—unless she planned on spending all day, every day, sitting and waiting. No, there must be another way.

She was about to leave when she saw a familiar face in the car pulling up next to her. A middle-aged, respectable-looking man got out and entered the building. She didn't know where she had seen him, but she knew she had. He walked with a purpose, a man used to being in control. She waited to see where he would go and held her breath as he approached the PO boxes. Just then a woman stopped in front of her car, fumbling in her handbag for her keys. Hannah couldn't see past her. Frustration almost caused her to honk her horn, but before she reached that point the woman moved on, leaving Hannah a clear view of the man. And yes, he was at box 137. Now all she had to do was find out who he was and where she had seen him.

Fortunately, the line at the counter had dwindled to only one person. When Hannah reached the counter she put on her best old-lady routine and said, "I need a roll of stamps, please...You know, I'm so forgetful these days. I can't remember the name of the man just leaving. I know he's a friend of my husband. Do you know who he is? It's so embarrassing to forget names. My children are always teasing me about being forgetful."

The young woman behind the counter was sympathetic. "Oh, we all have those moments. That's Jameson Lowell. He's a lawyer with that big law firm—Lowell, Snyder, and...somebody."

"Oh, of course—Jim. Thank you so much."

She paid for the stamps, smiled at the young woman, and left, pleased with her accomplishment. Deceiving, while wrong, was a lot of fun. Maybe she could have been a spy.

• • •

As she drove to the library, she tried to remember where she had met Jameson Lowell. He was a lawyer, but that didn't help—the only lawyer she knew was Paul. "Oh yes," she said out loud, "the lawyers' banquet." And who was the third person in Lowell and Snyder? Well, she'd know in a few minutes, she thought, as she turned her attention to driving.

The library was empty; the only person visible was the young woman behind the desk, who had shown her how to use the microfiche machine. Not wanting to deal with her again, she decided to try the microfiche machine on her own. How hard could that be?

Much harder than she thought, it turned out. After three attempts to bring up anything on the screen, she conceded defeat and approached the young woman, who recognized her.

Not good, thought Hannah. *She probably remembers me as a first-class nuisance. But I'm a citizen entitled to use the library, and she's paid to help me.* Confident of her rights, Hannah explained her request, which the young woman answered by walking over to the microfiche machine, turning it on, and setting it up for Hannah—all without saying a word.

"Thank you," said Hannah, hoping that the young woman was not planning on a career in public relations.

Seated at the machine, she scanned for any mention of the Good Nanny. The only reference to it that she could find was back in 2003, when it was established with a grant by the Lowell, Snyder, and Campbell firm—well, that saved her from having to look up the last partner in the firm. It was set up as a resource for "families seeking quality young women to care for their children."

Well, that didn't tell her much. Oh, she wished she had more hacking skills. Asking David for help at this stage was a clear no-no. She had involved him enough; to go any further would be irresponsible and perhaps even dangerous for him.

She picked up her purse, gathered the notebook she had not written anything in, and left the library. She stopped at Marty's for a few things for dinner and returned home.

Frustrated, but feeling she had tried her best, she rewarded herself with a cup of tea and a piece of last-night's blueberry pie, sat down in the recliner, and watched a rerun of a *Walker* episode. It wasn't long until she fell asleep, tea and pie forgotten.

CHAPTER 39

DAVID AWOKE EARLY and, hair dripping water, bounded down the stairs. Hannah was not in the kitchen. He ran to her bedroom but found it empty. He heard the back door open and raced back to the kitchen where he found Hannah with an empty pitcher in her hand.

"What are you doing up so early?"

"I was looking for you. Where were you?" a petulant David asked.

Hannah looked at him with raised eyebrows. "Where would I be at this hour? Having a party? I was putting water out for the birds—and Max. It's going to be another hot day. Max is your dog—you should think of how he feels in this weather...Anyway, why are you up so early?"

David looked around the kitchen, for food, no doubt, and seemed to forget why he wanted to talk to Hannah. She saw his look and smiled. "Don't worry. I'll get breakfast for you."

She put out the Cheerios that would be his breakfast, along with a cup of hot chocolate, and sat down across the table. She waited for him to finish the Cheerios, amused at the concentration he put into eating.

"Okay," he said, wiping away a hot chocolate mustache with his napkin. "Why I was looking for you was to tell you that I talked to Derek, and he's okay with talking to you. He'll be at the library this morning. He said he'll be there most of the morning—he's trying to find out how to fix a squirrel's tail."

"What's wrong with the squirrel's tail?"

"I don't know. Maybe it's broken—you remember he takes care of the animals in the park."

"Well, that's nice he should fix a broken tail. So he'll be at the library all morning. Good. I'll get breakfast going and go meet him. Thank you, darling. You've been a big help."

David got up from the table, took his bowl and cup to the sink, looked at his grandmother, and asked, "Do you need some more help with your investigation? I have some more time now—no soccer practice this week."

He looked at her, hopeful anticipation in his eyes, but his face fell when she shook her head.

"No, darling, I'm fine with the investigation…So what are you doing this week without your practice?"

"Probably go swimming in the quarry. Try the next level—Billy's catching up to me…"

Just then Janice entered the kitchen. "And mow the lawn," she added.

• • •

Hannah arrived at the library, stopped at the desk to ask where books on animals were, and received an exasperated sigh from the young woman who proceeded to tell her that there were many books on animals, in different sections of the library. What kind of books did she want?

Hannah reminded herself that this wasn't the real librarian, just a young woman with multiple piercings on her rather plain face. She smiled as the young woman looked up and said, "That's all right, dear, I'll find what I'm looking for," and marched off to find Derek. How difficult could it be? After all, it wasn't a large library.

After a brisk walk through the sections on fiction, science fiction, mystery, and romance—Derek wouldn't be there, she knew—she found him seated at a table, books piled high, engrossed in reading. A pad with notes rested on his right side, where occasionally he would jot down something.

Hannah stood there, looking at him. To all appearances, a young man intent on what he was reading, oblivious of his surroundings or what those around him were doing. The only difference from other patrons of the library was that his clothes were tattered, his sneakers were torn, and his long hair was dirty. Of course, many college students that Hannah had noticed recently didn't look very different.

Her heart went out to him. Here was a young man with a passion for life: his life and the life of animals. He should be in school, getting the knowledge and the certification that would allow him to pursue his passion. Yet he would most likely remain one of the invisible people living on the edges of society, surviving by his intelligence and creativity. *Surely we can do better for people like Derek*, she thought.

He looked up from the book, stretched his long arms over his head, and rubbed his neck. Hannah took that as the opportunity to approach him without disruption.

"Hello, Derek," she said. "I'm Hannah Lowenstein. We met before when…"

He smiled up at her. "I remember you. You're the lady who arranged that meeting about us—the homeless, I mean."

"Yes, that's right. I wonder if I could talk to you for a few minutes. You know my grandson, David, I hear. He's quite impressed with what you're doing for the animals in the park. So am I."

"Yeah, I'm really into that. In fact, I've learned a lot about surviving from them. You know, they live outdoors all year, even in the coldest weather. Sometimes it's too cold for them—they can't get enough water or they can't find protection from the cold—but most of the time they survive. It's sure taught me a few things."

"Like what?"

"Well, my cardboard 'home' is much warmer now that I've learned to fill it with twigs and newspapers and rags. At least I'm not sleeping on the cold ground anymore. And even though it's real crowded with all those rags around me, at least it's warmer."

He intrigued Hannah. She would have loved to hear more about his survival skills, but she needed to change the discussion to Sage's accident.

"David tells me that you witnessed that accident last week, the one where the young woman was hit by a car. I know the young woman and am trying to find out what happened. The police haven't been very helpful though, so I thought you might be able to tell me something. Would you mind?"

He pushed back the hair falling over his face and shrugged. "Sure, but I told the police that I saw what happened, and they never got back to me. Obviously, they didn't think anything I would say was important."

His eyes flashed as he said this. "I'm used to people ignoring me, but I thought that they would at least want to hear what I saw. They're always interested in telling me that I can't do what I'm doing. *No loitering. No smoking.*"

"Well, I want to hear what you saw. Maybe together we can solve this case—wouldn't that be a hoot: an old lady and a homeless young man doing better than the police."

Derek laughed at that and began to talk. "Yeah, I saw the accident. It was strange. There was nothing in the way of the car. The girl was on the edge of the road—there's no sidewalk on that street—and it looked like the car actually aimed for her."

"Could you see who was driving the car?"

"I think it was a woman—but it could have been a man with long hair. It wasn't that dark out, but the car had those tinted windows. You know the kind that lets them see out, but it's hard to see in."

"Could you tell what kind of car it was?"

"Oh, that was easy. It was one of those long black cars—clearly a luxury one: BMW, Mercedes, Lexus. You can tell from the sound. They have a purring sound even when they're going fast, and that car was going fast. That's what got me looking. I could hear it coming down the street, going way above the speed limit—at least fifty miles per hour."

"So you think it was deliberate, right?"

"Well, it sure looked that way to me."

"Anything else you noticed?"

"Yeah, I could see part of the license plate when it stopped."

"It stopped?"

"Only for a minute—then it speeded up and took off."

Hannah nodded and asked, "What was the license number?"

"It was a Michigan plate. It started with A-T-T and then maybe a one or a seven—I couldn't make it out. She drove off too soon. I don't know if that's going to help much though," he said as he expressed his disappointment with another shrug.

"Oh, it helps. It helps a lot," Hannah replied. "I have my suspicions, you know. Now I just have to get some more information. Thank you, Derek, You've been very helpful."

"Well, keep me in the loop. I'd sure like to know who that driver was. She could have killed that girl—I heard that she's okay, right?"

"Yes, she's alive, but was seriously hurt. She's still in the hospital but seems out of danger." She got up from the chair and smiled at Derek, who got up and extended his hand.

"Thank you—for caring. Not many people seem to care what happens to others. At least, that's how I see it. Don't want to criticize—I try to stay upbeat, but it sure isn't easy."

Hannah reached down to put her hand on his shoulder. "Don't give up. There are more people who care than you realize. They just don't know there's a problem."

• • •

"A-T-T something," she said to herself as she drove off. "That shouldn't be hard to track down." Now, however, she had to find out how to track it down. Her first thought was Charlie. Would he know? The more she thought about it, she decided he wasn't likely to have access to that information. Well then, how about Mac? Wouldn't a newspaper editor be more likely to have access to that information? It was worth a trip to the *Daily Sun*.

CHAPTER 40

"**M**RS. L—COME RIGHT in. Don't wait for an invitation," Mac exclaimed with dripping sarcasm, which was completely ignored by Hannah.

"Thank you. I hope I'm not disturbing something important, but I have a favor to ask of you."

"Of course. What could be so important I wouldn't want to do you a favor?" The sarcasm was getting deeper, but Hannah chose not to notice. Mac put down his pencil and turned his attention to her.

"So what's the favor?"

"I need you should look up a license number—see who it belongs to. I found out the number—or at least part of the number—from the eyewitness to the accident. Now if we can find out whose car it is, we'll know who did the hit-and-run. You can do this, right?"

"Well, no, I can't do that, but I know someone at the police department who I can ask. How did you find out?"

"Remember David said he knew this young man who had seen the accident and went to the police, but they didn't listen to him? Well, I just spoke with him—the young man, not David—and he described the car as dark and expensive and the driver was—well he thought it was a woman, but I think it was a man dressed as a woman—and he had the first part of the license: A-T-T one or seven. Surely there can't be that many cars like that with a license like that. A-T-T could be short for attorney, right?"

"So you think it was a lawyer's car?"

"Yes. And I think I know which lawyer, but I can't say—I'm sworn to secrecy."

"Secrecy?" Max asked. "So how secret is the information on the license going to be? I thought the point was to use the information to make an arrest—that's certainly not going to be secret."

Max took a deep breath, leaned over the desk, and put his hand on her hand.

"Hannah, please slow down. I'll do what I can to help, but let's get the whole story first. Okay? Start with the eyewitness, this young man."

After a half hour of Hannah explaining and Mac asking for more detail, Mac seemed satisfied that he understood enough to ask his friend for the license information. Before Hannah left though, Mac cautioned her about jumping to conclusions about who was driving the car. After all, he reminded her, the owner of a car wasn't always the driver.

● ● ●

Hannah left Mac's office convinced that they would identify Larry Campbell as the hit and run driver. The car would turn out to be his car, someone would have seen him driving it earlier in the day, he wouldn't be able to provide an alibi for the time of the accident, and he would be found guilty of attempted murder.

She drove home singing along with Frank Sinatra on the radio—an oldies station, one that played songs she knew the lyrics to. Maddie had tried to introduce her to some of the more current music groups, but Hannah complained that they all shouted too loud and that she couldn't understand what they were saying. Better to stick with what she knew.

She had intended to head straight home, but her excitement was too great. She had to share the news with someone. No one would be at home—and she wouldn't share it with the children in any event. So who? Ruby wouldn't understand, but Charlie would. Yes, that's what she would do: lunch at the Senior Center and talk with Charlie.

When she arrived at the Senior Center, she could barely contain her excitement. She parked the car as close to the building as possible, straddling two parking spots, and rushed into the building. It was not quite noon, but the food was set out, and a few people were lining up for lunch. Hannah looked around for signs of Charlie—the lunch line, the poker table—but he wasn't to be found. Well, maybe he'd come in for lunch, she thought as she sat down at an empty table, hoping to avoid making small talk with other people. Fortunately, she didn't have many friends at the Center. She attributed this to the fact that midwesterners were too polite and didn't appreciate her no-nonsense style.

After waiting a half hour, her frustration rising, she finally asked a woman she knew if she had seen Charlie. When she was told that Charlie and Ruby had gone to Saginaw for a day of shopping, she remembered. Ruby had invited her to join them, and she had never responded. Again guilt struck her. Ruby was her only real friend. How could she treat her this way? Ruby deserved better. Well, once this Campbell business was over, she would make it up to her.

She gathered her purse, left the Center, and sat in her car. What to do now? She sat there for what seemed a few minutes but was close to twenty. When someone tapped on her window to see if she was okay, she realized the time. Remembering to smile at the concerned tapper, she acknowledged that she was okay, only woolgathering—an expression she assumed he would understand. After all, he was as old as she.

Quickly starting up the car, she drove out of the parking lot with no idea where she was going. It was only when she saw the sign to the hospital that she made her decision: visit Sage.

She arrived at the hospital in less than ten minutes, making every green light along the way. Hannah wasn't superstitious, but she wouldn't sniff at propitious signs. After all, who knows what connections there were between apparently random events? Of course, she would only acknowledge the significance of these connections when it fitted in with her already formed beliefs—or desires.

She found a parking spot close to the entrance—another propitious sign—and took the elevator up to the ICU unit. She walked briskly to Sage's room, opened the door, and stood frozen in the doorway. It was not Sage she saw, but another patient.

She uttered a small cry, put her hand to her chest, and slowly backed out of the room—into the cart delivering lunch. The young woman pushing the chart was startled, but thank goodness she quickly realized that Hannah was having trouble breathing.

"Are you all right? Here, sit down," she said as she pulled a wheelchair stored against the wall over to Hannah. "I'll get a nurse. You just sit here," she instructed Hannah as she dashed off to find help.

Within a few seconds two nurses appeared. An old woman possibly having a heart attack was sure to get the attention of the staff.

Hannah recognized one of the nurses, who asked, "Are you all right, Mrs. Lowenstein? Any pain? Can you breathe?"

Before she could ask any more questions, Hannah raised her hands, palms outward, and said, "Where is she? What's happened to Sage?"

"She's fine; she was transferred to a regular bed. She doesn't need ICU any longer. If you're feeling up to it, I'll take you to her—but first we'd like to check you out. You've had a shock, and we want to make sure you're okay."

Hannah took a deep breath, sighed, and replied, "I'm fine now. Just panicked when I saw she wasn't in the room. Silly of me to react that way. I'd like to see Sage…"

"Just let us take your blood pressure and monitor your heart. It won't take long, and then I'll take you to Sage's room."

Hannah started to refuse but, with her heart still racing, condescended to be checked out. After all, it was a free checkup.

Receiving an all-clear report, she refused the use of the wheelchair and took the elevator to the surgical unit, where she found Sage sitting up in bed, looking better than the last time Hannah had visited. The bruises on her face had started to fade to yellow, and the cuts were healing.

"You almost gave me a heart attack when I didn't find you in the ICU unit. So how are you feeling? You look better. Are you still having pain?"

Hannah recognized that she was blathering, so she took a deep breath and smiled at Sage. "Okay, enough of my questions. Your turn to talk."

Sage laughed. "I don't mind your questions. It's nice to have someone talk to me. The nurses are nice, but they don't have time to talk."

"So how are you? Your face looks better—almost as good as new. But what about your insides? The last time I was here they said something about internal problems, right? Did they check? What did they find?"

Sage shrugged. "I don't know. They may have said something, but I don't remember—I sleep a lot and forget things."

Hannah looked at Sage. What she saw was a frightened young woman with no family or friends to be there for her when she needed help. Hannah suddenly realized that she was probably the only person who visited Sage, the only person who really cared about her—and she had absolutely no connection to her, except her nosiness. Well, that wasn't quite true. It had started out as nosiness, but she knew it had grown into something more. Concern? Compassion? Love? Well, this feeling she had for Sage didn't need a name. Whatever she was feeling, she knew that she would be there for Sage.

Changing the topic, Hannah asked, "Has Diane visited you?"

Sage looked away, obviously disappointed that Diane had not visited, but was quick to defend her.

"No, not that I remember. But she's probably real busy. You know she has to work in the summer even though there's no school. She might have called the nurses though. I don't know."

Hannah didn't pursue the issue, just nodded as if Sage's defense was quite reasonable, and again changed the topic. "So have they told you how long you'll be here?" *They probably haven't told you anything*, she thought, reinforcing her biases against hospitals and how they treated those who were not obviously "special."

Sage shrugged again, looking embarrassed. "I don't know. I just…"

Hannah jumped in. "Of course you don't know. How could you know? You've had a terrible accident. Your body's in shock. Your brain was probably shook up—no wonder you don't remember things. That's to be expected. So let me ask—do you want I should bring you something tomorrow? Something to eat? Something from Diane's house maybe?"

Sage smiled. "Well, if you could bring some cookies or something, that would be nice. The food here isn't so bad, but there's nothing that's really *good*."

"It's as good as done. Tomorrow I'll bring something *good*. Do you want some books or magazines, something to read? Clothes?"

"Magazines would be nice. I sleep a lot, so a book wouldn't be good— I can't focus very well. But *People* magazine or something like that would be nice."

Hannah nodded. "Okay, now I'm going to have a little talk with the nurses. You rest for a bit. I'll be back in a few minutes."

Hannah left the room and strode down the hall to the nurses' station. It was unattended, but Hannah resisted the temptation to ring the bell for attention. No sense antagonizing the people she was going to ask for help.

After an agonizing five-minute wait, a nurse appeared. Hannah smiled and asked, "Whom should I speak to in order to get some information on my niece? She's in room 225, the young woman from the car accident?"

The nurse pulled out Sage's chart, looked it over, and turned to Hannah. "She's doing fine. The breaks will obviously take time to heal, but the bruises on her face are healing well."

Hannah nodded and asked, "What about the internal problems? She was complaining about stomach pains the last time I was here. What did the tests show?"

The nurse scanned the file, shaking her head. "There's nothing here about any tests," she replied, looking over her glasses at Hannah. She closed the file and turned to leave. Hannah startled her when she grabbed her arm.

"I'm sorry," Hannah started as she released the nurse's arm. "I don't want I should be rude, but that's not right. Sage was complaining of stomach pains just two days ago, and nothing was done to check it out? She was knocked down by a car, has broken bones and bruises. Wouldn't it be possible she has some internal problems? Shouldn't that be looked into? What if she's got a broken spleen or liver or something? Shouldn't that be checked? At least blood tests?"

She turned to Hannah and asked, "Is your niece still having stomach pains?"

Hannah was embarrassed to admit that she didn't know. She hadn't asked Sage, and Sage hadn't complained.

"Well then," the nurse said, "let's go ask her."

They walked down the hall to Sage's room in silence. Sage was asleep when they entered, but the nurse gently woke her. "Sage," she said, looking at the name on the chart, "your aunt tells me that you had stomach pains the other day. Do you still have them?"

Sage, still groggy from sleep, murmured, "It still hurts, but I think it's not as bad as before."

"Show me where it hurts."

Sage lifted the bed covers and pointed to her lower abdomen. When the nurse pushed down on the area, Sage gave out a cry. "Yes, that's where it hurts."

The nurse pulled the bed covers up around Sage and smiled. "We'll check into that, honey," and left the room, followed by Hannah.

"So what do you think? They should do some tests?"

"I'll speak to the doctor. He's the one who has to make the decision, but I think he'll want some tests. You just go back to your niece and help her relax. We don't want to worry her unnecessarily."

Hannah thanked her, after extracting a promise that she would speak to the doctor as soon as possible, and went back to spend some more time with Sage.

CHAPTER 41

ANNAH RETURNED HOME, her concern for Sage overriding her excitement about the imminent demise of Larry Campbell, and plopped down in the recliner. *I should start dinner*, she thought, but didn't move.

"Grandma, are you okay?"

She vaguely heard David drop his backpack in the hall. He ran over to where she sat, purse clutched in her hands, held closely to her chest.

Hannah awoke more fully to find a frightened David looking down at her. "I'm fine, darling," she replied, anxious to relieve his fear. "I was just so tired I sat down and fell asleep right away. Come. Let's get you a little something to eat."

David looked at her in surprise, as if she clearly was not fine.

Hannah wandered around the kitchen, not sure what snack to offer David.

"I'm not really hungry. Maybe I'll just have a cookie," he said as he opened the cookie jar and took out two Oreos. "I have to call Billy," he mumbled, cookie already in his mouth as he ran off to make his phone call.

Hannah smiled as she helped herself to a cookie and sat down at the table. She was sorry she had frightened David, but she was also moved that he had been so concerned. Maybe he *was* growing up.

David, on the other hand, was still frightened. When he had finished both cookies, he dialed his mother's private number and waited.

Janice always kept her personal phone with her and answered it immediately. Family and close friends had the number, and they knew to use it only in emergencies.

"Mom? It's Grandma. Something's wrong." David's fear was clear even though his words were not.

"Slow down, David. What's wrong?"

"It's Grandma. I think she's having a stroke or something. She's not acting normal. Come home. I don't know what to do—I'm scared."

"I'm on my way. Just stay with her until I get there."

David put down the phone. It would take Janice at least fifteen minutes to get home. What if something happened before she arrived? He wanted to hide, to pretend that everything was normal, that Hannah was in the kitchen preparing dinner. He didn't want the responsibility of taking care of her if anything happened.

But he was the only one in the house. He didn't know what he could do, but he knew he had to be there just in case. And, he realized, he couldn't imagine life without Hannah. Drying his eyes, he took a deep breath and nonchalantly walked downstairs.

"Hi," he said. "I thought I'd tell you about my practice today." He reached into the jar for another cookie.

"Wonderful," she replied, "but enough cookies—you'll spoil your appetite."

Well, he thought, that was a better response. Almost back to normal. After about ten minutes of recounting every move he had made on the field, pausing to explain the significance of each action, he was relieved to hear Janice open the door.

Hannah was also relieved, having had trouble keeping her eyes open throughout David's monologue.

Janice was surprised to see them calmly sitting at the table. She hadn't known what to expect, but surely not this.

Hannah looked up. "You're early. Is everything okay?"

"Yes," she stammered. "Everything's okay. I just thought I'd make it an early day. So, what are you two talking about?"

"David was telling me about his soccer practice. Did you know that he made more goals—that's right, yes? Goals?—than anyone else on the team?"

Janice looked at David. "I'm sure he's very good. David, I have some packages to bring in. Come help me."

Once outside, Janice turned to David and asked, "What's going on? What's wrong with Grandma? She seems fine."

David shook his head. "No, she's not." he shouted. "When I came home, she was in the recliner, holding her purse to her heart. I thought she was having a heart attack. And then she told me to get something to eat—highly unusual, right?—and then she was sort of out of it as she wandered around the kitchen. It was like she didn't know where anything was. I thought she was having a stroke."

Janice hugged him. "You did right, honey. I think Grandma's okay, but it's good you called me. I'll talk to Grandma, see what happened today to upset her."

David nodded and went back into the house, forgetting to help his mother with the packages. Janice shook her head and retrieved them from the back seat.

"So, Mom, what's for dinner? Should we order something?"

"No, we had pizza the other night," she responded as she shook her head. "I'll make something."

"Janice smiled. "The pizza was two weeks ago. I think we can handle another take-out meal. How about something from that new Greek place? I hear it's pretty good."

"Will David eat Greek food?"

Janice took a deep breath before responding. "David will eat whatever we put on the table, or he can go hungry. Stop babying him." She stopped before saying anything more and upsetting Hannah. She saw no signs of heart problems or stroke, but there was something about Hannah that worried her.

"I know. I know. I forget he's not a baby any more. Okay, Greek food it is. You order—I don't know what the different things are."

Janice hugged her mother. "How about a cup of tea. We have plenty of time before we order the food. Come. Tell me about your day."

• • •

After a dinner of moussaka, feta cheese salad, and baklava for dessert, Janice recruited Maddie and Shelley to take care of the dishes and clean up. Dinner had been successful, everyone agreeing that the food was delicious—even David, who had helped himself to a second serving of the moussaka. The conversation was jovial, with Maddie and Shelley recounting the dilemma of one of their friends who was trying to date two boys without either one knowing about the other.

Hannah had smiled and laughed at appropriate times but had not participated in any of the conversation. She excused herself as the girls started to clear the table, claiming a slight headache, and went to her room to watch some TV.

Paul, always watchful but seldom interfering, pulled Janice aside and asked, "What's up with Hannah tonight? Is she okay?"

"I'll tell you later. I think she's okay, but...well, we need to talk after the kids are out of the way. I don't want them to get concerned."

Paul nodded and turned on the TV, catching up with the latest statistics on the Detroit Tigers, who were having a great season.

Janice checked in on Hannah to make sure she was okay and found her watching a rerun of an old *Matlock* program—another man Hannah thought reminded her of Leo.

Janice joined Paul in the living room and related her earlier conversation with Hannah: the concern about Sage and the belief that she knew who was responsible for Sage's accident, although she wouldn't give a name.

"I know she's fond of Sage and probably right to worry about her. With hospital staff so limited these days, patients need someone to be an advocate for them. Mom's concerned that Sage has some internal injuries that haven't been taken care of."

Paul leaned forward. "Well, that's a genuine concern. I'm glad she's looking into that. But that's not what worries me. I'm worried that she's in over her head on the accident. I know she can't sit quietly by if she sees an injustice, but I have a feeling she's jumping to conclusions about who's responsible. She has a good reason not to like Campbell, but if she is convinced he was driving the car that hit Sage and if she starts talking about that without any evidence, she could be in big trouble. That guy could make her life miserable, even file a slander suit against her."

Janice frowned. "What does she have against Campbell? How does she know him?"

Paul realized that Hannah had not told Janice about her belief that Campbell had sexually molested Sage. He hadn't told Janice either, assuming that his talk with Hannah had been confidential. He didn't want to violate confidentiality, but he had to say something to Janice.

"You'll have to ask her, but she does have some reasons to dislike him. After all, he's not squeaky clean. Even I know about some of the shady deals he's been involved in—nothing you can prove, but enough to make you wonder." Paul hoped that was enough information to ease Janice's concern and was relieved when she nodded agreement.

"Do you mind if I turn on the game?" Paul asked sheepishly. "They're playing Milwaukee and they're tied in the eighth. I just want to see how it ends."

Janice rolled her eyes and laughed. "Go ahead. I have some papers to read. I'll be upstairs—waiting for you," she said in a sultry voice.

"I won't be long," he replied with a smile.

CHAPTER 42

ANNAH WOKE REFRESHED after a surprisingly good night's sleep. She knew what she had to do and was anxious to do it. First, however, her morning chores.

The sky was overcast as she filled the bird feeders and watered the few plants that received special attention. Janice's idea of an ideal garden was one that took care of itself.

Hannah agreed but made exceptions for those plants that bore beautiful flowers. Like some children, they needed more attention if they were to reach their full potential.

Her morning chores finished, she started the coffee and set the cereal, fruit, and milk on the counter. This was going to be a help-yourself breakfast; she had things to do.

Showered and dressed, she quietly waited for the family to come down for breakfast.

First to arrive were Janice and Paul, each in a hurry for 9:00 a.m. appointments. Then came Maddie and Shelley, still in their pajamas, hair tousled, moving slowly.

"You're going to be late," Hannah exclaimed. "Here, let me get you some coffee."

Maddie walked over to the counter and helped herself to coffee, shaking her head. "No, I don't have to be at the clinic until eleven, and Shelley doesn't have to go in at all today."

Hannah turned to Shelley. "So what are you going to do all day?"

"Hang out at the mall, sketch—the usual," she replied.

"So when are you going to show us your new drawings? You must have a lot by now."

Shelley shrugged. "Yeah, I have a lot, but not all of them are good. I sent my best ones off when I applied to Michigan, and they haven't returned them yet. That's why I want to spend today at the mall. I'm hoping I can get some good scenes to draw."

At that moment, David charged into the room, looked around, and finally spotted the food on the counter. "Is that what we're having?" His disappointment was apparent.

"Yes, that's breakfast. Help yourself. I have to leave in a few minutes." Hannah was not going to give any more explanation; David would just have to make do with cereal.

Something in Hannah's tone must have cautioned David not to make a fuss. He went over to the counter, looked over his shoulder at his grandmother, poured some Cheerios and milk into a bowl, and quietly sat down at the table.

Hannah smiled. *Perhaps Janice is right. I do spoil him.*

• • •

Her first stop was the hospital. Before entering Sage's room, she stopped at the nurses' station to ask about the results of the tests. The nurse she had spoken to yesterday wasn't available, so she approached the woman behind the desk. "Good morning. I'm the aunt of the patient in 225. They were going to do some tests to see why she had pain in her stomach. Do you know the results?"

The woman looked at her and pulled out Sage's file. "I don't see anything here about new tests. The only tests that were done were when she first arrived here—to check for head injuries and broken bones, and those have been attended to. In fact, she's doing quite well—can probably go home in a day or so." She turned to some papers on the desk, politely dismissing Hannah.

Hannah was not so easily dismissed. "Excuse me. I don't want I should be a nuisance, but my niece is in pain, and the nurse who was here yesterday thought it was serious enough that some more tests should be done."

"I can't help you. Tests have to be ordered by a doctor. The doctor hasn't ordered any more tests. That's all I can say."

"Well, then I need to talk to the doctor. Where can I find him?"

"Dr. Kravich is making rounds now. She should be looking in on your niece within the hour."

"A woman? Oy, women now are as uncaring as men—such progress. I'll wait for the doctor."

Hannah walked up and down the hall in an attempt to calm herself. Sage didn't need to see an agitated, worried face. She needed to rest and get well.

It was almost two hours later that Dr. Kravich entered Sage's room. "Well, how are we today, dear?"

Sage smiled and said, "Fine."

Hannah interrupted. "She's not fine. She has a pain in her stomach—something is wrong. It's been hurting her for a few days, and it's not getting any better. You need to check it out. It could be a broken spleen, you know." Hannah had done a bit of Googling and knew about spleens.

Dr. Kravich looked at Hannah. "Excuse me, but who are you?"

Hannah gave a worried look at Sage and answered, "I'm her aunt."

To her relief and delight, Sage nodded. "Great-aunt, actually," she chuckled.

"Well, let's see what's going on there," Dr. Kravich said as she lifted the sheet and gently poked around on Sage's abdomen. When Sage winced, the doctor pushed harder until Sage actually cried out.

"Hmm, I agree. We do need some tests. I'll schedule them for this afternoon." She looked at Hannah and said, "May not be the spleen, but it's something. It's a good thing she has you to speak up for her." Turning to Sage, she said, "Young lady, we're not mind readers. If something hurts, you have to tell us, not just say 'fine.' Okay?"

Sage nodded, embarrassment showing on her face. Hannah jumped in to defend her: Sage hadn't wanted to create more work for the hospital; she was a very considerate girl; she was grateful for the care she had already received. But, Hannah assured the doctor, looking at Sage for confirmation, she would be more assertive in the future. Sage nodded again.

After the doctor left, Hannah gathered her jacket and purse and got up to leave. "Rest, darling. I'll check back later to see about the tests."

She headed toward the door and stopped. "Oy, I forgot to bring you those things you asked for. I'll have them when I come back," she said as she waved good-bye.

Next on her list was a visit to the *Daily Sun*. Maybe Mac had information on the license plate. This was going to be a busy day.

• • •

"Hello, Mrs. L." Mac looked up as Hannah entered his office. "You don't need to ask. I have the information you wanted," he said as he waved her to the chair in front of his desk.

Hannah sat down and waited. After three seconds, she asked, "So? Tell me."

Mac chuckled. "Ah, a woman with patience—how rare. Okay, it's licensed to Lawrence Campbell, an attorney in town. The full description is: A-T-T 1-S-T—kind of modest, huh?

Hannah ignored the sarcasm. "I knew it. I knew it was him." Her heart was racing; she couldn't catch her breath. She just sat in the chair, bobbing her head up and down. "It all fits in. I knew it."

Mac opened a bottle of water and went over to her. "Here, have a drink. I'd give you something stronger, but you don't look like a person who likes scotch."

Hannah took a sip. After a few seconds, her breathing approached normal, and she looked at Mac with raised eyebrows. "Don't judge an old lady by her looks. Scotch is my favorite medicine."

"So do you want to tell me what's going on? Why you thought it was this Campbell guy?"

She hesitated. How much should she tell him? Would he print what she told him? Would it interfere with the police investigation?

"I'll tell you only if you promise to keep it private—you know, off the record."

Mac sat back in his chair, arms barely crossed across his chest. "Okay, for now, off the record. Shoot."

Hannah recounted the events that led to her suspicions about Campbell: the fact that he had sexually molested Sage; the suspicion that Sage's wife probably knew about his involvement with Sage; the fact that they had accused Sage of stealing the necklace (which Hannah assured Mac was simply not true); the fact that after Sage had been kicked out of their house, Campbell had offered to put her up in an apartment and pay all her bills; and the fact that Campbell's car was seen hitting Sage. To Hannah, it was obvious: Larry Campbell had tried to kill Sage.

Mac was silent. Hannah worried that he hadn't heard her and started to talk, but he interrupted her. "No, I heard, I understand what you're saying. I just don't see enough evidence to build a case against him... No, let me finish. First, the only evidence we have that it was his car is the eyewitness account. Now, don't get excited, but a homeless young man with drug convictions is not the most credible witness. Second, how do you know, what evidence do you have, that this guy molested the girl and that the wife knew about it? We can go to the police, but they're likely to ask these same questions, and if we can't answer them, they'll ignore us."

Hannah smiled. "You said 'we.' Does that mean you think there's at least something to what I said?"

Mac sighed. "Yeah, *something*. But not enough."

"So what do we need? Can't we have the car checked to see if there is any blood on it, things like that?"

"Well we can't do that. The Police would have to order that, and with nothing to back up our suspicions, I can't see them doing that. I did a little digging when Campbell's name came up. He's a big shot in town. They're not likely going to go after him unless they have more evidence than you provided."

"Can't we at least find out what he was doing that night? You know, maybe someone saw him leave the house, and someone saw him in that part of town..."

Hannah was floundering, trying to think of something that would keep Mac involved. She didn't have the means to get this kind of information; she didn't have access to the world that Campbell lived in. She hoped that Mac did.

He picked up a pen and started to write. "Remind me of the date, time, and place of the accident. I'll see if anything comes to mind. In the meantime, leave it alone. If you're right, this is not a guy you want to tangle with. Go home. Make me another chocolate babka—my wife loved the last one."

Hannah ignored the implicit sexism in his remarks and simply nodded. "Okay, I'm leaving. Let me know what you find out."

It was only eleven when Hannah left Mac's office, too early for lunch, too early to return to the hospital to find out the test results, too early for any action. Frustrated, she drove home. Maybe baking a babka for Mac would help her think.

CHAPTER 43

BABKAS COOLING—WHY MAKE one when doubling the recipe was just as easy—Hannah sat at the kitchen table, sipping a cup of tea and enjoying the aroma floating through the room. She was trying to keep busy until she could return to the hospital. Her frustration had abated, but it was still there. So much to do, and yet she couldn't do anything.

At two she returned to the hospital, this time carrying cookies and *People* magazine. The nurse from yesterday was at the desk and recognized her. She waved Hannah over and said, "You were right to push for more tests. Your niece has a ruptured spleen." Hannah's gasp turned her from explaining to calming mode. "She's going to be all right. The doctor will explain everything to you. Your niece will be fine. She's awake. Go see her."

"Does she know?"

"Yes, the doctor explained everything to her. She understands what has to be done. Go on in. I think she'd like the company."

Hannah paced the hall a bit, calming herself before entering the room. Sage was sitting up in bed, watching what looked like a children's program on the TV. She smiled at Hannah as she received a kiss on her cheek.

"Don't mind the TV. I'm so used to watching kids' programs, it makes me feel good, like things are normal."

"So they tell me they found what was wrong. What are they going to do?"

"I don't know very much except they've scheduled me for surgery tomorrow." With a sheepish smile, she added, "Can you be here? I know it's asking a lot, but I don't want to be alone."

"What nonsense. Of course I'll be here. What time is the operation?"

"I don't know—sometime in the morning, I think."

"Well, I'll be here first thing in the morning. Okay, that's settled. Now I have to ask you some questions. Okay?"

"Okay."

"Has Mr. Campbell been in to see you since that first time? Any contact with him? Did he repeat the offer of paying for college and for an apartment?"

Sage looked away, tears forming in her eyes. "No, he hasn't. I haven't heard from him at all...Oh, I feel like such a fool. I really thought he loved me, that we had something special. But...I don't know. I think he's forgotten about me. He probably never really cared about me. An Indian girl wouldn't fit into his life, would it?"

Sage wiped the tears running down her cheeks with her hands and looked at Hannah, who wiped the tears from her own eyes.

"Darling, yes, you were a little fool, but how could you have known what he was like? He manipulated you into feeling that way. It allowed him to..." Here Hannah hesitated. She didn't want to say he had "used" Sage, but she wanted to convey the thought. "It allowed him," she continued, "to have relations with you without you protesting. That was his fault—really his crime—not yours. Now here's a Kleenex. Dry your tears. We're going to talk."

Their talk was interrupted when Dr. Kravich came in to give the good news that since Sage didn't have a swollen abdomen and didn't have severe pain—either of which would have complicated matters—they had done a CT, which showed only a small tear in Sage's spleen, easily repaired.

Satisfied with the doctor's report and satisfied with the information that Sage was now willing to share about her relationship with Campbell, Hannah promised to be there early in the morning. All the fears, worries, and even anger had left her. She now had permission to do what she could to hold Larry Campbell accountable for his actions regarding Sage—all of them.

She arrived home, settled in the recliner, and was just dozing off when she remembered the babkas. Oh well. Mac would enjoy them just as well tomorrow.

Hannah woke drowsily and shifted in the recliner. She could hear the girls giggling in the kitchen. "What's so funny?" she asked, which made them giggle even louder.

"We didn't want to disturb you resting your eyes." They giggled again as Hannah started to protest, only to give up with a smile.

CHAPTER 44

HANNAH PRESENTED HERSELF at the hospital at seven thirty, carrying a tote bag filled with a newspaper, a crossword magazine, cookies, fruit, and a thermos of coffee. She was prepared to sit there all day, if necessary.

Sage was still in her room, being prepped for surgery. She looked pale and frightened. Hannah took her hand, the one without the IV, and said, "I'm here, darling. I'll be here the whole time, and when you're awake, the first thing you'll see is me—after the doctors, of course. You'll be fine. I checked up on the doctors, and they're all top notch, so everything is going to be okay." She hadn't really checked up on the doctors, but she thought it would reassure Sage to say so. Sometimes little lies weren't really bad.

Three hours later, Sage was returned to her room. The surgery had gone well, Dr. Kravich announced as she entered the room. "It was a very small tear, no complications. She should be able to go home in a few days."

"Are there going to be any problems after—with the spleen, I mean?"

"There shouldn't be. The spleen should function normally, and there shouldn't be any negative effects. She was a very lucky girl. That must have been a pretty bad accident."

Hannah almost said it was no accident, but held her tongue. No sense in starting that conversation. She sat by the bed, holding Sage's hand, watching her sleep. She hoped she could get to the *Daily Sun* before it closed in order to give Mac his babka, but if Sage needed her, she would just have to make a fresh one for Mac—the family could eat the others.

When Sage was finally alert enough to realize that Hannah was there, she smiled.

"You're here," she whispered.

"Where else would I be? I told you I'd be here, and you know I don't break a promise. The doctor says you're going to be fine. It was just a little tear—all fixed—and you'll be out of here in a few days."

Sage nodded, her eyes closing.

"I'll leave now. You need your rest. I'll come by tomorrow," Hannah said to an already-sleeping Sage.

It was almost three. Enough time to go home, retrieve the babka, and see what news Mac had for her. Hannah tiptoed out of the room, stopped at the nurses' station to remind the woman there that she should be contacted if Sage's condition changed, and headed home.

• • •

Babka in hand, she knocked on Mac's door. "Enter," a booming voice responded.

Mac looked up. "You knocked. Are you all right?"

Ignoring Mac's sarcasm again, Hannah placed the babka on his desk and sat down. "For your wife—and for helping with the license."

Mac received the gift as if it were a delicate piece of glass. He grinned like a little boy anxious to open his present on Christmas morning. Hannah chuckled. Men were just little boys, only bigger, she thought. *It's good, however, that it doesn't take much to please them.*

"Have you heard any more about the accident? Are the police going to do anything? Have they arrested Campbell?"

"Whoa, let's take it slowly." Mac leaned across the desk and placed his hand on hers. "I do have some information, but it doesn't answer all your questions." He paused. Hannah indicated she was ready to listen. "Okay, here it is. I sent out one of my young reporters—a real James Bond wannabe. I'm sorry to have to tell you this, but Campbell was at a meeting the night of the accident—some group of investors or something. There were enough witnesses, so there's no question that he was there the whole time."

Hannah sat silently, not even trying to hide her disappointment. Finally, she nodded. "So, Derek was right. It was a woman driving the car."

Mac scowled at her. "What are you talking about? What woman? I thought you were convinced it was Campbell. Now you're talking about a woman?"

She shrugged. "If it's not him, it's her. It's clearly their car. Who else drives it? And Derek did say it was a woman. And it makes sense. She found out about what he was doing. She got the girl out of the house by framing her for stealing her necklace. She worried that he would keep seeing her, so she tried to eliminate her. Makes sense to me."

Mac scratched his beard and shook his head. "You know from anyone else I'd ignore what you just told me, but...You do have a way of seeing things others miss. "So, let's back up a bit. Tell me how this girl came to be a nanny for the Campbells. She's not from here, right? How did she get here?"

"Ah, I thought you'd never ask. Listen to this," she replied as she sat back in the chair and related the activity of the Good Nanny group.

When Mac heard that Sage had been recruited from Gladwin, and that she was Native American, his old investigative reporter nose started twitching, which fascinated Hannah.

"What do we know about that group?" he asked.

"All I know is what's on their website. But they never met Sage. She saw the advertisement, applied, and was hired. They paid for her bus transportation from Gladwin to Brewster, and that was it. No background check—on either side. Now who does that? Hire someone, sight unseen, to take care of their children? Nonsense. Something fishy is going on there."

Mac had started writing while Hannah spoke. He looked down at his notes. "I think I'll check into the Good Nanny and see what they're up to. But, Mrs. L, accusing Mrs. Campbell is just as dangerous as accusing him. Please be careful. Let the authorities do their job."

"Authorities? Who? The police? They're probably in his pocket," Hannah shouted.

"Calm down, Mrs. L. Don't get all *fartumelt*—you know the word? I'm just saying be careful. The police know the license plate belongs to Campbell—they'll check it out. Just stay out of it—at least until we see what happens."

"You're right," she replied, nodding her head. "I'm just so angry at how they've treated a young girl—barely fifteen when she arrived here—and then they try to kill her. I can't accept that they'll get away with it."

"We, you and I, will work together to make sure they don't—if they're guilty. But there's another issue here I'm interested in. That Good Nanny organization. I'm going to look into that. It doesn't sound kosher."

He looked at her. "You know Mrs. L. you remind me of my mother. Right was right and there was no excuse that could change that. I learned early on to trust the gut reactions of strong women and I'm proud to consider my daughter and wife in that group. And I guess you belong there too."

Hannah left his office with more optimism than she had felt for days. Sage would recover, and the Campbells would get their comeuppance—which she hoped was prison. Now all she had to figure out was where Sage would go when she left the hospital. Her belongings were still at Diane Cassidy's, but was that the best place for her? Diane hadn't once visited Sage—in Hannah's eyes, unpardonable—and, perhaps more relevant, Diane wasn't home during the day. Sage would need care for a while, and Hannah wasn't convinced she would get it there.

Her first inclination was to take Sage home with her. She could easily provide care for her, as well as companionship and someone to talk with. But there was no room. With Shelley sharing Maddie's bedroom, Janice and Paul in another, the only remaining room was David's. She couldn't ask him to give up his room for Sage; neither could she give up her room. Well, there must be another option, she decided as she put the car in gear and drove away.

CHAPTER 45

TWO DAYS HAD passed and no news from Mac. Hannah was fast losing her optimism—and her patience. She had managed to control her frustration by focusing on the homeless project. The Committee for Providing Shelter for the Homeless had been meeting every two weeks and had made some decisions. Committee members had recruited twelve churches that were willing to offer night shelter for a week at a time. Two had agreed to participate for two weeks. That would only provide fourteen weeks of shelter, but it was enough to start.

Much of the discussion at the last meeting had focused on when to start. Some wanted to start in November, at the beginning of the cold weather; others wanted to wait until January in order to provide shelter throughout the heart of winter. There was much discussion on the issue, until it was pointed out that either way, they could not provide shelter for all of the cold weather. It was then decided to open at the beginning of January, hoping that the fall season would be mild.

The Committee for Providing Shelter for the Homeless had received donations sufficient for the necessary supplies. All that remained was to find a sufficient number of volunteers to provide the necessary services. But the committee did not know who would be in charge. A program run by volunteers could not provide the necessary oversight and security that would be required. Clearly, someone with experience was needed, and that person would have to be paid. The committee needed more funding.

Suggestions were made and discarded. Bake sales wouldn't bring in enough money to justify the time spent. Ads in newspapers were too

expensive. Flyers around town wouldn't be effective. At last it was suggested that perhaps there were some grants that would provide funding,
at least funding for specific needs. A committee was set up and assigned
the task of finding grants.

Everyone felt better now that someone else was responsible for raising
money, and the meeting was adjourned. Hannah lagged behind, slowly
gathering her belongings. She wanted to speak to Reverend Dwayne
away from the others.

"Mrs. Lowenstein," he said, "what's up?"

"Well, you know I don't like to interfere, but I'm worried about how we're
going about getting donations. I don't know about grants, but I think we
shouldn't depend on them. And even if we got a grant, I don't know how
long it would take to get the money. So I think we need to think of something
else to do…You know, I'm new to town, but it seems to me there are a lot of
people with a lot of money here. Isn't there some way we could get to them?
Like have a contest and name the shelter after the biggest donor? Well,
maybe that's too crass, but, you know, somehow appeal to those people."

Dwayne motioned for Hannah to sit down as he folded his long body
into one of the chairs at the table. "I agree that we have to do something
more than the grants. You're right. We do have a number of wealthy indi-
viduals whom we could approach. The question is how to do so in a way
that's likely to be successful."

"Well, maybe if we got one rich person to talk to the other rich persons…"

Dwayne laughed. "Well, let me think on that. Finding a rich man who
wants to support a homeless shelter might be like finding the proverbial
needle in the haystack, but it's worth a try…But," he continued, "we could
approach the city for financial support."

Hannah looked puzzled. "What could the city do?"

He looked at her in amazement. "What do you think your city taxes
do? They're used to provide services in the community—and a homeless
shelter would certainly be providing a service."

Hannah smiled at him. "You're a *mensch*, Reverend Dwayne—what a
wonderful idea. How do we do it?"

"We'll need a proposal to present to the City Commission. I can get
one of my parishioners to help draft it—he's a lawyer and teaches political
science at the college. He'll know how to get started."

With that, they both rose and smiled at each other. "You know," Hannah quipped, "we got more done in these last ten minutes than in the previous two hours."

Dwayne nodded his head in agreement, but added, "Yes, but that's how committees work. Some people do the work and then present their ideas to the group, who then adopt them as their own. It's not an efficient process, but it does work—and it makes people feel that they're making a contribution. That's important if we want to keep them involved."

She sighed. "You're right. I get too impatient. My family tells me all the time, 'Slow down. Don't be in such a rush.' Well, I'm going to slow down. Let me know if you want I should do something to help—not write, but something else, okay?"

"Okay," he replied as he looked at her with a warm smile.

Hannah returned home, satisfied that plans for the homeless shelter were on track and comfortable that they were in the hands of Reverend Dwayne. Too bad he wasn't Jewish. He'd make a wonderful Rabbi.

• • •

The satisfaction that had lifted Hannah's spirits yesterday was rapidly being replaced by irritation. What were the police doing about Sage's accident? And what could be done about Sage? And which concern should take priority today? She decided that finding a place for Sage to stay after her imminent release from the hospital would be her first priority. Once she felt that Sage was in a good place, she could worry about the police.

Reviewing all the options she could think of, she realized that she didn't have any. She sat at the kitchen table, a picture of despair, when Janice entered.

"Mom, what's the matter?"

Hannah sat up quickly and turned a smiling face toward Janice. "Nothing, darling, just thinking. There's coffee and bagels. Do you want I should make something else?"

"No, that's fine. So what are you thinking about?" she asked as she helped herself to coffee and put a bagel in the toaster.

Hannah took a deep breath. How much should she share? Would Janice think her a meddling old woman for her concern about Sage? Was it really her responsibility to find a place for her?

At that point, she shook herself and said, "Okay, I'll tell you. You may not agree...no, don't interrupt...You may not agree, but I have a responsibility for Sage. She gets out of the hospital in a few days, and I have to find a place for her to live, and I haven't any idea where she can go."

Janice shook her head. "Why do you always assume I'm going to disagree with you, that I wouldn't understand your concerns? Of course we have to find a place for her. What about Diane? Wasn't she staying there before the accident? Couldn't she go back?"

Hannah explained her reasons for rejecting Diane's place as an option, leading Janice to raise her eyebrows.

"She never visited or called her? That doesn't sound like Diane. But I do agree that Sage needs someone to be with her, at least at the beginning, and Diane couldn't provide that level of care. But what about a rehab place? You know, where she would get help until she was strong enough to live by herself—which leads me to ask, does she have any ability to pay for a room or apartment?"

"Who knows," relied Hannah with a shrug. "She told me that Mr. Campbell had offered to put her up in an apartment, as well as pay for her college in the fall—but that was one time at the beginning, and she hasn't heard from him since then. Such an SOB, that man. So I guess the answer is no, she doesn't have money to pay for anything...But does this rehab place cost a lot?"

"In her situation it might not cost anything. She obviously would qualify for Medicaid. I'll check on that, but the bigger issue is what is she going to do once she's well?"

Hannah was silent. The mention of Campbell's offer to take care of Sage's financial needs led to a chain of reasoning that ended in a conclusion: he was guilty. Even if he hadn't been driving the car, if it was his wife, he knew about it. Perhaps at first he thought Sage had seen his wife in the car, and he was covering his tracks, relying on Sage's good feelings toward him. And now, since there had been no further indication that she knew anything, he had backed away, ignoring his first generous offers of help. Yes, that was it, Hannah decided, with the assurance of someone who actually had evidence. Now what should she do with this knowledge?

All of this went on in her head in less than twenty seconds. She turned to Janice with a smile. "Maybe there is a way she could pay for an apartment and go to college. Yes, there might be a way," she said, head bobbing up and down in agreement with herself.

Janice looked at her mother, obviously perplexed and concerned.

Hannah had already risen from the table, put her coffee cup in the sink, and was heading toward her room to shower and dress. She turned to Janice and said, "Thanks, darling. You've been a big help."

To which Janice replied, "Don't do anything foolish, Mom."

• • •

Well, what *was* she going to do? Confront Campbell and blackmail him into paying Sage? As tempting as that was—and it was tempting—she decided against that course of action. She couldn't see herself descending to that level. But, she thought, there must be a legal way to get him to pay.

Ordinarily she would have consulted Paul about the legal recourses open, but that would tip her hand on her involvement, and she wasn't willing to do that. Janice would worry and try to stop her. So what to do?

Well, what were the police doing? They certainly had enough time for them to conclude their investigation, if they had even started. Again, she thought of Mac—maybe he had some information.

CHAPTER 46

THIS TIME SHE didn't have to barge into his office; he was in the hall talking with a group of his reporters. He raised his eyebrows when he saw Hannah in the doorway and, with his head, motioned her to his office.

"I'll be there in a minute, Mrs. L. Take a seat," he shouted.

Hannah nodded and strode down the hallway, determination apparent in every step. She couldn't help but overhear Mac's conversation.

"This will take me a while, folks," he said. "We'll figure this out later. In the meantime, let's go with what we have for tomorrow's issue."

"Mac, is that the woman who's involved in the accident?" called out a young man's voice.

"She's not involved. She's concerned."

"Yeah, that's what I meant. But is the case closed? Do you need me to get any more info? It might turn into a great story—and we could have an exclusive."

"I'll let you know. In the meantime, keep on the latest on the parking issue."

"Okay—I just wanted to be sure that if there was a story, it would be mine," replied the young man.

"I said I'd let you know, Izzy," Mac replied with his usual grumpiness. "Now get to work."

He still acted grumpy when he joined Hanna in his office.

"These young pups, always anxious to get the *big* story—think it'll make them famous, get asked to write for the *Times* or something," he grumbled as he tossed the papers he held in his hand onto the desk, pulled up his chair, and sat down.

"Well, weren't you the same way when you were young," asked Hannah. "Dreams are important—even when we're old. And who knows—some of the dreams we had when we were young have maybe been replaced by other more realistic ones…"

"I'm sure you didn't come here to spout platitudes at me. What do you want?" he thundered.

Hannah pulled herself up to full size and said, "Don't you shout at me, young man. I'm old enough to be your mother, and I demand the same respect you give her—at least I hope you give her."

Mac shot her an embarrassed look and chuckled. "You're right. I apologize. My mother would not be proud of me today."

"So what's got you all *fartumelt?*

"Nothing important. Just got up on the wrong side of the bed, I guess. So, what can I do for you, Mrs. L?"

Hannah leaned forward in the chair. In a conspiratorial whisper, she shared her conclusion with him, being careful to include the reasons she had for each of her claims.

"Hmmm," he said when she had finished. "Interesting story, but I don't see any evidence for your claims. It wouldn't stand up in court with just your conjectures. We would need solid evidence."

"Yes, yes, I agree," she replied, "and now here's where you come in. We have to find out about the car: Are there any dents, or blood, on the front? Did they take the car to a repair shop right after the accident—you know, to get rid of the evidence? And what was Mrs. Campbell doing that night? You can find this out, right? You wouldn't have to do this if the police were doing their job right…Have you heard anything from them? Are they even investigating?"

Mac didn't reply at first. "Well, they do have a suspect—haven't arrested him yet, but from what I hear, it's only a matter of time before they do." He stopped here and waited a few seconds. Hannah leaned forward, eyes wide in anticipation. "It's that young man—Derek, I think you said. They think he's involved somehow." And then he waited for her reaction.

"Derek? What are they—the Keystone Cops? He doesn't have a car—I don't know if he even knows how to drive. He's the one who came forward with a description of the accident. He's the one who called 911. Why would he do that if he was guilty—why call attention to himself? They're just lazy—and prejudiced. How easy to close the case, blaming it on the homeless guy—who they never see except when it serves their purpose. Of course they don't want to accuse Mr. High-and-Mighty Campbell. He probably contributes to the police fundraisers—maybe even has some of them on his payroll…"

She was on a roll. All of her frustration was let loose, and Mac became the target of her rage. Her inner voice was telling her that it wasn't fair to take it out on Mac, but her rage was so strong she couldn't hear it.

When she stopped to take a breath, Mac interrupted. "Mrs. L, calm down. You'll have a heart attack. Here, have some water," he offered as he pulled out some bottled water from the bottom drawer of his desk. "Drink," he ordered.

Hannah could feel her heart pounding like a drummer at an Indian Pow Wow—she had been to one last year. She couldn't hear what Mac was saying, only aware that he was shoving a bottle of water at her and looking worried.

Her hands shook as she took the bottle. She fumbled with the cap until Mac reached across the desk to seize the bottle and, with one quick twist, opened it. "Here, Mrs. L. Drink."

They sat in silence, Hannah drinking water, Mac observing Hannah.

Her eyes filled with tears, threatening to stream down her face.

"It's my fault," she cried. "If I hadn't gotten him involved, he would never have been suspected. If he gets arrested, it'll be my fault."

He grabbed a tissue from his desk and walked around the desk to try consoling her. It was a clumsy attempt—patting her on the shoulder and murmuring, "It's all right. Don't cry"—but it did the job. Hannah took the offered tissue and wiped her eyes.

"Silly of me. I'm usually not so emotional. Must be that I'm coming down with something…Now that we know what's what, we can't expect the police to help us. We have to do it ourselves."

Max returned to his chair, sat down, and contemplated his fingers—at least that was what Hannah thought he was doing. Impatience almost caused her to interrupt his contemplation, when he looked up, pounded his hands on the desk, and yelled, "Izzy. Get in here."

Within seconds the young man appeared in the doorway. "You called, Mac?"

"You wanted to try for an exclusive? Well, you've got it. Now here's what I want you to do." The next twenty minutes were spent on Mac's instructions to Izzy, who grinned while nodding his head as he made notes on his pad.

"Wow, no way," he uttered over and over. Mac told Hannah that Izzy was about twenty-five years old and the first in a family of immigrants to finish college, and he was ambitious. "If there's a story to be told here, Izzy will find it," he concluded.

Mac turned to Hannah. "Well, we've begun. Go home, cook, watch TV, or go shopping. Do something relaxing and forget about being a detective. I'll let you know when I know something."

Hannah wiped her eyes, blew her nose and, with a nod of thanks to Mac, left the room. Imagine, she thought, actually being able to prove the Campbells guilty of attempted murder. The emotional ups and downs she had experienced in Mac's office had so exhausted her that all she wanted at the moment was to get home, take off her shoes, and curl up in the recliner. No more thinking, no more worrying, no more frustration. Something was going to be done, and, with the utmost confidence, she knew they would nail the Campbells.

CHAPTER 47

JANICE CAME THROUGH with setting Sage up in a rehabilitation program, paid through Medicaid, which solved the immediate problem of where she would live, leaving the larger one, however, unsolved. But at least that gave them some time to consider the options.

Hannah had to use all of her control to keep from checking up on what Izzy had found out about the Campbells' car. A week had gone by since their meeting, certainly enough time to have found out something, she thought. Well, one more day, she decided. *I'll wait one more day. Then I'll call.*

Having made that decision, she tried to focus on the homeless shelter project. She had attended a meeting of the Committee to Provide Shelter for the Homeless the previous evening and was pleased that four of the churches had agreed to sponsor a second week in the rotating program. That made almost four months of shelter possible, allowing them to open earlier than planned.

Reverend Dwayne's lawyer had written a proposal asking the City Commission for funding for a permanent shelter in town. Dwayne would ask the commission to put the proposal on the agenda for the August meeting. Everyone agreed that they would need to round up friends, family, and any potential supporters to be present at the meeting.

All in all, it had been a productive meeting; Hannah went home comforted by the thought that they would be able to provide shelter for at least some of the homeless population in Brewster.

Today she would focus on food: freezing the berries that were plentiful this year and baking enough cookies and pies to take them through the hot spell predicted for next week.

By one thirty she had frozen and baked enough to last for a month, although she knew that the supply would most likely be demolished within two weeks. When she sat down at the table after taking the cookies and pies out of the oven, she realized she hadn't had lunch. No wonder her stomach was growling and her eyes were coveting the cooling cookies.

She opened the refrigerator, hoping to find an interesting leftover, but was disappointed to see that there had been nothing left over from last night's dinner. So much for serving a dinner everyone liked so much that they asked for seconds. Now she would have to prepare something for her lunch. That thought seemed to drain all the energy from her body. She plopped down onto the chair, looked around the kitchen, got up, grabbed her purse, made sure the oven was turned off, and left the house. Surely the Center would still be serving lunch, she thought as she started up the car and drove off.

People were still lingering over coffee when she arrived. She glimpsed Ruby sitting with a group of women, none of whom Hannah wanted to listen to. All the talk would be about their grandchildren, their health, and how wonderful their doctors were. Boring. But the only other option would be to eat alone, and Ruby would think she had done something to annoy her, and she didn't want that. So she walked over to the table, pulled out the remaining chair, smiled, and sat down.

"Hannah," Ruby declared with a smile. "We were just talking about you."

"Only good things, I hope," replied Hannah.

"Of course, dear," she said with a mock scold on her face. "We were just saying that we hadn't seen you for a while. We hoped you weren't ill—although I knew you would have called me if it was anything serious."

Hannah smiled in response. "No, I've been fine, just busy." She turned the conversation to what she knew would interest them: "So how was lunch today? Anything worth eating?"

The ensuing discussion on the merits of the lunch menu—too much starch, not enough variety, same old cookies—led Hannah to say, "Well,

I'm hungry enough to eat whatever's left," and she got up to attack the buffet. She returned shortly with a plate of tuna salad on lettuce leaves and a piece of carrot cake.

The conversation veered to plans for the July Fourth holiday. The conversation flowed easily, allowing Hannah to finish her lunch without participating in the discussion.

When the other women got up and left, promising to see Ruby after the weekend, Ruby turned to Hannah and asked, "Are you really all right? You don't look all right—you look tired."

Hannah nibbled at the crumbs on her plate. How much should she share with Ruby? Certainly not her suspicions about the Campbells. But Ruby was her friend, perhaps her only friend. She had to offer some explanation for her recent behavior.

"Well, it's true. I am tired. I've been worrying about the young woman I told you about—the one who was hit by a car. I can't find a place for her to live when she leaves the rehabilitation place. Remember, she used to be a nanny for a family in town? But now she's on her own—no money, no job, and no place to live. I'm hoping it's just a temporary problem, that she'll get a job and have money for a place of her own, but in the meantime—which may be a few months—she has no place to live. We'd take her in, but with Maddie's friend staying with us, and with Sandy—Paul's daughter—coming in a few weeks, we don't have room. So yes, I'm tired, tired of worrying…Does it show that much?"

"Only to someone who knows you well, dear."

They continued to chat, enjoying their time together. *Why don't we get together more often*, Hannah asked herself. *I really enjoy her company. And she has a way of calming me down. I'm going to spend more time with her.*

Just then, Charlie walked in. "How are my two favorite ladies this afternoon?" he asked as he sat down at the table.

Ruby beamed with delight.

Hannah rolled her eyes. "We're fine, Charlie. You missed lunch. Where have you been?"

"Ah, it's good to know you noticed my absence. I was hitting a sixty-eight on the golf course. Best day I've had in years."

"Oh, that's very good. Some pros don't do that," said Ruby, adoration in her eyes.

"That's sixty-eight on nine holes I think, not the eighteen that pros play. Right, Charlie?"

He frowned at Hannah and whispered behind his hand, "Did you have to spoil it? I'm trying to impress her."

Hanna laughed. "She's impressed by everything you do—even your breathing impresses her, right, Ruby?"

Ruby just smiled.

Charlie got up to get refills on their coffees and a piece of cake for himself. When he returned, Ruby filled him in on Hannah's concern about Sage. "Just think. The poor girl has no place to sleep. That's just shameful. Everyone should have at least a room for themselves."

Charlie murmured agreement with his mouth full and returned to the last piece of his cake. Mouth finally empty, he looked up from his plate and asked, "How long would she need a place to stay?"

Hannah had withdrawn from the conversation, focusing on her own thoughts, but perked up when Charlie asked his question. "I don't know, but probably until she can find a job that pays enough for a room or apartment. She's hoping to go to the community college in the fall, and if she gets financial aid, she could probably afford at least a room. So she probably needs a place for two or three months."

Charlie slurped his coffee and looked at Hannah. "You know, I've been trying to get this gal to move in with me," he said as he inclined his head toward Ruby. "This may be my best chance. Maybe she'll let me move in with her—for a few months—and this girl can stay at my place."

He turned to Ruby, whose face had turned a lovely red. "Come on, Ruby," he pleaded. "It's not as if I don't already spend a lot of time at your place. And this would be for a good cause—you like good causes, right?"

She hesitated, and Hannah could easily read her mind. Ruby would love spending more time with Charlie, but to live with him? It was almost as if Ruby spoke out loud, Hannah was so in tune to her thoughts. Ruby's home was lovely, everything in its place, no clutter, no mess. She loved the peace and serenity it provided her. Would that be disturbed if Charlie moved in? He was a wonderful man and, yes, she was in love with him. But he was a larger-than-life presence who sometimes left her exhausted. And he was a slob—left his clothes on the floor, didn't put things back where they belonged, and dominated control of the TV with sports programs.

Oh, what should Ruby do?

Hannah realized that Ruby didn't see Charlie's solution as positively as he did, and she broke the awkward silence by saying, "The girl's in a rehab center now, so we have time to figure out what comes next...Well, it's time for me to get on home," she said as she rose from the table. "I'd better put the cookies away before David gets home. That boy can sure eat."

She gave Ruby a hug, waved at Charlie, and left the Center. Once settled in the car, she thought, what a good suggestion that was. If only Ruby would accept it.

CHAPTER 48

HANNAH ARRIVED HOME to a house filled with the aroma of cookies and pies and the sound of boyish excitement. David was upstairs with his friend Billy, and they were obviously engaged in some serious video game competition. She ignored the whooping but made a mental note to speak to David about the cursing. Not a prude, she was known to utter a few cusswords herself, but that shouldn't stop her from reminding him that there was a place for such language, and it wasn't at home. Maybe she should pretend she didn't hear him and leave the disciplining to Janice—perhaps a cowardly approach, but after all, she was his grandmother, not his mother. The more she tried to justify whatever she did, the more confused she became. Better to ignore the whole thing, she decided, and called to the boys to come down for a snack.

Cookies and lemonade consumed in a flash, David and Billy thanked her and raced upstairs to continue their battle. Hannah smiled at their retreating backs, having already forgotten about their language.

● ● ●

It was almost five when she received the call from Mac. She was in the midst of the preparations for dinner—a new chicken recipe that called for a lot of chopping—and ran to the phone, drying her hands on a towel.

"Mac, you have news?"

"Hello to you too. Yes, I have news. My boy Izzy came through. He's going to be a great reporter if he doesn't end up in jail first. Yes, I have news. The Campbells' car was taken into a chop shop—that's not just a repair shop. It's where they basically dismantle the car and use the parts. Since it was only two years old, it's strange that they would want to get rid of it—unless they were trying to hide something. So I think it's time to go to the police. Do you want to come with me?"

Hannah didn't reply. Usually she would have jumped at the opportunity to confront the police, to argue her case. But unexpectedly, she hesitated.

"Mrs. L, what's the matter? You should come. It was because of you that I pursued the issue. You should be there to take credit. We've got good grounds for the police to at least question the Campbells…and you could use a little good publicity for yourself. Come on. Don't get squeamish now."

She sighed and agreed to join him. "When are you going?"

"How about tomorrow morning? I could pick you up—say about nine?"

"Okay, I'll be ready…and thanks, Mac."

"See you tomorrow," he replied and hung up.

Well, there was no turning back now. She was nervous—frightened? But that was nothing unusual. She had the same reaction whenever she confronted authority. She just had to take a deep breath, calm down, and do what had to be done. But first, she had to be sure she was prepared, had all her geese—or whatever—in a row.

She returned to her chopping, rehearsing what she would say when she met the police. The last thing she wanted was to seem like a dotty old woman who couldn't present her case coherently.

• • •

The meeting with the police went surprisingly well. Hannah left the meeting confident that there would be a genuine investigation into the so-called accident and that they would look into the involvement of both of the Campbells. She remarked to Mac as he drove her home, "That went better than I expected. Maybe the police aren't as corrupt as I thought."

Without turning to look at her, he replied, "Mrs. L, you've got to give up your suspicions about everyone in Brewster. Sure there are some bad apples, but most of us are decent, hard-working blokes. We may fumble, and we may be too provincial for you, but get to know us better. You'll find that we're not all like the Campbells."

Hannah was chagrined. Mac was right. She was unfairly judgmental. And she really didn't know many people in town. She needed to change that—although she didn't know how.

She nodded in agreement and said, "You're right. I keep forgetting all the people who have been helpful—not just now, but since I came here. Leo, my husband, used to tell me the same thing. He'd say, 'Hannah, give people a chance to know you. Don't judge them so quickly.'"

Mac smiled. "He must have been a very wise man. Did you ever listen to him?"

"Once in a while—when I remembered." She chuckled.

• • •

The police investigation underway, Hannah could focus her attention on Sage. She was scheduled to be released from the rehab center the following week, and Hannah still had no idea where she could stay. She also had no idea if Sage had officially registered for financial aid as well as for classes in the fall.

Well, she thought, the person who could at least help with that was Diane Cassidy. Hannah had kept her distance from Diane, disappointed with her apparent lack of concern for Sage, but, she reluctantly decided, Diane was someone who could help Sage with the whole college situation.

She got through to Diane immediately and, after explaining the situation, solicited her help in checking Sage's application and financial aid. Diane thought that Sage had already submitted her application, and Diane reported that she had already given Sage the necessary papers for requesting financial aid. She was sure that Sage would qualify for financial aid and perhaps even more.

Hannah hung up the phone, thinking more positively about Diane than before. It looked like the Campbells were going to be held responsible for the hit-and-run, but what about his sexual abuse of Sage? She hadn't shared that with the police. Was that a card she could still play?

CHAPTER 49

THE REHAB CENTER was in Whiteville, a slightly larger town than Brewster, twenty-five miles away. She checked that all the ingredients for the night's dinner were on hand, grabbed her purse, and took off for Whiteville after setting her GPS system.

Sage was in the recreation room, the only person under the age of sixty, watching the Food Channel with the other residents. She wheeled over when Hannah entered the room, and gave her a hug.

"You look wonderful," Hannah declared as she returned the hug. "You wouldn't know anything was wrong."

Sage laughed. "Nothing is wrong anymore. I'm eating regular food, and my arm is just about normal. They say once the cast is off my leg, I should be walking without a limp. I'll just be glad to be out of here. Oh, everyone's been kind to me, but it's quite boring…Most of the people here," she whispered, "are quite old. They sleep a lot and can't hear very well."

"Come. Let's find a place where we can talk," Hannah said as she took Sage's arm and led her to the door. "We need to talk about what happens when you leave here."

They went back to Sage's room. Her roommate was in the recreation room, allowing them to have the room to themselves.

Hannah started the conversation by telling her that Diane was looking into financial aid for her and that she, Hannah, was looking into a place for her to stay. She was relieved that Sage didn't ask why she couldn't continue to stay at Diane's, an acknowledgment that Sage was aware stay-ing there wasn't an option.

When there was no more to say about Sage's financial situation, Hannah turned the conversation to Larry Campbell. "So has Mr. Campbell been in touch with you?"

Sage looked her in the eye. "No, and I don't expect him to. I realize I was foolish to think I meant anything to him—in fact, thanks to you, I real-ize he used me. I don't hate him, but I certainly don't like him and have no desire to see him again."

When Hannah told her about the Campbells' involvement in the hit-and-run—or as Hannah called it, the attempted murder—Sage turned pale. "My God, they hated me that much? Why? I never hurt them. I took good care of their children. I actually liked them, thought of them as my family. God, I was stupid."

Hannah went over and put her arms around Sage. "No, you weren't stupid. They were evil. Good people like you can't imagine that there are people like that.

"But that's what I want to talk to you about. I remember your saying that Mr. Campbell had offered to pay for your school and do something about an apartment for you. I know that was before any of this came out about their involvement, but if he made the offer again, would you accept it?"

She could see clearly Sage's confusion on her face, starting with an expression of repulsion, to one of embarrassment, ending in anger. "I don't know what I would do," she responded "but I doubt he'd make the offer again."

"But if he did?" Hannah persisted

Sage sighed. "It would certainly be nice to have some money, but...I don't know. It feels dirty."

"Nonsense. It would just be a way of his admitting he took advantage of you and that he's sorry. There's nothing wrong with that."

Sage bit her lip and shrugged.

"Well, maybe he won't make the offer, and you won't have to decide. It was just a thought." Hannah didn't want to push the issue but thought that she detected at least the possibility of Sage considering the option.

And even if she refused the offer, think how good she would feel at rejecting it. Yes, Hannah knew what she had to do.

• • •

The next morning she received a call from Ruby. "Hannah, I couldn't sleep after our talk the other day. I'm so confused. Of course I'd like to help that girl, and you know how much I love Charlie—but the thought of his moving in just scares me." She paused for a moment. Through the silence, Hannah could hear her breathing.

"Of course you're scared" she said. "It's a big step, even if it is for only a short time." She emphasized the "short time," hoping that would ease some of Ruby's concerns.

"But what if we find out that we *can't* live together—that we're too different. Will he feel the same way about me? Will he think I'm too prissy, too set in my ways? I don't want to spoil what we have."

"I understand," replied Hannah, using her soothing-a-child voice. "But you don't have to do anything. Charlie will understand, and I'll find a place for Sage. So don't worry."

The silence this time was broken by Ruby. "Tell me about the girl—what's her name?"

Hannah perked up. Ruby hadn't asked anything about Sage before. Perhaps she was reconsidering her decision.

"She's a lovely young woman, quite mature for her age. She just graduated high school and plans to attend college in the fall. She was a wonderful nanny for one of the lawyer families in town. She's quiet, neat, polite, intelligent, helpful—what more can I say? I'm very fond of her, as you can tell."

"Why can't she go back to the family she worked for?"

Hannah hesitated. How much should she tell Ruby? She didn't want to mention the necklace incident—that would frighten Ruby—but she didn't want to lie to her either.

And she certainly didn't want to talk about sexual assault over the phone.

"You know, dear, I have something in the oven," she lied, "so why don't we get together later for coffee and one of those delicious pastries at that new café. That way we can have a real conversation without my worrying about burning my buns. Can you meet there at, say, three?"

"Oh, what a good idea. I've been wanting to go there for weeks. It's right next to that adorable new shop—the one with all the beautiful floral arrangements in the window. Yes, I'll meet you there at three."

Hannah hung up the phone. Was it possible to change Ruby's mind, she wondered. She didn't want to push her into making a decision she would regret. Well, she decided she would explain Sage's situation and leave the decision up to Ruby.

It was only nine thirty; she had almost the whole day ahead of her. Enough worrying about housing for Sage. She had to focus on another matter.

• • •

It was now two. She had been sitting at the kitchen table since the phone call from Ruby, pondering options with no success. How could she get Larry Campbell to honor the offer he had made to Sage? It seemed clear to her that he had made the offer to keep Sage from talking to the police, but once it had become clear that she had no idea he—or his wife—was involved, he saw no need to follow through. Blackmail was such an ugly word, she thought as she considered blackmailing him. Was there a more positive way to describe what she was considering doing?

She looked up at the clock, surprised at the time. Her third cup of tea had cooled, and she had forgotten to have lunch. *Well*, she thought as she got up to leave, *maybe I'll have two of those delicious pastries.*

• • •

When Hannah walked in the door, Ruby was already seated at a table by the window, laden down by brightly colored packages. Hannah smiled at her and pointed to the packages.

"I see you found something to do while waiting for me," she teased.

Ruby held up one of the packages and opened it. "Isn't this the most adorable hat?" she asked, as she pulled out a straw hat with pink roses on the brim. "And look at this," she exclaimed, pulling out a scarf from another package. "Look at these colors—aren't they like a Monet painting? The blues and greens and the touch of mauve?"

Hannah nodded, trying to remember which paintings were Monet's—or was it Manet? But she had to admit the scarf was lovely, and it certainly looked good on Ruby, who was holding it up against her face.

"Have you ordered?" she asked Ruby.

"No, I just got here. What are you having?"

"I think I'll have one of their cannoli to start with...and a coffee. I'm starving—I forgot to have lunch."

"You should have something more substantial—soup or a sandwich. Then you could have dessert."

Hannah rolled her eyes. "What are you—the food police? It won't kill me to skip lunch and have dessert. That's what being a grown-up is all about. So what are you having, Miss Healthy Eating?"

Ruby shook her head and replied, "I think I'll have coffee and a cinnamon roll."

"Good healthy choice," snorted Hannah.

They chatted about family—who was doing what, how the grandchildren were doing in school—and compared the new aches and pains of aging until the waitress delivered their food. Conversation ceased while they dug into their respective treats.

Hannah's desire for a second dessert had disappeared after the cannoli. She wiped the remaining cream from her lips and sighed. "So you want I should tell you about Sage, the young woman we were talking about. Well, let me start at the beginning."

After a description of Sage's background, how she handled her job as a nanny—without the mention of Larry Campbell's behavior—she had decided to tell Ruby about Sage's being accused of theft—how else would she explain her being fired, which led to her being homeless? She also told how Sage was the victim of a hit-and-run. Hannah tried to draw a picture of Sage's character. She knew that Ruby would be sympathetic to the situation that Sage was in, but she also knew that the kind of person Sage was would be the key point in deciding if Ruby would allow Charlie to move in.

Ruby listened quietly as Hannah explained Sage's situation. She frowned, nodded, shook her head, and teared up at appropriate moments.

She sat, picking at the crumbs on her plate, and didn't say a word for a few moments. When she finally spoke, it was with a sigh.

"Such a terrible thing for such a young person. To be accused of something you didn't do and then to be homeless. And to be in a serious accident without any family to take care of you. Terrible."

"She's a wonderful young woman: intelligent, caring—she treated those children as if they were her own—and did the cooking and the housekeeping too. I'd ask Janice to let her stay with us, but we're running out of bedrooms."

Ruby listened quietly, nodding her head as Hannah spoke. "From what you've said, she seems like a nice young woman. Do you think she would want to live with me?"

Hannah sat there with her mouth open. "Live with you? I thought we were talking about Charlie moving in and her using Charlie's place."

"Oh no. There's no way I want Charlie to move in. That wouldn't work. But I do have that other bedroom that the girl could have. In fact, I could even pay her a little for helping around the house. You know, help clean, maybe even help with the garden, if she wanted."

"You are the most amazing person I know—puzzling and frustrating, but amazing. I never thought of this. It's perfect." Hannah was looking at a new Ruby, or at least seeing a side she had not noticed before. The woman knew what she wanted—or didn't want—and held firm. No Charlie moving in. That was definite.

"Have you thought this out?" she asked. "You're not used to living with someone, you know. And what about Charlie? Will he understand?"

Ruby waved her hand as if swatting a mosquito. "She's not going to be there forever. A few months won't be a problem. And I can handle Charlie. This is less threatening to our relationship than his moving in would be."

"Well, if you're sure, I'll mention it to Sage, but not until tomorrow. I want you should be sure about this."

They left the café, agreeing to talk again, and Hannah headed home while Ruby continued her shopping at the local boutiques. There was always something she could use.

• • •

Hannah was still stunned at the solution Ruby had proposed. She drove home with a new respect for Ruby. She had always admired her gentle, kind friend, but had seen her as passive, dependent on other people for her opinions. She now realized that there was a core to Ruby that was strong when something was important to her. Perhaps she was passive because she really didn't care about many of the things others were concerned with.

Hannah hooted out loud, "Thank you, Ruby. You've made my day," as she sang along with the oldies on her favorite station all the way home.

CHAPTER 50

NOW THAT SAGE'S housing situation was solved—assuming Ruby didn't change her mind and that Sage would accept Ruby's offer—Hannah turned her attention back to Larry Campbell while she prepared the evening meal: cold cuts and cold salads. With a loaf of rye bread from the bakery and ice cream and fruit as dessert, she wasn't expecting any complaints.

Later in the evening, she approached Paul as he headed for the living room. "I don't want I should interfere with your Tigers game, but do you have a few minutes?"

"Of course. What's on your mind?"

They sat down, he on the sofa, she on the recliner. "Well, I don't know if you heard, but the Campbells are being investigated for the accident a few weeks ago, the one that put my friend in the hospital..."

"I've heard that they were being interviewed. I figured it was more than just a polite talk." He stopped and stared at her. "I'm afraid to ask. Did you have something to do with that?"

"Not much, just asked a few questions, you know, that sort of thing," she replied, hoping he wouldn't pursue the issue.

"I bet," he responded, shaking his head. "Well, go on. What about Larry Campbell?"

"Well—she leaned forward in the recliner—"do you remember what I told you about his having sex with the nanny? Well, when he visited her in the hospital the first day, he offered to pay her way through college. He also offered to put her up in an apartment, but we're not going to discuss that. Anyway, I think he was afraid she knew that his wife was driving the car that hit her, and he wanted to sort of bribe her to keep quiet. But once he found out that she didn't know anything, he stopped visiting her. He never visited again—"

Paul interrupted her. "I'm not sure where this is going. He certainly has the right to change his mind about his offer. It wasn't legally binding, if that's what you're asking."

"No, no, I know that. What I want to know is if there is any way we can get him to honor that offer? To do the right thing? To ease his conscience, maybe? Remember, he had promised her that he would pay for college, from the time she was hired. Surely that's like a contract, no?"

"No. If there was no written contract or proof of a commitment, he's not legally bound to pay. It may be unethical, wrong, dastardly—but it's not illegal to go back on a promise."

Hannah leaned back into the recliner, disappointment written on her face. "So that's that." She sighed. "Okay, I just needed to know…There should be a law: a promise should be kept even if it isn't written down and signed, and witnessed, and all that stuff."

She pushed herself up from the recliner, thanked him, and went to her room.

• • •

Hannah sat on the edge of her bed, going over the conversation with Paul. *So that's it; the son of a bitch gets away with it. Well, not if I have anything to say about it.*

• • •

Hannah's resolve dissolved in the morning light as she galumphed around the kitchen, banging pots and pans, preparing the traditional Sunday breakfast: buttermilk pancakes, maple syrup, and bacon. She knew there was no need to call the family to the table. Once she started broiling the bacon, the aroma would serve as the wake-up call. What she barely realized, though, was that her galumphing and banging had already done the job.

Everyone seated at the table, plans for the day shared, Hannah sat quietly enjoying her family.

"Earth to Grandma. Are you with us?" Maddie laughed.

Hannah looked up to see all eyes focused on her. "Mom, we've been trying to get your attention for the last few minutes. Are you all right?"

"I'm fine." She smiled. "Just thinking about how lucky we all are. We have food, a beautiful home, and we have each other...But enough of that. Anyone want any more pancakes?" she asked as she started to get up from the table.

David raised his hand, his mouth too full to speak. Janice put her hand on Hannah's shoulder. "Sit, Mom. I'll get it."

Conversation had stopped, no one sure of what to say. Hannah broke the uncomfortable silence by commenting on Maddie's plans for the day. "See, I was listening: you and Shelley are going swimming at your friend's pool, right?"

"Right."

"So you know you should wear sunscreen, right?"

Maddie rolled her eyes. "Yes, Grandma, I know."

After that interchange, the mood in the room lifted, and conversation resumed.

Janice recruited the girls to clear the table and do the dishes, so Hannah headed to her room.

"So, Mom," Janice asked as she followed Hannah into her room, "what are your plans for the day?"

"Oh, nothing special. I'm going to meet Ruby for lunch at the Center. Did I tell you? She might be willing to have Sage stay with her when she gets out of the rehab place this week. I'll find out if she's made up her mind when I see her."

"That's great. I know Diane is looking into the financial aid situation. She should know something shortly."

Hannah smiled. "Well, it looks like things are falling into place for Sage...You haven't met her, have you? You'd like her. She's quiet but quite mature for her age. I think she could have a good life once she gets on her own feet."

Janice hugged her mother and left the room. Hannah sat down on the bed and sighed. She still had no idea how to approach Campbell. If only she could run into him at some social function. She could drop a hint about what she knew and hope that he picked up on it. Then maybe he would see the wisdom of repeating his offer. But they didn't run in the same circles, and she couldn't think of any other way to talk to him except to confront him in his home or office. Even she knew that was unwise.

• • •

Long lines at the buffet tables greeted her. She spotted Ruby and Charlie in the corner and made her way through the crowd to join them.

"What's going on? I've never seen it this crowded, especially on a nice day like this. You'd think people would want to be outdoors."

"There's a special today: barbecued pork. People are lining up to get some for takeout. I guess they're going to have picnics at home," Charlie replied.

"They can do that—take it home?"

"Who's going to stop them?"

"It just doesn't seem kosher." She shrugged.

"Is barbecued pork ever kosher?" He laughed, eliciting a giggle from Ruby.

"Funny," Hannah replied with a roll of her eyes. "So what are you two up to? Any exciting plans for the rest of the day?"

Ruby spoke to Hannah but looked at Charlie. "I've told Charlie about my decision to have the young woman move in with me. He thinks it's a great idea, don't you, dear?"

"Yeah, that'll probably work better than my giving up my place." Hannah noticed that his body language didn't match his words, but she said nothing. If Ruby thought things were fine, she wasn't going to dissuade her.

"Aren't you going to get something to eat?" Charlie asked. "You'd better get up there before it's all gone. It's like a feeding frenzy among the zoo animals. I'm going back for some dessert before that's all gone too." And with that pronouncement, he got up from the table and headed for the buffet.

Hannah moved her chair closer to Ruby. "So tell me—how did he receive the news? Was he upset?"

Ruby removed her glasses and rubbed her eyes. "I think he was a little upset…but when I explained about not wanting to ruin our relationship, I think he understood. We're going to play miniature golf later today and then go out to dinner at the new Thai restaurant. So I think things are okay."

"I'm glad. I wouldn't want you and Charlie should break up because of me."

"Oh, don't worry about us. We've become like an old married couple, without the marriage and the living together. It's actually better than my marriage was," she declared with a laugh.

Hannah smiled. She knew enough about Ruby's marriage to know that it wasn't a happy one. She was pleased Ruby had found Charlie—or vice versa. They were good for each other.

"Well, I didn't come to eat. I had a big breakfast this morning. I just wanted to stop in and find out what you decided. I really appreciate this, Ruby. And if there are any problems, you have to let me know. We can always find another way," she said, not believing a word of what she said. *What other way?*

She waved at Charlie, who was returning to the table carrying a plate of cookies, and left the Center. Now she had to make sure Sage was agreeable to the arrangements.

CHAPTER 51

I T WAS AN open visiting day at the rehab center, and the lobby and recreation room were filled with visitors. She walked down the hall and stood in the doorway to Sage's room, watching. Sage was sitting up in bed, the lunch tray pushed away, still loaded with soup, salad, and a small sandwich. She appeared sad, just staring at her hands on the bedcover.

Hannah knocked and entered without waiting to be acknowledged. "How are you doing, sweetheart?" she asked as she advanced toward the bed.

Sage looked up and gave her a radiant smile. "I'm so glad you're here. I was getting bored."

Hannah knew it wasn't boredom but loneliness that Sage was experiencing, but didn't correct her. "I have some good news for you."

Sage looked up in anticipation. "Really?"

"Yes. My friend has an extra room in her condo, and she would like you should move in with her. She's a lovely older lady, quiet, and kind. And it won't cost you anything. As you get stronger, she'll pay you for helping with chores around the house—and gardening, if you like. She's a wonderful gardener, takes care of the big garden the condo has. Anyway, if you agree, you can go there as soon as you leave here. So how does that sound?"

Sage burst into tears. "Oh, my dear," Hannah cried out. "You don't have to go there if you don't want to. It was just a suggestion…"

Sage reached for the box of tissues on the tray, wiped her face, and blew her nose. "No, that's not it. It's just that I'm so happy. I've been so worried about what would happen to me. This sounds wonderful. And tell her that I won't make a mess, I'm quiet, I can cook and clean, and I love gardening, especially flowers. Oh, this is so much more than I had even hoped for."

"Well, that's a relief. For a minute there I thought I was back to square one."

"Oh, Hannah. I love you. You've been more than a friend…"

"Yes, I know—like your grandma." She laughed.

• • •

Hannah left the rehab center in high spirits. Sage would be all right—Ruby would see to that. Now Campbell was her only problem. She would have to think more on that one.

It was after two, and she recognized that rare feeling in her stomach—she was hungry. The pancake breakfast was wearing off. She put the car in drive and took off for the Bistro. Just a little something, she promised herself.

Traffic was light on a Sunday afternoon, and parking was available in front of the shop. She sat down at a table by the window and ordered coffee and a bear claw—not quite the "little something" she had planned, but rather the treat she felt she deserved. She pulled out a small pad and pen and started to make a list of groceries to buy.

Within ten minutes, she was the only customer remaining. She started to gather her belongings, when the door opened. She looked up out of curiosity and was startled to see Larry Campbell. She didn't recognize him at first, having only seen him once before. He was a pale shadow of how she remembered him: he looked ten years older, his skin was pallid, his hair seemed grayer, and his arrogant air was missing.

Her first thought was a compassionate one: pretend she hadn't seen him—he had enough problems on his plate now. Her second thought, though, reminded her of her mission: get him to offer to pay Sage's tuition. Mustering her courage, she approached him.

"Mr. Campbell, isn't it? I'm Hannah Lowenstein. We met at the lawyers' banquet a while ago."

He looked up. "Yes?"

She almost lost her nerve, but taking a deep breath, continued. "I've just come from visiting Sage—your former nanny. You know she had that nasty accident, but she's recovering quite well. Lovely girl—I think of her as my granddaughter. She hasn't had an easy life—but then you know that." Hannah hesitated at this point. How much further should she go?

"Look. I'm glad to hear about Sage. Now let me drink my coffee in peace." He turned away, dismissing her with a toss of his hand.

That did it. "Sorry to bother you," she said, saccharine pouring out of her mouth. "I know how busy you are. But I just wanted to thank you for your generous offer to pay for Sage's tuition. She's very excited about going to college in the fall."

His head jerked up at her words. "She told you that?"

"Oh yes, she told me *many* things—but I'm sure you don't want me to discuss them here. Well, have a good day, Mr. Campbell."

She walked away, wishing she were taller. It was difficult intimidating people at five foot one inch with a pudgy body. No matter how straight she stood, how high she held her head, how majestically she tried to walk, it wasn't intimidating.

Her heart was pounding as she left the café. She stopped at her car and stood there, trying to calm herself. Had she been too subtle? Too vague? Should she have told him she knew what he had done to Sage? She took a few deep breaths, opened the door, and plopped down onto the seat.

Filled with self-doubt, she fought the urge to cry. What was she thinking? *Confront the man, and he'll fold—confess to helping his wife commit murder, confess to raping Sage, maybe even confess to running a sex-trafficking business.* Janice was right: she was watching too many cop shows.

She put the car in gear and headed for home. Enough meddling for the day.

CHAPTER 52

FTER A NIGHT of fitful sleep, she awoke to a glorious sunrise washing the backyard with a golden glow, highlighting the morning dew on everything. The grass seemed greener, the flowers more vivid, the leaves on the maple trees more glistening. Even the birds seemed to chirp more loudly as they fed at the feeders.

The remonstrations of the previous day disappeared as she viewed the beauty in her backyard. *Well,* she decided, *I've done what I could. Now it's time to get on with my life.*

Nodding her head in determination, she started the coffee, fed Max, and let him out for his morning run—with a mental note to remind David that Max was *his* dog, not hers—and returned to her room to get ready for the day.

By the time the rest of the family descended on the kitchen, she was dressed and on her second cup of coffee. Janice and Paul each grabbed a bagel smeared with cream cheese, gulped down a cup of coffee, and left for work. Maddie and Shelley came down next. Neither one wanted any breakfast but succumbed to Hannah's protests that they should at least have half a bagel—already prepared. Experience had clearly taught them that it was easier to give in a little than to argue with Hannah.

David was still in bed, so Hannah took the opportunity to indulge in a third cup of coffee—and half of a second bagel—while the house was still quiet. She took her second breakfast out to the deck overlooking the backyard and sat there, watching Max chasing butterflies, and remembering the events of yesterday.

All in all, she concluded, it had been a productive day: Sage had a place to stay, and she had at least confronted Campbell. As she relived the conversation with him, she remembered how he had looked when she mentioned that Sage had told her many things. His already pallid skin had paled even more, and…was that fear she had seen in his eyes as she started to walk away?

She sat back, more comfortable with her accomplishments than she had been yesterday. She was smiling as David barged through the door, asking, "What's for breakfast?"

• • •

The next few weeks flew by. Hannah was busy with plans for the start-up of the rotating shelter program, which was scheduled to open in December. There were still many details to work out, and Hannah had agreed to work on the Subcommittee for Details—a not-so-clear description of what its charge was. But, she thought, better that she be there than leave it to the other people who had volunteered. Nothing would be ready if left to them, she grumbled.

• • •

Sage had moved in with Ruby, and it was love at first sight. The two of them had so much in common it was amusing to see. Hannah had dropped by the previous day and found them in the garden, making plans for the fall foliage.

"Hannah, over here," called out Ruby. "We're in the garden."

Hugs all around, Sage explained the current project they were involved in, going into more detail than Hannah could, or wanted to, digest.

'You see," continued Sage, "we need something that will stand out against the dark green of the holly bushes."

"Yes," followed Ruby, "you can see that it can't be red—too Christmassy—and it can't be too subtle—it wouldn't show up against the dark green. So we're looking for something bright but not too bright."

Here Sage picked up the thread and said, "We were thinking of a yellow or gold, but we can't think of a fall plant with that color."

They continued discussing various plants, the advantages and disadvantages of each, and finally agreed that they needed to return to their sources, which—thanks to Sage—were now on the Internet.

Hannah was delighted to see how well they got along, but she was bored with the conversation. "Isn't anyone going to invite me in for something to drink?" she asked.

Ruby was mortified. "Oh, I'm so sorry. Where are my manners? We get to working on something and forget the world around us. Of course. Come on up. I just made some fresh lemonade."

The rest of the visit took place on the small balcony outside Ruby's apartment. Sage brought out the lemonade and some cookies she had baked.

"These are delicious," Ruby gushed, taking a cookie from the platter Sage was passing around. "This girl is amazing in the kitchen. I haven't eaten so well since I was a little girl—my mother was also a great cook."

Sage sat down, a smile on her face. "I have some news," she started. "I spoke to Diane Cassidy this morning, and she told me that my tuition for the fall is all paid up—tuition, room, and board, with a separate account for things like books and extras. Isn't that great?"

Hannah looked at her. "Did she say how it got paid? Financial aid, maybe?"

Sage looked puzzled. "No, she had helped me fill out the application papers—I got accepted—and when she checked on financial aid information, she was told that everything was already paid for. She didn't say anything more...Is there a problem?"

"No, dear. No problem. That's good news. I'm so pleased for you."

"But that means she won't be living here with me once school starts," whined Ruby. "I tried to convince her to stay here, but she's decided to move into one of the dormitories."

"Residence hall," corrected Sage.

"Well, whatever it's called, it's a good idea," interrupted Hannah. "She needs to be with people her own age, join clubs, get to make friends. That's what college is for: meet different people, learn new things. Besides, you could invite her over for dinner or whatever—maybe even make a standing date."

Sage chuckled. "Oh, I'll be over so often you'll get tired of me."

They all laughed and continued talking about plans for the fall. Hannah joined in occasionally but let the two of them carry the conversation. She was absorbed in in wondering who had paid Sage's bills. Had her conversation with Campbell paid off?

CHAPTER 53

THAT EVENING AT dinner Paul announced the latest news on the Campbells. They—both of them—had been arrested: Mrs. Campbell on a felony assault charge for intentionally running Sage down, and Mr. Campbell on a charge of obstruction of justice for helping to hide the evidence.

"I don't know anything more, just that they were indicted and there will be a trial. One of my partners was tapped for the defense, but he's trying to get out of it. Doesn't much like Campbell."

"Can he just refuse? What if no one wants to defend them?" asked Maddie.

"Well, that's not a problem. They could always be given a public defender. But I don't see that happening. They could certainly afford a top-notch criminal defense attorney—probably someone from out of the area…This is a serious charge. A conviction on a felony assault charge can carry a ten-year sentence. And if they up the charge to attempted murder, a life sentence is possible."

"Wow," exclaimed David.

Hannah had been silent throughout the discussion. Paul looked at her and asked, "How is Sage with all of this?"

"I saw her yesterday, and she didn't mention it. Does she have to be involved? She doesn't really remember anything."

"I don't know. It'll depend on what evidence they'll be using. Even though she doesn't remember anything about the accident, she might have information that would be relevant. After all, she worked for them for a few years. Had there been any bad feelings between them? Anything that might show intention to harm her would be relevant."

Hannah didn't want to mention the issue of the stolen jewelry at the dinner table. She planned to share that with Paul in private. Instead, she just shrugged and pleaded ignorance.

She turned the conversation to Shelley's plans for the fall. She had received an art scholarship, which covered her tuition, but still had to pay for rent and food, as well as her share of the utilities. She, however, didn't seem worried about that—which worried Janice and Hannah.

To question Shelley about where she would get the money would be rude—especially since Maddie's expenses were paid by Janice. *But, thought Hannah, we're talking about a significant amount of money. Was Shelley aware of that?*

She looked at Janice and raised her eyebrows as Shelley explained the scholarship she had received.

"They liked my sketches," she was saying. "Said I had real potential but that I needed to develop other techniques than sketching. They suggested I take classes in other mediums—like oil and watercolor—and see what I could do. It sounds exciting. I've never had paints to work with, just pencils, so it'll be something new."

"What other classes will you be taking?" asked Janice.

"I'm not sure. I don't have to register until August."

"Maddie, what did you have to take the first year?" Janice continued.

"Well, there are these general education categories that everyone has to take something in. You know—science, humanities, social science. And then there are competency courses in math and English that everyone has to take—or CLEP out."

"CLEP? What's that?" asked Hannah.

"Oh, if you can show that you can pass an exam—a CLEP exam—you don't have to take the class but you get the credit. It costs money though, so lots of students take the class and get an A, which helps their GPA—grade point average."

"So Shelley, you'll probably have to register for some of those classes. There's usually a lot of classes in each category, so you have some choices. What interests you besides art?"

Janice was bordering on rudeness. Hannah tried to get her attention, but she was so focused on Shelley that she didn't notice her mother's warning signs. Hannah got up from the table and announced that she wanted a second helping of chocolate cake. Did anyone want to join her? As she had hoped, David jumped at the opportunity of more cake, as did Paul, and so the focus on Shelley's classes was transferred to the chocolate cake Hannah carried to the table.

Hannah knew her daughter well enough to realize that she didn't want a second piece of cake and would understand that it was Hannah's subtle way of changing the topic. Besides, Hannah thought, it really didn't matter what classes Shelley took—surely the advisers at the university would handle that. What concerned her was where Shelley would get the money to pay for rent and other necessities.

Later that evening, Hannah mentioned her concern to Janice,

"Well, she doesn't have any income. There's no family supporting her. She wouldn't even have to take out much of a loan. There are plenty of grants she would qualify for. In fact, I'm embarrassed that I didn't think of that. Thanks for bringing it up. I'll talk to her tomorrow—set things in motion."

She smiled at her mother and got up to join Paul in the living room.

• • •

Hannah stood in the doorway for a moment before entering the room. "Is this a bad time?" she asked.

They both laughed. "I'm just leaving, Mom. He's all yours," Janice said as she got up from the couch. "I assume you want to get some of his free legal advice," she teased.

"Come on, honey. You know it's not free. We have a quid pro quo arrangement: she feeds me, and I give her legal advice. I think I get the better of the deal."

Hannah didn't know what a "quid pro quo" was, but she could see from Paul's affectionate look that it was something okay.

She settled down in the recliner and leaned forward. "Since we have this "quid" relationship, does that mean that whatever I tell you has to be kept confidential?"

Paul smiled. "'Quid pro quo' means we have a deal: I give you something. In return you give me something. If you want to tell me something in confidence, give me a dollar—then I'll be your official legal counsel."

"So cheap? I can afford more than that."

Paul laughed. "No, you just have to pay me something to become my client. Then it's official, and I'm bound by attorney-client privilege...So, what's up?"

"Well," she began, "I'm worried about Sage getting involved. She doesn't remember anything about the accident, and I haven't told her about the Campbells. She'll probably hear about it when it's in the papers though. Anyway, I'm sure she doesn't want to talk about the sex stuff, especially in front of other people..."

"That needn't come up in the trial, unless she wants it to."

"But what's the motive then? Why would Mrs. Campbell want to hurt her? It makes more sense if they can show that he was having sex with the nanny, and that she found out about it, and at first made up a phony charge of robbery so she could get her out of the house, and then tried to kill her when she found out that he was making plans to keep seeing her..."

"Whoa, I'm getting confused. What robbery? What plans?"

Hannah took a deep breath and continued. She told him about the missing necklace and how it was conveniently found under Sage's mattress. She told him about Campbell's initial offer to put Sage up in an apartment. And then she told him of the anonymous tuition payment—which she assured him was from Campbell.

"How do you know it was from Campbell?" he asked.

Reluctant to admit that she had talked to Campbell, she avoided a direct answer. "Who else could it be from?"

"Hannah, remember this is confidential. I can't reveal any of this conversation, so I need the whole story."

"Okay. I did something that maybe I shouldn't have. I ran into Campbell a few weeks ago and sort of let it slip that I knew what he had been doing with Sage and reminded him of his offer to pay her tuition—I didn't remind him of his offer to put her up in an apartment, like a kept woman...Was that blackmail?" she asked.

He hesitated before responding. "Technically no—you didn't threaten him, at least not overtly. But, Hannah, you took a foolish risk. If someone is willing to commit murder, or at least cover it up, can't you see that confronting him, even if you didn't make it overt, could be dangerous? What were you thinking?"

Tears were forming, but her voice was steady. "Maybe I wasn't thinking. Or maybe I was thinking how unfair it was that he could get away with what he did. And he did make the offer when he thought she might be able to remember the accident. That was sort of like a bribe, wasn't it? That 'quid' thing, right?"

"I'm not saying that what you did was illegal or even morally wrong. I'm only saying that it was dangerous," Paul replied in obvious frustration.

"Okay, I guess I wasn't thinking. I don't mean to worry you and Janice. It's just that sometimes I act before I think things through. Leo used to say the same thing to me—but I usually remembered too late."

"Well, getting back to the original point, it would be good if they could use the sexual assault and jealousy as the motive, but if Sage doesn't want to mention that, the Campbells certainly won't…But if we could find that he paid her tuition, that would at least indicate something was going on— yes, it could be seen as a bribe."

"So you can find that out?"

"No, I can't get that information. But I could mention it to the prosecutor, who can get it. But you have to realize that if they use that as a motive, it's likely they're going to want Sage to testify—at least to the fact that he offered to pay her tuition. It would be a stronger case if she would testify to the sexual abuse, but…"

"No, I don't think she'll do that. But it wouldn't hurt to ask her, right?"

"Right," he nodded as he watched her lift herself out of the recliner and wave good night to him.

CHAPTER 54

THE NEWS ABOUT the arrest of the Campbells was the lead story on the front page of the *Daily Sun*. Max told Hannah that Izzy had done a follow-up on his initial investigation.

"I gave Izzy the go-ahead to get as much information as he could and he convinced the garage owner to admit that Campbell had paid him extra to destroy the car rather than to use the parts. And yes, it's clear that the car had hit something.

"Izzy also interviewed the new nanny for the Campbells. He knew that Campbell had an alibi—he was at some meeting—but he found out that the wife didn't. Her new nanny reported that she had taken the car that evening and returned within the hour, clearly upset. She had yelled at the nanny for letting the children stay up, even though she had previously agreed they could watch some movie." Max chuckled. "It seems the new nanny doesn't really like Mrs. Campbell and had a lot to say about what a bad mother Mrs. Campbell is and how she, the nanny, was already looking for another job."

"So what happens now?"

"Well, once the police were notified of the results of the interviews, they took it from there. Told me not to print anything until they investigated. I agreed but had Izzy write up a front-page article to be printed as soon as we got the release. I'm always willing to go along with the police but not at the cost of losing the opportunity for an exclusive."

• • •

Hannah was becoming more and more uneasy as she read the paper. How would Sage react, she wondered. To think that someone would try to kill you, someone you thought liked you. Well, maybe it would help to end any lingering feelings she might have about Campbell.

She waited until nine before calling Ruby, who she knew was a late sleeper. "Yes, it is a lovely day, but listen, I have to talk to Sage, and it would be better if you were there. I'll leave in about twenty minutes... Good. And could you maybe make some coffee? I'll bring a little some-thing—these talks go better with snacks...I'll explain when I get there."

Hannah arrived to find a worried Ruby and a puzzled Sage. "Hi, Hannah," Sage called out as Hannah entered the apartment. "Ruby's all upset, but she won't tell me why. Is something wrong?"

"No, darling, something's right. But let me put these cinnamon rolls down and get myself some coffee. Here, help yourself," she said, offering the rolls to Sage and Ruby.

Sage took a roll, but Ruby declined. "I can't eat a thing. My stomach is so upset. What's happening?"

"Nothing bad. I just wanted to be the one to tell Sage—she shouldn't read it in the paper first." Hannah sat down with her coffee and cinnamon roll, and she proceeded to recount the events that led up to the arrest of the Campbells. She was careful to focus on Sage's reaction as she talked, ready to stop if it was too much for her to hear. But to her surprise, Sage listened impassively, occasionally nodding her head as if she already knew what Hannah was going to say.

"I'm sorry you had to learn what kind of people they are, but it's better to know, right?" she asked when she had finished.

"Much better," Sage replied. "You know, I've had a lot of time to think these past few weeks. I guess the accident was a good thing—"

"Good thing?" interrupted Ruby. "It's a terrible thing. You could have been killed."

Sage leaned over and put her hand over Ruby's. "Yes, but it didn't kill me, and it helped me to see things more clearly. If it hadn't happened, I would have believed that I had done something wrong, something that had turned these nice people against me. That it was somehow my fault. But to try to kill me—that's not the behavior of normal people. I wasn't harming them. They had already fired me. What harm could I do? Even if I protested my innocence, who would believe me?"

"It's not about the missing necklace, dear," Hannah answered, looking over at Ruby. How much did Ruby know? *Well, it's going to come out in the trial, so no point in being squeamish now.* She just hoped that it didn't change Ruby's attitude toward Sage.

"It's about Mr. Campbell's behavior. His wife was jealous. She saw you as a threat to her marriage. The necklace was just her excuse for getting you out of the house. One can only imagine what Mr. Campbell said when he found out you had been fired. Probably enough to allow her to still see you as a threat."

She looked across the table at Ruby, who sat in silence. Hannah wondered if Ruby had understood what they were talking about. "Ruby?" she asked.

Ruby looked across the table and put her hands over Sage's. "The bastard," she blurted out, tears filling her eyes and slowly falling down her cheeks. "You poor thing."

Hannah was taken aback. Ruby had figured out what she had tried to be vague about. And here she was, saying "bastard" as if she said the word all the time. *I would have never thought to hear such a word coming out of her mouth,* Hannah thought. Well, no need to worry about Ruby's attitude toward Sage. *She'll probably overdo her solicitude and make Sage uncomfortable.*

• • •

Hannah was in a jubilant mood when she left Ruby's. Things were falling into their rightful places: Sage would be going to college, fully paid; the Campbells would stand trial—and most likely be convicted; Sage had indicated that she was willing to help at the trial. Shelley seemed to be set for the fall after talking to Janice about financial aid. Maddie and David, as usual, were doing fine. And the Committee for Providing Shelter for the Homeless was set to open shelters in December. Life was good, she reminded herself as she drove home.

She inspected her pantry to ensure that she had enough ingredients to make a chocolate babka for Mac. While sipping a glass of iced tea, enjoying the aroma drifting through the kitchen, she realized she needed something for Izzy. Without him there wouldn't have been a case to present to the police. But perhaps something less Jewish for him. Chocolate chip cookies, she thought. Everyone liked those.

By the time the babka and the cookies were cooling, Hannah was exhausted, emotionally as well as physically. It was only two. Plenty of time for a little nap before going down to the *Daily Sun,* she decided as she sat down in the recliner, feet up, TV turned to a *Dr. Phil* show. Within minutes, she was asleep.

Awakened by the banging of the screen door, she yelled out, "Don't slam doors."

"Sorry, Grandma. It slipped. What smells so good?"

"That's not for us. It's a gift for someone else, so don't touch it."

"What's for dinner?" he called out as he headed upstairs to his room.

"Dinner? Oy, I didn't realize it was so late," she said, looking at the clock by the fireplace. Not only wouldn't she be able to deliver the babka to Mac today, she hadn't even thought of dinner. In fact, the thought of dinner drained whatever energy she had left. Obviously a three-hour nap hadn't been sufficient to rejuvenate her.

Okay, she told herself, they get Chinese takeout tonight.

CHAPTER 55

"**M**OM, WHY ARE you in such a hurry this morning? Sit down. Don't stand at the sink with your coffee."

"I have things to do today. I don't have time to sit down."

"What things?" Janice persisted.

Hannah sighed in exasperation. "Things. Like taking the babka and cookies to Mac at the newspaper. I planned on doing it yesterday, but… well, I got busy. And if I don't get it to him today, it won't be fresh."

"So an extra hour will make it stale?" Janice teased.

"No, of course not. But I'm just…I don't know. I need to be doing something, and sitting down is not what I need to be doing."

Janice smiled. "Okay, don't sit down. Is everything okay?"

Hannah considered her answer. "You know, everything *is* fine. I really don't know why I'm all atwitter. Maybe it's because there's nothing I really need to do," she replied, bemusement showing on her face. "Isn't that strange?" she asked as she sat down across from Janice.

"I'm sure you'll find something to do," chided Janice. "There's always someone who needs your help. And remember Sandy will be arriving next week. She's back from camp and is spending the weekend with her mother. She'll come here on Monday. I don't know how long she'll be staying, but we should set up the back room for her. If I know Sandy, she'll want to stay for a few weeks—and I don't think her mother will object."

"I forgot all about her visit. I'd better make some of those cherry wink cookies she likes so much."

• • •

After sharing a second cup of coffee with Janice, Hannah took off for downtown. The parking lot by the *Daily Sun* was filled, requiring her to drive around the block to find a spot. Car parked, babka and cookies in her right hand, purse in her left, she marched into the office.

Ignoring the receptionist's request that she wait until she announced her, Hannah waved as she strode past her and stood in the doorway of Mac's office.

"Are you busy?" she asked.

"Not for you, Mrs. L. Come on in. Sit down."

"Such a good mood. Should I assume you're gloating? An exclusive on the Campbells?"

Mac laughed. "Damn right I'm gloating. Not only did we have an exclusive, we've been picked up by the state papers. A murder involving a prominent right-wing lawyer! Everyone's eating it up."

"What do you hear about the trial? Is there a date?"

"No date yet, but they have been indicted. Given the low number of cases the court has on the docket, I'd guess that there shouldn't be much of a delay."

"So they're in jail?"

"No, they're out on bail. They probably had to put up their house as collateral. But the argument was that they weren't flight risks and so jail time wasn't required. But there's an interesting bit of news. Judge O'Connor found that there was enough evidence against Mrs. Campbell to proceed to trial. Campbell, however—nice guy—pled out, gave testimony against his wife in exchange for a lesser sentence. He'll probably just get probation, but that most likely means his days as a lawyer are over."

Hannah frowned. "They should both be in jail. What kind of a man squeals on his wife?"

"I'm sure he'll find losing his license to practice law a significant punishment, Mrs. L," Mac responded.

"That son-of-a-bitch—pardon my language—will somehow land on his feet...Oh, what am I doing?" Hannah exclaimed as she fumbled with her package. "Here, I made a chocolate babka for you and some cookies for Izzy. You know if it wasn't for you and that young man, the Campbells would have gotten away with murder—or attempted murder."

She handed the packages across the desk and watched as Mac opened the wrappings to smell the babka and eat a cookie. "Delicious," he pronounced with his mouth full.

He wiped his mouth with a tissue and looked at Hannah.

"Mrs. L," he began. "I've been doing some investigating on my own."

She watched him with expectation. "What investigation?"

"That agency you mentioned, the Good Nanny. I had one of the young women on the staff pose with Izzy as a couple in search of a nanny for their two young children. All you do is sign up online, tell them what you want in a nanny, and they send you a list of possible people. You choose one, and they set up the meeting, although it's not really a meeting. It's all done online—the people never meet each other until the nanny arrives in town. At least they pay for the transportation.

"But it sounded 'off.' Something didn't sound right, so I did a little investigating. It's run by a group of businessmen and lawyers, mostly from this area. I was able to get their financial statements—don't ask how. And it doesn't bring in a lot of money. So the question was not *how* does the agency keep going, but *why*."

"So what did you find out?" Hannah had leaned forward in her chair, impatient to hear his answer.

"I looked at the list of possible nannies that Izzy had gotten, and did some follow up. All of the women on the list were young, attractive—at least those who had driver license pictures to see—and came from families living below the poverty line, on public assistance, and, in many of the cases, classically dysfunctional: alcohol and drug abuse in the family, father in prison. It wouldn't surprise me if most of the young women looked at an opportunity to work for an affluent family as the way to get away from home."

"But so what? Is there any proof that they're doing anything wrong?"

"Well, yes there is," he shouted, pounding the table. "I checked on those girls—or as many of them I could find. And guess what?"

"What?"

"Two of them were working for families in town. One went from family to family, staying six months at each place. I can't find where she is now. The best information we have is that she's in Saginaw, working as a prostitute. But we can't track her down. The other woman left after a few months and works as a maid at the Super 8 on Mission Street. Izzy talked to her and found out that the husband made advances, and she was uncomfortable being in the house when he was there.

"The interesting thing is that the main clients for the Good Nanny are the same people who run it—businessmen and lawyers mostly from town. How convenient. You form an agency. It doesn't make much money, but with only a website to manage, you get your pick of a pretty young thing to take care of your children and maybe take care of you too. I don't know that I have enough for an indictment, but I can sure put the spotlight on them. And that's what I'm going to do. It's just coincidence that I'm going to do it before the trial starts."

Hannah looked at him in amazement. This would make it easier for Sage to testify, she thought. It would show that Campbell intentionally targeted her, and if the other woman in town were to also testify, that would give more credence to Sage's testimony. Oh, this was good news.

"Say something, Mrs. L. Tell me I'm brilliant, I'm a paragon of journalism, that I belong on the editorial staff of the *New York Times*. Say something."

"I'm speechless. Yes, you are brilliant. I never even considered going after that group. I knew it was not right—who hires someone sight unseen to take care of their children? But I had no idea you could, or would, do this. You've made a believer of me, Mac. There *are* good people in Brewster."

"Okay," he bellowed, "out with you. Time to get back to work."

He got up from behind the desk and walked over to Hannah. He stretched out his arms, and she walked into them, each one holding on to the other as they rocked back and forth in celebration.

• • •

"David, I need your help," she shouted as she entered the house. Hannah had come straight home from Mac's office. It was nine thirty, and the chances were that David was still in bed, but Hannah couldn't wait. She had to do this, and she had to do it today.

David came running down the stairs, hair standing up in spikes, panic on his face. "What's wrong, Grandma? Are you okay?"

"Oh, I'm sorry, darling. I didn't mean to scare you. I'm fine. I just need your help in finding Derek."

"Jeez, I thought you had fallen or something. Don't do that," he complained, panic being replaced by anger.

"You're right. I'm sorry…But do you know how to get in touch with Derek?"

"Yeah…why do you need to see him?" Now curiosity had replaced anger.

"Come. I'll make you breakfast, and we can talk."

He followed her into the kitchen, helped himself to a glass of orange juice, and sat down. "Okay, so let's talk."

Hannah cut a thick slice of bread, whisked an egg into a froth, seasoned the egg, melted butter in a pan, and made David a breakfast of french toast, which he smothered in maple syrup. Devouring that in less than a minute, he smacked his lips. "Any more?" he asked.

She smiled. "No, but there's fruit if you're still hungry."

"Nah, I'm okay. So why do you want to see Derek?"

Hannah poured herself a glass of orange juice and sat down across from David. "You remember telling me about Derek witnessing an accident? Well, he was the main reason they were able to arrest the people who tried to kill that girl and so I want to tell him that and thank him. And I'd like to do something for him."

"Like what?"

"Well, I don't know. He seems like a nice young man—intelligent, kind. He's just had a rough life. Maybe help him finish school, get a job—something like that. Being homeless, especially at his age, isn't right."

"Okay." Then he moved on to the more interesting part of Hannah's explanation. "So they got the bad guys? Are they in jail?"

"No, they're out on bail…but enough talk. Get dressed and help me find Derek."

CHAPTER 56

THEY FOUND DAVID in the park, tending to an injured squirrel. He was attempting to splint the damaged tail with a twig and an old bandana, and the animal wasn't cooperating. When he saw Hannah and David, with Max, approaching, he gave up his Good Samaritan attempt and got up to greet them, allowing the squirrel to scamper away.

"Hi," he said, wiping his hands on his stained jeans and bending down to rub Max's ears.

"I see you're still taking care of the wildlife," Hannah said as she smiled at the retreating squirrel.

He smiled at her and nodded. "I try. Sometimes they don't let you help them though. I guess they're scared. Anyway, what brings you out here?"

"Is there some place we could sit down and talk?" asked Hannah.

"I'd invite you to my home, but it's a little messy right now," he joked. "But there are tables in the pavilion, and no one uses them much during the morning, mostly in the afternoons for picnics. It's right over there," he indicated with a toss of his head, still petting Max.

Seated at a picnic table in the pavilion, Hannah recounted her conversation with Mac, thanking Derek for his role. She was surprised when she learned that the police had not contacted him. After all, it was his remembering the license plate number that had given Mac the information to start the whole investigation. How had Mac explained knowing that, she wondered—reporter protecting his source?

Derek thanked her for the update and turned his attention back to Max. David started to get up, ready to leave, but was stopped by Hannah, who suggested he take Max for a run while she talked some more with Derek. He called to Max, and they both dashed off toward the dog park area.

Smiling at their energy, she watched them run. When they were out of sight, she turned to Derek. "There's going to be a City Commission meeting on funding a more permanent homeless shelter. It's on Thursday. I don't know if it'll pass—probably not—but I'd like you to become involved in the committee that's setting up the rotating shelter program. You heard of that, right?'

"No."

"Oh my. I've got to speak to the publicity people. Anyway, we've got a program where some of the churches in town will open their doors for people who need a place to sleep. It'll start in December—we don't have enough churches to start earlier—and go to probably the end of February, maybe early March. You should tell the other homeless people about it. And you should consider using it. No sense sleeping in a tent during the winter if you don't have to."

Derek looked interested, so she continued. "And I was thinking. You told me you dropped out of school because it was hard to keep up being homeless. I'm concerned about other young people who are dropping out or thinking of dropping out. You could be helpful in getting me, and others on the committee, to understand what the young people would need to stay in school. Like help getting the GED—I think that's what it's called—or like foster homes, but not foster homes, just a place where they had like a temporary home. I don't know…that's why you could be helpful.

"And while we're on the subject, what about you finishing high school? Getting your GED? Without some credentials today, it's impossible to get a real job. It would open at least some possibilities that are closed to you now."

She sat back and took a deep breath. "Anyway, what about helping us on the committee? Or at least talk to some of us. Give us some ideas on how we can keep kids in school. Would you do that?"

"I don't know that I'd be much help," he answered.

"Well, think about what would have helped *you* stay in school. Do you know other kids who dropped out of school or who stayed in school, who were homeless? Maybe if you talked with them, pooled your experiences—like made a little committee that could help us understand. Could you do that?"

Derek thought for a few minutes, not saying anything, looking down at his hands. Hannah didn't interrupt his thinking, controlling her impatience by focusing on the abundant wildflowers flourishing in the area.

When Derek looked up, he smiled. "I'd like that," he whispered.

"What part?"

"Both parts—talking about what would have helped me and getting my GED."

"Wonderful," shouted Hannah. "You talk to whoever you can, and I'll talk to the committee. And I'll get my daughter—she's the principal, you know—to explain to me what you have to do to get your GED."

She beamed at him. "And I want you should come to lunch tomorrow. There's no reason you can't have a good home-cooked meal while we're discussing plans…And bring some other kids. There'll be plenty to eat."

After confirming the address and time, they both got up: she to round up David and Max, he to whatever he did with his days.

• • •

Derek had obviously taken his charge seriously. The next day, promptly at noon, he and three other young people arrived at the house. The two young men had dropped out of school two years ago and were living on the streets; the young woman was still in school, barely getting passing grades, staying with her boyfriend of the moment.

Hannah had prepared a hearty meal. Not knowing how many people would show up, she'd decided to make a spinach chicken and penne casserole, large enough to feed whomever Derek brought. And if it was just Derek, there would be enough left over for the night's dinner.

She rounded out the meal with a salad, pies—one peach and one blueberry—and ice cream. There wasn't enough of anything left for dinner.

After lunch, they assembled on the deck and talked about their experiences: why they were homeless, the difficulties of staying in school, why they dropped out. In fact, they were more open in sharing their situations than Hannah has expected. They didn't get to the issue of what would have helped them stay in school, but Hannah thought they did pretty well for a first meeting. By the time they left, they had all agreed to meet again, to brainstorm about what the Committee for Providing Shelter for the Homeless could do to help.

CHAPTER 57

THE CITY COMMISSION meeting had started with the usual business items, keeping the audience filled with supporters of the shelter program on edge. Finally, the chair turned to the discussion on the proposal to put on the ballot a five million dollar millage for a permanent homeless shelter in the city.

Reverend Dwayne was the first to speak, followed by other supporters. It looked as if there was general support and that the City Commission would likely agree to put the issue on the ballot in August.

Then a loud voice from the back of the room thundered, "What about our children? Do you want these people living next to your children?"

"No" was heard by a voice up front, followed by a chorus of "no" throughout the audience.

The chair, struggling to maintain order, pounded the gavel, instructing people to be recognized before speaking. It did no good. Within minutes, the meeting had been hijacked by an organized group spread throughout the audience. When one finished reporting a bad situation he or she had heard of with a homeless shelter in a residential area, another would pop up to continue the attack. No one else could get the floor. The chair in desperation called the meeting adjourned, and the commission members left the room. No action was taken.

Pandemonium broke out with supporters accusing the opponents of unfairly sabotaging the meeting and opponents reciprocating by calling them ignorant do-gooders, child haters, and other invectives.

Hannah didn't get up from her seat until she felt Janice's hand on her shoulder.

"Mom, come on. Let's get out of here," she shouted, trying to be heard above the din. "They've called in the police. It's getting out of control. You don't want to be caught in the middle."

Hannah nodded. As she rose from her seat, a small woman with hatred plastered on her pinched face and spittle foaming from her mouth confronted her.

"You're the bitch that started this whole thing, aren't you? You should rot in hell for all the trouble you're making for the good Christian folk in this town."

She was shortly joined by a group of similarly minded people who proceeded to harangue Hannah, who was being pulled by Janice toward the door. They reached the exit just as the police arrived.

Three large men and a medium-sized woman entered, and within a few minutes order was restored. Janice hurried Hannah to the car, where Paul was waiting.

Once in the car, Janice turned to Hannah, "Are you okay, Mom?"

Hannah, breathing hard, nodded. "Such hatred. I don't understand how they can call themselves Christians."

Janice gave Paul a brief description of the attacks on Hannah, exaggerating, in Hannah's eyes, their seriousness.

"Now don't get Paul thinking they were going to do anything to me. It was just angry, hateful talk—which I've managed to survive before."

Janice sighed in exasperation and turned to Paul. "So what happens now?"

He shrugged. "They could bring it up again," he replied, "but with that much opposition, it doesn't look promising."

"What are you going to do, Mom? It's dangerous for you to stay involved—"

"Dangerous? Not really. Of course, I'm disappointed, but it's not the end. We just have more work to do. Changing people's minds always takes time. Most of the people tonight were afraid. They've been told a bunch of lies, and they're scared. We need to do a better job at explaining next time...I just hope the committee doesn't give up. People don't understand how change happens...you need patience, and that takes time to develop."

Paul smiled at Janice and put his hand on hers. "I think we all need to take a deep breath and think before any decisions are made." Turning to Hannah, he said, "The main thing is to make sure you're okay. There were some very angry—even crazy—people in there. They could be dangerous...and yes, I know you're not afraid of them, but you don't want to be foolish. After all," he added with a wink at Janice, "what would the Committee to Provide Shelter for the Homeless do without you?"

"Yeah, they need me—like a fish needs a bicycle, they need me. But you know, a permanent shelter isn't really the ideal solution. What those people need is their own place. And if I can get the landlords in town to drop the cost of their apartments—they always have vacant units—and if the city would subsidize a good portion of that, we wouldn't need a permanent shelter. The rotating shelter program could continue for emergency housing, but people could eventually be moved into housing of their own at no, or little, cost to themselves. It would help restore their dignity and give them an address so they could receive mail. And don't forget—the young people are working with the committee to find ways to help them stay in school."

Hannah looked at Janice and Paul in the front seat. "Don't worry though. I'm not giving up. But I'm not stupid. Enough talk. Drive. I'm in the mood for another slice of that pecan pie we had for dinner."

THE END

Made in the USA
Monee, IL
04 March 2023

29182645R00174